A Close Run Thing

DAVID DONACHIE

Allison & Busby Limited
11 Wardour Mews
London W1F 8AN
allisonandbusby.com

First published in Great Britain by Allison & Busby in 2018.
This paperback edition published by Allison & Busby in 2019.

A CIP catalogue record for this book is available from
the British Library.

10 9 8 7 6 5 4 3 2 1

ISBN 978-0-7490-2253-2

Typeset in 10.5/16 pt Adobe Garamond Pro by
Allison & Busby Ltd.

The paper used for this Allison & Busby publication
has been produced from trees that have been legally sourced
from well-managed and credibly certified forests.

Printed and bound by
CPI Group (UK) Ltd, Croydon, CR0 4YY

To Mark Quinn and everyone at Quinn Estates
From myself and all at Deal and Betteshanger RFC
In recognition of your support

CHAPTER ONE

John Pearce scooped up his uniform coat and naval hat, aware of the need to move swiftly. At the same time he registered someone had made a basic and very foolish error: whoever had command of the detachment sent to arrest them should have been more restrained. Clattering on the door, which sounded as if it was being done with the hilt of a sword, while shouting that it should be opened in the name of the Revolution, was pure folly.

An old stone-built house, in a border fortress town like Gravelines, it had been constructed with a sturdy, inches-thick oak door, naturally fitted with substantial locks, so all the idiot did was alert his quarry. Not that such knowledge provided reassurance to Pearce or his fugitive companion, the fellow he knew as Samuel Oliphant.

'National Guard or soldiers?' he asked, as he slipped into his silver-buckled shoes.

'It makes no difference,' Oliphant snapped. 'Unless our host has a way out, we're trapped.'

The person alluded to came in to the kitchen at a bustle, one not so very different to his previous mode of behaviour, to then indicate that his guests should follow him. He was a fussy sort of fellow of indeterminate years, not young, stooped in posture and wearing a set of spectacles, which seemed at risk of falling off his nose – the very opposite image anyone would apply to a dangerous conspirator.

Both men were quick to tail his disappearing frame, but not without grabbing slices of the fresh-baked bread, which had been part of their breakfast. On the run, and they were surely that now, who knew when they would eat again? They found the man's young and appealing daughter, Eugenie, was already in the stable yard, wearing a hooded cloak to cover her blonde hair. She was carrying a large, bulging canvas bag and looking, Pearce thought, unnaturally calm.

More angry shouting and thumping had him glance at the substantial double gates that enclosed the yard, relieved to see the long sharp metal stakes that arced outwards along the top of the wall. These doors too were made of thick oak and, added to the heavy wooden bar set across the join, meant forcing them open, or overcoming them, would be difficult.

They were led into the sole empty horse stall, in which the straw on the floor, as well as the raised banks around the edges, lay undisturbed. The servant who'd taken their mounts the day before, they now curious onlookers in the other stalls, was holding the panniers that had been given to them outside Paris. They had been repacked with the military uniforms in which they had travelled, added to personal items plus pistols. He also held their swords, which were handed over.

At a command from his master, a section of one of the straw banks, pulled out, revealed a trapdoor, quickly if not easily lifted by a metal ring, the morning light exposing a set of steps leading down to a tunnel. Lowering himself, the servant struck at a set of flints to light a lantern, this handed up to his master, who then beckoned the men and his daughter to join him in the descent. Once everyone was down, the trapdoor flap was quietly lowered, with the daughter pulling on a line as soon as it had been secured with heavy metal bolts.

An enquiring look from Pearce elicited the information that the rope would haul back into place the bundle of straw and hide their escape route. Though it would not remain undiscovered, the concealment would buy precious time, as would the need for axes to smash the trapdoor itself.

Pearce spoke softly, in French, addressing the girl. 'You are abandoning your house and everything you possess?'

'What do you suggest they do?' was the querulous enquiry, in English, from his companion, 'Hand us over?'

Their still unnamed host might not speak the language but, having understood Pearce's sentiment, he obviously got the sense of what Oliphant was saying in response, his rejoinder in his own tongue brusque.

'We must move quickly, there is no time to explain matters.'

That said, he was off, servant and lantern to the fore, his daughter at his heels, Pearce and Oliphant following, like them, at a crouch. The tunnel, which had several tight turns to both left and right, was low and narrow. The old man stopped for a moment, raising a hand to check on something. Coming closer, Pearce picked out a rope basket full of rocks, set into the tunnel roof. The pause was brief and progress resumed, only for their elderly guide, two dozen paces on, to stop once more and let loose a rope from a cleat set in the wall.

The sound was unmistakable: rocks tumbling down, Pearce assumed to shut off the passageway, his supposition soon confirmed as a cloud of dust began to fill the air. A man of few expressions outside concern, in the small circle of light from the oil lamp their host now looked positively smug, which had Pearce reckon the stratagem had been his idea. Those in pursuit would find the tunnel blocked in such a way as to make the clearing of it, if it could be done at all, a job of several hours.

In minutes they were at a junction by the base of a second set of steps, the narrow passageway going on into darkness, the servant reaching up to unbolt a second heavy trapdoor. Fully opened it fell back with a crash, the tunnel filling with light and again Pearce examined Eugenie's expression. She still appeared calm, as though what they were about was an everyday occurrence. Was that indeed the case – for she and her father lived in a febrile world, made doubly dangerous by their obvious opposition to the ruling revolutionary regime?

Climbing brought all five into an open space, once a substantial dwelling of several storeys. Now it was charred walls, collapsed floor and roof timbers, above it an open grey sky, giving it an appearance of having been burnt down some time past. They were admonished to wait while father and servant disappeared, leaving his daughter to usher them into the half-remains of a room. There, for the first time, both men could seek to make some sense of what had just happened. The conclusion was obvious, if unwelcome.

Their escape from Paris had obviously been engineered for this very purpose, using them to expose a chain of opposition to the rule of the Jacobins. Looking back, everything that had happened previously now appeared part of that ruse. The effortless departure from the Temple, the famous and ancient Paris building, which had served as their prison, followed by the smooth way each part of the journey down the River Seine had been facilitated.

Then came the provision of those horses, now abandoned, the military uniforms into which they could change and finally, a *laissez passer* signed and bearing the seal of Lazare Carnot. A powerful member of the ruling clique in the Convention, he was the de facto Minister of War. No one would dare to question that permission to travel north, towards a zone of recent conflict for a pair of cavalry officers. Thus their passage to the port of Gravelines had been unhindered.

Pearce felt like a chump and said so. 'Humbugged.'

'By clever people, Pearce,' was Oliphant's reply. 'If you cannot love them, at least admire them.'

Using lumps of debris and a baulk of timber, Oliphant began to construct a seat on which they could rest. Then he looked pointedly at the girl. 'But it seems we are in the care of folk of equal if not superior wit. That escape route and the blocking of it was near to genius.'

'What a price they are paying.'

Reverting to French and addressing Eugenie directly, Pearce made the same point he had made on entry to the tunnel, apologising too, which got from her a knowing smile. Shy and, up till the present, not one for many words, now was an exception.

'The house was not ours, monsieur. It was the property of an early victim of the Terror, a fine upstanding man, a physician of repute. But he was outspoken in the name of justice for the King, too much so for his own well-being.'

She looked around the shell of the building, her expression sad.

'As was the owner of this grand manor, the local tax farmer for King Louis.' At the mention of that name she quickly crossed herself. 'The mob burnt it the very day he was guillotined, but not from revolutionary passion, more to loot his possessions.'

'So you and your father took over both?' Pearce enquired, cutting across Oliphant, who looked set to say something which, by his irritable expression, would be objectionable. His effort was wasted.

'Is he really your father?' he demanded, in what, to John Pearce, was an inappropriate tone. About to check him for a lack of gratitude, he was stopped by the old man's return, with no sign of the servant.

'The plan we had to get you away will no longer serve. We were to sneak you onto a boat this morning, just prior to it floating out on the tide, which will begin to recede around noon. The port will now be on alert and, being daylight, it is too dangerous to go there. It would put at risk, if you were caught, everything we seek to accomplish.'

He looked pointedly at Pearce's naval clothing, the garments in which he'd come to France, the blue coat and distinctive hat, white waistcoat, breeches and stockings as well as the very obvious and gleaming silver buckles on his shoes. To progress through a town

12

garrisoned by Britannia's enemies, they would not serve. There was brief thought to change back into the French cavalry uniforms, packed in those panniers, this soon discarded; the pursuit would be looking for that.

'Now we must take you to a place where you can hide and where, perhaps, a boat can be found to pick you up. We have no idea what is known to the authorities and, until we are sure . . .'

The rest of the point was left hanging as the servant returned, carrying a good-quality boat cloak which Pearce could put over his uniform, as well as an ordinary tricorne hat. The two Frenchmen then moved away and fell into a quiet conversation from which the escapees were excluded.

'How much easier to be a servant, Pearce,' Oliphant said with a smirk, pulling at his own, poor-quality garments. 'No need for a disguise.'

'You may be clad like one, but I have seen no evidence you're willing to act so.'

'I am obliged to do so only in circumstances that merit it.'

Oliphant fixed Pearce with a defiant look, intended to remind him of a pertinent fact: whatever differing roles they had played in this venture, they were equals and Pearce would have struggled to disagree. If he had been handed the primary role in the mission, it had too often depended for success on the wiles of his companion. And he was a man he had known – what was he saying, thought he had known – for no more than a couple of weeks.

Pearce was not even sure of his name. He'd been Oliphant when they met in London, but Régis de Cambacérès, the man who had arranged their 'escape' from Paris, knew him as Bertrand and there was no certainty that was true either. When it came to intrigue, he was the expert and Lieutenant John Pearce of King George's Navy was the novice. Their relationship had fluctuated mightily from the outset, swinging between common purpose through to open quarrel and, on one occasion, near descending into violence. Where it lay now was moot; they had only one common aim, to get away from Flanders and back home.

'For which we are wholly in the hands of our hosts,' Oliphant said with a grim expression when Pearce made the point.

'You don't sound pleased.'

'It's never a comfort to be entirely dependent on others. I should have thought you'd have learnt that by now. Added to which, when the old man said he must find a boat to get us away, how was it conveyed? I do not recall any assurance it would be either quick or easy.'

Pearce looked at the girl, the only one close enough to hear the exchange, to see if she had picked up on Oliphant's downbeat assessment, having shown no sign of understanding English prior to this. But the events of the morning, added to how it had come about, rendered him cautious in regard to everything. The glance and expression were noted by Oliphant.

'I reckon us safe from being understood, but it is as well you show concern.'

A decision had been made in the quiet conversation. The servant would take Oliphant to the required destination, a couple of ordinary folk passing through the streets, who should attract no attention. At a decent interval Pearce, in the company of Eugenie, would follow. He was to be armed with the cavalry pistols, now extracted from those horse panniers.

'The rest of the contents we will leave here,' the old man said, with a finality that brooked no argument. 'They can be safely stored elsewhere.'

'And you?' Pearce asked.

'I will go about my affairs, monsieur, as I do every day.'

There was a temptation to ask what that might be. But with a man who'd never even gifted them his name, there was likely no point. Impatient, the old man bustled his servant out of a postern door, with Oliphant in tow. That closed, he set himself to loading the pistols, talking all the while, making the point to Pearce that he and Eugenie would not walk together, but would do so twenty paces apart. If the enemy was looking for anyone, it was not an attractive young girl.

'Monsieur, you must act as my daughter does in all respects, for to do otherwise is to endanger her as well as yourself. Should it be necessary to use these' – the pistols were held up – 'then she will seek to save herself and will not stay to aid you. You will then be on your own and, if you're captured, I ask only that you say nothing about us or how you came to this house.'

A small leather purse containing some coins was pressed into Pearce's hand, though no explanation followed, just a command. 'Now you should go.'

Eugenie stood, this as Pearce took the pistols to secrete them in the deep pockets of his coat; thus they were hidden under his cloak. She exited first, he at the required distance, to emerge into the grey morning light, though there was evidence of a low watery sun in the eastern sky. Pearce, who had been in Gravelines before, sought, without much success, to establish his whereabouts. A haven for English contrabandists in peacetime, it had remained so even in war: the gold and silver brought in by smuggling was of great value to a nation suffering a naval blockade. France was so short on specie the government had been obliged to print a form of paper money called *assignats*. It was one widely mistrusted by the citizenry.

The town, set inland from the sea, was dominated by a star-shaped fortress, designed and built for Louis XIV by the Marquis de Vauban, a type of defensive structure replicated all over Europe. It had a deep moat surround with the town an exterior sprawl, and he was relieved to discover they were outside that water barrier. With its very necessary bridges, it provided many natural choke points at which papers and purpose could be demanded by the ubiquitous National Guard.

The position of the sun told him Eugenie was heading west, proven when they came within sight of a long, straight canal, the outflow of the River Aa, which ran from far inland to the North Sea. At this point the quayside was a wooden construct, bordered by the kind of enterprises that supplied the needs of a seaport and fishing fleet, with numerous boats tied alongside and many more downstream.

Prior knowledge told Pearce these upstream vessels were local; the part of the canal used by English smugglers was, for the purposes of discretion and safety, closer to the sea. Eugenie turned sharply and descended a set of steps, which had Pearce hurry to follow; by the time he got to the edge he could see her taking a place in a small boat. This was manned by a solitary, weary-looking and raggedly dressed individual, to whom she was proffering a coin.

That small, gifted purse from her father now made sense; money was needed to pay the boatman. Once he was seated in the thwarts, Pearce nervously offered a couple of sous, pre-revolutionary coins, which he feared might engender curiosity. They were taken with a nod, to be pocketed in a leather waistcoat, before the oars flicked to cross what was not a very great distance to the southern side of the canal.

Eugenie was out and away first, heading at a brisk pace, he on her heels, past the houses bordering that side of the canal. She then darted into a narrow alley, which led to a twisting and turning route through many more. They made their way through backstreets lined with increasingly unkempt dwellings, their walls high enough to make it difficult to be sure of the heading.

Finally, they thinned out to reveal open land, first sparse coastal woodland. This turned, after a short distance, into undulating sand dunes, mixed with low scrub bushes and strands of tough grass. Sea and the flat expanse of beach were occasionally visible on the rise, with the odd hut dotted around above the high-tide mark. These were not places to live but shacks to be occasionally visited when the owner wanted to fish, one of which proved to be their destination.

As he came abreast of the door – if a tarpaulin sheet could be called that – it was pulled back to reveal Oliphant. A flick of the man's head drew him into the gloomy interior. The first thing to strike him, other than the lack of daylight, was the strong smell of fish and not fresh at that.

'The servant?'

'Gone,' Oliphant hissed. 'As I assume is the girl by now.'

'Did the servant say anything more about a boat?'

'He repeated that efforts are being made to find one, but when I asked him how long that might take all I got was a shrug.'

'We just have to trust them,' Pearce insisted. Even in the gloom he could pick up Oliphant's misgivings. 'They've stood by us till now, have they not? They could have easily used that tunnel and left us to our fate.'

Eyes now adjusted to the gloom, he was examining his surroundings – not that it took long, for they did not amount to much. There was barely enough room for both men and only one cot, with a grubby blanket. In one corner sat a tiny, much-scarred table, which looked as if it had been used for gutting fish. Under it sat a small barrel, which probably would serve as the only place to sit. To the side of the entrance there was a charcoal brazier on which the owner could, if he wished, cook his catch.

'Food?' he asked, as that pointed to a need.

'Will be brought, and water.' Oliphant paused before adding. 'And there are rods outside with which we can fish.' There was a lengthy pause before he added, 'We're not in a safe place Pearce.'

'Which hardly needs to be said.'

'I don't mean this hut.'

'Even if I agree with you, I cannot think how we are to go about improving it.'

'So you're content to rely entirely on the old man?'

'Content no, but certain we must.'

'I disagree.'

'Something you're prone to,' was the acerbic response.

'I hope, as do you, they will find the means to meet our needs, but what if they struggle? I grant you they've been clever and, I'm as sure as I can be, their identity is unknown to whoever was clattering on that door. But who are they and how many do they constitute? Is it one old man and a girl, or a large and active conspiracy? What if we are in the hands of the only people in the whole of this part of the world who can aid us?'

The silence that greeted the point encouraged Oliphant to continue. 'I've told you I'm never happy to be dependent on others. I would go as far as to say I'm only alive now because I have had a care to avoid being so.'

The response was larded with irony. 'Do I sense a proposition?'

'On the way to this hovel, the servant and I moved with little difficulty, down and across the canal, this at a time when the local forces were supposedly on the lookout.'

'People whom we last heard hammering and demanding entry and they will still be occupied. It will require the door to be broken down and they'll find nothing. In time they'll surely discover the tunnel entrance, but that has been blocked so will lead them nowhere.'

Oliphant acknowledged the point; preoccupied, those doing the chasing might still be looking for them in the wrong place. He then moved onto another point, namely that such a situation would not last.

'I have no idea which route you took, but it revealed to me a large number of boats lining the canal. If what you told me on the way here is true, some must be crewed by our fellow countrymen and the intention was to get us away just after the turn of the high tide?'

The plan, obviously, had been to put them aboard a smuggler: who else would be sailing out of Gravelines on course for England? An immediate set of questions then arose: which one had agreed to the plan, how could they locate them and was there time to find out?

'It was said plain such a course was no longer safe.' That

engendered another possibility. Were they now seeking a replacement, and if not, could they find one without help? 'If we can, we could perhaps offer them money.'

Pearce pulled out the small purse and threw it to Oliphant. 'Unless you have means of which I'm unaware, that's all we possess.'

'A tempting sum could be offered . . .'

'From where?'

Oliphant barked at him in reply, given Pearce was being obtuse. 'Henry Dundas, the man who sent us on this damned errand.'

'You repose more faith in him than I do.'

'Would you accept it is worth the attempt?'

'Only if we have no other recourse. But we are not yet so desperate. Let's wait and see what our friends can arrange.'

CHAPTER TWO

Between these two men, with time to kill – and they had been gifted with ample before now – normal conversation tended to be stilted. Quite often there was none at all, mainly because Oliphant was secretive to a high degree. Anything regarding his background or prior actions, just like his true name, were never to be openly discussed. Pearce had no inclination to air his own concerns, past exploits or discuss his previous life. This left only that which had occurred between, as well as to them, since they first met. Naturally, much of that had been covered on their journey. There was not much more to say.

Oliphant spoke eventually, ending a long silence 'I still think we should plan to escape unaided, as a precaution.'

'Why?'

Pearce asked this wearily, given the same point, in various forms, had been briefly alluded to more than once. Sat on the barrel, the folded cloak easing the discomfort, he was no more content than his companion, but less inclined to say so on the grounds that speculation was useless. Oliphant was not to be put off.

'I fear I must repeat that when getting a boat was mentioned, it was not put forward with even approaching certainty. The same with the servant who fetched me here. A blank look and a shrug is all I got when I enquired, and that does nothing to provide reassurance.'

'He's a servant. It requires to be arranged, but by his master, not him.'

'A boat, the old man said, not a ship. What do they mean by a boat?'

'He said boarding in the port would be too risky now. I would guess they mean a rowing boat to carry us from the beach to a waiting ship.'

'And how long will that take, when we are at imminent risk of discovery?'

'Whatever time is required,' was the reply of a man clearly becoming exasperated.

'Time we might not have. Those pursuing us will start searching the town when they find the house empty. Since we're not there to be found, how long before the search extends to the country around?'

'A bridge to be crossed when the need arises.'

Oliphant looked him up and down. 'Not dressed in that garb. It would help, either way, to get you some more suitable clothing.'

The small purse was alluded to once more. 'There's barely enough in here to buy a loaf of bread.'

Silence descended once more, each man lost within their own thoughts, but it was clear Oliphant was chafing at the inactivity. He clearly craved to be doing something, anything, other than sitting waiting for the efforts of possible unseen rescuers, not aided by his obvious anxiety they might never arrive. When he spoke again his voice was more cheerful.

'It occurs we're better found than you know, Pearce. Those silver buckles on your shoes will fetch a pretty penny. Even your breeches and coat can be sold.'

'Sold?'

'A change of clothing is something I've been obliged to find in the past, and in a hurry.'

'I'm tempted to ask why.'

'While I will say, if you cannot guess, you're a fool. Clothing identifies you: it's not a face that betrays a man to a stranger, but the colour and cut of his garments as described. Need I refer to what you're wearing?'

Pearce was left with no choice but to shake his head. He had no doubt that, undisturbed this morning, and in executing whatever plan had been put in place, he would have been obliged to discard or cover up his uniform. If they were to be taken off by a smuggler, and he could not see it being carried out any other way, the sight of a naval officer was not one to comfort men intent on cheating the Revenue.

'I reckon it a good notion to purchase garments similar to mine, and I'd expect, selling what you possess, to have funds left over.'

'You're surely not proposing to go back into Gravelines?'

The reply was full of irony. 'Unless you can find a market outside.'

'You do not apprehend that being dangerous?'

'Of course it's dangerous. But you stepping out as you're now dressed, and without that cloak you're sitting on, would be fatal.'

'Our friends are aware of the problem.'

'Once more you are content to rely on them. Believe me, it's never wise.'

'While wandering around a town where we're being looked for is?'

'Sitting here doing nothing I cannot abide. So let me try to affect something, which will be necessary anyway, especially if we suddenly find soldiers approaching this hut and we have to flee.'

'And what do I do?'

'Wait, what else can you do?'

Sat on the low cot, wrapped in the boat cloak, John Pearce felt absurdly vulnerable. Oliphant was right; if the local soldiery did not find them in a search of the town, anything bordering the sea presented an obvious place to look, and he had a morbid fear it might happen soon. The thought of being captured was not a pleasant one in any case, but to be taken in nothing but your small clothes seemed to add extra humiliation.

His companion had departed with his buckles and outer clothing; all he had left were the buttons prised off his coat and a naval scraper no one in this part of the world would choose to be seen in. If Oliphant had seemed sure of what he was about, the owner had been much less confident and became less so as time wore on. Surely those in pursuit would have an eye on the kind of places where such things as clothes were pawned, bought and sold?

Normally he possessed too active a mind for gloomy contemplation. Pearce was struck with that now, not only gnawing on his present concerns, but reprising how he had come to this wretched state. He cursed himself for allowing that slimy politician, Henry Dundas, to talk him into the mission, only to remind himself it had not been him alone. William Pitt had been equally instrumental in selling the proposition.

It seemed to be flattery now, the notion he could help to bring about an end to a war going far from well, one which was costing Britannia a fortune. This was not only in its own military expenditures, but also ballooned by subsidies disbursed to its allies, without which they would not, could not, fight the common enemy.

Being under a cloud at the Admiralty had also been a factor, of course. Pearce had been lucky previously to be in receipt of a command – more than one, in fact. Circumstances and the particular needs of fighting in the Mediterranean had been a major factor. Now he was home, in colder climes, and that applied not just to the weather, which induced a degree of rising resentment. His rank might have come about in a manner his naval peers found questionable, but surely his successful actions, so many of them carrying the risk of death or serious injury, should have moderated the animosity.

'And where in the name of the devil is Oliphant, anyway?'

He said it out loud, in an attempt to both ease his mood, as well as shift his mind away from such depressing ruminations. Also at the centre of his concerns, and too hard to dismiss, sat Emily Barclay. He needed to prove to her his ability to make his own way in the world, without laying a finger on the money she had inherited from her swine of a husband.

Pearce could never bring himself to curse the mother of his child, but he had no trouble in damning her insistence on respectability. They could have been happy without the bounds of matrimony and the constraints of her being a recent widow. Society demanded she behave in the prescribed manner and would be scandalised if she did not. This she could not abide. He didn't give a damn.

Round and round whirled these thoughts, while being cut off from the only people with whom he might have been able to share them didn't help. And that only served to raise another concern. Were his friends prospering or, had he, by his manoeuvres, and not for the first time, exposed them to risk? The faces of Michael O'Hagan, Charlie Taverner and Rufus Dommet swam before his eyes, along with the memory of the foul winter night, years past now, in which they had been taken from the Pelican Tavern by a press gang. How much they had shared since – and it might never be any more.

Sailing on a privateer, maybe they were at sea and in profit, not idle and sitting in harbour. Yet such employment was hazardous to a massive degree. The boats issuing from the small port of Shoreham were not, as he had noted on his first visit, deep-sea vessels, destined for long voyages to open waters. This was a less hazardous pursuit. Far from home, the chance of encountering an enemy warship was minimal, with captures being easier due to the laxity of merchant captains. From what Pearce had observed, the man under whom they were serving, given the size and ordnance on his ship, would be obliged to seek his quarry in the confined waters of the English Channel, occasionally maybe venturing south into the Bay of Biscay.

These were, of course, waters patrolled by the Royal Navy, an always present Inshore Squadron to watch the port of Brest. But they were also a hunting ground for French sloops, corvettes and even frigates, which took no account of enemy letters of marque. They lived by preying on British trade and some of them were likely to be better armed and manned than their English rivals.

In conjuring up an image of the trio, he wondered how they would react to his present situation, which lightened his mood and brought forth a grin. There would be some sharp and disparaging comments from O'Hagan; the huge Irishman had never been shy of telling him if he thought he was being a fool. Charlie Taverner would exercise his cutting wit while young Rufus Dommet, less accomplished in the article of jocularity, would probably say something inappropriate or incomprehensible.

'What in the name of the Lord are you grinning at?'

Oliphant asked this from the pulled-back tarpaulin. Pearce just shook his head, not wishing to share his thoughts, staring instead at the bundle his companion had under his arm. The look, when the direction was noted, had Oliphant pull a crabbed face.

'This is a godforsaken spot for poverty, Pearce. There's scarce enough coin for the locals to purchase the means to eat never mind clothe themselves, and poor is the stuff being sold.'

'Yet you obviously managed to trade.'

'Had to be done with a sharp eye out. But the men set to watch for us, if indeed they were that, stood out like Job's wife. Pillars of salt would have had more subtlety. I have to admit, those from whom I was buying were as alert to their being around. Most of my exchanges were done in deep doorways.'

'If you can forgo the boasting, how did we fare?'

'*I*,' Oliphant responded, with great emphasis, 'have done better than expected.'

'So?'

'I refused to trade for those useless paper *assignats* issued by Paris, hence the length of time I was gone. Got a good exchange in Prussian crowns for your broadcloth coat, lack of buttons notwithstanding. But the buckles were the bonus, even if the rogue who bought them tried to dun me by denying they were true silver. Said the hallmarks could have been forged.'

'They're Italian.'

'I suggested he weigh them and that stymied the sod, though he haggled for an age. I had to take his price in the end, for it came in Dutch guilders and a half-Louis d'or. Pity, they must have set you back a great deal, but you have to accept I was never going to get the full value.'

Acknowledging the truth took Pearce back to Brindisi, on the Adriatic, the previous year. He was flush with his share of the spoils from the sale of a couple of fat French merchantmen, sold as prizes to the local British trading fraternity. Since he was trapped in the port, with a seriously wounded captain, he had decided to travel to Naples to see Emily, residing in the home of Sir William and Lady Hamilton.

The purchase of the buckles, to replace his previous plain pair, had been an attempt to impress her with his new-found prosperity, making the point about self-sufficiency on which he had so recently been ruminating. All he could recall now was the somewhat cold reception, added to the fact that she hadn't even noticed the new adornment, while his joy at her being pregnant was not really shared either. He was distracted from this return to a melancholy mood as various items were thrown on to the cot.

'There you are: good flannel breeches and shirt, a leather waistcoat and a cap of liberty, so you will look the honest revolutionary. As to the time gone, I had another errand to fulfil and one, if you had the wit, you would see as necessary. I examined the boats tied up along the canal and tried to make out which were local and which might be owned by our fellow countrymen. I'm set on not sitting around and hoping.'

'Then might I suggest,' Pearce growled, 'before the light goes and now I have suitable clothing, we examine our surroundings? Should we have to run, a knowledge of the terrain would be an advantage.'

Oliphant was reluctant to admit it both right and something he should have thought of, so agreement was slow in coming. With pistols stuck in waistbands they exited, to check there was no sign of any threat from the town, nor was there any evidence of other humanity using the various huts they could see.

So they set off, over ground often so soft and sandy it tugged at their feet, soon to observe that the surroundings were poor for concealment and they extended a long way. The beach ran for miles to the south and, with the tide out, it was deep. The whole landscape was utterly devoid of cover, bar the obverse side of a dune, or a bit of scrub or seagrass on the top. This might serve to hide in, but not for any time.

'I feel less secure now than I did before we set out,' Oliphant said, to which Pearce could not take issue. 'We're like game birds for anyone with a musket.'

With the light fading in a clear sky, they made their way back to the hut, with an occasional wistful look out to sea. Their clothing was being tugged at by the kind of breeze on which Pearce could imagine a brisk rate of sailing. Inside it was near Stygian black, with no more than a modicum of approaching twilight coming through the gaps in the driftwood slats. Pearce found and then lit a stub of tallow, achieved by much sparking of flints, which revealed a basket laid under the cot. Opened, they found it contained bread, part of a smoked ham, as well as a flagon of what turned out to be cider.

'One must wonder what they thought to find us gone.'

Oliphant lowered the flagon and waved it under Pearce's nose. 'Perhaps it would be good riddance.'

'Will you ever afford these people some gratitude? They are risking their lives for us.'

'No. They are risking their lives for a cause to which we are no more than a means to an end. Shielding us from capture is to ensure their own survival as much as ours. It is sentimental to think otherwise.'

'I bow to your superior knowledge in the article of deceit.'

'Will you bow to the point that, with the gaps in these walls and in full darkness, anyone who might be looking for us will know this hut is occupied?'

That meant killing the light, while the presence of the single narrow cot established that one of them was in for an uncomfortable night.

'A toss of the coin would seem to be the answer,' Oliphant suggested.

'Not one of yours,' Pearce barked, reaching for the small purse. 'And I will mark the passage of the moon, so that we may both have a share.'

* * *

Pearce had declined forcibly the suggestion that, having lost the toss, his companion in misfortune should have both the cot and boat cloak. Once more wrapped in said cloak and perched on the barrel, he soon became prey to another set of gloomy reflections, this mixed with fitful dozing in a near-silent setting, there being no more than a faint hint of wind whispering through the less-than-sturdy structure.

How different this was from being at sea, where it was never quiet given a light breeze hissing through the rigging, even less the screaming of a strong gale. Cordage was never soundless as it stretched and contracted regardless of wind, and the ship's timbers would continually creak. If a change of course was called for, and it often was at night, the soft noise of bare, running feet would register enough to open an eye. On a taut-run ship, with trained hands, what followed would be muted: with a yet-to-be-worked-up crew, it would be all hell let loose in the amount of shouting and cursing.

Dozing, Pearce picked the odd sound, though nothing like those to which he was accustomed. Yet something brought him near to full consciousness and the realisation he needed to relieve himself. With the taste of cider still on his tongue, he pulled back the tarpaulin flap and stepped out, falling headlong and emitting a loud curse, which woke Oliphant.

'It cannot be time to change places,' came a groan from the cot.

No immediate reply followed. Pearce was on his knees, examining by moonlight what had caused him to trip. The realisation of their shape raised first his curiosity, until the nature of when and how they had been delivered, surreptitiously in the early morning hours, brought on a depressing thought.

'Might I suggest you rise and come outside, Oliphant?'

'In God's name why?'

'I think we've been delivered of a message.'

Oliphant staggered out to see Pearce, kneeling by two objects, easy to identify by their shape. The two sets of panniers lay squat upon the sandy ground. That they should be returned was not in itself a cause for alarm; that they had been so furtively left for them to find was very much so. Opened, one revealed enough food to last them several days. The other had the uniforms in which they'd come to Gravelines.

It took Oliphant no time at all to voice the conclusion. 'We're being told we must contrive to find our own way to cross the Channel.'

'I'll call up a hot-air balloon,' Pearce suggested, his tone arch. 'I'm sure the Montgolfier brothers will spare us one.'

'We could still seek out a smuggler.'

'By traipsing up and down the canal and asking?' Pearce growled, thumping one of the panniers in frustration. 'You must know that's too dangerous, doubly so without any means to produce the kind of payment it would require just to get aboard. And don't mention Dundas and a promise of future reward.'

'We could tell them of our connections and our reasons for being stuck in Flanders.'

'If men who follow that trade thought there was a price on our heads and, who knows, there might be, they'd just as likely turn us in. I have experience of these people, you do not. They are not to be trusted.'

Expecting a string of questions from Oliphant about said experience and at least some vehement protest, Pearce was surprised at how calmly he reacted, though he didn't speak for what seemed like an age.

'Then we must go via Calais. There's a regular neutral cartel sailing between there and Dover. Getting aboard is not easy, quite the opposite, but it can be done and, once on the ship, we should be safe.'

'You seem very sure.'

'Why would I not be, when I have used the route to get out of France before?'

CHAPTER THREE

'Mrs Barclay, there's a fellow at the door who says he has come with letters from your father.'

The message from the house steward caused a frisson of alarm: for Emily's father to send a servant, rather than using a postal service, boded ill. It quickly put an end to the chucking of baby Adam under the chin, which was a pity. The child was much given to smiling and gurgling when tickled.

'Thank you, Cotton.' A final peck on a full cheek was accompanied by, 'Please call the nursemaid to sit with my son while I attend to it.'

Emily, still full of concern, made her way down the wide staircase to the front door, where stood another servant of Heinrich Lutyens, a livered footman, holding the handle of the closed door.

At a nod, it was pulled open to reveal a fellow of middle years, immediately identified.

'Tom Whetton, is it you?'

The cap that had been on the man's head was swiftly whipped off, revealing greying hair, while a hand was held up containing said letters, one in particular pushed forward.

'Your papa begged me bring this by hand, as he would not trust it to strangers.'

'It does not speak of distress, I hope?'

That engendered a tooth-missing smile as Tom got the drift. He too lived in a world where death and disease could strike suddenly, even to the heartiest soul. The cheerful reply came in his warm Somerset drawl.

'How would I know, ma'am, not being lettered, but all were hale when I set out, may God preserve them whole.'

'Then I will not have you stood on the doorstep.'

Those words and a nod saw Tom Whetton step inside, not without a swift skyward look from the footman, his feelings plain that someone of Tom's standing should not be allowed through the main doorway instead of the basement. The sudden yell, loud and speaking of serious discomfort, startled Tom and had him look with alarm at the closed hallway door, from behind which it had emanated.

'Pay that no heed. It is merely Mr Lutyens treating a patient.'

The look that got, one which made Emily smile, was a silent plea to never be prey to such medical ministrations. Heinrich, in whose house she was staying, had become a very fashionable physician in the last two years, with a string of wealthy clients paying goodly sums to suffer his attentions. She knew, of old, he was not a gentle practitioner. That had been so when he'd been the surgeon aboard HMS *Brilliant*. So, regardless of the depth of a purse, alleviation, if it came at all, was generally accompanied by a degree of distress.

'You must be sharp set, Tom, from your travels. Can we provide you with a bite to eat and something to drink?'

'That'd be most kind, Mrs Barclay.'

The footman was instructed to ask of the cook that both be provided, to be fetched to the drawing room. It was an order obeyed, but it came with a significant pause to register further disapproval: the drawing room indeed! Not for the first time, and especially with Tom Whetton standing cap in hand close by, Emily registered the gap which existed between servants such as him, from a rural setting and almost part of the family, set against the sort employed in London, whom she was sure looked down on their paymasters.

Once they were alone, Tom handed over another tied packet, which bore her address, as well as the superscription of her late husband's prize agents, Ommaney and Druce. But he added in a serious manner, 'The first message, ma'am, the one that so worried your papa. He was keen it should be read right off.'

Emily broke the wax on the folded letter, indicating that Tom should be seated, which saw him perch uneasily on the edge of a satin-covered chair. Opening it revealed an enclosure, a rather grubby slip of cheap paper, which looked as if it had been much handled. She recognised her father's sloping writing in the main missive and read the words, which said no more than that he had received the enclosure by hand. It being unsealed, he had taken the liberty of reading it. The contents had so shocked him he felt it necessary to send Tom Whetton to London as a safe bearer of the insinuations, which he would not trust to a public service.

Emily was amused by his caution, not unusual in a parent who was given to being easily discomfited, for John Raynesford lived a very ordered life. Anything untoward took on dramatic overtones they rarely warranted, and this was probably an instance. Unfolding the enclosure and reading it soon wiped both the smile from her face and the sentiment from her mind.

Aware Tom was watching her closely, she composed her features to smile at him and enquire after everyone at home in Frome. This was continued over tea and cake as she had a look at the other letters relating to her business affairs. The old Raynesford family retainer seemed much flattered to be drinking a valuable brew he might never before have tasted. At home the tea caddy was locked and her father had the key.

'You must be weary, Tom, and I would not hear of you seeking a bed other than in the attics. I'm sure Mr Lutyens will oblige.'

'Oblige what?'

The question was posed from a door, which had opened noiselessly, to reveal the owner of the house, which had Tom, who knew quality when he saw it, leap to his feet. He also, no doubt, took in the small stature and features, which had about them a vagueness, the expression on his face one of curiosity and somewhat fish-like in enquiry. Emily provided a quick explanation and the request for a bed was rapidly acceded to, on the grounds that she may wish to send a letter back to her father.

'I'll leave you, Emily, to ensure Cook knows to lay another place for the servant's dinner.'

A bell was rung, the same footman appeared and Tom was taken away to be accommodated. As soon as the door was closed behind them, Emily, her look serious, passed both her father's letter and the enclosure that had so shocked her to Lutyens.

'Gherson, for all love!' he exclaimed, on reading the superscription on the grubby note.

'Indeed.'

Lutyens read on, his brow furrowed. 'Do you give credence to what he is seeking to tell you?'

'It has never been my inclination to trust him.'

'Wise, Emily, very wise.'

If Cornelius Gherson had figured little in Heinrich Lutyens life, he had been a bane in Emily Barclay's. Pressed into HMS *Brilliant* on the same night as John Pearce, though not from the Pelican Tavern, he had proved to be the most mendacious creature imaginable, utterly untrustworthy. He was also excessively vain, sure that she, when he made his interest in her plain, would not be able to resist either his comely looks or his oleaginous charms.

That had earned him a rude rejection, but it had failed to stymie his attentions, so it had to be repeated on more than one occasion until he finally seemed to accept rejection, something not taken well. He had wormed his way into her late husband's regard and ended up as his clerk. This had Emily decide, since Ralph Barclay had proved to be a marital despot and had turned out to be a less than suitable husband, they were made for each other.

'If you recall, Heinrich, with the duties he carried out for Captain Barclay, he was certainly in a position to act as he claims and it suits his dubious character.'

'Which is a long way from accepting that a respectable firm of prize agents, well known in the naval community, conspired with him to dun your husband out of the full dues on his investments.'

'Do you think I should go and see him, as he requests?'

That brought forth a thin smile. 'I have long ago come to accept, Emily, and this applies just as much to John Pearce as you, that any advice I proffer is usually ignored.'

'That's unfair.'

'Which leads me to suspect you are going to Newgate.'

'Do you think he could be, as he claims, innocent?'

'Hard to tell, my dear. John, when he spoke of it to me, was incredulous and he knows him better than I. But my opinion? I do not like him and would never trust him, but I too cannot see him as a rapist and murderer who would, after gratifying his lust, mutilate a woman's body.'

There was no conclusion one way or the other from Emily, more a look of confusion, as Heinrich Lutyens turned to another subject, one as a physician he felt qualified to pronounce upon. It was a subject he had challenged her with since she first became his guest.

'Are you still wedded to the folly of feeding your own child? It wearies you and deprives you of much needed sleep. I tell you once more, you'd have no trouble engaging a wet nurse and I will set in motion moves to find one on your word.'

'Why would I forgo it, Heinrich, when it makes us both so content?'

'I'm not sure contentment in an infant is good for his future well-being.'

Thinking that for all his erudition and ability in the medical line he knew nothing about children, Emily replied, 'I'm hoping by doing so he grows up to be like his father.'

That got a cackling, good-humoured laugh. 'Then God have mercy on his poor little soul.'

Adam's father, along with Oliphant, was trudging through soft, dry sand at the head of the beach, staying as close to the dunes as possible, each carrying one of the panniers, Oliphant with a fishing rod over his shoulder. It had been his contention that alone conferred an appearance of innocence; what could be seen as wrong on a beach, about an angler and his companion looking for a good spot to cast their line?

John Pearce was once more being gently upbraided for not seeing the world as it really was, this as both men kept a weather eye for anything that could spell danger. So far, nothing had appeared to pose a threat. They were on a beach that ran all the way from Gravelines to Calais and were not the only people about. Out on the wet sands a whole host of human clusters were digging for cockles and worms, seeking their tradeable bait and molluscs before the tide came in.

Beyond them, out to sea, but not far offshore, sat dozens of small fishing boats, while further out they could see billowing sails, as coastal traders plied a course as close as they could to land, one that would allow them to run for shelter if an enemy vessel appeared on the horizon.

'You feel betrayed, Pearce, but look at the matter from the point of view of those who saw a need to abandon us.'

'I am angered by the method more than the act.'

That got a soft chuckle. 'Hardly true. If you are uncomfortable at all, it is with your own erroneous assumptions, your strong belief in their honest intentions. But I say again, they have concerns that make their actions, to my mind, perfectly rational.'

'No doubt you will now explain to me why.'

'I will also clarify what made me see it as a possibility from the very outset, even before the noise of that idiot clattering on the door yesterday morning.'

'Do not hesitate to enlighten me on that too,' was delivered with a tone lacking in anything like enthusiasm.

'Was it perhaps deliberate, to drive us into the open? A ploy to match that we had already been duped by?'

'Our hosts?' Pearce insisted, not wishing to contemplate he might be wrong about that too.

'They went to some lengths to avoid identification, did they not? And before you mention the girl, I suspect Eugenie was not her real name. Hark back to arrangements to get away, not least the tunnel. It speaks of organisation and foresight, which means they knew taking us in represented a risk.'

'Why do I sense hindsight becoming foresight?'

'Curious, those tunnels. They were far from fresh hewn.'

'No doubt they're the same as exist on our own coasts. Taxes are, as that American cove Franklin said, the only thing as sure as death. The French must have a revenue service too and, I daresay, their citizens are just as adept at avoidance of duties as our own.'

'Hence the connection to the English fraternity,' was expressed as if it came with enlightenment. 'Our own people would trust and deal with another smuggler, for sure, whatever the nationality.'

There was a pause while that was considered. 'But to continue and, as I do so, I wish to remind you of the number of times you checked me either by word or look, when I did not replicate your unbounded faith.'

'Which,' Pearce snapped, 'I put down to your habit of being discourteous when it was uncalled for. We were dependent on their good offices.'

'But it was right to be so.' That got no response from John Pearce, who was still unwilling to be open about how wrong he had been. 'We were sent to a house that was not theirs, which, by the way, the girl should not have admitted was the case. Then we were whisked away to one previously abandoned and by a route that made pursuit impossible. Where you see a degree of dissimulation, I see something to admire.'

'It would please me if you'd get to the point.'

'The point is, Pearce, we don't matter. Arrangements had been made to get us away, of that I'm sure. But they took precautions against us being part of a plot, in order to protect themselves, soon established by the speed with which they apparently came to arrest not just we two, but those harbouring us. The organisation of which they are part is, I now take leave to assume, royalist, widespread and made up of a substantial body of people of some standing. What they have done, by forsaking us to our own devices, is to ensure that it is not any further penetrated.'

'There's scant doubt it's infiltrated.'

'Of course it is. Cambacérès had already exposed the Parisian conspirators. We were sent on our way to flush out the rest – perhaps not all, but certainly a major part – and, no doubt, to shut down a means by which the conspirators can communicate with England. I wouldn't be surprised if the whole plot that brought us to France originated in Gravelines.'

Pearce wondered, in the ensuing silence, if Oliphant was doing the same as he, reprising the whole escapade from the outset. The contrived capture; code words that would allow them to make contact with people who claimed to have the ability to bring about the fall of the Jacobins. And there waiting for them was Régis de Cambacérès, a regicide as well as a survivor of the Terror, still whole when many of those who had voted to guillotine King Louis had themselves fallen to the blade.

Pearce had been fooled into believing Cambacérès had a soft spot for him: not only a physical attraction, given he was an open pederast, but a degree of sympathy for the way his father had perished.

Oliphant, obviously experienced in the game of duplicity, he had met for the first time in Whitehall as the man who would accompany and guide him. It had been an occasionally fractured relationship in getting to where they were advised they needed to be and that had not diminished. Pearce could not forget that Cambacérès had identified his companion too, and named him as Bertrand, which had Pearce demanding to know if that was his real name. He was still waiting for an answer.

'Dundas and Pitt were equally deceived, then?'

'It would seem so.'

'Do you not mean obviously so?' All that query got was a smile. 'I look forward to telling them.'

A man who'd been calm, and not short on being smug, barked at him with real venom. 'I've already pointed out that is the wrong message to deliver. There is opposition to the Jacobins, extensive opposition, we have just been in their hands. That is what Pitt and Dundas must be told.'

'Would that be because your future depends on it?'

'Are your prospects so rosy that you can comment upon mine? Do you think I failed to ask about you before we set out, to seek a reason why you were being groomed for a task such as that we have been part of? If I wanted to know, all I was required to do was find a naval officer and mention your name. So perhaps, my ever-so-lofty friend in misfortune, your future depends on it too.'

If Oliphant had wanted to make Pearce miserable, he could not have touched on a more sensitive spot. But before he could brood on that, he got a shock, as his companion put forward another proposition.

'I wonder if, *in extremis*, they might have killed us rather than let us fall into Jacobin hands?'

'That I cannot even countenance.'

'Why ever not? For them the fate of their country is paramount. They are people with a cause for which they will willingly sacrifice their own lives. What makes you think, if that cause was in peril, they would spare us? Beware those who put an ideology above their own well-being, Pearce, for they will care naught for yours.'

The tone of his voice changed from morbid speculation to one of cheer. 'If you look ahead, you will see the walls of Calais plain now.'

The spire of the cathedral had been in sight for some time. Now they could see the walls through which they would have to progress, at which point Pearce posed a question he had been dying to ask since they set out.

'I'm bound to ask you, why did you not mention this as a possible route to escape until we were abandoned to our own fate?'

'Given what I have just been telling you, I invite you to speculate?'

If the conclusion was not long in coming, it was far from a warming one when arrived at. 'You would have left me to my fate, if I had been captured?'

'I would, and given you have no idea of this means of getting out of France, you would have been unable to betray it and me.'

'It does not occur that I would have remained silent?'

'Easily said, Pearce, when no one has a knife at your eye, with one already gouged out.'

'You have said you have been seeking to educate me. I thank providence I have the character to stay an ignoramus.'

Oliphant threw back his head and laughed, before dropping his pannier packed with provisions. 'By all means sacrifice yourself for me, Pearce, just don't expect it to be returned. Now, let us at least praise our conspirators for being generous with the means to assuage our bellies.'

CHAPTER FOUR

Fortified since time immemorial, the town of Calais had long spread beyond the old medieval walls, thus entry to the outer environs came without difficulty. The problem, Oliphant explained, would arise in trying to get through the gates and into the old town, without which there would be no access to the waterfront and harbour.

'It's still seen as a way out of the country for those at odds with the regime. There are watchers on the gates, keeping an eye out for known agitators or unfamiliar faces in a town where the same people make their way in and out regularly.'

They were heading towards one of those now, obscured from authority by a crowd gathered at the entrance, presumably queuing for permission to pass through, something that would appear to be taking time, which was quickly referred to.

'That does not speak of guards who will just let pass two unfamiliar fishermen. For certain, these panniers we're carrying will invite search. Not only do we have those uniforms, but each one contains a pistol.'

Oliphant took a firm grip on Pearce's arm and hauled him off the roadway into a narrow alley, one devoid of humanity and hemmed in by low, windowless buildings, where he began to outline how they were to proceed.

'I have a contact, one who has aided me in the past when I was on my own. I must warn you, us being together may complicate matters.' He waited in vain for Pearce to speak; the man should be demanding more. 'You're silent, I find.'

'You're still husbanding information it would do no harm to share.'

'Has everything I have said to you previously been wasted? If I'm to make an approach, it has to be done without you.' Oliphant looked hard at a less-than-happy companion. 'If I can sometimes carry concealment to excess, it is the only safe way to act in order to protect others, in this case a person I hope is still able to provide assistance.'

'How?'

'One bridge to cross at a time. We must part company for a while. I wonder how that sits with you.'

'I've had a need to be cautious in this country before,' Pearce snapped, sick of the endless condescension. 'And I have been content to depend on my own wits.'

If he'd hoped his tone would check Oliphant, he was disappointed; the man spoke with more than studied calm. 'I suggest we dispose of the rod.'

With that he threw it so high it landed, to get embedded, on the thatch of a low roof. From a pocket he extracted some of the coins left over from the sale of Pearce's clothing, a couple of Dutch guilders.

'More than enough for a bottle of wine and some food.'

'There is no danger in using such currency?'

'They will be welcome in these parts. The whole of France trades in what coinage they can acquire, anything to avoid useless paper money. Calais is a port like Gravelines and they are accustomed to foreign coinage, just as they are adept at giving less for it than its true value.'

Oliphant moved on, Pearce following, until they came to a small square and the destination: a tavern with a low doorway and tables outside. Pearce didn't need anyone to tell him inside was best. Food pannier in hand – Oliphant would take the second one – he entered and sought the darkest corner, a table deep in the interior of the low-ceilinged room, much scarred on its top where previous customers had carved their names.

He sat well away from the doorway, a favoured spot and occupied by chattering customers, men who had barely spared him a glance on entry. Approached by a buxom mademoiselle, he ordered wine, bread and sausage in a gruff manner, designed to prevent any attempt at conversation. With that delivered he was alone again with his thoughts and recollections.

It had been a place not dissimilar to this from which he'd been pressed into the navy by Ralph Barclay. The images of that night, of a mass of sailors rushing in wielding clubs, had him ease open the catch on his pannier, which exposed the butt of his pistol. It had been jammed into the rolled-up boat cloak in a way that allowed it to stay primed and loaded. If anything threatened him, as it had in the Pelican Tavern, he was determined he would not go quietly.

The outside of Newgate Prison had been designed to intimidate, with its reinforced walls and few windows, giving it an air of deliberate and brutal vulgarity. There had been one attempt to soften the outline of the more comfortable part, the State House, with statues in alcoves of various famous lawgivers. But since they all wore grim expressions, it hardly moderated the whole.

The carved chains over the entrance to the Common Gaol were designed to instil terror into those who, about to be incarcerated, saw it for the first time. For a visitor, entry presented no such fears; nevertheless Emily, having coached from Harley Street, with Tom Whetton as an escort and companion, took a deep breath before descending and making to cross the threshold.

'Stay close, Tom.'

She imparted this to a man trying to hide his own reservations. Newgate was known to all in his hometown. It was likely, when named, to induce a feeling of fear in a place much given to rioting over these last decades. This had occurred several times when the price of wool, the main staple of trade in the county, fell so far as to make starvation for those on the lower rungs of the community a real danger.

Houses were torched, storerooms sacked and those seen as hoarders and exploiters forced to flee. Such disturbances inevitably led to broken heads and, on the odd occasion, much worse – violence enough to bring in the soldiery to impose law and order. Thus, some of the most vicious offenders of Frome had ended up here, awaiting judgement for their crimes at the nearby Old Bailey.

Well supplied with warders at the gate, it was mandatory, according to Heinrich Lutyens, who often visited for the purpose of study, they be slipped a small coin for the trouble to which they did not go. This, once the name was given and the location of the prisoner identified, consisted of calling to a boy and telling him to lead the lady to the common cells of the Men's Quadrangle.

'Which are occupied by many more than one prisoner, surely?'

'Have to be, ma'am.'

'Would it be possible for me to see the man I'm visiting in private?'

She might look young, sweet and naïve, and certainly pretty, but Emily Barclay had seen and done things at which this fellow could only guess. As John Pearce knew, there was a core of steel within that delightful frame. So when the doorkeeper said, with a deeply worried expression and an insincere manner, that he 'should' ask the warden, Emily was certain the answer was in his gift. The next words he imparted confirmed his purpose.

'An' he ain't here, as of this moment, ma'am. Saw him out this very gate not an hour past.'

She did crestfallen well, but the simultaneous slipping of her hand into a decent-sized purse was what drew his eye. When a hint of silver appeared, it produced an expression that had Emily register she was in the presence of an accomplished performer. His face went through various expressions from an inability to oblige, a query as to the cruelty of the fact, to finally arrive at what was in his mind.

'Warden likes, for special privileges, that visitor's show a bit of charity to the unfortunates under his care. Now it ain't my duty to press his desires but . . .'

Emily's hand came fully out of the purse, producing a shilling, which would be half a week's wage to this fellow. His expression went from concern, through to the almost beatific, before the coin was taken, this as if it was the Papist host, though it disappeared into a pocket, not his mouth to check the metal. Emily knew that to laugh would not serve, but it was hard in the face of such hypocrisy to keep her features straight. Thankfully the warder had looked away to loudly repeat his instructions to the limping youngster previously called forth.

'Take this sainted lady to the State House and the warden's anteroom, then have someone fetch the prisoner Gherson to that place as well.'

'He'd have done it for two pence, Mrs Barclay,' Tom whispered, as they were led away.

'I know, Tom, and I doubt the prisoners will see any of the so-called charity.'

'Happen the wrong people are given the rope.'

They followed the lad to a first-floor landing, he hobbling through corridors of closed cell doors, all studded, with unopened and barred viewing panels. The sound of an indifferently played violin came from behind one, but that soon faded and silence reigned. The door to the anteroom was different; made of heavy, varnished and much-carved oak, panelled and with nothing of the prison cell about it.

It opened onto a room that was comfortable, if not very well appointed, with a long table bounded by several leather-covered

51

chairs, with heavily barred windows overlooking noisy Newgate Street. The wait was uncomfortable; Emily might have steeled herself to face Cornelius Gherson, but it had never been a pleasant experience in the past – quite the reverse. With it now imminent, the feeling in her chest of a dubious enterprise embarked upon became oppressive.

When he did arrive, he was accompanied by another warder and dragged by a set of shackles, his escort a burly, heavily bearded fellow with a club. The feeling of dread evaporated at once: never had she seen anyone so diminished. His clothing, normally something in which he took excessive pride, consisted of tattered rags. The blonde hair was unkempt, matted and long and, where it joined his forehead, showed the blueish remains of several bruises. Below that, even with his head part bowed and eyes cast down, she could see tangled and wispy blonde growth on a previously close-shaved chin.

'I wish to speak with the prisoner only in the company of my servant.' As the warder looked set to protest, Emily added quickly, 'I made the arrangement with the fellow at the gate that this was to be a private visit.'

The burly warder's eyes narrowed under a beetle brow; it was as if he sensed money had changed hands and he might be in for a share. Yet he was concerned to leave a prisoner alone with just a slip of a lady.

'Your man there a'stayin?'

'He is.'

The warder looked past Emily to Tom, who had good broad shoulders. 'Then he'll be no trouble, an' if he is, you'se my permission to bruise him a bit more than he is already, for he's a mouthy sod, saving your presence, ma'am.' The shackles got a shake as he stuck his face to within an inch of Gherson's. 'You heard that?'

A meek nod, with eyes still downcast. 'Right 'en, ma'am. I be outwith the door.'

The head came up slowly as the warder exited, and there it was: a look of defiance which was more like the Gherson she knew. She sent Tom as far away as the room would allow, to stand by the window, before addressing him.

'Do you wish to sit?'

'Do you think I require your permission?'

'Should I call the warder back and tell him you lack manners?' As he sunk timidly into a chair, Emily did likewise, pulling from inside her bag the grubby missive he had sent. 'I require you to explain this.'

'Does it not say enough? Captain Barclay was systematically dunned for a percentage of his dividends and some of the investments made on his behalf are speculative to a less than sound degree.'

'All carried out by you.'

'I merely ensured they attracted little attention. The actions were contrived at by the agents supposedly working on his behalf.'

'People I take to be as wretched as you.'

'Come, Mrs Barclay, I suspect you have either been to see them, or have been in correspondence, perhaps on the subject of my letter.'

She was not going to answer his enquiry: that it might be her next port of call was for her alone to know. 'What a sorry specimen you are.'

'Fit to see to your husband's affairs, by his estimation. I am bound to ask you what took you so long to come.'

'You will want for an answer.'

Sudden passion was muted; he dared not shout for fear of the warder, so it came out as a snake-like hiss. 'Do you know what I've sacrificed to get that note to you, every stich of decent clothing I possessed? I have been living like a pig in a sty for two weeks.'

'If the courts were in session, Gherson, you would have been hanged by now and I would have been spared this interview.'

Gherson could not contain himself. Spittle flew from his mouth and there was no more hiss; this was a shout. 'For a crime I did not commit!'

The door swung open and Gherson, who had been sitting forward, his face contorted, suddenly shrank into a ball, like a threatened hedgehog. The warder, his club swinging in his hand, looked at Emily, who shook her head to say there was no need for him to stay. As the door closed once more Gherson sobbed.

'Please believe me, you must believe me.'

'You say you can prove both your innocence and what you assert in this letter?'

'You have been robbed and I can get back for you every missing guinea.'

'And what do you want from me in return?'

'My freedom. A search for proof that I'm not a beast.'

'The first is not in my gift. As to the second, who am I to say?'

Suddenly he was gabbling, about the night Catherine Carruthers died. First, her unexpected arrival at the Covent Garden bagnio in which he was taking his pleasure, a woman

54

whom he had not seen for years and one far from pleased, indeed furious, to note both his inebriated state and the company he was keeping.

'Of the kind for which the Garden is famous.'

'Not something I would know about.'

Being too noisy they had repaired to a private room where he could calm her down. Within less than ten minutes, and before he'd had a chance to persuade her of his continued regard, two brutes burst in and felled him. He knew nothing of what followed, but awoke to find his one-time mistress lying on her back on the floor, with her clothing ripped and her intimate parts exposed.

Emily was no shrinking violet, but she did then blush, while wondering what Tom Whetton was making of all this. Gherson had not finished. He sobbed, his misery increasing as he added,

'And the blood, Mrs Barclay. Her blood, all over the floor and me. And by her body lay a knife . . . not mine . . . theirs . . .'

The way he began to control himself, an apparent struggle, left Emily wondering if what had gone before was contrivance. Deep breathing first, then the clenched fists pounding his knees, as if he was fighting an internal battle, followed by the whispered coda.

'I may be many things, Mrs Barclay, but I am not a butcher. Certainly not of someone for whom I had a previous regard, a *tendresse*, as well as an intimate affection. She had given her body to me freely in the past.'

'So you knew the lady well?' was asked to cover her discomfort at so much disclosure.

'She was the wife of my one-time employer, Alderman Denby Carruthers. It was through him that I ended up aboard HMS *Brilliant*.'

That was a tale Emily knew well. It had become the talk of the ship on the voyage to the Mediterranean, so much so, it had even come to be talked about in the great cabin, where she resided with her husband. How Gherson had landed in the River Thames, right beside the boat taking John Pearce and his fellow pressed men downriver to Sheerness. Gherson was hauled out to be saved from drowning and, if he'd denied falling off the bridge, he had never said how such an occurrence came about. For the first time the voice was measured, low and flat.

'All I have to trade with is my cooperation in the matter of Captain Barclay's investments.'

'You seem very sure your being involved is necessary.'

'It is, for you'll be dealing with people well able to obscure figures.'

'And if I were to agree?'

'First, I need to be moved from the common cells to this State House, to a room where I can, with quill and paper, give you a list of questions to ask. These will be queries to which they will be unable to avoid a response, as well as some they must, for their own sake, decline to answer. Once I have proved myself to you, I hope to warrant the means to prove my innocence. A lawyer must be engaged and a plea put into the court for a delay in bringing me to trial. That will provide the time to uncover the truth.'

'You ask a great deal, which I must consider . . .'

The interruption was soft, but it was very insistent. 'I do

not have time for such consideration. Without I secure a delay, when the courts sit again, I will be brought before a judge, tried, convicted and hanged within days, no more than a public spectacle for a baying mob. If my words don't move you, I hope Christian charity will.'

'Tell me again what occurred.'

This time the explanation was more fulsome; he admitted he had been very drunk, in fact in such a state for days, spending money given to him by Edmund Druce, bribes to ensure his silence in the matter of her inheritance. It was also the case that his surprise visitor had been distressed at what he had clearly been up to with the ladies who entertained the customers of the bagnio. They might be a cut above street whores, but they would, if the terms were right, play the prostitute nevertheless.

'She was very vocal in her condemnation, which disturbed other clients, thus we were asked to shift to an upstairs room. It was there that the deed was done, her poor body mutilated . . .'

Emily had heard enough of that and cut across him. 'I was told of a will – a forged one, it transpired.'

'Created for me by a friend. With your husband gone, I needed a way to earn a living. The will was designed to force Druce to see to my well-being, for that purpose and no other. I knew it would hardly have held up in the Court of Chancery.'

Was he telling the truth? Emily was aware he had reverted to type, albeit his appearance militated against it. Gherson was master spinner of falsehoods and his growing assurance seemed an affront, an animation that had brought to the fore, through the grime, his absurdly, almost girlish, good looks. Yet she had been careful to show no overt sympathy, so he would surely know an appeal to her better nature was likely to fall on stony ground.

'From memory, tell me of one of the more egregious depredations played upon my husband.'

CHAPTER FIVE

Oliphant was taking too long. To sit alone eating in a tavern was one thing; to stay still and unoccupied for an age afterwards was not, especially when the bill had been settled. This was not like a London Coffee House, to which people repaired for many hours to discuss weighty matters and read the latest journals, or lose themselves quietly in a book. Locals stopped here for a limited time to take a quick and bracing eau de vie before moving on.

Customers drifted in, individually and sometimes in small groups, workers or artisans, some having loud conversations as they exchanged the latest rumours. The taverner saw to their requirements and they left again, this while Pearce sat on in his dark corner trying to look contemplative and relaxed, when inside he was seething with anxiety.

He sought to distract himself by thinking about the cartel they would try to board. The crossing being so short, there had been regular and heavy traffic between Dover and Calais before even Roman times. The French Channel port had ever been a bolt-hole for those Britons running from their debts, or writs against their name like the radical agitator John Wilkes. Some, when hostilities broke out, would have had no option but to remain; to leave Calais was to exchange their accommodation for a prison cell.

Very obviously, even if they were at war, there must be a need for some form of communications, otherwise what could be the purpose of a regular cartel vessel? Were there still diplomatic messages passing back and forth between Britain and France, if for no other reason than possible moves to call a halt to the war? Or enquiries regarding the well-being of prisoners, the kind of correspondence that might lead to an exchange. This would be something of more value to the French than Albion, given they lost more ships and crews in battle. But it was probably a two-way and mutually beneficial affair.

Such prevarication could not go on for ever. In the end, knowing the day would some time soon begin to turn to night, he picked up his pannier and made his way out to the small square, which was hardly much better in terms of being exposed. All he could think of doing was to pace round the perimeter, an act which, if it became repetitive, would expose him to curious scrutiny.

'Pearce.'

The voice, emanating from the dark recess of the narrow walkway, the one by which he and his companion had originally entered the square, made his heart skip a beat. If his mood was far from sanguine, it went down several notches when the same voice hissed.

'By damn, you took your time.'

A hand shot out and grabbed Oliphant by the throat, to push him back and out of sight against the wall. Pearce followed up and pressed with such force the man's eyes showed serious alarm, which brought no sympathy whatever. Frustration was added to sheer rage at the discomfort and worry Pearce had been suffering.

'I've a mind to see you damned to hell.'

'For the love of God,' came out as a gasp.

'You choose the wrong deity to appeal to.' Having said that and forcibly made his point, Pearce eased his grip. 'I have been sat in there for an age, wondering what had happened to you.'

'I reckoned it best not to come in. Safer.'

'For you?'

'For us both,' Oliphant insisted. 'There are eyes everywhere. I had to make sure the tavern was not being watched, knowing you had to come out eventually. If anyone had sought to apprehend you, I would have been able to come to your aid, or at least distract them.'

There was something not quite right about the excuses, but Pearce had learnt on this very day that to ask for the truth was pointless. 'Which you could have advised me about before we parted.'

'How, when I had no idea how long I would be? Anyway, I have good news. The Dover vessel is berthed as we speak. If the weather remains clear and the wind stays in the north-east, the plan is to sail on the tide at first light. We are to be provided with the means to get into the harbour before it weighs.'

'What about payment?'

'Has been made and we had it all along without knowing. It was in the pannier I took with me. The uniforms will, in the future, come in useful to the people I know. But even better, the pocket of your jacket revealed that passport from Lazare Carnot. It was signed for the day we left Paris, but had no end date, which makes it a truly priceless document.'

'And how are we to get aboard?'

'Trust that it will happen. Now compose your features, abate your anger, and follow me.'

Oliphant didn't wait for agreement, which left Pearce trailing him once more. He moved at a brisk pace through a series of narrow alleys, occasionally crossing wider streets but never once turning to check if his companion was keeping up. Finally, in a quiet backstreet, he stopped outside the gates of what looked like a warehouse. It had a beam and a pulley above an upper-storey doorway, by which goods could be hoisted onto the first floor. The series of staggered knocks was clearly a signal, which caused a tiny viewing panel to open, so whoever was inside could identify the caller.

The clattering sound of a bar being removed was followed by the gate swinging open. Pearce followed Oliphant through and into a covered and gloomy courtyard, most of which was taken up by a pair of carts, fully loaded and covered with tarpaulins. The fellow who opened up nodded they should proceed, then sat down in the place he occupied. He had a chair and beside it a musket resting against the wall, which was presumably loaded.

The horse stalls were behind the carts, all occupied but with a corridor between. This led to a sizeable chamber packed floor to ceiling with bales, chests and barrels, the overarching odour being of a miscellany of wines, tobacco and spices. The door at the rear required no knock, so Pearce followed his companion into a comfortably appointed room. This was lit by several ornate oil lamps, dominated by a large open fireplace full of burning logs, making it somewhat oppressively warm.

'Marie, this is the fellow I told you about.' There was a pause before he added. 'For all our sakes I will not use his name.'

The woman he'd addressed rose from a wing chair she occupied to examine him, Pearce doing likewise. He took in her solid frame, encased in a brown brocade dress, which did not speak of being in anyway gross, more of the natural shape of a woman who'd never been slender. She had a mass of ginger curls, which fell to frame the face, while her pallid skin told him her age was past the peak of youthful beauty. Yet there was a clear trace of a woman who must have been striking in the past. The eyes were brilliant blue, steady and piercing, the mouth tight and unsmiling.

'For the risks being proposed, you must be someone of importance.'

Oliphant spoke gently, before Pearce could reply, not that he would have done, given he had no idea what his companion had said about him. 'The less said the better, Marie, you know secrets kept hidden cannot be revealed.'

That produced a ghost of a smile, accompanied by a look aimed at Oliphant, which had about it a degree of longing. Well versed in the way people regarded each other, Pearce was left to wonder at the possibility of a relationship.

'Take your friend to another room, Oliver.' Oliver, not Samuel! Yet another name, though it could be a given, birth one. Was he really Oliver Bertrand? She broke through these thoughts as she addressed Pearce directly. 'It would be good that you rest, for once the light begins to go, you must get ready to depart.'

Oliphant took her hand to lift and kiss it, engendering a smile, which was soft and benevolent, this as a hand came out to gently stroke his cheek. Told by a gesture to follow, Pearce was taken to a small adjoining parlour, this too with an open fire.

'I must leave you here for a while, I have a duty to perform.'

John Pearce was in little doubt as to what the duty consisted of. 'If I'm asked who I am, since you seem to have made up some tale about me, what am I to say?'

'You will not be asked.' With that Oliphant departed, saying over his shoulder. 'Sit down, take your ease. You're safe here.'

Given the strain of the last forty-eight hours and an indifferent night's sleep, Pearce did as he was told, occupying a comfortable armchair and laying back, eyes closed. With the heat from the fire, he was soon asleep, woken by a shaking of his shoulder, the light from a hand-held lamp causing him to blink.

'Time to get ready. If you wish to shave, as I have done, there is a bowl of hot water on the dresser and a looking glass. There's a change of clothes as well.'

Pearce could not resist a jibe. 'The perfect servant, for once.'

The response was a gratifying growl. 'Don't tempt me to leave you behind.'

The lamp was placed by the looking glass and water, which was indeed hot. He extracted his razor from his pannier, to find the act of shaving off two days' growth truly refreshing. That done, he examined the clothing, a threadbare black jacket laying over black breeches. Neither were a good fit, the former too tight and the latter a couple of inches short. Likewise round the waist, the top button could not be secured. Once dressed he waited, full of curiosity, until Oliphant came back, he too dressed all in black.

'Come, we need to help get those carts we passed out of the yard and the horses harnessed. Don't forget to pocket your pistol, but leave everything else.'

There was no sign of Marie as they made their way through the parlour, then out into the yard. This was now occupied by a quartet of men, all working in silence and not wishing to exchange greetings. They helped to back the carts out into the backstreet, which, in twilight, appeared deserted.

The horses were brought out, sturdy animals fit to pull a load and seemingly passive-natured with it. Backing them into the spokes and fixing the traces was achieved without equine protest, at which point they were ordered to take a seat on the lowered back tailgate. Two of the men sat astride a horse on each cart, while the other pair, having hooked substantially sized lanterns on high, rigid poles that oversaw their heads, took to the box seats.

A crack of the leather traces set the mounts in motion and, if facing backwards didn't permit any sight of the route, it did get them a wave from that musket-bearing sentinel as they passed him at the end of the street. Moving at no great pace, they slipped onto what was a busier thoroughfare, passing numerous people walking, the pair nodding and smiling, getting like greetings in return. It all seemed so innocent.

'Do you know where we are headed?'

Oliphant nodded, but provided no explanation, so they sat in silence in the fast-fading twilight. The wheels, which had been making a deal of noise on the rutted road, turned silent as a layer of sand absorbed the sound, no doubt a gambit to allow those living close by to sleep in peace.

In full darkness now the cart slowed to a halt, those carriage lanterns providing the only light, not much of which extended to the rear. The sound of voices came floating back and, within short order, a heavily moustached fellow in National Guard uniform appeared, to brusquely order them to climb down.

With access given, he untied and pulled back the canvas covering the load, poking the various bales with his fingers, tapping a couple of barrels with his knuckles, to finally grunt in satisfaction and drop the covering. Oliphant moved forward as he departed to retie the ropes, saying softly, as Pearce joined him, 'For show, no more.'

Back aboard, there was a tense wait before the wheels creaked and the cart began to move again. Within minutes they were under the arch of an old city gate, eyes cast down to avoid contact with the rest of the uniformed men who manned the position. Inside the walls the road was cobbled, which made for a lack of comfort as the unsprung cart bounced and swayed.

Oliphant pointed out they were not yet safe: another medieval gate, leading to the harbour, had to be negotiated. But any concern was misplaced; the sequence occurred as previously, a cursory look at the cargo, before it was waved through. Once he could be sure they were out of sight of the gate, Pearce was told to jump off, this being as far as they would go. On foot they watched till the cart disappeared.

'That's the first hurdles taken.'

'I sensed there had to be more,' Pearce said.

'The Dover ship is fully guarded by the military and the

inspection of papers is rigorous. We can't just approach the ship and march aboard, even if we could get past such scrutiny. That takes no account of our own countrymen, particularly the officer in command. The cartel operates under the strict rules of neutrality, by which they must abide – conditions which do not permit the aiding of escapees, regardless of nationality.'

'They might refuse us passage.'

'I expect they will be sympathetic, if we can meet with them in the right circumstances.'

'Which are?'

'Unobserved by their French counterparts.'

The radiance from a clear sky and the Milky Way – there was only a sliver of a newish moon – allowed for progress through deserted buildings, as well as a number of warehouses used for cargo storage, until they came to the landward end of a great mole. Halfway down, they crouched behind the base of a tall derrick, one of several that lined a wooden and much weather-battered structure. This jutted out to sea, buttressed on both sides by huge timber baulks driven into the mud, forming the berth at which vessels tied up.

They could pick out several ghostly shapes of trading vessels down both sides, but the cartel, its prow towards them, was obvious by being lantern-lit along its upper works. This was busy, with men going about various tasks, both on deck and in the rigging, the reasons plain to a seaman.

'They're preparing the ship, right enough, prior to weighing.'

'You sure?'

'Allow that I know my trade, as well as you know your own.'

Two guards, musket-bearing French soldiers, bayonets attached, stood at the bottom of a sloping gangplank, their presence alluded to by Oliphant. Pearce then drew his attention to the point where it joined the gangway, for there stood a rigid marine guard. One of the ship's big lanterns illuminated his red coat, white crossed belts, the light bouncing off the polished wood of his musket, as well as the steel of his tall bayonet. Did he represent another apparently insurmountable obstacle to making it onto the deck?

A strong light came from the open door of a wooden hut, one of a pair, Oliphant suggesting it probably housed the official, likely to be political, who would be the final arbiter of who was, and who was not, allowed aboard.

'There will be more than two guards,' Pearce whispered, adding they must rotate the duty, pointing out the light leaking from the windows of the second, larger hut. 'I would guess the rest to be accommodated there.'

'Very likely true,' was the low-spirited response.

'How did you get aboard before?'

'Does it matter?'

'Of course it matters.'

A lengthy pause followed what was an obvious question, yet Oliphant seemed to be wondering what to say, which came down, Pearce thought, to whichever suited best: either lying or telling the truth.

'I was taken out by boat to meet the cartel, once she'd cleared the anchorage.'

'A method not vouchsafed this time.'

'There's a good reason.'

'Would that again be something you're keeping to yourself?'

'I am bound by my word to do so this time.'

'No doubt because of my profession.'

In nothing but starlight Pearce couldn't see much of Oliphant's face, but he felt he had no need of an explanation. Carts loaded and moving in darkness, passing through guarded gates with seeming ease, begged the question as to where they were headed. It did not take a genius to work out that, inside the harbour area, the cargo was about to be put aboard a ship, probably one preparing to smuggle those bales, casks and spices into England.

'I sense,' he said softly, determined not to sound ungrateful, 'that the ship before us is not the only non-French vessel that has leave to come and go from Calais. I also sense it is one we cannot be allowed to get close to.'

'While the last thing to be welcomed,' came the equally quiet reply, 'would be a serving British naval officer witnessing both the loading, as well as the nature and name of the ship. I had to tell Marie of your profession, if not your name. She agreed to get us into the docks, but not beyond. That, to keep her trust, I have to respect.'

Pearce wanted to say that the precaution was unnecessary. The Royal Navy had no interest in smuggling: very much the reverse, that was a job for the Revenue Service and there was no love lost between them. But there was no point.

'And now you don't have a plan?' The silence was eloquent. 'So we are relying on good fortune.'

'I had an idea we could haul ourselves aboard by the hawser holding the ship to the mole.' Pearce would have laughed if the situation had allowed, which it did not, as Oliphant added, 'If the rats can do it . . .'

Pearce could not resist the interruption or the barb. 'Which leaves you the one person I know who possesses the natural and required attributes.'

'Damn you,' came the wounded reply.

The insult did merit an apology, but none was forthcoming from a man too busy thinking. It was obvious they could not stay in France, especially with the possibility of continued pursuit, which might not have abated. Once it had been accepted they were not in Gravelines, the next obvious places to look were the ports to the north and south.

If there was some kind of relationship between Marie – was that her real name? – and Samuel Oliphant or the newly minted Oliver, it would not extend to excessive risk. They were in a country where the penalty for nefarious activates was so far from gentle, the guillotine would be seen as clemency. What help had been given was safe to provide and no more. It now came down to their own devices and surely this was a situation where Pearce was required to come up with a solution.

'If you'd clapped eyes on a hawser you'd know why a rat can climb it, where a man will most likely fall. First, if it's been in the sea, it's wet and covered in slime so a grip is impossible. Added to that, the weight of a human will cause it to dip and sway, making it doubly hard to keep hold of.'

'I was told by a tar once it could be easily done.'

'Then you were likely being practised upon. It's a common game played on lubbers like you for the price of a pot of ale. Can you swim?'

'No.'

'Then you'd likely drown.'

Pearce realised he was being too hard on his companion, so he set out to soften his response. 'I daresay it has been managed for a wager and under perfect conditions, but I have no mind to make the attempt. Nor can I think of a method by which we can get aboard otherwise.'

'Then we best go back to the place we dropped off and wait for the carts to return.'

'Arranged?'

'We won't be turned away.'

'So not arranged?' Again there was an eloquent silence of several seconds. 'Were you offered a way out, if you chose to go alone?'

'If you're asking if I'm a fool, the answer is yes.'

'A thought you no doubt gnawed on when I was in that damned tavern, which means I'm obliged to offer up my thanks, given you did not just walk away.'

'Gratitude for which, at this moment, I have little use.'

Pearce was thinking back to the day he and his father had arrived in Calais, fleeing from England at a time before the madness of endless judicial murder gripped France. The ship that brought them from Dover had tied up at this very mole and, if he could not see it now in the darkness, he could well recall the structure. Barnacle-covered timbers below the highest tidal mark, green- and weed-covered above that line.

'If you wish to retrace your steps, on your own, I will not seek to stop you.'

The reply came with a touch of asperity. 'Has anyone ever told you your sanctimony can be infuriating?'

'Not for that, as I recall, but exasperating as a person, many times. The thing is, Oliphant, I reckon I can get aboard unseen, if I'm alone.'

'How?'

'Listen,' was all Pearce said, the note of alarm in his voice obvious.

CHAPTER SIX

The imminence of the approach, signalled by a babble of conversation, had both men dip into a pocket and produce a pistol. Next came the glim of a lantern, bouncing off the warehouse walls, before a six-strong party emerged to make their way onto the mole. The base of the derrick was substantial, as well as square, and this, combined with inching movements, allowed them to remain unseen.

They stayed well hidden until the group was well past and had reached the first hut, into which they disappeared. There they remained for some time, before reappearing again. With everyone calling loud farewells, two of the party made their way up the gangplank, to be greeted by the lifted hat of a fellow in a blue coat, who had come to join the marine sentry. He examined their papers before escorting them further on and out of sight.

The pair had to conceal themselves once more as the four remaining visitors made their way back, past the derrick, until they too disappeared, to become nothing more than a murmur of voices. Oliphant then repeated the question he had posed to Pearce prior to the noise of their approach, which produced an explanation and a method his companion acknowledged, albeit reluctantly, excluded any participation by him.

'You have ever chafed at my being a burden, Oliphant. Now I see it as best you are relieved of the need. How long before the carts make the return journey?'

'They must be out of the gates before six.'

'When the guard changes,' Pearce mused, Oliphant acknowledging the obvious point. Such a routine event would bring to the duty a group not in on the illegality or the bribery that had to go with it. 'You have ample time to rejoin them.'

'There's no certainty you will succeed.'

'True,' came the reply, from someone fully aware of the risks, but one who knew he needed to sound hopeful. 'But if you had ever been to sea, you would know uncertainty is what sailors live with every day. Capricious superiors, unpredictable weather and the hazards of battle to name but three. Added to which, my life, prior to being press-ganged, was just as precarious and I daresay your own has not been without hazard.'

There was another noisy distraction to interrupt this whispered conversation, as the guards at the gangplank were changed, this being done with punctilious military ritual. The door of the larger hut had opened to disgorge the replacement pair, as well as an officer, who called them to attention before engaging in a fussy inspection.

The distance to be covered might only be measured in yards, but it was done at a slow march. This was followed by the requisite shouts and salutes, as two men moved forward and the others took up their place. Those standing down were marched at a similar pace back to the hut, to be dismissed.

'What to say to Dundas,' Oliphant whispered, 'is a subject I have raised before, and you may well get to London before me.'

'You still wish to manufacture a conspiracy?'

'I wish them to know there is opposition to the Jacobins, that it is well organised and a possible source of future upheaval, which might merit support.'

'Which would require contact and employment for a fellow who knows how to make and maintain it.'

'Perhaps a pair, rather than an individual?'

It was an inappropriate place and situation in which to chuckle, but Pearce did just that. 'This after I have proved to be such a liability?'

'I would see you as one quick to learn.'

'I can't see fabrication as being a skill I am keen to acquire.'

'Then leave it to me to paint a picture, one that will meet their aspirations.'

'You are assuming us both to be in a position to do what you require. That, right now, is a distant concern.'

The truth of that was acknowledged: neither of them might get to London, but Oliphant made the point nevertheless. 'It would ease my mind if the matter was settled.'

'I'll seek to be obscure, indefinite, on the grounds of your being better informed and more experienced in the ability to judge matters. But the men we deal with are well able to spot anyone

75

seeking to dissemble and deceive them. They are politicos and practise such arts on a daily basis themselves.'

'I think you'll find, Pearce, the easiest person to deceive is a habitual dissembler.'

'Maybe so.' Pearce handed over his pistol, which would be of no use to him. 'You'd best go now.'

The injunction was acknowledged with no more than a grunt, as if wishing his companion luck was likely to bring on the opposite. Oliphant scurried away, the sound of his departure fading quickly. Knowing he was in for a long wait, Pearce sat with his back to the derrick, facing east. It was from there the timing of his plan would be fixed, which gave him the space to wonder if he could, or should, despite what he'd said to Oliphant, concoct a tale to deceive those who'd sent both of them on this mission.

If it was a selfish thought; it really came down to that which most favoured his own future prospects. Oliphant was bound to act likewise, there being no doubt that he would, so loyalty and honesty were not germane. In order to progress, Pearce needed employment and that came with a strong desire it should be in command of a ship.

With time to kill, he conjured up a touch of pure make-believe, though it was a dream common to the profession, the kind of coup rarely gifted to a naval officer. He imagined the taking of a prize so valuable it would set him up for life. He and Emily would, in this reverie, be married and damn the social norms, the parents of several hearty children, domiciled in a substantial manor house, red-brick and sun-blessed, in the middle of an estate bursting with both produce and profit.

The dream lasted long enough for him to sense, in such a

situation, he would likely become quickly bored, for knew himself to be wedded to risk. He recalled the number of times his life had been in danger since that night in the Pelican, as well as the feeling induced: that of being fully alive.

As a boy and budding youth, he'd had a precarious, peripatetic existence, on the move with his father, a man known for his passionate polemical speeches and pamphlets, and not always with affection, as the Edinburgh Ranter. Addressing a crowd, he was as likely to be booed as cheered for the message he sought to convey to those he saw as exploited and downtrodden. If such a life had periods of boredom, it had also flared up many times into sudden and dangerous excitement. Naval service felt the same.

A hint of grey to the east told him the time had come to make his move, so it was once more necessary to concentrate on the activities aboard the cartel vessel. The bell, which had pealed intermittently throughout the night, rang eight times, which would bring on a change of watch. Not that it would mean leisure for those who'd been on duty. If the captain decided, once he'd seen the sky and assessed the state of the weather, to cast off from the mole, they would be required to participate. It would be all hands to unmoor and get the ship out to sea.

He took off the too tight black jacket, running over in his mind the various activities said manoeuvre required. The ship was prow on to the shore, so the first task of much of the crew would be to take to the boats. They must bring round her head to face the gap between the twin breakwaters, these forming a reasonably safe anchorage against most winds and currents, including the prevailing westerlies.

Even with a favourable wind, and Pearce could feel the chill of the north-easterly on his face, those boats would continue warping the ship, beyond the chance of fouling anything anchored, or drifting too close to the stones of a breakwater. Only then would a wise captain drop his topsails for a cautious exit to the open sea, not that all peril would have been laid to rest.

He recalled the approach he'd witnessed years ago, one of careful and slow calculation. There were dangerous sandbanks just offshore, marked by buoys to show the safe channels for both entry and exit. Such underwater obstacles tended to shift over time and could be made even more hazardous by a sudden gust of wind, a common occurrence in these waters.

There was a degree of speculation in his aims, but he reassured himself they were based on knowledge, not wishful thinking. He could put himself in the position of the fellow in command, carrying out a movement he had personally overseen many times. Various commands were being issued, far from faint, even at a distance. The orders had gone out to haul in the boats to seaward and in that lay his opportunity, the one he'd outlined to Oliphant.

The boat crew must climb down the man ropes and battens to take their places. By that method they would get back on deck again once their task was complete, which left the gangway open. As the ship was hauled off the mole, what tars remained would be engaged in fetching in the mooring cables, which put them below decks, either on the capstan or laying out said cables in the bitts. With good fortune and everyone occupied, he could get aboard without being seen.

That omitted several possible negatives. If timing was essential, the ability to match his actions to those of others was far from straightforward, this while he was immersed in water he knew to be seriously cold and that could hamper movement. The tow would be at the prow, swinging the bow round being the primary task, the mole cables only being cast off when the tow ropes took up the strain.

Those plying the oars would hopefully be too preoccupied with the task, not an easy one, of getting a vessel of many tons to begin to move. Would they see a head in the water in a harbour likely to be full of flotsam? Pearce had to get between them and the ship before it was hauled too far round and away; any attempt to board had to be made out of sight of the guard detail or the officials on the mole.

Being spotted by them, with the officers aboard alerted, would see him hauled out and handed over, a requirement of the conditions of service as outlined to him by Oliphant. A strictly neutral obligation meant his nationality would provide no shield; the only person choosing such a way to depart France must be either an enemy of the regime, a spy or an escapee.

The boats should be awaiting the men to man them, for him the signal to act, and it would surely come soon. The captain would want to make as much use of daylight as possible in order to try to complete the entire crossing before darkness fell. The wind might be favourable now, but it could turn foul at any time, in waters notorious for fast-changing and unpredictable weather. Few were the harbours that could be entered with any degree of safety at night. Dover was one, with its own well-documented and lethal peculiarities, contrary currents on an exposed headland that made such a landfall one of high risk even in the daytime.

A shouted order was forthcoming, which had to be the one for which he was waiting. The last thing for Pearce to discard were his loose-fitting shoes, which would hamper him in the water; he left them by the derrick. Off came his stockings too. He then crawled to the edge of the mole, easing himself over, his body hidden behind one of the great, square upright pile-driven baulks that secured the edifice to the seabed.

He could recall the nature of the mole, even if it had been observed a long time past. Easing in aboard the ship, and a curious youth, he had spotted the horizontal gaps, formed over time between the lateral timbers, places where he hoped, with both hands and feet, he could get a grip, using them to lower himself down to the water. Jumping in was a sure and noisy way to alert those he sought to avoid.

Lying on his belly and easing his body over the edge, he felt with his toes for just such a gap, glad when they slipped into an opening with which he could support his weight. Grasping the rough edge timbers, he lowered himself further, searching again with one foot for another rung and having trouble locating one. Pearce knew he was not gifted with time; in his mind's eye he could envisage the ship's boats fully manned and standing off to commence the tow. It would take a matter of minutes, no more, before the ship began to move.

Desperation forced him to go lower without caution, leaving him unsure if he'd found another foothold. His weight was now being borne on a hand thrust into the opening previously occupied by his toes, those now feeling for another gap. Uncertain, he had to take a risk on what could only be a possibility, one he soon came to realise had failed.

Lacking any secure footing there was no option but to push off with all the force he could muster, this to avoid a painful and possibly crippling contact with the outwards slant of the mole's base. He was falling towards the water, with no idea of what he would come into contact with – possibly not water, but some hard and maiming object.

He hit the water with the loud splash he had earlier sought to avoid, momentum taking him below the surface, the icy cold penetrating his being. He was never to know the noise it made coincided with, and was masked by, the spliced end of the prow cable. Lifted off its bollard, it had been thrown with force, landing on the surface at the same time as him.

When he came to the surface to look for the reaction from those on the mole, there was none. So Pearce struck out, noting, even at sea level, the gap between the prow and the mole was opening up. A powerful swimmer, he had to restrain his strokes: in the now strengthening light, being too forceful would cause noisy splashes and they could attract attention. Because of that restraint, he came very close to failing in his first object, to get to the outer side of the ship. Only a thrust-out hand on the very prow, below the figurehead, saved him, taking him out with it.

The ship would, in a very short time, be stern on to the shore. As it continued to swing, the side by which he hoped to get aboard would become visible on the mole where people might be watching. Or would such a common sight as a vessel off to sea mean attention would turn elsewhere? He could not know and nor could he take the risk.

If the copper lining the ship's bottom kept out worm, it was not immune to barnacles and weed, enough to provide purchase for his bare feet. With a combination of swimming and pushing, Pearce made his way along the side towards the man ropes and battens, this as the prow continued to swing outwards, acting to shorten the time he had to succeed.

He made the point below the gangway to find, while the foot battens continued below the waterline, the ropes were set for entry to and from a boat, not a man lifting himself bodily from the sea. He attempted a sort of leap with nothing but water to push off from and his right hand got hold of a rope at full arm's length. Pulling hard got him far enough up to get a hand on the left side line. Then, with feet scrabbling on slippery weed, he managed to get one foot on a batten.

The effort so far expended had sapped him to the point where he could only hang there immobile. But the imminent prospect of coming into view from land gave him the motivation to pull himself up, hand by hand, foot by foot. He made his way slowly and deliberately up the side, until his head came to the point where the gangway met the timbers of the deck.

Another half-heave allowed him a snail's eye view, thankfully with no sign of legs or feet; the gangway was unguarded. His aim was to crawl aboard, hoping to be unseen until he could get below, not that he reckoned to be able to remain a stowaway for the entire crossing. As soon as the cartel cleared those breakwaters, he would be out of French waters and could declare himself to the captain, he hoped with no risk of being put back ashore. He was halfway to where he needed to be when a gruff but commanding voice spoke.

'And who, sir, in the name of creation are you?'

Dripping wet, hair plastered to his face, there was no option but to get onto the deck and stand upright, to see before him a naval officer of quite advanced years, white hair peeking out from under his scraper, added to bulging eyes and a seriously crabbed expression. At something like attention and with a direct look, the reply came out with as much force as he could muster.

'Lieutenant John Pearce, of his Britannic Majesty's Navy, at your service.'

CHAPTER SEVEN

The elderly officer before him spun round to look towards the stern. There, gathered at the taffrail, stood a party of those departing, all civilians looking towards the mole and the shore they were leaving, one fellow vigorously waving. None were looking in the direction of the officer and the dripping specimen he was far from shielding. If the several men around the wheel, those both steering and supervising, had noticed his arrival, they were ignoring it.

'Damn you man, get below and out of sight.'

Pearce required no second bidding; all it would take to raise curiosity, if not actual alarm, was that one of those saying farewell should turn. The lanterns as always were lit below; daylight was never of a strength to make its way to the main deck, even with the ports open, and they were tight shut now.

Mess tables were down, awaiting the men who'd occupy them once the ship was clear of the shore and breakfast could be consumed. It was under one of these he dived, not that it provided much in the way of concealment.

There he crouched, ready to spring away if necessary. The sight of shoes and white stockings on the companionway nearly sent him scurrying, but a voice, calling for him to reveal himself, was doing so in English and could surely be no threat. He emerged to find the same fellow who had previously damned him, still glaring and still far from happy, judging by the growling tone of his voice.

'Do you, sir, have any idea what you have risked?'

'I have risked my life.'

'While putting into jeopardy that of many more by your action. The captain has a damn good mind to send you ashore.'

'From the tone of that, sir, I discern that you have spoken to him and he's not going to do so?'

The look and jerk of the head to this response, indicated he thought his superior mistaken. 'Follow me.'

The squat figure stomped off, heading along the deck towards the marine sentry guarding the wardroom door, a man whose eyes, very deliberately, made no contact with either Pearce or his escort. Good discipline or caution, Pearce couldn't tell. The wardroom, once entered, was deserted; everyone who resided here would be occupied at such a time and so should be the lieutenant who had brought him here. His years and the worn state of his apparel indicated the rank to be one he had held for some time.

'Your name again?'

That provided, he demanded, 'You carry nothing to identify you?'

Pearce held his arms out; where on his person would it be? 'I fear you must take my word, sir.'

'The date of your commission?'

That provided, Pearce was happy to note two things: it caused no negative reaction, while the satisfied look indicated the man before him was, by time served, his superior.

'And how do you come to be in enemy territory?'

Here the truth served very well. 'I was taking part in a cutting out expedition at Le Havre, but failed to get away when our boats pulled off.'

'On which ship?'

'HMS *Circe*.'

Quickly aware of the proximity of Deal, from where the frigate had sailed, and the port of Dover, the danger existed that this fellow would know the captain and officers of that vessel. He waited with some trepidation for an enquiry, relieved when it didn't come.

'I was not part of the ship's company,' was added, as a precaution and, as for truth, it required to be discarded in favour of invention. 'I was visiting a relative, heard of the proposed operation and volunteered to take part. I do believe it was a success, but I can't say for certain. I sought to hide as soon as I realised I could be taken prisoner. My task then was to find a way of getting out of Le Havre and to Calais, which would surely provide me with a higher chance of getting home again.'

That got raised brows, which were hairy enough to hang right over eyes full of disbelief. 'You managed to make your way from Le Havre to Calais?'

'Partly on foot and also by a series of lifts on carts with the locals.'

'You did not fear exposure?'

'I'm lucky enough to be able to speak good French and I had quickly discarded my uniform. What clothing I am wearing now was stolen.'

That induced a pensive response, then a command. 'Wait here.'

The lieutenant wasn't gone long and, when he re-entered, it was in the company of two marines and a petty officer in a tarred hat. 'Master-at-arms, take this fellow to the cable tier and put him in chains.'

'Why?'

'I suggest you may be an imposter.'

'I protest,' was the feeble response.

'You may do so as much as you wish, sir, but I find your tale you tell to be one that is not credible. To journey from Le Havre to Calais without interference, in such a heathen country, at such a time? If we must guard against exposure when one of our own seeks to escape, we must also allow for the possibility of the vessel being used to smuggle scoundrels into England, people who are intent on doing the nation harm. Master-at-arms, carry on.'

'Could I request some dry clothing?'

'Damn your effrontery.'

Edward Druce had before him a report from the man he had despatched down to Somerset. Hodgson had been sent to find out if there was anything untoward in the life of Emily Barclay that would be of use to the firm should they be in dispute with her. His man could only say that, after a few days, she had departed for

London and, lacking anything to observe that was in any way out of the ordinary, and having elicited no information of note, he felt it best that he return.

In this he had inadvertently acted as Druce would have ordered; the reasons for his mission were no longer of concern. These had evolved around a will, produced by Cornelius Gherson, which had subsequently been established to be a forgery. The seeking of less than flattering information on Emily Barclay was now unnecessary. She was the true and undisputed heir to Captain Barclay's legacy and, more importantly, was about to call on him.

She was received in the manner reserved for a wealthy client, fulsomely and with insincere humility. This was carried out even if, in his heart, there was a degree of reserve. There had to be a chequer in her past, even if he had no precise knowledge of what it could be. He knew for certain her late husband had asked him to find her when she went missing, a clear indication she had been estranged from Captain Barclay.

Hence the employment of Hodgson, a well-known and successful thief-taker. His enquiries had failed to find her, but had raised the name of a certain John Pearce as a possible lover. More recently, given certain facts to which he was definitely privy, like a list of dates and the location of the people involved, there was room for serious doubt that Captain Barclay was the father of her child.

None of this must be referred to: if she wore the mask of respectability, when she had been anything but, then he must accept it and deal with her accordingly. But first he had to allude to the unfortunate matter of the forged will and how it had occupied both himself and his partner, as they had set out to disprove its validity. That he had delayed meeting her, while he waited for any dirt to emerge, she would never know.

'But this you will know of from my correspondence, which I sent to your family home, letters which I assume have brought you up to town.'

'Correspondence that I received only yesterday. I have been in London for over a week.'

'Then being in town, I'm curious as to why you did not make contact prior to this.'

'It was not any reservation on my part, Mr Druce. I was waiting for you to contact me. I do believe that was agreed with your clerk. It was the very day when news came of the unfortunate death of your sister-in-law. Your man informed me how that had taken you from the office and was likely to occupy you for some time. I asked that you should write to me when you were able to attend to your affairs and left my London address.'

The lie was delivered with well-practised ease. 'Such a message was not vouchsafed to me.'

'How odd.'

'Whatever happened, I must thank you for your indulgence.'

'A terrible affair,' Emily responded.

'Made worse by becoming a public humiliation, with the name of my relative bandied about in the streets.'

Given the nature of the crime and the standing in the city of Alderman Denby Carruthers, the grisly details of the event were now the subject of lurid pamphlets. These were being hawked in the streets for a penny, with added drawings of the scene and the dramatis personae. The villainous murderer, the grieving husband

and most shocking, a drawing of the dead victim as imagined by the illustrator.

'Naturally her husband is distraught and my own wife, his sister, has taken to comforting him within our home. He cannot face a night in his own house. Quite apart from being importuned by strangers, it evokes fond memory and a veritable cascade of misery.'

The Denby house was an object of public curiosity, with endless streams of folk passing by, some even rapping on the knocker, in the hope of eliciting from within some intimate, scurrilous detail unknown to the common herd.

'You have my condolences, of course.'

'I am glad to find you in London. This will save me corresponding with you on the subject of some investments requiring attention.'

'The very matter that has brought me here today, sir.'

Emily had determined before setting out she would act normally. Yet she found that difficult when actually faced with this man, given the information provided by Gherson. This had driven her back to the papers that had been in her husband's possession when he died. Previously examined in order to discredit the false will, she had gone back to them after her visit to Newgate, seeking to establish if what he implied was true, which left her uncertain. Emily was made aware she did not possess the kind of skill required to establish matters one way or the other.

There was a certain respect for her father, whom she had never seen as very adept with such things as investments. Yet he had pointed out that canal trusts were high risk, not that he had any experience of such things as financial transactions. He would have picked up the information from his frequent visits to the town coffee shops, where the people who did took their beverages and their news.

'Now I am here and, since the previous business of the will has been discredited, perhaps you can advise me of where I stand.'

'You're a very wealthy woman, Mrs Barclay, but I assume you know that.'

'It would please me to have that established, not only in value, but also in a breakdown of what investments I hold and how they are performing.'

'I had assumed a figure continually and monthly updated would suffice?'

'Detail will suffice, Mr Druce.'

The way he looked at her, like an indulgent parent, dealing with an awkward child, was irritating. 'I'm sure you would be less troubled if you placed your faith in us, as did your husband.'

'It may be I'm of a more enquiring disposition than Captain Barclay.'

'Detail?'

'Nothing less.'

Druce paused for some time before nodding and ringing a bell, to bring forth the very clerk who had seemingly failed to pass on her message. Given the exchange on that was so recent, it seemed odd Druce did not enquire on the reason. Instead he asked that the relevant files be fetched, adding, with a direct look at his factotum, 'All the files.' His gaze swung back to her. 'Legal documents included, for we are still in dispute over that merchantman taken in '93. You may recall they are insisting their vessel was salvage, not a prize.'

'Still?' was posited with amazement.

'The Admiralty Prize Court moves slowly, Mrs Barclay. Also, one must have a care that lawyers' costs do not eat up all that is there to be fought over. We spend half our time fighting to deny the opposite advocate's applications for fees.'

The taking of that ship was as fresh in her memory as the day it happened, yet in a year which seemed a lifetime away. How different she had been then: naïve, not long wed and trusting of her husband, sure her marriage would be successful. Druce talking brought her back to the present.

'I hope you're not pressed for time, Mrs Barclay. There is much to examine. In the meantime, I have been remiss in not offering you some refreshment. Would you prefer tea, coffee or wine?'

'Tea, please.'

The bell was rung once more, the beverage ordered and Druce's partner sent for to be introduced. Ommaney was a substantial man, large of belly and jowl, sleek and well garbed, with a palpable sense of his own importance. He also had a condescending attitude, giving her an arch look when told of her request to fully examine her legacy. It was as if to say she should not worry her head about such things; that was business for men.

'A fine upstanding officer, Captain Barclay, and a credit to the service. You must greatly miss him.'

The lie was smooth and, by now, well practised: she had been required to respond many times to those expressing sympathy at home. 'Of course I do, Mr Ommaney, every waking hour. But now, as a widow, I must look to the future and that of my son.'

'Rest assured,' Ommaney boomed, 'we are here to advise

you and, should you find it burdensome, you must allow us to relieve you of tasks that are onerous and time-consuming. Markets move upon the hour and rare is the person of commonplace interests who can devote the time to keeping abreast of such things.'

'But I'm eager to learn, sir.'

It required a small trolley to bring all the files and, even if she knew her husband had been a success in the article of prize money, the pile was daunting enough to make her wonder if she had time to do that for which she had come. Ommaney gave the trolley a quizzical look, frowned at Druce, made a few more flattering remarks about her late husband, and departed.

'There is much to cast an eye over and, as for detail, I would say it might take a whole afternoon and even then it could only be cursory.'

'Mr Druce, you must have other business to attend to and it would be remiss of me to occupy your office. Perhaps, if you could have the papers transferred to another room?'

The lips twitched, not towards a smile, but as evidence of resolve. 'No, no. I would be failing in my duty to you if I was not on hand to answer the numerous questions that are bound to arise.'

Emily knew it would not serve: not only was the pile formidable but she was far from sure she could make head nor tale of the contents. Ommaney might have talked down to her, but he had the right of it. When it came to accounts she was out of her depth. She needed to cut to the chase.

'There was a venture to which I was privy and one which made me curious.'

'And that is?'

Did he notice the way she took in a huge amount of air, brought on by nerves, before she responded, for he was giving her an odd look, part curiosity, part an indication of unease.

'I would wish you to explain to me the details of the shares taken out in the Bingham and Waverley Canal.'

The lips tightened into a narrow line. 'Might I enquire why?'

'I wondered why funds were taken out of three per cent government Consols, to be committed to a type of project which is, by common consent, highly speculative.'

The look she was receiving had a hard edge now, which made her continue to speak, when silence would have served her better, especially when what she then implied was pure invention.

'And there were other placements, vouchsafed to me by my husband, of which I have a vague knowledge.'

Druce could not resist the rejoinder, given what he suspected regarding her behaviour as a wife. Nor could he keep a sarcastic edge out of his voice. 'Captain Barclay obviously placed great trust in your opinion, Madame, even if you were rarely in the same place together.'

The strong emphasis on the last two words had Emily blink. This pleased Druce and it showed. He felt he had found a way to get back on top of the conversation.

'That particular canal investment was done with the full knowledge of Captain Barclay.' A hand was waved towards the trolley. 'Indeed, I could, given time, show you the very correspondence allowing us permission to employ a portion of his funds in that venture.'

Druce went back to his previous avuncular tone, forcing Emily to supress her irritation. 'And, I would add, it is quite common for a portfolio as extensive and well funded as that of your late husband to have within it both safe investments such as Consols and those of the nature you describe. We would, in the future, perhaps recommend similar opportunities to you. Should they come to full fruition, they are highly profitable and the risk is thus justified.'

'For Ommaney and Druce as much as a client, I suggest.'

'We take our commissions, which are set by prior arrangement.' The trolley was alluded to again. 'The documents in question are there to inspect, though it will take me a while to locate them.'

'There's no need. I clearly recall that particular projection carried the signature of my husband's clerk.'

'Who would surely have been instructed by Captain Barclay?'

'I had a pleading note from Gherson.'

That threw him. All he could say, eyebrows raised was, 'Surely not from Newgate?'

'Where else?'

'And plead he should, but to the Lord Almighty for his soul.'

'He claims to be innocent.' Emily made the next point in a calm voice, as if she was questioning her own view. 'He refers to the arrival of two brutes, who first felled him, then ravaged and mutilated Mrs Carruthers while he was unconscious.'

Edward Druce should have reacted loudly and with outright disbelief at such a claim, but he failed to do so. His actual response came as almost a whisper, his eyes cast down as well for – and she was not to know this – his mind was in turmoil.

'All such scoundrels claim innocence. It is the nature of the criminal.'

'But if it's true, it would mean someone else is responsible for the cruel and foul death of your sister-in-law.'

'Poor Catherine,' was all he said.

CHAPTER EIGHT

As accommodation, the cable tier, on what was a small vessel, was far from comfortable, yet Pearce was loath to think of it in a negative way. Where it might have had slung hammocks, given the crew was not required to fight, their numbers were small enough to render this unnecessary. He was, after all, on his way home and what was an obvious error would soon be corrected.

Being amidships, the pitching of the ship was muted, but yaw and sway it did, the timbers creaking mightily. In this lay evidence of the state of the English Channel, a stretch of water unpredictable and rarely calm, with a particularity all of its own in the choppy nature of the waves, which could render seriously seasick even experienced blue water sailors.

The level of movement came from the swinging lantern, the

tallow wad both smoky as well as smelly, without which he would have been left in total darkness. Food had been provided: boiled pork, duff and bread rather than biscuit, fresh from the bakeries of Calais. With a small beer to wash it down, even shackled, he made the best of what was a rudimentary berth.

Naturally, he wondered how Oliphant was faring, but his main focus was on his own immediate needs once he got ashore. He would have to make contact with Alexander Davidson, who, like most prize agents, had some form of representation in all the major ports. On the sending of a letter, funds could be released to pay for better clothing and for onward travel to London.

In truth what he required should come from Henry Dundas; he was after all on government business. But Pearce had no notion to wait till the Minister for War, never a man to be fond of, got round to meeting his obligations. A bill he would certainly present, which even if it were acknowledged would not be met until sometime in the very distant future.

Most of the time he was stuck in another one of those longueurs, of which he'd had so many in the last few days, with time to gnaw on the same problems over and over, in what seemed to be a rotating list of worries and aspirations, none of the latter certain of fulfilment. But nature would reassert itself and he would eventually come round to counting his blessings.

Reprising the words of Oliphant on the mole, put against what had happened to him indicated many inconstancies. Was it possible, as his companion had implied, that he had been picked up from a boat just outside the harbour? It seemed far-fetched. More likely he'd got across the Channel with the smugglers connected to his Marie, a fact he kept hidden, just another example of the man's propensity to muddy everything to do with his activities.

The temptation to sleep, albeit uncomfortably, was hampered by the rats, ever at home in the hold and bilges just below the orlop deck. Already much enlivened by the smell of his meal, they would do more than just investigate his bare toes if he closed his eyes. Thankfully, the man who'd brought his food was sympathetic. As well as refreshing the lantern, he brought with him some grease to ease the friction of his ankle chains, as well as a long broom handle with which to keep the pests at bay. A chatty soul, a mate to the master-at-arms, he reassured Pearce that good progress was being made: the ship was eating up the twenty-two miles needed to make Dover harbour.

'With this wind, we'll raise it well afore night falls. Happen you'll soon be in a shoreside gaol, instead of here.'

'I will be thankful for that,' Pearce replied; he deemed it unnecessary to insist he would be sleeping in the comfort of a tavern.

'Many a time it's taken a week at sea and never to make a landfall, with trying to get back into Calais a waste and Dover deadly as ever with its crossing currents. That's without a westerly gale. Once we were blown so far north, we made our landfall halfway to the Humber.'

He paused and peered at Pearce, as if in by doing so enlightenment would follow. 'Word t'ween decks is you're a Frenchie.'

No mention of officer rank? But he had only vouchsafed that to the man he encountered on coming aboard. Best keep it to himself. 'Word is wrong, friend. I am a true son of Britannia, which will be established as soon as we tie up.'

'Better be, brother, for they'll ship you back across and hand you over if you ain't. Won't be the first time. Got to keep Johnny Crapaud happy.'

'Who decides?'

'Some blue coat from the Port Admiral will come aboard when we dock. Has the job of inspecting what we carry. Miserable sod, all say.'

'Then it will be my task to cheer him up.'

Emily was sure she had played a good hand with Druce, keeping to herself the fact she had actually visited Gherson. She would have been less happy on her way back to Harley Street if she could have seen into the workings of his mind. Thinking on what had just passed between them, Druce had come, after lengthy deliberation, to a troubling conclusion. The late Captain Barclay's devious clerk, who had represented risk before his confinement, could still do so now. What was he doing writing to Emily Barclay?

In consideration, the claim to be au fait with the aforementioned document, on the canal investment, just did not ring true. Husband and wife had not shared such a relationship for two years. Had she stumbled upon something in among Barclay's personal papers? Surely, if that were the case, she would have said so and not claimed memory. If the information regarding that piece of market manipulation had not come from Barclay, then where? It was not quite a jolt when Druce saw his original line of thought to be utterly awry.

Ralph Barclay should have been in the dark about the true nature of that piece of speculation, which was why it was signed off by Gherson. This was part of an arrangement that allowed both the clerk and the company to profit. Ergo, he was the only person who could have passed on the facts. How and when? Only the clerk, still alive because of the court recess, could provide a clue.

The notion of visiting Gherson in Newgate himself was swiftly abandoned; he was related by marriage to the victim of the crime for which he was sure to hang, which brought to mind, much as he would wish it otherwise, that claim of innocence. Gherson, even with his manifest faults, was not the murderous type. A thief yes, a lecher too, who had seduced Catherine Carruthers while employed by his brother-in-law.

An image of Denby Carruthers: irascible, and the manner of his reaction to being cuckolded engendered a train of troubling scenarios and memories he was quick to repress, speculations he was determined to avoid for the possibility of where they may lead. The Gherson business must be attended to first, so the bell was rung to fetch his clerk.

'You have had occasion to call at Mr Hodgson's lodging before. I wish you to do so now. Ask him to call upon me at his earliest convenience.'

'Now, sir?'

'Immediately.'

As the man departed, Druce went to the trolley containing the Barclay paperwork. They would need to be filleted so the man's widow, or anyone acting on her behalf, only had sight of that which he, Druce, wished them to see. He could not entrust the going through of those to anyone but himself, which meant there would be much burning of midnight oil.

Added to that, certain arrangements of a questionable nature might have to be liquidated, prior to their maturing in the way

such creatures as this trio with such force they would beg for his forgiveness, which was gleefully never forthcoming. But life was no reverie and being the man he was, with his vivid imagination, which saw pain or death everywhere aimed at him, he was fearful to an overarching degree. Yet he knew how to survive, how to deflect the threat he was now facing, even if he could not keep the tremor out of his voice, or control his trembling knees.

'My bruising was remarked upon in that room,' he said, to deflect any chance of an immediate blow. 'Someone so sweet on me might have a word in high places.'

'Warders' taps, Gherson,' Joshua scoffed, 'ain't what we would be handing out if the mood took us.'

If they had been informed about the private meeting, they must also have been told of the third presence, of the rough-looking fellow who had stood silently by the window. So all this talk of carnality was either for show or their own amusement.

'I have a high hope to soon be in a place better than this, away from the common cells.'

'An' here's me thinkin' you took to our company. Like a brother, I reckoned.'

Joshua – Gherson knew of no other name – who had produced this ironic jest was the prime malcontent of this lot. But there were many more to do his bidding, enough to make even the warders have a care around his person. Being close to the sod meant better food, an occasional bit of baccy and other treats, usually taken from newly incarcerated and weaker prisoners. The life they lived was not much better than the collective lot, but in Newgate, the margin of improvement did not have to be high.

'I could be in a position to share a bit of comfort.'

'Easy to say back to the wall, Gherson. But once you'se away from the reach of my fist . . .'

'No one stays here for ever, Joshua, and I have no mind to be ever on guard when walking the streets.'

'You'll not be troubled by that, with your neck stretched.'

Gherson's reply was fervent, a combination of hope and belief. 'That will not happen. I shall be freed from here long before I face a beak.'

'Blameless, is we?'

'Did I ever tell you, Joshua,' Loomis sneered, in response to the query: it was his turn to jest, 'I is here by error? Had up for a bit of thievery done by another hand and never my word taken.'

'Same as every other sod in this yard, I reckon. Best we lift what's on offer now than hold to false promise.'

'What can you get out of me now, Joshua? The rags I have or my portion of bread? Take it if you must, but if silver was handed over today, for word not to be overheard, who's to say it won't be gold on the morrow?'

'Which metal lines your tongue?' Loomis spat.

Joshua put his nose near to touching distance. 'Be careful of what you promise, Gherson. Gold, eh? If it turns to glister, there'll be no call for a rope.'

'Get moving, you lot,' called a warder. 'You'se here to exercise your legs not your jaws.'

It being a command best obeyed, Gherson was able to rejoin the circle of prisoners for the remainder of their hour. It was near time to return to the cells when his name was loudly called, his stomach contracting in fear and his legs nearly giving way, fearing a special court was in session and it presaged a trip to the scaffold.

'You got another visitor, an' private like afore.'

He should not have gloated, it was unnecessary. But he could not help himself. The look he aimed at Joshua and his fellow ruffians said in words what he was thinking and relishing.

'You swine can die in here, for all I care!'

Hodgson, a bounty-seeker of repute and fresh back from Somerset, had been found, not at his nearby lodgings, but in a neighbouring tavern to which the clerk had been directed. Having been employed and well rewarded by Ommaney and Druce over a period of over two years, and with no pressing and profitable villains to pursue, he was quick to answer the summons.

'You sent for me, Mr Druce.'

'I require you to take a message to that fellow Gherson.'

'All know he's in the cells of Newgate, Mr Druce, for foul murder.'

The reply was acerbic. 'I'm aware of that, man. I wish you to go there, get him alone and impart to him that I am concerned for his welfare. Just that and no more. What I want is his response.'

The man Druce was addressing, who had not been invited to sit, possessed a mind as devious as any of the criminals he had collared in a long career. A business that had, at one time, been very lucrative, it was less so now that the likes of the Bow Street Runners were increasingly the fashion. Working for Druce had turned out to be a damn sight easier and even better rewarded, especially when he had been well paid *not* to find the fellow just mentioned. His task had been to produce false sightings and information, credible enough to keep the search alive, which had been altered only weeks past, changed in favour of seeking dirt on the widow of Captain Barclay.

Hodgson needed a face of carved stone to deal with Edward Druce on this day. His mind was racing, for the murder for which Gherson stood accused had followed very soon after the commission to find him was terminated. His name had then been added to that of Emily Barclay as someone to watch out for in Frome, but there had been no sign of him there. Obviously he had never left London.

Of a naturally inquisitive disposition, Hodgson had, over the time he had been working for Druce, sought to uncover the purpose of his strange engagement. He could not enquire of the man who had given him his instructions, but then Druce did not pay him directly; that fell to an accounts clerk, working on instructions. Hodgson totted up his costs, travel and food, then presented a bill, which Druce was required to approve.

There had never been any kind of query, something he had mentioned in a casual way to the clerk. No previous person who had employed him had been so lacking in curiosity about costs, only to be informed that the expense was being borne, not by the company, but by another. That imparted, there was no attempt to discover more: it would have probably caused the fellow to clam up.

But, over time, as they had become more familiar, he had extracted the name of his real paymaster: a powerful man in the city and brother-in-law to Druce called Denby Carruthers. The name had meant nothing to him and really he cared little. But he had come back to a ghoulish London to find the city excited by a celebrated crime, and the name of the victim, linked to that of the perpetrator, was too coincidental.

The thinking must have gone on too long; Druce gave him a challenging glare. 'Do you comprehend the instruction, Mr Hodgson?'

'Very clearly, sir.'

'Then I'm at a loss to know why you're still here in my office.'

'I'll see to it, right off.'

As Hodgson departed, Druce went back to examining a pile of papers on his desk, there being no farewell or smile, which rankled. In previous encounters, not numerous it was true, he had found the man courteous enough to offer him to sit and, on one occasion, he had been availed of the contents of the decanter. The change of mood was another matter to ponder on as he walked the distance between the Strand and Newgate.

Though not great, it was full of the usual bustle of hawkers and beggars, sharps and dips, mingling with folk going about their lawful business. Hodgson found a fellow selling penny pamphlets and bought the one relating to the Gherson case, repairing to a coffee house to read it. He absorbed the details of something that had certainly pricked his interest, but no more than that. It was all there in lurid detail: the name, the crime, the mutilation, the plea of innocence, treated as the natural entreaty of the guilty.

Mid-afternoon found him at the entrance to Newgate, dealing with the same warder who had extracted a shilling from Emily Barclay for the use of a private room, which was required for a second time. Such a rigmarole as she had gone through did not wash with Hodgson. He had experienced life in pursuit of the dregs of humanity, in order to hand them over to justice.

Newgate was a place he had called into many times before,

though not in the last couple of years, usually to see incarcerated some wanted miscreant, so he was well known throughout the district. He had taken his ease hard by the prison, in the taverns of the nearby Old Bailey, drinking ale and eating freshly cooked sausages, usually awaiting a conviction, which would bring him payment for his services.

He had become well enough known to the court and prison officials to address them by their given names, though this fellow manning the entrance was a stranger, a newcomer and openly avaricious. He had probably purchased the position from his more familiar predecessor, given it was a good place to extract gifts from those visiting relatives.

'Happen I'll come back when Sir Jerrold is here and ask for a room personally, given I know him of old. He's never denied me that for which I asked in the past. I wonder how he'll take to my being dunned for a coin for that which he would grant me gratis.' Presented with a fallen face, Hodgson produced a penny and a smile. 'For your trouble.'

When Gherson was brought into the same room in which he had faced Emily Barclay it was with a swagger, his bruised face bearing a superior and triumphant grin. This immediately disappeared, to be replaced with a look of utter confusion. Before him was a total stranger, a burly fellow with a square face, the scars of healed wounds upon it, a direct and unblinking gaze, the possessor of large hands and powerful shoulders.

Bareheaded, his hat on the table, he was wearing an expression that gave nothing away, the green eyes fixing the prisoner with a cold look. Gherson was still muddled when he was jammed in a chair, something not eased when the warder was requested to depart. This left him to stare at his non-speaking visitor, a man who knew that silence, in such a situation, generally paid dividends.

Having read through the whole Gherson affair, it had thrown up too many things that did not smell right. Here before him was the supposed committer of a most heinous crime. To say the fellow was pathetic was only the half of it. Hodgson had sent quite a few killers to the gallows and, if he could not say they fitted a type, he still felt he had a nose for guilt and right now it was not twitching. First, he needed to carry out his instructions. Using the exact words of Edward Druce, they were repeated back to him in a soft and solemn whisper, though there was something not quite right about the tone.

'Druce cares for my welfare?'

'That is what he requested I say.'

'And who are you?'

'What does that matter? D'ye have anything you wish to send back to him in response?'

Gherson's head dropped to his chest, but not in fear or supplication; he was thinking and took his time to do so. If he had hoped Hodgson would say more, give him some indication of what was required, he was to be disappointed. After several minutes the head came back up again, to fix this stranger with a direct look.

'Tell him you are not my first visitor today. A certain lady called upon me, at my request, seeking information. She is bound to do so again, very shortly.'

'For what reason?'

The way Gherson responded demonstrated just how much his attitude had changed. Whatever conclusion he had arrived at in his ruminations seemed to alter completely how he saw the balance. He spoke as if he was in command.

'You are a messenger, nothing more. Carry the message.'

Observing the sneer, in a face overly suited to such an expression, Hodgson was tempted to stand up and give Gherson a clout round the ear. No one addressed him in that manner, not even someone who engaged him and was willing to pay. That had to be put aside as the man continued; he must have realised more was required.

'If Druce wishes for my services, then he must outbid her.'

'It would be necessary to know the bid and the name.'

'The name will be known, without your being privy to it. The price for what he wants? Apart from private quarters, I need his aid to prove my innocence.'

'A tall order. I've just read this.'

The penny pamphlet, with its lurid drawings uppermost, was thrown on the table, to be picked up and read by Gherson. A hand went to the throat, no doubt when he reached the part detailing his coming retribution.

'Lies, all lies.'

'Which you wish Mr Druce to disprove. I would say askin' for the moon.'

'An essential condition, tell him. Without that, his problems will certainly multiply.'

'Anything more?'

'With the room granted and my innocence established, anything more will come in time.'

Hodgson decided, if there were questions requiring answers, this was not the place to find them. He stood and picked up his hat, moving close to Gherson, to tower over him.

'I have known of you for near two years and wondered all the while who and what you are. Now I have, for the first time, exchanged words with you, I will tell you this. If you ever adopt the manner you have shown to me this day on another occasion, you'll end up as a Thames corpse. I will see you on a surgeon's teaching table, being cut up, with the boatman who fishes you out of the river pocketing his half-guinea reward.'

The blood draining from Gherson's face was telling to Hodgson, as was the way his body shrank into itself. He was dealing with a weakling who had buckled at what was an invented threat. Jamming his hat back on his head he called for the warder to let him out.

'You may take this turd back from whence he came.'

CHAPTER NINE

Pearce could only imagine what was happening outside the bulkheads of the cable tier, but he had good reason to believe the crossing was going fairly smoothly. The pitch and roll were regular for hour after hour, to then turn into one of constant change, indicating much tacking and wearing as the captain, he surmised, sought a safe way to enter Dover harbour. It was soon followed by no movement at all, even the timbers ceasing to creak, which indicated they'd come within the arms of the breakwater. Expecting to be released from his chains, the amount of passing time, indicated by the faint and regular ringing of the ship's bell, was frustrating, so much so that he began to shout, demanding to be set free.

When the master-at-arms finally appeared, he had behind him a fellow with one peg leg, this first indicated by the tattoo of wood on wood as he approached. As they entered the small pool of lantern light, the affliction was confirmed, but it was not the only one. A naval captain, the fellow had an eyepatch and a much-scarred face, which might have struggled to look benign under any circumstances. Right now there was no attempt to do so: the one good eye was glaring at Pearce and the voice was a rasp.

'Swam aboard, you say?'

'Did that, your honour. Got hisself up the man ropes, an' all.'

'Would it be possible to unchain me?' Pearce requested.

The response was not really a laugh, but it was derisory. 'They might come off in Calais harbour and not before.'

'I'm a King's officer.'

'With all the appearance of one.'

'I may not be dressed as such, but I am.'

'Who tells a tale of crossing half of France and not being apprehended in a country full of internal borders and cut-throat Jacobins.'

'Have you come to condemn me, or to ask if what I say is true?'

That got an unpleasant bark. 'You would do well not to demand of me, sir.'

There was a moment when Pearce wondered if pleading and supplication might serve to soften the attitude of this sod. But it didn't last. He was never happy to suffer ill-treatment, and rank be damned. He spoke with as much force as well as an utter lack of respect.

'I demand to know your name, Captain, so that I may in future visit upon you the consequences of your attitude. I demand to be released from these chains, taken ashore and allowed to contact the representative of my prize agent. I also need to urgently get to

London, where I am due to report, in person, to Henry Dundas, the Minister of War.'

'You come aboard in a suspicious manner, dressed in common garments of low quality, with nothing upon you to give a clue to your identity, then make loud claims to be a naval officer with high connections. Do you really expect that to be believed?'

'I do, sir, and I expect to be asked the kind of questions that will establish my bona fides. I have already given a fellow officer the date of my commission and if you'd care to examine the Navy List, you will find that alongside my name. This is quite apart from the fact that I carry a certain amount of notoriety in the service for the manner in which I was elevated to my rank.'

'I require you to explain that.'

Struck by the flat tone, Pearce had no option but to oblige, to name the vessel in which he'd been a midshipman, the battle, date included, in which he had participated and its outcome. He went on to describe the way he'd been rewarded by King George with a lieutenant's rank, without the need to sit the mandatory examination. He did not add this had been gifted him for conspicuous gallantry: even in such a situation, Pearce was not one to boast.

'Who was your superior?'

'Lieutenant, now Captain Colbourne, who lost an arm in the action, an officer I'm still in dispute with over my share of the prize money.'

'Your agent is?'

'Alexander Davidson.'

'Who acts for many naval officers, can you name one?'

'Captain Horatio Nelson, alongside whom I very recently served.'

'His command is?'

'HMS *Agamemnon*. Eggs and Bacon to the common seaman.'

The one good eye blinked at that soubriquet. The voice, when he responded, wasn't friendly, but neither was it the rasp with which he'd begun. 'Unlock the shackles.'

'So you now believe me?'

'Aye. But knowing for certain now who you are, I would dearly like to leave you locked up and hand you back over to our enemies, an act for which I would receive the approbation of every officer in the service.'

He made to leave, his final words delivered over his shoulder. 'You may make your own way ashore.'

'Which I did, still in near rags and obliged to seek out Davidson's proxy. It was far from easy to convince him to provide the means to find a place to eat and sleep, pending a reply to the letter I wrote.'

Heinrich Lutyens looked pensive, which did little to flatter his rather pinched looks. 'I find it hard to accept the way you were treated.'

'Necessary, I was firmly told. Once I had some funds and could dress properly, I called at the Navy Yard and sought out the sod who'd interrogated me.'

'To no doubt expose yourself to more abuse?'

'Not so. I first made it plain the outcome of that would be him and I in a field at dawn, accepting pistols since a peg leg can hardly fight with a sword.'

His friend looked to the ceiling, as if to say what folly, as Pearce related the excuses provided and the outcome. The connection between France and England had to be kept scrupulously free from taint. It was not to be used for nefarious purposes, lest it be curtailed by one or the other who took benefit from it.

'What better way to smuggle a spy into England than in the guise of an escaped naval officer?' Pearce emitted a hollow laugh. 'I suspect it to be so much stuff. I reckon, on being told my name, he decided to make matters as uncomfortable as he could. It was all show.'

The sounds from the hallway indicated Emily had returned and Pearce went to meet her, his eagerness somewhat muted by her reaction at the sight of him, which bordered on the disconcerted. Lutyens, left in the drawing room, was wondering what she would say, given John was likely to ask where she'd been. He knew, but when enquired of it earlier, he had pleaded ignorance.

'You're home?' Emily said, actually biting her lip.

The reply was forcibly cheerful; Emily had been far from happy when he departed, as much because he sought to deceive her as the fact of doing so. He was exposing himself to danger, unnecessarily so in her estimation. All the problems of their relationship seemed to be in the manner of the greeting: reserved when it should be joyous.

'As I said I would be, and in one piece.'

'For which the Lord be thanked.'

'Are we to converse in the hallway, Emily?' The fact of it being witnessed by the servant waiting to take her cloak needed no mention.

'I am about to go up to Adam.'

'Then I will happily join with you.'

They were in Adam's little room and the nursemaid gone before anything more was said. Pearce was nonplussed by the lack of conversation, even if she was fussing over their son. There was no enquiry as to the success or failure of what he'd been about, added to a distinct air of something not being revealed, which prompted him to ask.

'Has anything happened while I've been away?'

'What could possibly have occurred?'

'Any number of things. I'm assuming you've stayed in London waiting for me?'

'Adam has,' she replied.

The swaddled child was handed over, which naturally occupied him for several minutes of cooing and asking questions he was too young to answer, revelling in the slightest hint of a reaction: a winning smile, even if he knew it was likely caused by wind. Yet he was also aware of the stillness of Emily, a sort of rigidity to her posture, which was not natural. He was tempted to ask again, to then be made cautious by the air of a pending statement, which he suspected would not be one to cheer him.

'I had a letter from Cornelius Gherson.'

He was genuinely surprised; in the number of things he suspected he might be in line for, rebukes being foremost, that was a real bombshell. He swung Adam a few times to cover his confusion, before the obligatory, 'From prison?' She nodded. 'Saying what?'

'That I, or rather my late husband, has been regularly cheated by his firm of prize agents.'

'I can think of no one more deserving,' was the bitter response.

Not a hater by nature, Ralph Barclay, even dead, fell four-square into that category.

'Which means I too have been dunned.'

'Do I have to point out to you how dishonest Gherson is?'

'No. But it meant I had to see him . . .'

'You went to Newgate?'

'How else was I to find out if he was being truthful?'

'Gherson never tells the truth where a lie will serve. He was that way from the very first day I encountered him, though I was slow to see it.'

'Don't make the mistake of thinking I trust him.'

She half-turned away and was silent for a moment, obviously considering what she was going to say. 'I've never told you this before, but do you recall on first being brought aboard *Brilliant*, you wrote a letter? It was in French, to the radical John Wilkes, asking him to intercede and get you released from impressment. Like his African servant, I recall you saying.'

That induced an odd feeling in Pearce's gut: it was Gherson who had undertaken to get the letter ashore. 'If you know of that letter, it could not have got to the intended destination, which would explain why nothing ever came of the request.'

'Gherson made sure it came to my husband by a trusted hand. He, lacking good French, asked me to translate it.'

'Which you could have refused to do.'

'Why would I, John? We were not long married and I was in a strange world. It was before—'

Emily stopped and blushed, no doubt recalling the moment on the deck when he, a common seaman to anyone observing them, in total contravention of respect for her position, had spoken a few words to her. Had there been an immediate attraction towards him? This was a thought that had never before occurred, but the notion was flattering. Or was it what a couple of innocent comments had led to over time: this room, the child he was gently swinging and all the subsequent problems of their relationship?

'So you went to see him. I cannot think he requested that you do so without naming a price.'

'A move to a private room and help to clear his name.'

'By damn, you'd need all the angels you believe in to establish that. I was pressed to buy any number of salacious pamphlets on the way here and his name stinks.'

'Gherson claims he's innocent.' She spoke again before Pearce could respond. 'You said yourself, it was hard to believe him capable of such a crime.'

'Which does not mean he is blameless.'

Emily explained what Gherson had told her about the arrangement with Ommaney and Druce, in which he was to be rewarded for keeping Ralph Barclay in the dark about the investments being undertaken on his behalf.

'He gave one example.'

Pearce listened as she explained how they had used her late husband's money, as well as some of their own, to set up a canal investment. Further funds were committed by the firm, over time, to raise the share values. Once thought to be at peak, the prize agents would sell out and pocket the profits, leaving the likes of Ralph Barclay to stand a loss when the scheme collapsed.

'How would they explain that away?'

'That fell to Gherson, who would also profit. He would reassure my husband, who was no virtuoso in the financial line, that in a large portfolio, where a portion was, by agreement, set aside for high-risk ventures, such an occasional loss had to be borne. As long as the whole was profitable there was no reason to complain.'

'Then?'

'Having seen him, I went to the Strand to see Mr Druce.'

'I suspect you have a lot more to tell me, Emily. Perhaps if we were to sit down.'

That was acceded to, which found them upright in two high-backed chairs. Emily described in more detail the meeting with Gherson and the questions she'd been primed to ask, adding her feeling that she had succeeded in discomfiting Druce when the canal investment was named.

'But nothing concrete.' A slow shake of the head, and another followed when he asked, 'Did you tell him you were planning to shift to Davidson?'

'No, but I did say I intended to inspect all the paperwork, of which there was a great deal. In truth, if I can give Gherson what he desires, it will not be necessary. He will tell me what I need to know.'

'I sense you're minded to do so.'

It was Adam who saved her from a reply. With that suddenness with which an infant goes from contentment to distress, he began to whimper and that soon turned to wailing, causing Emily to take him and prepare herself to feed. Something Pearce had always witnessed with pleasure, the possibility was denied by a knock at the door, one which obliged him to respond to through no more than a crack.

'Gentleman asking after you, sir.'

He turned and smiled at Emily, mouthed he would soon return

and exited, to find Oliphant stood in the hallway, hat in hand, smiling like a Cheshire cat, creating in Pearce a feeling he'd been humbugged once more.

'I had not expected you for weeks.'

'I possess the luck of the devil, Pearce, do you not perceive that by now?'

About to speak and berate him, Pearce restrained himself; he would not give the sod the satisfaction. It was obvious, if he was here now, Oliphant had got out on the very ship loading that night and it had nothing to do with luck. He'd known, when he left Pearce on the mole, the way out was immediately open to him. But he had not, as was his habit, revealed the fact.

'All I see is that you were less than honest again.'

The vessel on which Oliphant took passage would have sailed, not the same morning, but in darkness on the following tide. The same benign conditions would have favoured the smugglers as it had the quick passage of the cartel. The unknown was where it made its landfall. This could have added a day or two to his journey, and again, wherever it disgorged its cargo would also be in darkness. The conclusion was obvious.

'Did you manage to convince Dundas of the success of our mission?'

A wide grin, an open acknowledgement that the inherent supposition was correct. 'I said you're a quick learner, but you will understand my reluctance to allow you to relate our adventures because, for all your gifts, I reckon you to be poor at storytelling.'

'Falsification, you mean.'

'Call it what you will. I have exercised control where I reckon it was needed and it has paid dividends. Dundas wants and is eager to see you.'

'Does he?'

'Aye, and I would say his mood, given the praise I heaped upon you, is positive. We have an appointment for this very evening and I expect Pitt will be there too, although that was not admitted.'

'Praise?'

Oliphant, in jest, pulled a face that implied conspiracy. 'It was not fitting that I should tell the truth in that regard.'

'One day someone will horsewhip you before ducking you in the trough.'

If he'd hoped to dent the man's insufferable air of confidence, Pearce failed. 'It will not be someone who is left feeling they owe me a great deal.'

'That being?'

'You will find out tonight. Shall we say Downing Street, at seven of the clock?'

'And if I choose not to turn up?' Oliphant treated that for what it was: bluff. Both men knew Pearce would not be able to resist such a meeting. 'You better tell what it was you said about me.'

That got a slow shake of the head. 'That would never do. I have painted for Dundas a picture that meets with his needs. In querying your version there should be discrepancies and I think I can rely on you to produce them.'

'One might be the truth.'

'You have no more knowledge than I. But act as Dundas would if the positions were reversed. Look to your own advantage. It will do no harm for me to impart to you that there is much of that to be had.'

'You're keeping something back again,' Pearce responded vehemently. 'I now know you too well.'

Again that infuriating grin. 'Never in life, Pearce. You don't know me at all.'

Oliphant looked over his shoulder, forcing Pearce to turn. Emily was descending the stairs, which necessitated an introduction.

'Mrs Barclay, allow me to introduce to you Mister Samuel Oliphant.'

'Charmed,' was his reply, as Emily made the last step. That was followed, when faced with a strikingly beautiful woman, by a deep nod of the head. 'Do I find myself addressing Lieutenant Pearce's hostess?'

Pearce should not have blurted out the negative for, as he did so, he observed a glint in the man's eye, quickly masked, that was discomfiting.

'I too am a guest here, Mr Oliphant,' Emily replied. 'Visiting London from Somerset with my infant son. Our host is the physician, Mr Lutyens.'

'A mutual acquaintance, then.'

'Indeed.'

A look around the well-appointed hallway was followed by, 'And a remarkably successful one, it seems. Few in the medical line can run to such luxury.'

Pearce was brusque. 'Seven of the clock, Oliphant.'

The dismissal was taken with another grin; what was the swine thinking, what was he calculating?

'I look forward to it.' Another deep nod, in lieu of a real bow. 'And perhaps, Mrs Barclay, to making your further acquaintance. In our time together, Lieutenant Pearce never mentioned he shared his accommodation with a person of such remarkable beauty.'

Emily blushed and allowed her eyes to flick towards her lover, which was precisely the wrong thing to do.

Sat facing Hodgson, Edward Druce was in a quandary, while reflecting on the various strands of difficulty posed by Gherson's demands. He had been correct: Emily Barclay had been disingenuous when she visited him but that provided little in the way of solace. Understanding the message was easy: it was a competition.

Gherson had told her about one dubious canal trust and would tell her of more questionable activities unless he was indulged. He must have good grounds to believe she was preparing to meet his terms. That must be prevented at all costs, but it raised many other problems, so the solution was less easy!

Keeping his composure with Hodgson standing opposite was exceedingly difficult. Edward Druce felt as if he was in the grip of a metaphorical vice, one which was being wound to a close, as the strands of his difficulties coalesced in his mind, all of them relating back to Cornelius Gherson. He had, years past, obliged his brother-in-law by providing him with a trio of toughs, members of a press gang. The task was to dish out chastisement to the ex-employee who had stolen from Denby and who, into the bargain it later transpired, had seduced his young wife.

It had seemed justified and politic at the time; the thief deserved a sound beating and besides, a goodly slice of the investment money that had allowed him to join with Francis Ommaney had come from Denby Carruthers. There was always a suspicion that failure to oblige him could result in a sudden demand for repayment, which he would struggle to make, to the point of facing a debtor's prison.

It subsequently emerged that the aim of the supposed punishment was much more serious. It was also the case that what had been planned had failed, and this at a time when Gherson had become a valuable and profitable conduit, acting as he did in the manipulation of the prize funds of Ralph Barclay. The solution, seemingly so neat at the time, had been the employment of Hodgson, at his brother-in-law's expense, to search for Gherson, with the express brief that he was not to find him.

This had been easy to engineer given the quarry was at sea, first in the Channel, finally ending up far off in the Mediterranean. Why did the sod have to turn up like a bad penny, with his employer dead, producing a will that disinherited Emily Barclay and demanding he be supported financially? The dilemma of the will had been solved, but not the problem of the progenitor of that forgery. So Druce had told his brother-in-law that Gherson had turned up and that he was whoring in Covent Garden.

He now had to admit he had deliberately closed his mind, for reasons purely selfish, to the consequences of that admission. Yet his reasons remained, to him, sound.

The reputation of Ommaney and Druce was paramount and Gherson, merely by his existence, threatened it. Without that being above board, they would be unable to conduct business. Their clients would disappear and with them the fees, which spelt ruin, certainly for him.

All the Barclay business had passed over his desk and through his hands, so bore his signature. His partner Ommaney might have colluded in and approved of his activities; in addition, he may have said he was willing to lie to Denby Carruthers and take responsibility for the failure to find Gherson, but that would not hold. What would be his reaction if he discovered what Druce had done? He would surely deny knowledge of any unethical behaviour and would dump his partner to save himself. As for Gherson, he deserved whatever fate awaited him.

Hodgson had stood silently as he cogitated. As much to stop his train of thought as for any other reason, Druce fixed him with a cold look. What was he thinking, what services were necessary and what could he provide? If there was another truth out there, who was best qualified to unearth it? Added to that, he must avoid, if he opted to do so, dealing with Gherson personally. The thief-taker had thus become valuable.

'You must forgive me, Mr Hodgson,' he said, standing up and smiling, 'I am remiss in not offering you both a chair and a glass of wine. We have decanted a really fine claret today, of which I expect you will approve.'

'Obliged,' was imparted without expression; Hodgson, as he took the chair, was wondering what was coming and far from certain he wanted any part of it. But there would be payment and that should not be sniffed at.

'How do you see the plea of innocence?' Druce asked, as he poured the wine, his back to his visitor.

'As commonplace, Mr Druce. Never met a scoundrel who did not claim to be as pure as driven snow.'

'Is it possible Gherson could be telling the truth?'

There was no turning round when this was posed. Had the face been visible, its distinctive feature would have been the obvious tightness of the jaw.

'He's being written off as cold of blood, Mr Druce, when I

would say we are talking of a crime of passion. I take it you've read the tracts being hawked in the streets?'

'How can I, when they make such scurrilous accusations against my dear sister-in-law? They imply that her behaviour would not shame a trollop, quite putting aside that she was seduced from her marital estate by a rake of the most despicable sort.'

Druce struggled to compose his expression as he turned round, adopting a look of polite enquiry when taking a crystal glass to Hodgson.

'I will admit it is only by implication, but can I really credit that she went to meet a person of the nature of Gherson voluntarily? That she was not enticed by him into the place where she was slain?'

'I know the bagnio in question, as well as the owner.' Hodgson took a sip of his wine, to immediately acknowledge its superior quality. 'If you wish, I could enquire.'

'Discreetly?'

'It is ever my way.'

'Then I will engage you to do so. The private room in the State House? You can arrange that?'

'I can as long as I can pay the governor's fees. I would guess also, that Gherson would want proper food and better clothing. He is presently clad in rags.'

Druce turned his back again, ostensibly to recharge his glass, really to hide his face and his internal turmoil once more. 'We will provide the means to do both. If you do enquire on the matter of Gherson's guilt, I would want anything you discover to be vouchsafed only to me.'

'Mr Druce, if you're paying me, it would thus be remiss to hand anything over to another.'

'I cannot tell you what all of this is about Mr Hodgson, but it is of great moment to myself and the firm.'

'I have no interest outside my instructions,' Hodgson lied. 'I will attend to the matter this very evening.'

'More claret, Mr Hodgson?'

CHAPTER TEN

Aware he had left behind a deeply dissatisfied Emily – she had questioned what he was about and had been fobbed off with feeble excuses – Pearce engaged a hack to take him to Downing Street. As he bounced along he was turning over in his mind what he might say to Dundas. It would have been easier if Oliphant had been more forthcoming, but seeking that was like asking for the moon.

The best course of action, he reckoned, was to say as little as possible, in the hope that any information imparted would be revealed to him. To that he could respond in the manner that seemed appropriate. But what was appropriate? He had apparently been praised and this to a fellow who would scarce credit it. Dundas had known his father since their youth. Both Scots, that was the only thing he and old Adam had held in common and the dislike had been applied to the son.

When it came to devious politicos, Dundas, who could bring to the government the support of the Scottish faction of MPs, was in a class of his own. He stood as the antithesis of everything the Edinburgh Ranter believed in and argued against. Corrupt governance, in which the rich lined their pockets while the poor starved. Rotten boroughs, controlled by bribery and titled thievery. Parliamentary votes traded for sinecures, which paid a stipend to the recipient but required no actual effort.

'Once more,' Pearce said to himself, as he stood outside the door and rapped the knocker, 'you enter the lair of the Devil.'

'Pearce,' Dundas cried, as he entered the room, coming forward to take and pump his hand. 'By damn I am delighted to see you.'

Which caused the recipient to blink; they had rarely, over several years and in previous encounters, exchanged a civil word, this while Pearce prided himself on his ability to get under the skin of the man. Dundas demanded respect, which was not only far from forthcoming, but usually held back, responses larded with a demeaning insult. Oliphant, standing to one side, got a nod, to then be referred to.

'Our friend here could not praise you enough for the way you carried out your task. Saved the opposition to the Jacobins from any rash actions, which would have seen them destroyed. Live to fight another day, eh?'

'They do not possess the strength they aspire to,' was all Pearce could say, which had the virtue of being the truth.

'Never thought you had it in you to be so calculating.' Pearce could only maintain a blank look, as Dundas carried on. 'But with the link you've set up, we can maintain contact, so when the time comes . . .' What would happen when the time came was an expansive wave of the arms. 'Anyway, you've earned your reward. Never say that Henry Dundas does not keep his word.'

The temptation to respond as he would have done previously had to be curtailed. He really wanted to say that when it came to making and breaking promises, Dundas was a master craftsman.

'Billy Pitt has spoken to Spencer and you're to have a ship, not that the sod was pleased. He knows I'm behind it. We do not see eye to eye on much, quite the reverse. I'm told you're resident in Harley Street. It is to the address Oliphant has provided that your commission will be sent. It will also come with the trio of named exemptions you requested.'

Pearce looked at a beaming Oliphant. What in the name of creation had he said? There was no time to ponder, Dundas was speaking again. 'We have another mission we wish you pair to carry out.' Oliphant's smile changed to a wide smirk; this was what he had played for. 'You mentioned, Pearce, when we last met . . .' There was a pause then; was Dundas recalling the acerbic remarks John Pearce had aimed at him? 'You mentioned you know the creature Godoy.'

'Know of him, yes. Sir David Rose told me of him when I stopped at Gibraltar.'

According to the Governor of the Rock, Manuel Godoy was a commoner risen to prominence in the governing council who, in all but name, ruled Spain. Reputed to be the lover of the queen, he held the whip hand over her feeble monarch of a husband. Loaded with titles and money, Godoy was held to have no end to his ambitions, even to the point of coveting the crown.

One thing was known; he was antipathetic to the alliance Spain had with Britain, one which flew in the face of historical precedent, given how often the two countries had been mortal enemies. Sir David was in receipt of intelligence that Godoy was going to sign a treaty with Revolutionary France, to end fighting in the Pyrenees. If he went further and allied Spain to France, the Rock would be at risk of siege, as it so often had been in the past. And so would the British fleet in the Mediterranean, faced with the combined forces of two nations.

'We think the upstart is still playing ducks and drakes with the French, without yet committing himself, so we need to keep an eye on them both. You are to have a sloop, I'm told, so I want you two off the Catalan coast observing what's going on.'

'We two?'

Dundas swung to scowl at Oliphant, who'd posed the question. 'If Godoy allies with the French, he's not going to shout it from the rooftops, is he?'

It was Pearce who answered. 'Not before he has launched a surprise attack in the Mediterranean.'

'I never had you as the owner of a brain. I am moved now to think I was wrong.'

'A gift inherited from my sire.'

Dundas was about to object and with some passion; he had held old Adam to be an impractical fool, the radical orator against the master of placemen and influence peddling. But he held his response in check as Oliphant spoke, his voice sounding indignant.

'What about the opposition we uncovered in France?'

That got a dismissive shrug. 'You said yourself they are far from ready to act in any meaningful way. Thanks to Pearce here, we have

133

the means to keep their hopes alive. But that is all about promises, which will be hard to presently fulfil. We shall keep them warm while their strength grows to become a real threat to the regicides.'

'Without we keep close contact,' Oliphant protested, 'they may wither.'

'A possibility, I grant you,' Dundas muttered. 'Right now, the defection of Spain is the most pressing danger.'

Oliphant was struggling to contain his anger, which was patently not easy, so his voice had a strangled quality. 'Neither Pearce nor I speak Spanish, as far as I know.'

'What does that matter?'

'How are we to manage anything when we don't speak the language?'

Dundas raised his eyes to the ceiling in frustration, addressing them both.

'I want you off the coast of the old principality of Catalonia, and they don't speak Spanish either. Part of that old Barcelona patrimony is in France and it crosses the Pyrenees. If there is skulduggery it will be around that border. There is where you'll find if the French and the Dons are colluding. If they are, your task will be to see how far it extends and, if it is an alliance, to alert Sir John Jervis so he's not caught napping.'

'A watch on the Spanish Fleet in Port Mahón might serve as well,' Pearce said. 'They have been singularly inactive of late. If they weigh and head east for Corsica, it could point us to the nature of their game.'

'I do not suggest you have to always act in unison with Oliphant. He can see to matters on land. You'll have a ship and the ability to act as you see fit. Jervis is committed to the defence of Italy and keeping the Toulon fleet from mischief. He lacks the means to carry out the task of watching the Dons himself.'

'Funds,' Oliphant said, his voice still strained. 'Bribery trumps observation.'

A bit of the old Dundas emerged then, as he glared at Pearce. 'They will be provided. It is to be hoped they're better managed than the monies you pissed away in the Vendée.'

Tempted to respond in kind, Pearce once more held his tongue. It seemed churlish to remind a man, who'd just told him he had a ship, that the way the money had been wasted was his own fault.

The streets of Covent Garden were rarely quiet, even in the small morning hours before the carts began to arrive with produce for the market. If the area was a hub for the distribution of vegetables and flowers, it was also a home to every sort of drinking and entertainment den: playhouses, taverns, brothels in warrens peopled by pimps and trollops. There were also bagnios of various levels of refinement, where such activities were carried out with some discretion, leavened with music, singing and a good dinner.

That it was a hotbed of crime went with the district. It was no accident the Bow Street Runners had been set up from the nearby courthouse of that name. Catching a pickpocket, a thief or a sharp, in these streets, could be as simple as reaching out a hand for a collar. That said, the dips, cutpurses and filchers were of all ages from stick-thin children to rosy-cheeked and prosperous-looking burghers: you could never tell who was what.

The whores who paraded the streets in daytime, and they were numerous, ranged from the elegant and expensively clad, to the

135

occupants of dark alleyways, from near-starving waifs to long-faded beauties of the type who would see to a man's needs for a copper penny.

Hodgson had plied his trade in the area for years, with many an excursion out into the country, in pursuit of some felon seeking to escape the grasp of the law. Well known, the tradesmen, shopkeepers and stallholders tended to smile and nod, honest folk who saw in his presence a degree of protection. Most of those who roamed the streets avoided him; those of criminal intent were never sure if he was on the hunt, the bearer of a warrant, or just out for a stroll.

It was evening and the light was fading when he left Edward Druce, lanterns being lit in the windows of the buildings, as they had to be by statute, to illuminate the streets, which were dangerous. In the dark, and there were many places such lights did not penetrate, they could be fatal, especially to strangers to London, drawn to the Garden for its dubious and scandalous reputation.

In these streets they would pass hawkers and peddlers selling everything from nosegays of rosemary to apples, trinkets and gimcrack souvenirs. Lottery ticket sellers, both honest and crooked, would tempt them with the chance of a fortune, enough to buy a carriage and four. From the doorways and lower windows every type of carnality would cry out to entice them, even to the guarantee of a virgin child, if that was required for satisfaction.

It would have been difficult for a stranger to saunter past Lady Barrington's bagnio in Long Acre. This was housed in a narrow five-storey building, which contained space enough on the ground floor for the various pleasures provided. Above lay the rooms, which both accommodated the girls and gave them a place to entertain their well-heeled clients; the services they offered did not come cheap.

The queue outside was long and noisy and there was a fellow on the door, calling out the attraction, even if there was no need to tout for business. A party of four, two couples, were emerging as Hodgson approached, gabbling excitedly at what they had been allowed to examine: the very room in which Catherine Carruthers had been so foully slain.

He had no need to queue. A nod to the doorman had him stand aside to permit entry. The sound of the harpsichord reached his ears, accompanied by a charming and trilling female voice. The staircase to the upper floors was in use, the next quartet ascending to view the scene of the foul deed. He passed on to enter the main salon, the fug of pipe smoke causing him to catch his throat. It was, as usual, busy with clients, some eating, others mauling the girls, but that held no interest. He set out to find the owner, Daisy Bolton of Southwark parish, who for the purposes of trade styled herself Lady Barrington.

The card room, to the rear of the salon, once he had closed the door behind him, was a haven of silence. Serious-looking coves sat round the baize, either hunched over cards – they were losing – or acting expansive, fellows who had in front of them a decent pile of winnings. Daisy was fussing around, ensuring her clients had full beakers and probably glancing at the cards in their hand as she did so.

Walter Hodgson was not a frequent visitor. He was a man who had no need for the pleasures on offer and nor would he gamble, especially when he suspected that one of the players at the table worked for the house and was not beyond cheating. These were matters he saw as no concern of his, but he had often found information in this kind of establishment, which had made easier the apprehension of his quarry.

'I'm not on the chase, Daisy,' he said, when he got her far enough away from the slap of the cards to talk. 'Nice to see the murder of that poor woman is bringing in so much coin.'

Daisy had been a beauty once, but the years had ravaged those looks: now she sought to mask her lined face with rouge and powder. She had a large and no longer fashionable beauty spot on her cheek; the lips too were rouged and not much given to smiling, which would expose her toothless gums. Her hair was dyed orange, which did not make for an attractive whole, but then Daisy was long past the need for physical charms.

'A windfall indeed, Walter,' she murmured, nodding towards the green baize table. 'I am making more on the door than I will from this wagering.' There came a glint in her eye. 'We have a special tableau later for a guinea. Special guests only.'

'With a body, I suspect.'

A chuckle praised his sagacity. 'In the very spot where that poor creature was found and laid out in the shameless way she was abandoned, her parts on display, as they were after her ordeal.'

'And Gherson?'

'An actor playing the dead dog.'

'He claims he was clubbed and the deed done when he was unconscious.'

'Do I not know of it? He was screaming the very same as he was led away.'

'What chance he was telling the truth?'

The rouged lips pursed; the notion was unwelcome. 'If he

was, it is no concern of mine, nor, I would imagine, yours.'

'He will hang for sure when the courts resume sitting.'

Daisy shrugged. 'I'm sure he is sinner enough to deserve the rope for crimes past, so it will be justice.' Picking up from the pinched look on his face, she added, 'My concerns are here, Walter, in this establishment of mine, for which I pay a great deal to people we both know of, for peace and quiet.'

'They cannot have a stake in this crime.'

'They decide what takes their fancy, not you or I. They will take their share of my extra coin for the tableau.'

'I am asking permission to enquire, Daisy.' That was open to long consideration before anything emerged. 'You cannot deny his custom.'

There was no need to identify whom he meant. 'Gherson had been here on several nights, much favoured given his spending.'

'Was he armed, a sword or a knife?'

'Not a sword – for the other, who would know?'

'And the girls?' A shrug. 'Come, Daisy, who did he consort with?'

That got a hollow laugh. 'You'd as well ask who he didn't. He was like a man starved. There were two of my belles on his knees when the Carruthers woman arrived, which did not go down well.'

'His state?'

'Drunk, what else? For that and the girls, he was berated with tears. She started screaming imprecations about what she had sacrificed to him, with no doubt about what she was referring to. She was making a scene and refusing to leave, which obliged me to shift them out, for the sake of my other custom.'

'To the room where she was slain?' A nod.

'I allowed Gherson the room, aiming to charge him for it later.' That got a prune-like expression. 'I'm still waiting.'

'Who found the body? Or bodies?'

'I went to tell Gherson he could have the room if he paid, but if not, for both to leave.'

The memory, and it must have been a horrible sight for all her granite exterior, made Daisy suck in hard. 'I sent to Bow Street right away, which had the whole place in uproar, folk fleeing for fear of their own lives or ghouls crowding in for a look.'

Hodgson waited a while before he posed his next question. He could see she was struggling with a depth of emotion that he would have scarce credited. 'Daisy, I know you depend on regular custom.'

'Where would I be but the workhouse if I did not?'

'Then, if there were strangers around, you would know of it, people who may never have brought you custom before that night and have not been back since.'

The answer was even longer in coming, several deep breaths preceding it. 'I might have.'

'Dammit my beaker is empty,' came a cry from the table. 'Am I to be catered for or left to die of thirst?'

'He will die of poverty the way he plays his cards,' Daisy whispered, as she slipped away to attend to his needs and those of the other players. It was some time before she rejoined him. Clearly she had thought about the question he had asked in the meantime.

'I will not stand for any distress, Walter.'

'You know me well enough to be sure I will bring none down upon you.'

Again the pause was long, her words being well considered.

140

'There was a couple of hard bargains in that night, not of the type who make up most of my custom.'

'So they would stick out?'

'I would have them as men of the sea. Their gait and hair ribbons gave it away.'

'You marked them well?'

'For their quiet, their lack of interest in my girls, nor could they be tempted to sing when we came to responsive verses. They were not given to gaiety.'

'I would like more?'

Daisy waved her gnarled hands, as if she'd said enough. 'They sat, they drank but little, did not eat and, between themselves, barely spoke and that in whispers. There was a likeness, as if they were related, and one was heavily scarred on the face.'

'Did they stay until the murder was discovered?'

'They departed not long after Gherson and his lady had gone upstairs.'

'Speak any words on leaving?'

'None that I can recall. Paid their tariff and left.'

'This you should have told to the magistrate.'

The response was sharp. 'Not a man whose company I seek out, given the number of times I have paid his fines. Anyway, the deed was done and it had me a'feared for my trade. I thought no one would cross the threshold of a door that had seen such a horror. My girls were in terror, as well. Two of their number left that very night. I reckoned I faced ruin.'

'Which has happily turned to profit.'

'Which I did not see at first, only when callers came seeking to view the room and offering to pay.'

'Was there a knife in the room?'

'I can't recall seeing one, but happen the Runners took it.'

'Daisy, if I sent a limner round to you on the morrow, would you aid him in making a drawing of your pair of quiet sailors?'

CHAPTER ELEVEN

The packet, delivered by a naval messenger, bore a seal that had John Pearce draw a happy breath. He weighed the heavy document in his hand before he broke the wax. There it was, from the Lord Commissioners of the Admiralty, telling him by name that he was required to proceed forthwith and with all speed, at his peril, to Sheerness, there to take command of His Majesty's Cormorant Class sloop, HMS *Hazard*.

What followed was the usual words regarding his responsibilities to both the navy and his sovereign. But there were no other instructions as to what duties he was to perform and nor was he designated to sail under any flag officer. This meant he would be under Admiralty orders, as he had been in the past, which debarred anyone other than their Lordships from interfering in his assignments by giving him contrary instructions.

He was still reading it when the door knocker sounded again and another letter arrived, this time with the seal of the government. It was from Dundas, requiring him to take on board whichever vessel he was to command a special representative of the Ministry of War, Mr Samuel Oliphant. He would bring with him verbal instructions as to what was required of Lieutenant Pearce and his command.

There was a difference here: in all his other dealings with Dundas, both in the Vendée and that from which he had just returned, the nature of the task had been a deep secret. Certainly there had been nothing in writing. In his hand was a record of both his involvement and, no doubt in time, the aims and aspirations of the mission would also be on record.

'A busy day, John,' Heinrich Lutyens said as he emerged from his consulting room, where he went every morning to make up his notes. 'And we have yet to receive the first post of the day. Good news, I trust?'

'For me, yes – for harmony, we shall see.'

Heinrich threw his eyes to the ceiling as the knocker rapped again. This time it was that first post of the day, a substantial packet, which required to be paid for from the pot of coins kept in a hall table for the purpose. It was addressed to Emily, with a superscription to say it came from Frome.

'She will still be abed, Heinrich. Adam, I think, is teething and he had a restless night.'

That got a shake of the head from the physician; to him, employing a nursemaid and allowing your own sleep to be disturbed was folly. As they made their way to the dining room to take breakfast, he made the point by allusion.

'I do often think that Emily has read too much Rousseau.'

'While she would say that is impossible. She is a proponent of a more modern form of child rearing than that with which we were reared. The child means a great deal to her, indeed to us both. Do not doubt she feels deep Christian guilt about our liaison. Adam justifies it.'

That got Pearce a tap on the chest. 'I would search in vain for Christian guilt in that quarter, John.'

'Or concerns for society's norms,' came the reply as, having laid the various deliveries on the table, Pearce helped himself to some ham, a pigeon breast, kidneys and kedgeree, as well as a large cup of coffee. 'Hypocrisy is their abiding principle.'

About to expound on the basis for that statement and with venom – it was a matter that much exercised him – he was obliged to remind himself that Heinrich Lutyens had connections at court. His father was the minister of the Lutheran Church, which was attended by Queen Charlotte and quite often the whole royal brood, so he forced himself to make his point in a composed tone.

'Who stands at the apex of this hypocrisy, if not the very people who should lead by example?'

His friend did not have to guess of whom he was talking. 'Come, John, you cannot fault the King and Queen for probity.'

'And nor would I try. But what of their offspring? It's close to common knowledge the Prince of Wales conducted a secret marriage with a Catholic, and it is rumoured there are children of the union. Clarence, our doltish Sailor Prince, lives openly with his mistress and their brood – six I heard at the last count. Yet the rest of society is supposed to abide by a set of rules I cannot think suit anyone but the most joyless prude.'

'I have never been called that before.'

Having entered silently, Emily had overheard the remarks. She was not offended, indeed there was a twitch of her lips to indicate she was holding back her amusement. Besides, she knew her lover too well to be at all surprised at his trenchant opinions.

'You slept, I hope?' Pearce asked.

'Enough. More important, Adam is now laid down and I hope for a good couple of hours.'

'You have had delivery of yon packet, Emily.'

Lutyens said this, his eye fixing the unopened object in front of his friend's plate. There too lay the opened missive from the Admiralty. Having been married to a ship's captain, it was of a design and shape Emily had seen before.

'Orders for a ship.'

'So I see, John.'

There was no twitch of humour in that, quite the reverse. If was imparted with a stony expression. Pearce picked up the other missive, which would serve to change the subject. It might not be any more comfortable, but it would at least take conversation away from the coming departure his letter implied.

'From your father, no doubt more of the documents you were left.'

'Do have some breakfast, Emily.' Lutyens intervened; he was acutely aware of the tension and was trying to ease it. 'As a mother you must feed yourself.'

She moved to the table, back to the room, filling a plate from the serving dishes, to ask in quiet voice, 'I assume you will be on your way shortly?'

'You know what orders are like, Emily.'

'Proceed directly to, at your peril, is it not?'

'It may say that, but I must await another. That fellow Oliphant to whom I introduced you. Perhaps you should open your post.'

As he turned, plate in hand, the look John Pearce got, from an adamantine pair of eyes for again seeking to change the subject, had him concentrate firmly on his food. Sat down, Emily took the packet and broke the seal, which caused several documents to drop out, these examined as she forked food into her mouth. For both men present the silence was oppressive, for it was larded with Emily's disapproval. That her lover should be made to feel uncomfortable was perhaps deserved, but not Heinrich Lutyens and Pearce wasn't having it.

'I doubt we have thanked you enough, Heinrich, for allowing so much licence in your house. I really feel it might have been best if we sought somewhere to rent ourselves.'

Fixed with those fish-like eyes, there was no response forthcoming, hardly surprising given Pearce and Emily Barclay could never have taken lodgings together without causing the kind of scandal she feared. He felt it incumbent that she required to be reminded of his hospitality: Emily prided herself on her manners; it was about time she showed some. The document she was reading was dropped to reveal an apologetic impression.

'You really must regret having us as guests, Heinrich.'

'On the contrary, you are my two dearest friends.'

There had been a time, Pearce was sure, in Toulon, with her helping him nurse wounded sailors, when Lutyens had harboured hopes of his own regarding Emily. It was remarkable that had morphed into what their triangular relationship was now, for the statement just made was palpably true.

'But I do wish,' he added, 'you could see you are never going to agree, and live with the consequences. There is nothing more tedious than all this sniping.'

Emily made to speak, only to face a held-up hand. 'I have never known two people so separated by their manifest qualities. Agree to differ, allow each other their opinion and see that time will take care of everything.'

'I think we have just been very severely admonished.'

Pearce said this once they were alone. Emily came close and they embraced, she speaking quietly in his ear. 'Perhaps rightly so. I do want the same as you, John, and with as much desire.'

'Adam?'

'You cannot wish for your son to be known as a bastard?'

That was not a proposition to which he could claim indifference. In many areas it mattered little, but in others it was an irremovable stain. Who knew what their son would grow up to be, what positions he would seek as he made his way in life? Emily was determined such a burden could not be thrust upon him. If his father said he didn't care, he had to acknowledge he was likely being selfish.

The front door knocker was loud enough to resound through the house and it was little surprise when it was followed in under a minute by a soft knock on the door to their room.

'A Mr Oliphant calling for you, Lieutenant Pearce.'

The under-footman had a sort of faraway look, as if he was determined not to notice what was before him. Two people, seemingly not intimately related, in the same room, door closed and not seated separately in a way decorum demanded. Their true relationship was hardly a secret in this house and it was perfectly possible that some of the servants disapproved. Many below-stairs people Pearce had come across were more prudish than their employers. There was and always had been a devil in him, which came out now.

'Ask him to wait in the drawing room, please, and fetch him some refreshments. Tell him I have some pressing business to attend to.'

'Dammit, Pearce,' Oliphant protested, when he finally appeared, 'the hall clock struck twice while I've been sat here.'

'You can hardly claim discomfort.'

'It does not please me to be kept waiting. You will have seen my chest in the hallway, which means I am set to go wherever it is we're off to.'

Pearce was tempted to say what had tested his patience had been extremely enjoyable, but that was a private matter. His response was, however, delivered with a level of good humour, which came from being both sated and happy. Perhaps he and Emily had finally struck a degree of mutual understanding.

'If you crave activity, you will go mad on a ship, unless I rate you a topman and set you to trimming the sails.'

'You choose to be jocose.'

'Oh, I don't know, once we're away from the shore a captain is king on his quarterdeck.' The voice dropped, even if the humorous note remained. 'Not a man to chastise.'

'Stuff and nonsense.'

'Words said before, but never repeated, after a keelhauling.'

'Enough of this. What are your orders?'

'To repair to Sheerness and take command of a sloop.'

'Is it a suitable vessel?'

'I suspect you too have instructions, so maybe you can tell me. All I will say is that the vessel is fairly new built and well armed.'

'So we've nothing to fear?'

'Except your condescension.' Seeing him about to dispute, Pearce stopped him. 'I will have a hack ordered to take us to Charing Cross and from there we will go to Shoreham.'

'Why not Sheerness?'

'If I am to take command of a ship of war, I fear it would be more than tempting providence to do so without what I would call my talismans.'

'Sounds mysterious.'

'Which no doubt tickles your interest. On the way I will tell you a tale and you will hear of a place called the Pelican Tavern and a night that changed my life for ever. Now, order more coffee, while I pen a couple of letters, finish packing my sea chest and say my farewells.'

All this was done out of Oliphant's view. The letters went to Alexander Davidson and Admiral Peter Parker, commanding at Portsmouth, to tell them of his appointment. The missive to Portsmouth was pleasant to compose. Parker had shown Pearce a degree of compassion and understanding on his return from the Mediterranean, with a warning he was likely to be beached and remain so. It was good to be able to tell him he had a ship.

Goodbyes followed, to Emily with a tearful kiss, from Heinrich with a wish for his well-being and an admonition to make sure he had a physician aboard his new ship.

* * *

If John Pearce had a reservation regarding his detour, it was not that he was heading in the opposite direction to that demanded by his superiors. He worried that his friends would be at sea. In that case, he would be required to return and fetch them; there was no way he would put their official exemptions, which would replace the questionable certificates they'd acquired in Portsmouth, in the hands of another. They were simply too valuable.

He was as good as his word on the part of the journey in which they were the sole inside passengers on their second coach, a relatively uncomfortable unsprung affair between Brighton and Shoreham. He was determined to be open for the very good reason he felt what he had to impart could not be kept a secret. A ship was no place for such things and his Pelicans would inadvertently let parts of the story slip. So it would be better coming from him.

The point at which he named Ralph Barclay as the culprit in his impressment was instructive: Oliphant said nothing, but the stiff cheeks told Pearce he was making the link with the name he'd been given in the hallway at Harley Street. So Pearce made the connection for him, from how matters had begun, all the way to the conception and birth of young Adam.

'We have been discreet, but you can never be sure of success in that area. Out in the Mediterranean, given the time we spent there and what took place, I suspect there is more rumour on the subject than at home.'

'I would be inclined to say you have been successful.'

'How would you know, either way?'

Oliphant produced one of those reactions that sounds something like a laugh, one that makes the lips flap slightly, but is instead an allusion to the foolish nature of the question. 'In my game . . .'

'Which is?' could not be avoided and got an irascible shake of the head.

'I'm not one to take risks, Pearce . . .'

'Or be honest and open, I recall.'

'Stop making what passes in your feeble mind for a jest and listen. When I found I was going to have to be responsible for you' – Oliphant anticipated the objection and cut off any protest with a sharp gesture – 'I felt the need to find out what I was being landed with.'

'Landed? How flattering.'

'If I was to ask your opinion of the average naval officer, what would it be?'

'Hidebound, unimaginative and damn sure of his own opinion.'

'I could not have put that better myself. So here I am, going into the belly of the beast, with a person of whom I have no knowledge, on a mission in which my life is at risk.'

'So you enquired about me?'

'Damned right I did! And what I heard would make your ears burn.'

'I think not. My peers are far from shy in letting me know their sentiments.'

'Trust me, I would be embarrassed to pass on some of the more forthright opinions. Suffice to say, there is not a satanic presence that can compare with you for double-dealing, chicanery, theft, buggery and every sin in the canon.'

Pearce laughed. 'I do object to the last in that list. So, having been told all this . . .'

'I saw it as a recommendation. You are known to be insubordinate, indeed the higher the rank of those I questioned the more that came up. Given how you're loathed at the Admiralty, I was actually amazed Dundas got you a ship.'

'I cannot gainsay that.'

'With all I was told, you seemed to me ideal for the task.' Oliphant produced the kind of arch look that presaged a sally at which he himself could laugh. 'Shall I say not hidebound, you don't lack imagination but, by damn you are sure of your own opinions.'

About to respond, Pearce was obliged to hold back as the coach ground to a halt. The door opened and a head, under naval hat, poked in to see who was aboard, to merely grunt at the pair and close the door. Once they were moving again, Pearce explained that Shoreham, being a base for Letters of Marque, had a watch out for naval deserters.

'If they can get aboard, it can be a place of safety combined with employment.'

Now they were on a road that should not have been granted the designation, so bumpy was the ride. It ran along the seashore of what was, in essence, a lagoon, inland waters protected by a sandbank just offshore. With an enquiring mind, Oliphant sought more and listened as Pearce explained that Shoreham had at one time been a busy and significant harbour.

'Henry the Eighth sailed from here for war with France, but silting has rendered it too shallow for deep-hulled vessels, either for trade or fighting. But the privateers use shallow keels and sail on a tide that allows them to clear the banks. Shoreham also has the virtue of allowing them to see any approaching threat well in advance. A night-time excursion by a press gang, even in boats, would as like end up beached. Certainly, there's no chance of a short-handed captain of anything larger than a cutter seeking tars here.'

'But you have said quite clearly those who sail out of here are exempt from the press.'

'Just like the Liberties of the Savoy, Oliphant,' Pearce snapped, 'and what good did that do? That is home to Thames Watermen and the like, supposed to be inviolate even to a tipstaff. I was taken from there, as were the friends of mine I hope you're about to meet.'

'I know of the Liberties.'

'From taking refuge there?' was the impish enquiry.

The response was sharp. 'I should have added opinionated and too damned nosy.'

'Guilty.'

The quay – there was no real port – lay on the west bank of the River Adur, a typical huddle of seaside cottages, various enterprises to supply the needs of those going to sea, as well as a couple of inns, one of which was the destination for their coach. Oliphant and Pearce alighted, the former going straight indoors to escape a stiff and cold breeze, Pearce making for the muddy banks that formed most of the shore, to look out for a particular vessel.

His heart lifted to see the barque on which he had enlisted his Pelicans and he felt a pang of something rare. The feeling that without he had them by his side, he was somehow not complete. He would require a boat to get out into the midstream, where they were anchored in deep water, but first he decided to eat. Also, he had to enquire about the return coach, the one in which they arrived having its horses unhitched. Glad to find it would not depart until the morrow, he decided to wait to take food. How much better to order a capital dinner for five.

CHAPTER TWELVE

John Pearce was not exactly welcomed aboard the privateer vessel on which his Pelicans were serving; someone had alerted the owner/master, a one-eyed brute called Maartens, to his imminent arrival. If they recognised him, which was unlikely, or were perhaps confused by his naval attire, it was not something vouchsafed to anyone else aboard and whoever was acting as lookout had disappeared. So he clambered on to an empty deck and made his own way aft to meet Maartens, who had emerged from his cabin, that single basilisk eye fixed on him, steady and unfriendly.

'Captain Maartens, we met not long past.'

The voice was as rough as the man's appearance: weathered and scarred skin, where it was not hidden by his beard. 'You being clad as you are bodes ill.'

'I am come here for my friends.'

'Then you're here for three of my crew, purpose not yet stated.'

When he'd brought his friends to this place, he had told a gathering of privateer captains his own background and to some extent that of his Pelicans, acting as open as he'd been required to be, but no more. His main aim had been to get Michael, Rufus and Charlie into a berth that provided a modicum of safety, with the caveat that no such security totally existed.

Having brought them back from the Mediterranean, by means not entirely proper to a very strict navy, they could technically have been rated as deserters. Another complication: the exemption certificates they had were forgeries, excellent examples of the art but counterfeit nonetheless, so always at risk from deep scrutiny. None of this would have mattered if he'd had any real expectations of a new command, one in which he could claim them as personal followers.

On getting clear of Portsmouth, the trio had once more taken refuge in the Liberties of the Savoy. Indeed, he'd joined them in the very Pelican Tavern from which they had been pressed years past. Remaining there provided no solution; they would struggle to make enough to live on within the confines of the Liberties, while to venture outside the narrow boundaries risked being had up.

John Pearce had money, but not enough to support them for ever, so a way had to be found to alter matters and, thanks to Charlie Taverner and his easy way of talking to anyone, the Thames Watermen had suggested a solution. Shoreham was home to Letters of Marque and was left alone generally by the press so they could operate. The information was quickly acted upon.

Many of the ships were owned by syndicates of powerful men, merchants and London guild masters, the kind who had the connections to ensure their profitable enterprises were not interfered with. At sea, in swift-sailing vessels and with highly competent crews, a sharp eye would be kept out for risk. The sight of a naval vessel demonstrating interest would see any privateer captain up his helm and get as far away as possible, to avoid being boarded and the hands checked for their papers.

'I wish to ask if they'd be willing to join me in a new ship, Mr Maartens.'

'Then you will permit me to answer for them. No.'

Pearce had never thought this would be plain sailing. There was a limited supply of tars for this kind of game, thus they were as precious as the men who manned the King's ships. He had, on his way here, in between educating Oliphant, worked out various ways in which he might overcome opposition.

'If we were aboard said vessel, Mr Maartens, I would be inclined to offer you a glass of wine.'

He might look like something out of a rare fairground rendition of a pirate comedy, but Maartens' appearance hid what Pearce suspected to be a sharp mind and a bloody nature. The one eye didn't blink, but nor did his visitor and for some time. Pearce was aware during the mutual stare of the way the ship was rocking. On the low, still waters of a tidal river, this implied much movement below decks.

'Do I sense an offer?' Maartens growled.

'You sense an eagerness that we should both be satisfied.'

His eye switched, to glance over Pearce's shoulder, confirming his suspicions: they were no longer sharing an empty deck. Word would have spread, so there was a very strong chance that the presence to the rear included the Pelicans. He could not turn to check and give greeting; for what he was about it would not serve. The business came first.

If an invitation to follow Maartens was issued, it was so gruff and low as to stay within the confines of his beard. Pearce went through the low doorway at a crouch, to enter a space surprisingly refined in its furnishings. There was no desk of any kind, in fact it smacked of the east and even the seraglio. The wall hangings looked to be Turkish and the impression was backed up by the elegant, silk-covered and tasselled divan on to which Maartens threw himself.

Pearce was invited to sit on a low stool, likewise upholstered in silk. A thick intricately patterned carpet covered the deck planking, while the oil lamps, which backed up the daylight coming through the tiny casement windows, were overly ornate in their glister.

'So, satisfy me.'

'Can I ask if you have ventured to sea in the last few weeks?'

'You can and we have.' Pearce waited to be enlightened as to how the ship had fared; he waited in vain, so was obliged to ask if it had been successful. 'That's for me to know and for you to guess.'

There was no mystery to the ploy; a successful sortie into the Channel – there had been no time to go further – would mean Maartens was in funds. A dry run on the other hand and he could be stretched. Unlike many of his Shoreham contemporaries, this man owned his ship, one of the reasons Pearce had asked him to take the Pelicans on board. An owner who had to bear all the costs of running his ship was more likely to be a hungry hunter.

'What makes you think they'll be interested in being King's men? With decent fortune, this is a better berth by far.'

'I pride myself on my knowledge of these men.'

Maartens waved a hand to encompass not only his immediate surroundings but the trade in which he and his peers were engaged. 'And give up this? For myself, I'd want more than your word.'

Pearce smiled in that way a man does when he plays a winning card. He pulled from his pocket the commission appointing him to HMS *Hazard*, to then pose a question.

'I'm curious to know what value you would put on an exemption certificate.'

Maartens shrugged, but it appeared to be play-acting to Pearce. 'They're not easy to come by.'

'And my friends, if they join me, have three they will no longer require.'

'So you say.'

'The mere presence of these, plus my rank, will stymie any of the watchmen on the way out of Shoreham. Once they are aboard HMS *Hazard* and on the ship's muster roll, they have no need for such documents.'

If the smile stayed on Pearce's face, there was a degree of internal turmoil. Did this fellow captain know the certificates alluded to were forgeries? If he did not, if he rated them genuine, they could be used by others and so had sale value. Pearce made much of looking around the cabin, at the elaborate way in which it was appointed, which utterly belied the physical appearance of the owner.

He knew the time had come to make his offer and so did Maartens, hence the ensuing silence. The last thing he wished for was a dispute, yet there were factors to take account of. Even if the privateer crews were supposed to be free agents, it was never that simple. Any profits shared would be quickly expended on pleasure in the manner of sailors everywhere: navy tars were likewise spendthrift in a 'tomorrow you may die' fashion. They caroused until every last penny was gone and all hope of credit exhausted.

'How much are my friends owed?'

It was Maartens turn to smile. 'You're sure they're owed anything?'

'Happen they owe you.'

'That could be closer to the truth.'

'It cannot be much after so little time.'

'The exemptions freely given will suffice.'

Pearce was slightly thrown by that: he always intended to give them up gratis; he had, after all, the genuine article in his pocket. Maartens had obviously surmised he was going to have to pay for them, which underlined their value. To look pensive was necessary, to sound worried likewise.

'Then I would need to ask my friends . . .'

'Friends?' came the quick response, the one eye taking in his uniform.

'My rank is of no moment, as long as it's acknowledged in public. In private I see us as equals.'

'Happen you're on the wrong side of the Channel? The levelling is done on the French shore.'

'I need to talk to them and out of earshot of the rest of your crew. That can only be done ashore.'

'You may have my cabin.'

In other words, 'They're not to set foot out of this ship until I have my part of the bargain.'

For all its Levantine decor, Maartens' cabin was as tiny as those normally occupied by John Pearce. So, when the Pelicans were crowded inside, Michael O'Hagan naturally taking up the most space, there was no room to swing the proverbial cat. There was, though, scope to shake hands and have his hand near crushed by the Irishman.

'Uniform, John-boy,' he said. 'Not the garb for Shoreham.'

'I have a ship, Michael, and a place on it for all of you.'

There was a long silence and no joy in their expressions. The spoken response came from Charlie Taverner and with it a slight shake of the head. 'Don't know that appeals.'

Rufus Dommet backed him up with a glum look. 'Good berth here, John, in grub and space to hang your hammock. Better than a King's ship.'

'Sure, and right good mates we've made,' O'Hagan murmured.

Pearce didn't know whether to be angry or sad as he reflected on this unforeseen reaction. If he had risked his life in France for his own ends, it had been on behalf of this trio as well and there was a real temptation to tell them so. They were all looking at him with a touch of defiance, as if to say, how dare you take us for granted, enough to allow for a lump in his throat at the notion of sailing without them. Certainly he had done so in the past, but he held them to be a band of brothers, in the way spouted by King Hal before the walls of Harfleur.

'Well, I am pleased to hear it,' he lied. 'I had hoped you would see your way to joining me but, if that's not to be, I have something for you.' He pulled the three proper certificates out of his pocket. 'These, unlike those you now carry, are genuine.'

'And you'd be as well to use them to wipe your arse.'

Charlie added a physical gesture to go with the slur. That shocked John Pearce and it showed. His blood began to boil: he was not one to be so treated even by those for whom he had such regard and had shared so much. Just about to respond in kind, he picked up the fact that Rufus's shoulders were shaking, this in an effort not to laugh. He couldn't hold the air in and once he went the others did too.

'You bastards!' was aimed at a laughing trio.

'Holy Mary, it takes one to know one, John-boy.'

Hands were clasped again and mirth turned to smiles.

'Have you squared us departin' with Cyclops?' Rufus asked.

'I said you'd leave behind your exemptions, the old ones.'

'How in the name of Jesus did you get a ship and us free if we want it?'

'A long story, Michael, and one that must wait till we're off this barky. So gather up your ditty bags and let's get into the boat I have waiting.'

Maartens, having taken possession of the certificates, went off, John Pearce thought, to make sure the Pelicans were not leaving with anything not their own. There were no fond farewells in the noisy sense, just quiet nods, some murmured good wishes and the odd glare, which made Pearce curious, though he put it down to the short time they'd been aboard. They were halfway to the shore when Charlie admitted some of the crew would likely be glad to see the back of them.

'Why so?'

'Well now, John-boy,' Michael informed him, 'there were a couple of sods aboard seeking to rule the roost an' thinking us easy prey. Happen not me, but Charlie and Rufus.'

'We put them in their place,' Rufus added, making a fist. An arch look from Michael got the admission it was he who'd done the chastising. 'But it was more their hangers-on who suffered most. Lost their swagger.'

'Hard to know who was happy and who was put out,' was Taverner's opinion.

'You had a cruise?'

Charlie was quick to pronounce on that. 'Slim pickin's out there, John. Frogs sail close inshore and run to beach themselves to avoid being taken.'

'Which had us near grounded alongside them,' Rufus added. 'Maartens was desperate, I reckon, needs to go deep blue but is short on the money to buy in stores.'

'So you took a ship?'

'We did, but not much of a cargo. Still, he paid you out of what we was owed. Came special to tell us.'

Michael was looking at Pearce when he said this and, if he had spoken with confidence, it lasted only seconds before the face fell. 'Jesus, you're not sayin' . . . ?'

The protest sounded feeble, even to the man making it. 'You should have said something.'

Charlie's head was shaking, his expression part wonder, and part misery. 'I don't know what has become of you, John Pearce.'

'True, Charlie,' Michael added, with a sympathetic, almost pitying look. 'Dunned like a bairn.'

'You're as much to blame as I am.'

They started to laugh again, telling Pearce he was being guyed again, with Michael adding, 'Must be the blue coat. Was a time he could see a jest a mile off.'

Rufus wanted his say. 'Been away from us too long, I reckon.'

'I can't wait to get you on board *Hazard*. I'll show you what a jest is.'

The first task was to bespeak rooms for the night, book the coach for the morrow, to then order a meal fit for a prince, before rousing out Oliphant to meet the Pelicans and to inform them.

'This fellow will be sailing with us.'

It was amusing to watch them, their reserve, for Oliphant was not like some fellow tar: his dress alone marked him out as closer to a gent, while his hands were delicate where theirs were rough. The Pelicans were quite open about much Pearce still would have kept back, but they had the sense to stay off the subject of Emily Barclay, and to some extent her sod of a husband.

Sitting back and listening, only occasionally interrupting to dispute some claim of exceptional behaviour, Pearce noted a slight and worrying glint in the eye of Charlie Taverner, though nothing was said. It was unfortunate Oliphant was a trifle arch and acting superior for, in truth, the Pelicans were an easy-going lot if treated right.

He'd obviously decided he must establish he was a superior sort of person. Pearce wished he had warned him; to the Pelicans no such body existed, but it was too late now. Matters deteriorated over the feast and obviously, with much drink taken, the various attributes of all parties were exaggerated.

Oliphant became near to insufferable and all attempts by the host to soften the way he was presenting himself went right over his head. But it was Charlie who produced the spoke in the wheel. Normally the most garrulous of the trio, as well as the most flippant, he'd been unusually quiet during the meal, leaving the others to make what running was required.

Because of their positions at the table it was some time before Pearce realised he was watching Oliphant the way a cat eyes a bird. That was until he sat forward, elbows on the table, and said in a cold tone, 'I has a notion I've clapped eyes on you afore.'

There followed the briefest moment of fluster in the man thus challenged, before he managed to produce a look of disdain, quickly adding a humourless chortle.

'I cannot for the life of me imagine where that would be. We don't look the type to share a social milieu.'

The use of that last word annoyed Charlie and his tone reflected that. 'The Strand, Covent Garden, happen where the Fleet meets the Temple.'

'I can hardly deny having been in such locations, Mr . . . er . . .'

'Taverner,' Pearce said, finding it hard to believe Oliphant had forgotten a name he'd used a couple of times already.

'Charlie will do. Can't fix it, though. Daresay it'll come to me.'

'What will come to you, Charlie, is more porter.'

Said loudly and with false bonhomie, a jug was slid down the table, with it a look from Pearce to tell Charlie that, if enlightenment came, he was to keep it to himself. Unsure if he liked Oliphant – the man was too devious for his own good – Pearce knew his presence was necessary.

If he had been given HMS *Hazard*, Dundas's emissary came as part of the package. They would all be on a cramped sixteen-gun vessel, with a compliment of close to a hundred souls if the muster was full. The mood required to be lightened, so Pearce lifted his flagon and cried out, 'To HMS *Hazard* and all who sail in her.'

All the other flagons came up in a toast, one of many, which ensured it was a happy party that made their beds. It was less so in the morning, but the hangovers kept conversation to a minimum, for which John Pearce, with a thudding headache, was grateful.

CHAPTER THIRTEEN

As the Pearce party were crossing Kent in a series of mail coaches, Emily Barclay was on her way to Newgate, in order to bespeak private accommodation in the State House for Cornelius Gherson. With nothing substantial in the papers she owned, it was obvious any worthwhile information was going to come from him. An individual cell, decent clothing and the provision of food from outside the prison seemed the easy part; his requirement that steps be taken to prove his innocence was much more complex. The errand she was undertaking was not one with which to engage the fellow on the door: it was within the gift of the governor to grant a comfortable chamber for single occupation. A note had been sent ahead requesting an interview so, on arrival, she was shown the way to his apartments, traversing the very same corridors as she had passed through previously. Indeed, it took her past the very anteroom in which she had confronted Gherson.

'Mrs Barclay,' the governor boomed, as she was shown in.

He was a giant of a man in all respects, height and girth, but there was nothing slack about him; he filled out his well-cut garments, down to the heavy thighs over wide-spaced feet, with his head covered in what seemed like a long, quasi-judicial wig. The voice was a deep *basso profundo*, which seemed to emanate from his boots and bounce off the oak-panelled walls.

'Sir Jerrold Crossley at your service, ma'am.'

Invited to take a chair, Emily complied, declining the offer of refreshment, to put forward her request, which had a confused look sweep across the somewhat corpulent face.

'Odd, ma'am, very odd. Gherson has, this very morning, been moved to the State House and a private cell.'

'On whose cognisance, pray?' was the shocked reply.

'Mr Walter Hodgson.'

'That name does not register.'

'It would, Mrs Barclay, if you were unfortunate enough to know much of this place. Mr Hodgson is a thief-taker of some repute. We have been in receipt of many of those he has laid hands on over the years.'

In the mass of thoughts racing through Emily's mind, there was one obvious fact: she had been outplayed. If someone else was paying for a private cell, it was to ensure Gherson remained silent and that could only have been facilitated by Edward Druce. If she'd harboured any doubts there were frauds being committed, and she had few, they were now laid to rest.

'A wealthy man, Mr Hodgson?'

'Not to my knowledge. He is a fellow for hire, so I suspect he is acting on behalf of another, someone who does not wish his name to be attached to the request.'

'An unusual act?'

'Not so. When someone of high standing is apprehended, we often receive multiple applications for favoured treatment, not that I would put Gherson in that category. But he must have friends, and clearly you are one of them.'

The temptation to vehemently deny such a thing had to be suppressed. Also to be ignored was the arching of a suggestive eyebrow, a hint from the governor as to her motives. He must think she had feelings for Gherson, being an attractive woman and him a good-looking cove when brushed up. What she said next did nothing to dent that suggestion.

'Would it be possible to call upon him?'

The grin, one which implied Crossley had guessed right, was infuriating. 'I can send a request, if you so wish it.'

'I do.'

A bell was rung, a servant appeared and once instructed, he departed. This left Emily in the company of a man about whom she knew nothing, which was mutual. The wife, more so the widow of a naval officer, did not move in the kind of social circles peopled by the likes of Crossley. In fact, Emily was acutely aware that she did not move in any such circles at all, if you excluded the provincial gatherings of Somerset.

'Your husband chose not to accompany you, ma'am?' Emily suspected this was put forward as a way of fishing for information on her relationship with Gherson.

'My husband, Captain Barclay, is no longer with us. He was

killed on the quarterdeck of his man-o'-war, some months past.'

'The name registers. He was in command of HMS *Semele*?'
A nod. The next question was posed in the manner of a person
lost for something meaningful to say. 'You reside in London,
Mrs Barclay?'

'No, my home is in Frome, but I am lucky enough to have as a
friend the owner of a house in Harley Street and I have the use of
a suite of rooms. You may have heard of him. Heinrich Lutyens?'

'The physician fellow?' came with palpable relief, it giving
common ground. 'Heard great things about him and, should I
ever need a medical man, I might call upon him.' A fist thumped
the substantial chest. 'Thank the Lord my health is robust.'

'Tell me more of this Mr Hodgson.'

'What's to say? He's good at his work, though I must admit he
has fallen away from it in the last couple of years. Used to bring in
villains regular, but not recently.'

'Was it he who apprehended Gherson?'

'Not to my knowledge.' The brow furrowed in thought. 'It was
the magistrate at Bow Street who sent him to us, I recall.'

'A good man, an honest man?'

The question threw the governor slightly, an indication that he
did not think of Hodgson, very much his social inferior, in that
way, so the response was tentative. 'I would say so, yes. But then
our relationship is entirely a professional one, if you can term his
activities so.'

A knock and the door opened, to tell Emily that the inmate
Gherson would be happy to see her in ten minutes.

'Sir Jerrold, I am keeping you from your duties.'

'Nonsense, Mrs Barclay,' he lied, with a facility borne of long

171

practice. 'Pray tell me about the part of the world from which you hail, for I do not know it at all. Good hunting country, is it?'

Emily knew good manners when she encountered them, but she obliged nevertheless.

If Gherson's frame was diminished by a lack of decent food, the clothes he now wore were elegant enough to disguise the fact. Gone too was the straggly beard; he was clean-shaven and his hair had been dressed as of old. In terms of arrogance he was also fully restored, judging by the familiar smirk that graced his features.

'How nice it is to receive you in proper surroundings.'

The cell was not spacious and neither was it attractive, consisting, as it did, of bare and whitewashed brick walls. But the cot looked comfortable and was well supplied with bedding. There was a table, a comfortable winged armchair, as well as another high-backed seat for visitors, while the large, barred window let in a decent amount of daylight.

'You find me early in my occupation, but there are some hangings on order to break up the misery of the brick.'

The look accompanying that seemed to send a message, to drive home the point, to tell her she could have provided all this but had been too slow. It needled her, so the response was pointed.

'I did not call to discuss your furnishing requirements.'

'Can I not offer you the armchair?'

'You may offer me the services you said you'd provide.'

'Alas,' Gherson said. The raised hands opened in a gesture, palms on view, this added to a glance up at the arched ceiling, a pointed reference to his new circumstances.

'I came this morning to bespeak for you this very accommodation.'

'What a quandary I'm in, with two supplicants bidding for that which I know.'

'My aim is to expose it as fraudulent.'

'While mine is to extract maximum value from what resides in here.' He tapped the side of his head with a finger, this as a lecherous sneer filled his face. 'I am now wondering what it is you can offer me that would bend me to your cause.'

The lips were wetted and there was clear hunger in his eyes. How many times had she crushed this slug for the very suggestion he was advancing now, the notion that his charms were so overpowering she must, as others had done, succumb to his carnal desires? It took a steel resolve not to slap him down once more.

'The chance to right the wrongs you have perpetrated might serve.'

'I have had enough of thin gruel.' The voice altered, to become contemptuous. 'You have scorned me in the past. If you want my aid now, you will have to pay for it with your virtue. That is, if you have any left, after you betrayed your husband with Pearce to the point of bearing his bastard.'

'Odd, is it not,' Emily replied, in a very calm voice. 'Betraying my husband is the only thing we have in common.'

He made to move in on her, the glint in his eye that of a man who would not be denied. Her scream stopped him dead and had him retreat several paces, as the door opened and an alarmed warder appeared.

'Heinrich,' Emily insisted. 'There was really nothing to be concerned about. It would hardly aid his cause to have my rape

173

added to his tariff, a crime for which you can also hang.'

'You seek to make light of it, but I see nothing amusing. If John finds out, and for God's sake keep it from him, he'll break into Newgate and string Gherson up with his own hands.'

'If I visit him again, I could perhaps take one of your footmen as a guard.'

'Surely you will not expose yourself to a repeat of what just happened?'

'I was joking. There is nothing for me in Newgate. Now I must pen a pair of notes, one confirming my request that Davidson, John's prize agent, takes over the management of my affairs. A second must go to Ommaney and Druce demanding they release my papers to him immediately.'

Emily did not mention the third missive. A request to Crossley had produced an address for this mysterious Mr Hodgson.

The limner hired by Walter Hodgson was a man he saw as a competent painter of shop and tavern signs, which did not ask that human features be of too accurate dimensions, or that the sign for a trade aspire to high art. His customers got what they paid for: the head and chest of the latest naval hero, a royal sibling or a newly created duke. He could also do a fair representation of the animal kingdom, as well as spreading oak trees. It was thus surprising the drawings he was being given now, in charcoal, were quite detailed and would have stood as decent sketches on which to begin a portrait.

'You missed your vocation, Louis. Why do you not do portraits in oils?'

'If I were paid for a true likeness, I can do them, but the

174

purse of my custom does not extend to such things.'

It would have been churlish to point out that Louis Beleau was the author of his own travails, he being a slave to gin. Of Huguenot descent, but fully English, given his forbears had fled France several generations past, he would very likely take Hodgson's fee and head straight for a gin shop to purchase a flagon. He was sat now, hands clasped tight together, in order that their habitual shaking was concealed, a trembling that made it remarkable he could paint or draw at all. Yet he had done so with the charcoal.

The two sketched faces did not register, which had dashed one hope. As a man who flirted with the criminals of the city, Hodgson had harboured a vague anticipation that anything approaching a resemblance would trigger a memory. Daisy had said the pair were not much for gaiety and this was reflected in the grim expression Beleau had produced on her instruction. He could also see the similarity she had alluded to; they looked like an older and younger brother, the latter with a deep scar on his cheek.

'Lady Barrington asked that I tell you, she's done as asked and not to seek more.'

If that got a nod, it was only because her words were of no account. Further questioning, if there was to be any, would not come from Hodgson, but from the magistrate at Bow Street and she'd decline to answer him at her peril. The old Blind Beak might have been gone these last two decades or more, but Sir John Fielding had set up more than just his Runners to curtail crime. His successors were required to investigate as well as to pass judgement, not that they showed much skill in the former.

'Are these to be printed off, Mr Hodgson?'

'No idea, Louis, but rest assured, I'll pay extra if they are.'

'They'll fly out by the hundred, given they relate to such a prominent crime.'

Hodgson smiled: Beleau was trying to extract as much value from his work as he could and, ideally, he would like to be in receipt of it now. 'Which will be reflected in what I will pay you.'

'Except . . .' was the diffident response.

'Except you have debts?'

'For paper and paints, to those who're not beyond the use of the horsewhip.'

Hodgson reckoned the need for gin to be a more likely craving. If he had been paying, he would have reacted negatively. But the bill would be met by Ommaney and Druce and they had never questioned any of his previous demands. Added to that, it did no harm for a man in Hodgson's profession to spread a little goodwill where he could, especially at another's expense. So half a guinea was paid for the drawings, instead of four shillings, but there was more required.

'For that sum, Louis, I want you to do a quick sketch of yourself and someone else you know well. Not me.'

The 'whatever for?' was on his lips, but there it stayed. Hodgson watched as the limner opened his portfolio case. The strokes were quick and economical, what was required being provided with commendable speed.

'Myself and the Barrington doorman.'

Hodgson nodded in recognition of the latter, seeing it as suitable for his purpose. He then referred to the two originals. 'Mark these faces, Louis: if you clap eyes on them on your wanderings, I want to be told.'

With the limner gone, Hodgson was left wondering what all

176

this would lead to. The drawings Louis had made from Daisy's description had him staring at a pair of right villainous-looking coves, but that counted for nothing. He was not one to subscribe to the notion of a criminal face; you only had to recall Gherson to dismiss the very notion.

Nor did what he had been told the previous night imply anything, other than a possibility. There were people he had to show these drawings to, Gherson being one, though he would need to employ care there. Another was Edward Druce – and what would he make of them and the reasons they had been composed? He would do Gherson this very day and Druce once he had been given permission to call: even if he had been warm on their last meeting, just dropping in was not to be considered.

Gherson was eating a large beefsteak and washing it down with a good wine, obviously content to live like a prince when he was free from the expense. The initial experience of meeting him had set the tone for Hodgson's approach, which was strictly professional. This sod knew he was the messenger. If the name Druce had not been mentioned, there was no mystery between them as to where the funds were coming from.

Hodgson took him through his tale again, asking him to describe the fellows he claimed had clubbed him, not that his replies were entirely satisfactory. Asked over and over again, getting shirty at the repetition, his descriptions varied, which Hodgson put down to him being so drunk he barely recalled anything with clarity.

The time came to produce the first image, this taken from a hard-bound folder, which had drawn Gherson's eye on entry, an object that rendered him deeply curious. Extraction was executed with a slow and deliberate movement, the image slid across his table.

'Do you recognise the face?'

'Barrington's doorman,' was the firm reply. 'Surely you don't reckon him to be my assailant?'

'It is ever my way, Gherson, never to assume anything. This one?'

The image he was looking at was quite clearly the older of the pair, as described by Daisy, a man with an angry and choleric air about him, not aided by a heavily pockmarked face, which could be put down to the impression he had made on the bagnio owner: even the most evil cove could smile. Hatless, his hair was worn long and curled, framing the face.

'Who is he?'

Hodgson shook his head at such a stupid question. 'Do you recognise him?'

The pause was long as Gherson stared at the second drawing. Eventually fingertips went to his forehead to rub hard in frustration. 'There is a vague recollection . . .'

'This one,' Hodgson said firmly, pushing the drawing of Louis Belau under Gherson's nose.

The response was immediate and positive. 'Now this fellow looks likely. Yes, I see him now, coming through the door, marlin spike raised . . .'

'Marlin spike?' Hodgson interrupted. 'You're sure it was that with which they clubbed you?'

The lips curled and the tilted nose lifted enough to imply stupidity in the query.

'Allow that I have been a sailor and a damn fine one! God only knows the number of times I have acted to save the ship I was on with my skills.'

And I'm the Ruler of Tartary, Hodgson thought. The notion of Gherson being an efficient sailor jarred as much as his being a butcher, but he did reckon the fact of a marlin spike significant. The fourth drawing was produced, to a query as to why they were so numerous, if he had only been assaulted by two people.

'Tell me how an unconscious fellow knows how many men crashed into the room?'

'I sense you accept that I'm innocent.'

The way that was delivered troubled Hodgson, it was too confident. To say either yes or no was not wise, but it was a question that required an answer, given the expression of certainty, which to his mind should have been hope, on Gherson's face.

'I am prepared to allow no more than you may be telling the truth.'

'Damn you, may be is not good enough. Do I have to remind you of the factor of time?'

The reply was hard. 'You can choose to damn me, Gherson, then you will swing without my help.'

'Druce's help!'

Hodgson made a point of looking around the cell. 'I don't see him here, do you?'

Gherson got the point and the confident look evaporated; Druce may be funding Hodgson, but it was being done at arm's length. His life was in the hands of the man before him. The subsequent apology was all grovel.

'Forgive me, I beg you, but . . .'

Only professional experience stopped Hodgson from telling him where to poke his regrets. There was a job to do and liking or disliking the sod was irrelevant.

'Look at these faces again.'

CHAPTER FOURTEEN

Nothing, not even a bright sunny day, could make the distant sight of the Isle of Sheppey look welcoming when seen from the crest of Detling Hill. It consisted of flat marshland, surrounded by grey waters, the narrow Swale and the broad River Thames. Sheppey was home to cattle and sheep, plus any number of nefarious activities, many to do with the building and maintenance of the vessels of the Royal Navy.

It was rumoured that, for every ship built or refitted in the local dockyards, a sound wooden house was constructed on the island, and that took no account of the purloining of stores. The inhabitants were known, and with good cause, to be wary of strangers, even if they were a common occurrence. Sheerness, his destination, sat at the north-west point of the island, forming part of the entrance to the River Medway, known to the navy as the anchorage of the Nore.

For many years the waters off Chatham and Rochester had been the main base for Britain's 'wooden walls', the enemy to protect against being the mighty fleets of the Dutch Republic. Though they had never languished, they had given way to Portsmouth and its southern English equivalents, Plymouth and Falmouth, this to keep an eye on the main current threat to Britain, which came from the base of the French fleet at Brest.

Now the forces of the French Revolution had overrun the Low Countries, to create what they chose to call the Batavian Republic, the importance of the Nore had been raised once more. This gave the Revolution not only the North Sea ports, but the warships and the seafaring men of the region, reckoned by their British counterparts to be a match in both skill and fighting ability.

As the coach dropped down toward the King's Ferry, Pearce, while reflecting on these facts, could reckon on one certainty: he had rarely suffered a less pleasant journey, this entirely due to his companions. Not that being rattled around in a coach was ever agreeable, but at least, in normal times, jests regarding the state of the springs and the roads would ease some of the discomfort.

The tone having been set in Shoreham, both sobriety and being crammed together had done nothing to make friendly a quartet who'd got off on the wrong foot to begin with. It was no good just blaming Oliphant, although he was the prime culprit. Pearce wondered if he saw sharing, with common tars, the inner seating of the various coaches in which they had travelled, demeaning. But his Pelican friends had made no effort to ease matters and had positively stymied any of his own to lift the mood.

Under normal circumstances, he would have engaged Michael, Charlie and Rufus on the aspects of the forthcoming mission, not that there was much to tell. But the presence of the other man precluded that; it was supposed to be secret, though Pearce, for the life of him, could not but wonder who would benefit from the knowing of it.

The King's Ferry provided the only route to the island for coach-bound passengers. The toll paid, the conveyance was run on to the low flatbed raft by hand, to save on extra payment for the equines. It was then to be lashed to the deck, the passengers grateful for the lack of anything approaching a wind. Even on a short crossing, a real blow would make it decidedly uncomfortable.

Back on land the coach required new horses, which entailed a wait while they were harnessed, Oliphant staying close to John Pearce, while the Pelicans stood apart and muttering.

'I cannot say the journey has had me take to your companions.'

Pearce, having been dying to say something for three days, took his chance to be forthright. 'The feeling is mutual.'

'Yet I gather you will depend on these fellows to help you sail your ship?'

'Them and a hundred others.'

'I am not an expert on naval discipline, Pearce, but do you not fear your familiarity undermines the need for efficiency?'

'I have told you, they are punctilious in public. And they are also what the navy calls prime hands. Be assured you too can depend on them, even if they do not show you much in the way of regard.'

The horses now hitched, the signal came to get back aboard,

the well-maintained surface taking them along the coast road, past Queenborough, and on to the tip of the island. Pearce wondered, as they approached Sheerness, if his Pelicans were thinking the same as he: this was where HMS *Brilliant* had been berthed when they were first dragged aboard as pressed men. If one seascape looked much like another, it could not help but invoke unpleasant memories.

The temptation to hurry aboard his new ship had to be avoided; there was another in command, a Lieutenant Milton, and courtesy demanded that he be given some leeway as to when to hand over his ship and crew. So it was to the Three Tuns they repaired, to bespeak a place to lay their heads and eat, Pearce immediately penning a note to Milton advising him of his arrival.

There was another communication to write, to the senior officer on station, a Captain Laidlaw, asking permission to call and pay his respects. The reply to that was swift; Laidlaw was fully engaged and Pearce was told to repair aboard HMS *Hazard* as soon as his situation permitted.

'Truth or disdain?' Oliphant enquired, when told of the response.

'To you, it makes no difference and nor, once we get to sea, will it have any effect on our mission.'

'Where are your so-called friends?'

'Doing what tars do when they know they will soon be confined to the innards of a ship of war for an unknown length of time.'

'Drinking and whoring?'

'Very possibly, which will at least spare you their company.'

What he meant was the precise reverse.

* * *

The drinking mentioned was being indulged in and, in the case of Michael O'Hagan, at pace; Charlie and Rufus were imbibing more slowly. The other thing mentioned was far from tempting in a place like Sheerness. As a naval station it was out on a limb, lacking the kind of entertainments to be had in the likes of Chatham or Portsmouth. The town did boast Assembly Rooms, where the officers and local worthies mingled, but it was short on the more raucous entertainments beloved by tars.

It was also the case that the trio were in a pensive mood and the subject was Oliphant, the question to which there was no answer being why was he included in their party and where in the name of Christ risen were they going?

'He's a rum cove, an' no error,' was Charlie's opinion, that not gainsaid by the others. 'It's drivin' me mad trying to place him.'

'Happen we'll find out what he's about when we're aboard,' Rufus suggested. 'It's up to you, Michael, you're closer than we are to John and he will allow you the question.'

'Rufus,' the Irishman insisted, 'if John-boy had wanted us to know, he'd have let it out already. If he has not, it's furtive an' like to stay as such.'

'Don't like the smell.' Charlie sniffed. 'That uppity bugger best stay in the cabin on a dark night, or I might just see him into Davy Jones' locker.'

The others didn't respond to the statement, seeing it for what it was. Idle talk.

'We don't have to go aboard,' Rufus pointed out. 'I'd not be happy letting down John after all he's done but it might be we has no choice. We could boat up to London and take service on a merchant ship, maybe an East Indiaman.'

An obvious reference to their being in possession of exemptions, the suggestion was sneered at. The aforementioned vessels were certainly large and spacious, but not for the crew, too much being given over to the passengers and the freight. The pay might be above that of the navy, but not so much as to tempt tars away from the prospect of prize money.

Added to which, the provision of food was down to individual captains; some would see their men well fed, others would skimp and pocket the money saved. On a King's ship the food was laid down by statute and it was regular, unless the vessel was on short commons by dint of time at sea and no chance to revictual. But in truth there were navy men and merchant seamen and they were rarely happy in each other's hammocks.

'We's got company.' Charlie was facing the door to the tavern, so was the first to see those entering, albeit Rufus and Michael felt the draught of cold air. 'And not charmers. Far from it.'

'Impress?' Michael asked, to get a slow nod.

It came as no great surprise to find such creatures in Sheerness. It was the kind of station from which they would operate, allowing them to roam up and downriver. They could raid in the docks of London, as well as both banks of the Thames. The estuary was a good place to pick up hands from incoming vessels returning from foreign climes. Charlie made a point of staring at his companions, which was the best way not to catch the eye of people of which it was wise to be wary.

'How many?' was the next question from the Irishman, to which Charlie spread four fingers on one hand.

They were noisy enough for twice that number, a testimony to their confidence. A home for the natural bully, the manner went with their inclinations, loud and vulgar jests mingling with demands for ale and food.

'Should we sup and leave?' Rufus asked.

There was no fear in the query, more what he saw as common sense. There were tales aplenty of men in possession of exemptions ending up in the bowels of a warship, one heading out to sea on a voyage of unknown duration. Only a fool would place absolute faith in a piece of paper, which could easily be stolen or destroyed.

'I'll not be shifted by turds,' was O'Hagan's slurred response.

It was a bit too loud, a consequence of the amount of ale he'd consumed; not that he was drunk, just far enough over the edge of sober to loosen his tongue. The look, warning him to be cautious, came from Charlie, who knew what Michael was like in drink. He was now wishing he'd shown him ten fingers.

'You fellow, did I hear you aright?'

'If you did,' Charlie said, 'it was on another subject, one unknown to you.'

'Best be.'

'Be still, Michael.'

It was wasted. The Irishman swung round to address the Impress man, a rough-looking cove with numerous scars. Unknown to his companions, it was not just ale that was making him act as he did; too much time with Oliphant and the frustrations of not being able to put the sod in his place was part of his resentment. Nor could he understand why John-boy did not do it for them.

'Sure, if you listen into the talk of others, being who you are, don't you go getting surprised at a bit of truth?'

'You angling for a pasting, Paddy?'

'If I were, you'd not be man enough to hand it out and nor would your fellow turds.'

It wasn't one angry Impress man now, it was all four getting to their feet at the same time as O'Hagan and they were up for bloody chastisement.

'Remind me, Rufus,' Charlie hissed, as he eased himself out from the back of the table, 'to never venture out to an alehouse with Michael, unless I have a barge crew in tow.'

The next words came from the one who'd overheard Michael's insult. 'It's the receiving hulk for you lot, once we've had our pleasure, an' then maybe we'll find you a flogger for a captain.'

The words were barely out of his mouth before the Irishman moved. He closed in to land him a blow to the cheek. Not that he stopped there, carrying on to spread his arms wide to take the other three backwards before fists flew. What followed was a melee in which it was far from easy to tell who was harming whom.

Rufus, who followed O'Hagan, was knocked backwards and obliged to roll away. He then picked up a solid-looking chair and used it to good effect, crowning the first man Michael had punched. He dropped onto his haunches, to get another clubbing, which took him out of the game. Not that Rufus got away free; a haymaker from one of his victim's mates took him on the ear so hard, it split open.

Charlie was using his feet – he knew he lacked a punch – seeking the sensitive parts of anyone who came within reach of his toes and his aim doubled over the fellow who'd clouted Rufus. No longer the callow youth of yore, Rufus stepped in, ignoring his wounded ear, and felled the sod, raining blows on him to prevent him getting back to his feet.

But it was Michael O'Hagan who was doing the real damage. There was no flaying of arms from him, he being a man who could take a blow and withstand it. His concentration was as sharp as it would have been in a bare-knuckle one to one, huge fists used to land blows that counted. If he sought the chin, a nose would do, for it bled copiously once smashed, or a belly easy to wind.

He had the ability to keep moving forward, even in receipt of punishment, as if he felt no pain, until the two remaining Impress men, sick of being pounded, found refuge in retreat. The fellow still being repeatedly punched by Rufus was obliged to crawl away to safety. The one comatose on the floor was lifted bodily by O'Hagan and thrown out of the door, this being held open by Charlie Taverner, to land on the cobbles outside.

'Jesus,' Michael cried, his chest heaving as he went back to his tankard of ale, any pain he felt, as well as the slow bleeding cut above his eyebrows, ignored. 'I feel better for that.'

Rufus, a hand clasped to his bleeding ear, was glaring at Charlie Taverner. 'How come you're the one free of blood?'

If he'd hoped to shame the man, it was not to be. Charlie grinned and claimed superior guile, before calling to the girl who had served them their ale, now cowering behind the serving hatch, to fetch some hot water, towels and refills.

'I hope this goes no further,' was the angry response of John Pearce, faced with the bruises and injuries of his friends, the remains of his dinner still on the table. Michael had two fresh scars above one eye. The skin on both sides of his nose was yellow and that, Pearce knew, would soon turn to black. Rufus had a bandage round his chin and ear.

'Thank you for the shaming of our ship, before I even set foot aboard. I doubt I'm in good odour with the officers on station, without you lot adding to my burden.'

'Got to have a bit of sport, John-boy,' Michael said, through swollen lips.

'Sport you call it. What would have happened if you'd lost?'

'Weren't likely, given the odds.'

Pearce shook his head slowly; there was no shaming this lot. 'At least you were wise enough not to hang about. I should think the whole of the Impress service round these parts is out on the hunt for you and in numbers you can't contest. Luckily, I have heard from Lieutenant Milton. I take over command of HMS *Hazard* tomorrow, at two bells in the forenoon watch.'

'A fine sight coming aboard they will be,' Oliphant sneered.

Pearce was annoyed with his Pelicans, so his mood was fragile. He'd had enough of Oliphant sniping and for once his anger boiled over. 'If you don't button your lip it will be you who's black and blue and I'll be the one administering the punishment.'

'You wouldn't dare.'

'Recall what I said to you once about the powers of captains at sea.'

The morning saw a stiffness in both Michael and Rufus that had not been there the night before, one that encouraged Charlie to guy them; that was until the Irishman, and not for the first time, put a fist under his nose. Pearce, having got his sea chest, Oliphant's trunk and the Pelicans' dunnage onto a cart, ensured there was nobody waiting to waylay them before he called them out to join him. The group, eyes peeled for an ambuscade, made their way towards the jetty, to take the boat that Milton would send for them.

There was no sign of such a craft, which at first confused Pearce. But, as time went by, it began to seriously irritate him. HMS *Hazard* was surrounded by boats, but none were heading their way, quite the reverse; they seemed to be filling with men and heading for the River Medway. In the end he had to bespeak a privately owned wherry to take them out, one that was somewhat overcrowded for the numbers and possessions it was obliged to carry, five souls and the two oarsmen.

A number of boats were still standing just off from the side, more than double the quantity belonging to *Hazard*, rendering Pearce deeply curious. But he was obliged to put that to one side, as well as pass up a chance for a close-up examination of his new command. He needed to compose himself, given he wished to come aboard with some dignity. To look less than competent in front of the crew would not do, men who would be just as curious about their new commanding officer.

Not that they were singular in that; every member serving on a man-o'-war, when it came time for a change of command, speculated on the nature of the fellow who would lead them. In the navy, a closed community for all its numbers, reputations and opinions were bandied about, rarely being far from the truth.

Tars were quite prepared to serve under a hard taskmaster, as long as he was fair. Yet it was not unknown for a crew to refuse a new appointment if the proposed captain was known as an overflogging martinet. The Admiralty could huff and puff, the senior officers on station could threaten all sorts of retaliation, but if the men remained unmoved and held to their guns, the appointment would be rescinded.

How much would these fellows know of him, for they would surely have been prewarned of whom they were getting? Probably only how he had been promoted, for none of his Mediterranean exploits would have made it back home yet. He reckoned, at best, to be an unknown quantity. It mattered not; their trust he would have to win if his tenure was to be a success.

It required the others to shift so Pearce could get into position to catch the man ropes and haul himself aboard. The officer he was replacing was stood just inside the gangway and had been visible for some time, as were the marines lined up behind him. The bosun was standing by, pipe in hand, for that familiar refrain accorded to captains and above coming aboard.

It all went smoothly; the pipes blew as he made the gangway, for him to raise his hat to the quarterdeck. He and Milton exchanged the required courtesies, Pearce deciding there was no point in raising the lack of a boat to meet him on the jetty. Two men emerged from the cabin carrying a sea chest, which was placed on the deck and a whip from the yard lashed on. It was then raised, swung over the side and lowered into a boat. He waited for an unsmiling Milton to invite him to his cabin, where they would no doubt share a glass of wine; he waited in vain.

'I ask that you step away from the gangway, Mr Pearce,' Milton said. 'If you do not, you risk being jostled.'

If he was even more curious, Pearce obliged, to hear orders shouted that brought a clutch of some two dozen men onto the deck, all carrying ditty bags. In a line they approached the gangway and exited, dropping down with practised ease to the boat which, without any orders, had come in to fetch them. As soon as one boat was filled and heading for the Medway, another took its place, it too soon filled and rowing away.

'What in the name of the devil is going on, Mr Milton?'

'Going on? I think I'm entitled to my barge crew and my servants.' Seeing Pearce still confused he added, 'I'm told you were given this ship on orders from the First Lord of the Treasury. If it is true, you should have asked Mr High-and-Mighty Pitt to provide you with a crew to go with it, for the navy declines to do so. If you doubt my word, ask Admiral Buckner.'

Milton lifted his hat but there was, judging by his sneer, no courtesy in the gesture. 'Now sir, if you will excuse me, you will observe I have a boat waiting. I will not request the use of what, until a very short time ago, was my barge.'

CHAPTER FIFTEEN

If the Admiralty had stripped out the crew, they lacked the power to shift the standing officers and warrants. The master, the gunner and the carpenter were appointed by the Navy Board, the purser by the Victualling Board. The cook, who was always a Chatham Chest pensioner, got his place, a highly valued one for a man often missing a leg, from the Commissioners of the Navy. The bosun, again a Navy Board appointee and the senior petty officer of the ship, belonged to the vessel and would stay with her whether in service or laid up in ordinary.

When John Pearce came face to face with these men, he found himself looking at a far from happy bunch. Their mates, the men on whom they relied to carry out their duties and whose positions were approved by the captain, had departed with Milton. When you listed what the sloop lacked it was scary; he was bereft in every area required to sail the ship and sustain the crew, never mind fight with it.

He required people of experience to fill the various functions: a surgeon to repair wounds and deal with common ailments, a sailmaker, an armourer, a rope maker, a caulker and a cooper, though some he could probably do without. He also needed experienced men for various leading roles, not least a yeoman of the sheets to supervise things aloft when it came to the setting and taking in of sails.

Right now he did not even have the manpower to haul inboard the ship's boats, which had been left behind in the water. The muscle to man the capstan and heave them inboard was lacking, as was the number of men it would need to haul the ship over her anchor.

'Rest assured this situation is temporary and will be rectified. I request that you go about your duties with that in mind and I will carry out an inspection of each of your purposes when time permits.'

Stated with a confidence he did not feel, the words were backed up by a determined look. Oliphant, standing to one side, sought to appear equally resolute, even when Pearce had told him privately the situation was dire.

'I shall first go to Chatham and beard Admiral Buckner who, if he did not issue the orders to strip out the ship, must certainly have known of them. I will demand of him that the requirements of the ship be made good.'

That got another dogged look, to which all four warrants responded in a like manner: their faces were stony masks and, such was their manifest doubts, they would not meet his eye.

'Gentlemen, you may have heard of me and I would not presume it to be flattering. But know this, you will not find an officer more resolute than I, or one more willing to engage with the enemy, be they the French or in the corridors of the Admiralty.'

'I know your bravery to have been praised personally by King George,' Oliphant bellowed. 'Was it not he who promoted you to your present rank?'

He was trying to help, only to have Pearce reckon he had achieved the very opposite. He had reminded these men of why he was so disliked by his naval peers. It was not just blue coats who loved the service. These men would too, for it was, in their various branches, purser apart, a lifelong career. It might be they resented him just as much as his fellow officers, but that worried him less, given he backed himself to win them over in time.

'Now I ask that you go about your duties as best you can, while I sort out what will turn out to be a hiccup.'

They still had not met his eye, nor responded verbally, by the time they filed out. Pearce turned to Oliphant, his expression conveying his thoughts. 'You can bet that lot have gone to write to everyone they know who might owe them a favour, asking to be shifted.'

'Pantry cupboards are bare, John-boy,' Michael said, having appeared as the others departed. 'Mouse would want for provender.'

That presented another problem. In normal circumstances he would have sent Michael ashore with the funds necessary to buy what was needed in food and wine. But his melee with the Impress men made that risky, the same applying to Charlie and Rufus. It seemed he would have to go and do the ordering himself. He pulled a ledger from his desk, listing the stores in the hold.

'It will do us good to eat as common seamen until the situation can be rectified. Michael, go to the cook and make sure his coppers are lit. You, Charlie and Rufus will have to haul out from the hold that which needs to be boiled.'

'If you're going ashore I shall come with you,' Oliphant pronounced. 'Such fare may suit you, but I am of a more delicate nature.'

'You will come ashore with me, but not to take your ease at table. If my interview with Admiral Buckner—'

Oliphant interrupted. 'If he'll see you. That fellow Laidlaw declined, did he not?'

'He'll see me, damn him,' Pearce responded with real force. He could only hope he was right.

It took another hired wherry to get him ashore and it entailed a much longer row than coming out from Sheerness. He was coming up two hours in the boat, huddled in his cloak to keep his best uniform clean. In some senses this was more demeaning than what had happened earlier: he should have been in his barge, being rowed by his own well-trained crew, under his trusted coxswain, able to approach the Admiralty Quay with a flourish.

Instead he came alongside at a whimper. Having helped Oliphant on to dry land, he strode off towards the C-in-C's office, part of the so-called officer's row, these a dozen substantial and handsome brick buildings, constructed in the reign of the first George. These housed both the administrative headquarters of the fleet as well as providing accommodation to the senior officers on station.

It was necessary to get past the ex-tars who'd managed to secure for themselves the agreeable jobs as doorkeepers. Passage for officers of his rank, with no arranged interview, was usually secured with a small bit of silver. Then came the more daunting obstacle of the civilian functionary, he who managed the business of the headquarters. He was the gatekeeper and long practised at refusal, which is what Pearce faced now. Politely requested at first, it soon became dogged.

'Then I require you,' Pearce insisted, 'to inform Admiral Buckner that my next destination will be the Office of the First Lord of the Treasury. He will, no doubt, want to know why his express wishes are being thwarted by an officer whose fitness for command could be called into question.'

That got Pearce a cold and disbelieving look from a dry stick of an official, with parchment skin and hooded eyes, a fellow who'd heard threats from many more whales of senior officers than this mere sprat of a lieutenant.

Oliphant added his weight, in a deliberately even tone, which was more effective than the Pearce bluster. 'It would be a mistake to see that as an idle threat. From Downing Street, the matter will go straight to the desk of Earl Spencer and, no doubt, given it is such a serious political problem, to the Duke of Portland as well.'

The name hit home; keep the gate he might, but this man was not going to lay down his future to keep it closed. He conceded in a sepulchral tone.

'All I can do is to send into the admiral and inform him of your request.'

'Then oblige me by doing so,' Pearce insisted.

A bell summoned another ex-tar who was handed a note just penned to take to the C-in-C, with Pearce asking, 'Where can we await his reply?'

There was the very faintest twitch of the lips; this fellow, put on the back foot, was working up to take pleasure from his response. 'I daresay this hallway will serve as well as anywhere. Or, if you prefer, Lieutenant, you may wait in the porch.'

John Pearce's blood had been boiling when he set of from HMS *Hazard*. It had, on such a long journey, cooled somewhat, but that remark sent it spiralling again. This disdainful dismissal, for that was what it was, sent his temper soaring to the level of rage. It was all Oliphant could do to restrain him as he pushed forward to the very edge of the desk, intent on clouting this supercilious sod.

'Come away, John. Taking out your ire on this low cully of an under-clerk will not aid the purpose.'

The icy and superior demeanour cracked. 'You dare term me a low cully, sir! And under-clerk! I would have you know of my seniority.'

Oliphant threw up his hands, as well as his eyes, in a faux gesture. 'Forgive me if I have inadvertently flattered you, for you are inferior to a scrub. Seniority? It is a truism that shit floats, to end up in the most surpassingly elevated places.'

This was delivered as a Parthian shot, as he pulled Pearce away from a man now spluttering imprecations. Oliphant was advising his companion that a too often recourse to his fists was unbecoming. Pearce wanted to respond by telling him how close he himself had come to meeting them. The waiting was done out in the fresh air, which went some way to alleviate the mood, despite it taking a measure of time before Pearce calmed down.

The call to see Admiral Buckner came eventually. Pearce, instructed to leave Oliphant behind, was led to his office, a large and well-illuminated room, due to the large sash windows and a clear blue sky. Buckner, of whom he knew little, was a burly fellow, with a crabbed expression. It was not just in the muscular upper body, but in the cast of the eye, a directness that seemed to eschew the guile that Pearce had found too often a trait in admirals.

He had about him the look of a man seeking to send a silent message that to cross him would be dangerous, and was standing, hands clasped behind his back, as if to guard against anything coming in his direction and he did just that. But first he had to admonish the sheer effrontery Pearce had shown.

'How dare you, sir, behave in the manner you have shown?'

'I have good reason to believe you are responsible for my lack of a crew.'

'Indirectly. I am merely an intermediary in this matter. The orders to strip out *Hazard* came down from Mr Marsden.'

'You take your instructions from the Second Secretary, sir?'

The full face filled with blood and the response was a shout. 'I take my instructions, young man, from the board upon whose directives he acts. And damn you, who do you think you are to come in here and challenge me?'

'I am an officer in command of a ship of war, which cannot weigh for want of the hands to do it. I see it as deliberate enmity.'

'From the little I know of you, you'd as well to see it as chickens coming home to roost.'

'I demand you provide me with the men I require.'

'Demand away, sir. How many ship's captains do you think I have in here daily, pleading for things I cannot provide, and among those people are those for whom I have a high personal regard.'

It did not have to be said that did not extend to John Pearce; the look was enough.

'Then I have no choice but to bring the matter, which I see as deliberate interference in what is a government task, to Mr Pitt personally.'

That got a derisive snort. 'Then I hope he has some hands hidden away, for I have none to spare, this when every vessel under my flag is short on its compliment. Even if I had them, I would not provide them to you.' That look of guile Pearce knew so well replaced exasperation and vocal bluster. 'It might be best for you to resign your commission to command HMS *Hazard*, then matters may right themselves.'

'You are not the first flag officer it's been my misfortune to deal with, but I see you as, by far, the least substantial by some margin.' The face reddened again, prior to an outburst, so Pearce spoke quickly to cut it off. 'Having overcome the malice of fighting admirals, I see no great difficulty in humbling one who has yet to lead a fleet into battle.'

The shouts of anger followed him down the corridors to the hallway, where he rejoined Oliphant, who fixed him with a look. 'I sense it did not go well?'

'It's Whitehall for you and immediately.'

'Not another coach – will my poor arse bear it?' Then his face brightened. 'At least I'll not be required to share it with your damned Pelicans and their hostility.'

By the time Pearce got Oliphant away on a London-bound coach, then visited the various chandlers and bespoke the needs of his personal stores and other necessary items, it was too late to return to the ship. So, despite the standing instruction, one which could only be waived by the commanding admiral, which stated officers must sleep aboard their ships, he booked himself into the Royal George.

That too had been instructive of how quickly rumours spread in a place like Chatham. Not a word had been said, but in the attitude of those listing and costing his requirements lay a degree of scorn at the quantities ordered, enough for a long voyage. Yet they accepted his credit and undertook to ship the goods purchased out to HMS *Hazard* on the following day.

Next, he had to deal with the fact his cabin was poorly furnished, Milton having removed his own possessions even before Pearce came aboard. These included his chronometers, and that needed addressing. So he visited the various emporiums where such used objects ended up, to bespeak several pieces that would make life more bearable, not least a dining table and a dozen chairs.

He bought a wine cooler and a couple of captain's chairs for individual visitors, with cushions to ease the hardness of the seat. A carpet would take away the stark wood of the decking and help to mask the sounds from the wardroom below, once he had the men to occupy it. A couple of tapestries always softened the appearance of a cabin, hinting at homeliness instead of the true function.

But it was the clocks that were essential and there no expense was spared. He wanted better timepieces than those supplied by the navy, one telling Greenwich Time, the other set by sextant to local noon, thus enabling him to establish the ship's longitude.

There was a certain amount of guilt about being ashore. He was staying in a comfortable tavern, eating a proper meal, while his friends were not. This he justified to himself by acknowledging the Pelicans had brought it on themselves. Had they been less at risk, he might have brought them along. For the others, he had to assume those Milton had been obliged to leave behind had their own personal stores.

Food consumed, he retired to a room and sat down to write to Emily, deciding against detailing his concerns for the forthcoming cruise. He followed with another letter to Sir Peter Parker, detailing how the forces of malice had contrived to render his command inoperable, though adding what steps he was taking to remedy the matter. On the page these looked to be more hopes than realities.

That done and cursing the navy and all its works, he went to bed, to dream of legions of admirals, all hanging from the sturdy branches of oak trees.

That same day, three men were contemplating letters they had received from Emily Barclay. The first was Alexander Davidson, to confirm the wish that he take over the management of her affairs. While the chance for increased business was welcome, there had to be caution too. Ommaney and Druce, a larger firm, would not take kindly to what they would see as encroachment. They could retaliate by seeking to poach some of his own existing clients.

The second letter had come to a bleary-eyed Edward Druce. He had spent too much time filleting the papers relating to the Barclay estate to welcome anything relating to it. An ultimatum had even come from home, to enquire where he was, one the work obliged him to ignore. The request, in truth a demand that the files in their entirety should be transferred to a rival, had him worry over his efforts, concerned that he might have missed something.

Several schemes to which the Barclay funds had been committed had now been closed out, the shares in various trusts, not all canals, sold at the best price that could be extracted in a quick disposal. One or two showed losses, but happily others were marginally in profit or at break-even. Remaining were two of the most egregious ventures, where seeking a quick sale would be disastrous. These required as much as a fortnight before they could be liquidated at a reasonable value. That done, if you excluded the propriety of the original investments, they would appear as acceptable risks.

The letter that went back to Harley Street requested time in which the firm could ensure that everything was in order. This came with the ritual words of dismay that their work on her behalf had failed to satisfy. But, in his heart, he was glad to be shot of the problem, there being no doubt that Emily Barclay, thanks to her one visit to Newgate, knew too much to be an easily dealt with client in the future.

Walter Hodgson got the third missive, having just returned from a tour of some of the less salubrious haunts known to a man of his trade. There were places in the city where information could be gleaned about the kind of villains he had spent his life in pursuit of. Such burrows were peopled by the dregs of a society that did not lack for low creatures, men and women engaged in every kind of criminality.

The best sources were the least successful at survival in that world. Those who struggled to subsist by wrongdoing watched their more successful brethren with a keen and envious eye. They could be willing to provide scraps, if the fee for betrayal brought profit and provided it was carried out with care to avoid retribution. These partial tips a clever investigator could fashion into a whole.

The whole he had conjured up this day told him the men in the drawings were not from the underbelly of the capital city. All he had asked for was recognition, not any crime that might be associated with the images. If you excused those so desperate they would concoct knowledge for the price of a pot of ale, he had drawn a complete blank. The result was not wholly discouraging; he had learnt where not to look, which could be just as valuable.

Daisy had intimated the pair smacked of the sea, so further searches would take Hodgson east of the City, to the docks lining the north bank of the Thames. If nothing emerged there, it would be a tour of the coastal towns of Kent and Essex. If they had come to her place of entertainment for a possible act of murder, and that had yet to be established, it surely would not have been from a far-off location.

During the day, he had toyed with the problem of what to pass on to Druce, coming to the conclusion anything partial would not serve. Gherson was still the prime suspect to all but him, but that only amounted to a reasonable if strong doubt about his guilt, based on a feeling in his lower gut. It was not a certainty. A visit to the usual clerk for funds to continue his pursuit would be necessary, and that would produce, as it had in the past, some useful gossip of the goings-on on the upper floors. But he would leave the principal alone until he could place before him undeniable facts.

He had been surprised on coming home to receive a letter from such a source and to wonder how she had got the address. As with the creature now lording it in Newgate, it came from someone whose name had been known to him for an age, while likewise being a person he had never actually clapped eyes on.

Here she was asking to meet with him, a proposition which, despite a high degree of curiosity, he saw as perturbing. He pursued a profession in which deduction equalled both persistence and information. Therefore he had, sometime past, come to see both Gherson and Emily Barclay as part of the same entanglement. Exactly how much so remained in the realm of speculation.

That she should write seeking his help, without naming in what capacity it would manifest itself, took the latter from deduction to certainty: she had to be the lady Gherson had alluded to in Newgate. After all, the name Barclay was common to both cases. In reflecting on that, he came to realise a deeper reason for avoiding Edward Druce.

It was a feeling of manipulation, of being involved in matters where he was being fed only what the prize agent wanted him to know: there had to be so much more. Given the gravity of the crime and the feeling of matters not being straightforward, he could not put out of his mind such a situation could leave him exposed.

Could talking to Emily Barclay fill in some of the gaps? Was it worth the risk of such a meeting becoming known to Druce, who would surely not welcome it? If done at all, it had to be carried out discreetly, and the Harley Street address, to which he had been invited to reply, looked to be the best for the purpose.

Taking his supper in his local tavern, he decided an affirmative reply was a good idea. He took out and looked at his drawings for the umpteenth time and an odd thought did surface. Would it not be remarkable if the person to put names to these images turned out to be Emily Barclay?

CHAPTER SIXTEEN

No advantage would come from waiting in Chatham, so John Pearce boated out with a portion of the stores he had purchased, knowing the rest would follow. He had, the day before, examined *Hazard* on approach, but it had been cursory, he too anxious as to how he would appear on coming aboard to give it the attention it deserved. Now, to save time, he had himself rowed around the ship, partly just to look at her lines, but also to check on her trim. If he needed to shift stores or water to correct that it was going to be quite a task.

Thankfully Milton had kept such matters well in hand, which left just the ship and that which he had learnt regarding her in the brief time he had been aboard. A Cormorant class ship-rigged sloop, she was in prime condition. Her timbers looked sound, while her cordage would, by now, have matured to taut perfection. One hundred and eight feet long in total, her beam was just shy of thirty feet, over a hold of nine foot in depth. An examination of the ship's logs had her service record, this mostly in support of the North Sea fleet blockading the Dutch ports under Admiral Duncan.

Requiring little water under her keel, she would have been very useful as an inshore observer, keeping an eye on the preparations of the Dutch fleet. With her sixteen 6-pounder cannon, *Hazard* had the means to defend herself should trouble appear, but the greatest asset of her class was speed.

Three-masted, her type could generally show any pursuit a clean pair of heels. Slowly being rowed around, he felt a craving, of a kind he had not felt since leaving the Mediterranean. There was real beauty in her lines; she looked sleek, especially with a full set of canvas clewed up on her slightly raked masts. HMS *Hazard* was his and he could imagine himself and her carrying out the kind of duties for which she'd been designed.

Finally aboard, while his purchases were being fetched on deck by the Pelicans, Pearce did that which the previous day's requirements had rendered impossible; he interviewed his warrants and standing petty officers. Not only did he quiz the master, Mr Williams, on her sailing qualities, he wished to be told of her quirks, for every ship had some peculiar to herself. It was necessary to know them in advance of their being demonstrated. Action left no time for education. Conversation with Williams left Pearce with the impression the man was competent, without being inspiring.

The cannon was inspected in the company of Mr Low, the gunner, Pearce first having been introduced to the man's wife, a woman of square build with a rubicund complexion and a ready and permanent scowl. She had the task, amongst others, of looking after the younger midshipmen when and if they arrived.

That done they moved on to the dozen half-pound swivels, set at various points along the upper deck. They were designed to fire small ordnance at close quarters, with the kind of telling accuracy that could clear an enemy quarterdeck. The quantity of shot in the lockers was checked too and the state of rust on the balls noted for later chipping.

Shoes exchanged for leather slippers, the magazine was next for a visit, the powder room too, with assurances being received that no evidence of damp existed. Likewise, Pearce was informed the powder barrels had been turned only two weeks before. This, carried out on a three-monthly cycle, ensured the various elements did not separate and render the whole ineffective.

Pearce let it be known he had been in action many times and had often worked and personally fired more than one cannon. To begin with, Mr Low's mood had been punctilious to the point of seeming stand-offish. Yet he was a gunner to his fingertips, a man who revelled in the position he held and the deep knowledge of his trade, acquired over years. Given a shared interest, he warmed to this new commanding officer, who knew enough on the subject of ordnance to provoke a lively debate on ballistics.

Crocker, the bosun, properly termed boatswain, came across as a real misery, the impression given of a man hoping for a better appointment. Had he been like that with Milton? There was no way of knowing and it mattered not. He was obliged to confirm the state of the stores and the condition of the rigging, blocks and sails. This included those in the locker in terms of quantity and weight of canvas, with a check on how regularly they were aired. Damp sails left too long could spontaneously combust and endanger the ship.

Crocker showed real surprise when, back on deck, his new captain threw off his blue coat and began to climb up the ratlines, eschewing the lubber's hole as he passed the mainmast cap. Pearce made his way out on to a couple of the topmast yards, sliding along the footropes to inspect matters, before continuing up to the very crosstrees, not something commanding officers, careful of their dignity, were supposed to do in Crocker's estimation. Pearce stayed aloft for a while, surveying the anchorage as well as the shorelines of Essex and Kent, before returning to the deck by sliding down a backstay, there to face a disapproving look.

'Wouldn't shame a skylarking mid,' was what Crocker later said to his confrères and it was not meant as praise.

One of those confrères, the carpenter, came next. Together they went from top to bottom of the ship, inspecting everything from mainframe timbers to the hanging knees, even the seating of the masts. He was required to list his stores of wood and the special tools needed to ply his trade, before they eased along the carpenter's walk to inspect the inside of the hull, which thankfully showed no sign or smell of rot.

Likewise the bilge was not malodorous, which could affect the health of the crew. Mr Towse, a former shipwright from Whitby, for that was his name and birthplace, had checked the level of water in the well once that day already, as was his duty, but was happy to do so again and to show the pumps, which he had the responsibility to maintain, were in good working order.

In all, the inspections were satisfactory, telling Pearce he had a competent set of inferiors who would do their duty and some might even smile in the activity. If they were not happy at his appointment, it mattered not one jot. They had tasks to perform and would carry them out diligently for the sake of their careers, if not his. The whole vessel had been properly cleaned by the now departed crew and the odour, as is should be, was a mixture of wood, resin, tar, hemp and diluted vinegar.

The purser, Pearce suspected, had stayed aboard to protect his investment, even if he could have applied to shift in the advent of a new commanding officer. Porlock, a Manxman, came to the cabin with his ledgers, to be offered a glass of newly purchased wine. His books were examined with what appeared to be an eagle eye, one that could not but make the man feel uncomfortable. Head down, John Pearce was thinking it would take a genius to find discrepancies: every purser known to man was adept at hiding anything that would make questionable their figures.

Responsible for victualling the ship in all respects, from food to tallow and candles and hundreds of other goods, he had as a basis of his income some twelve and a half per cent, this being the difference between what the Navy Board charged him for the provisions of the ship, as against that for which he billed the Admiralty. His private trade was in the provision of hammocks and bedding, slops and, most profitable of all, tobacco.

'Your weights comply, Mr Porlock, I trust?'

'A true sixteen ounces to the pound, sir,' came the confident reply.

Pearce could only hope that was the truth, though he would contrive a way to find out if Porlock was lying. Having acted as his own purser in the Mediterranean, he knew how suspicious tars were of being cheated over less-than-honest weights. Many of Porlock's breed used fourteen ounces to the pound as their measure, thus short-changing on everything they supplied. Pearce also knew the endemic risks of the purser trade. Get the figures wrong and you would soon face bankruptcy.

There was provision for the sloop to muster both a chaplain and a surgeon. Pearce would do without the former, but possibly find room for a schoolmaster and one willing to take Divine Service on a Sunday. This was a task all captains were obliged to perform, but one which went against the grain for him. He had no wish to deny another his faith, but his own doubts made him feel a hypocrite. He would certainly seek out a sawbones, plus an assistant, which would require a written application to the Sick and Hurt Board.

There was the question of junior officers and midshipmen, Milton having removed his with the rest of the crew, no doubt the whole going to a new vessel. He needed a marine officer and a party of a dozen bullocks, including corporals and a sergeant. Oliphant had been given a list of the ship's requirements, which included those vital elements.

Lieutenants and midshipmen at least should prove possible; there were any number of the former unemployed and on half-pay, as well as a queue of youngsters begging for a place on a ship. He had left notice at the Royal George saying what his needs were. That said, a crew – full if possible – was the prime requirement and that had to include a number of ship's boys, to carry out the functions of nippers when weighing and act as powder monkeys in battle.

* * *

Oliphant had presented the demands to Dundas; it would be up to him to involve William Pitt if it was deemed necessary. If Pearce was confounded by what had happened, his messenger was less so, being more conscious of the perennial infighting which characterised government. Pitt, a Tory, led a coalition which included the so-called Portland Whigs, with those of that persuasion who had stuck with Charles James Fox providing a very vocal opposition, not least in the way they diverged on the whole notion of the war.

To stay in power Pitt relied on the Duke of Portland and he had extracted a high price for his support. The King's First Minister had been forced to remove his own older brother, the Earl of Chatham, from the Admiralty, so the place could be given to Earl Spencer. It was therefore a truism that applying pressure to Spencer was fraught with risk. Dundas decided to bypass him and go directly to the recently appointed First Secretary, Evan Nepean, with a request-cum-demand that the needs of HMS *Hazard* be met.

'Spencer will hear of it, of course,' Dundas opined. 'But he's an idle sod, so I'm hoping he will leave it to Nepean to deal with.'

'With respect,' Oliphant replied, 'the order to strip out the ship must come from the same source as the proposed remedy.'

'Without a doubt, but I'm hoping that having made their point . . .' Seeing the look of curiosity on Oliphant's face, Dundas broke off to explain. 'They are telling me, in no uncertain terms, and not for the first time, that the navy does not come under the jurisdiction of the Ministry of War.'

The face clouded. 'I can't tell you the arguments we've had. The salts think that they can do as they wish with no recourse to cooperation. How can I despatch troops in their thousands to places like the Caribbean, without I have some say in who is to be in command of the expedition?'

The look of innocence on Oliphant's face was there to mask one fact: he knew very well why such disputes occurred. Command of a fleet was not within the gift of Dundas, because his choices were always overtly political. Military competence, to this minster, came second to loyalty to the Tory and monarchical cause.

The conception and planning of such expeditions emanated from his office, the navy then being tasked to get the designated forces to where they were supposed to be. Quite naturally, given it would be their ships that would be at risk, they insisted on the right to appoint a competent commander.

Trust, never high, was not aided by results. The Caribbean, and more recently the expedition sent to Quiberon Bay, had turned into expensive fiascos. In the West Indies, the soldiery had been decimated by yellow fever; at Quiberon they'd failed, once landed, to even get to their objectives.

Recriminations naturally ensued, but Dundas was like an eel when it came to responsibility, thus the ensuing censure was ever laid at another's door. The generals got the blame for failure in the Caribbean. In the case of Quiberon, it fell on an aggrieved and furious navy.

'If Nepean will not play, then I will have to bring in Billy.'

The look accompanying that demonstrated how unwelcome such an act would be, so Oliphant asked what, to him, was an obvious solution. 'Why not advise them of the mission and its importance?'

Dundas growled and shook his head. 'I might as well send a letter to Paris and tell them myself. Inform the Cabinet and it will be the talk of every club and salon within the day. Now, what does Pearce want exactly? I need to know what to ask for.'

The list was passed over to be scrutinised, Dundas nodding as he read it.

'Some of this I can satisfy myself, certainly in the article of a quartet of midshipmen. I'm plagued daily with pleas to find places for the sons of friends, those who cannot run to the cost of an army commission.'

The sons of political adherents of the Scottish vote, was Oliphant's conclusion. Pearce would no doubt be in receipt of a number of lads whose brogue could be barely comprehensible to an English ear. Still, the man was a Scot himself, so he at least should understand them.

'Lieutenants?' was expressed with ministerial doubt.

'Pearce reckons, if word gets out, both he and the Admiralty will be in receipt of endless pleas and, I'm informed, any appointments have to come from there.'

'Nepean should be happy to oblige, just to get some peace, if his post is anything like mine. Leave this with me, Oliphant, and I will deal with it as soon as I can.'

'Lieutenant Pearce did wish me to say the matter is pressing.'

'To which I would respond that Rome wasn't built in a day. Dealing with Secretary Nepean will require a degree of delicacy.'

It occurred to Oliphant, as he departed, that either the fellow mentioned was in pursuit of some favour from Dundas, or that one had already been provided and thus payment was due.

'It would do you well to know, Pearce,' he muttered to himself, 'that is how government works.'

* * *

There was little doubt the news of what had happened to *Hazard* had become common knowledge. She was anchored in amongst a number of other naval vessels, from 100-gun ships of the line and seventy-fours, all the way down to variously sized frigates, brigs and bomb vessels. It seemed that every boat setting off from another ship saw the need to row close to the sloop and cast an eye over her. What they hoped to see was a mystery, there generally being a true lack of activity on deck. Few of the common undertakings could be carried out without a crew.

Over a few days, of a morning, they would have observed the same quartet swabbing the decks in shirtsleeves, without realising that one of their number was the man in command of the ship. They would also not realise the duty was being carried out with much banter among the four souls, who had bonded as Pelicans over just such duties when newly pressed.

The warrants Pearce had dealt with reacted in different fashions; Crocker and Porlock saw it as demeaning that a man of rank should act like a common tar. Towse, as a carpenter, known by the soubriquet, Jack of the Dust, seemed unsure of how to react. Only the gunner was on hand to join in the jesting, though Mr Low refused the invite to swing a mop for fear of what his wife might say.

Later in the morning they would have observed the same quartet in the ship's jolly boat, heading for Chatham, Pearce in uniform but still on an oar. He had written yet another letter to Sir Peter Parker in what seemed to be a daily bulletin of his travails, the one reply he had received evincing much sympathy and understanding, while also detailing what he saw as the limitations of Charles Buckner.

But his main purpose this day was to seek out nippers-cum-powder monkeys and servants, the former from the sons of the common dockyard workers, who could not get them into a trade like their own. As in the navy, there were more applicants than places in the highly paid royal dockyards.

For captain's servants, even if they may never carry a tray, the requirement was different, an appeal to parents in the more elevated dockyard occupations; shipwrights, ironmasters, sailmakers and the more responsible storekeepers. With aspirations that their sons should rise to be gentlemen, they would be keen to see their offspring given a place aboard a warship.

Pearce chose the brightest among the obviously willing, those who dreamt, as all boys do, of endless good fortune. Eyeing them assembled, he wondered how many saw themselves dressed as he was in some rosy future, particularly those enlisted as a captain's servant. It was an entry point that could see a youngster of the right stamp rise to be a captain and to even fly an admiral's flag.

'I will hire boats to fetch you out,' was addressed to both groups, twenty boys in all. 'Please ensure your parents send you with everything you will need.'

He was right about one fact: the way news of his need for officers would spread. Within a day he received his first letter begging to be considered for a place and it made depressing reading. The correspondent, a Mr Peat, was a lieutenant of advanced years, the true number of which he was vague about: calculation put him in the second half of his fifties.

He listed the vessels in which he had served, from midshipman to his present rank, gained just prior to the loss of the American

Colonies and it was clear he had lacked employment since. He was clearly a fellow lacking in any kind of interest, a senior officer or someone of power able to push his case. With such a gap in experience, there had to be a reason: the recipient, even if he could be sympathetic, was forced to decline the request.

More soon followed, all having written to the Admiralty as well as John Pearce. He was requested to do likewise, in order to enhance their claim for, if the commander of a ship of war could decline an officer, he could not appoint one. It was not just local Medway residents who applied; relatives in Chatham must have written to needy brothers or cousins and advised them of the vacancies. Even more surprising were the letters that came from various worthies, one being from a belted Earl.

In the end, with no personal connections to give him guidance, Pearce chose to back half a dozen applications, writing to the Board of Admiralty with their names. While this was taking place, Oliphant was doing his best to harry Dundas and getting many a rebuke for his temerity. But his persistence, added to a thick skin, paid off. Before the week was out, the matter had been settled with the interlocutor wondering what price Nepean had extracted for compliance.

'None of your damned business, Oliphant,' Dundas had barked. 'Just be satisfied that it is done.'

'I shall write to Pearce immediately.'

Dundas threw a paper across his desk. 'These are his mids, who are as we speak on their way to take up their places.'

A look at the names told Oliphant he'd been right. They were not all prefixed with a Mac, but each name seemed redolent of Caledonia.

* * *

The line of half a dozen cutters was visible long before it could be established they were heading for HMS *Hazard*. Every vessel they passed brought forth to the deck an audience to mark their progress. It was when they'd cleared the stern of the last third rate that Pearce, called on deck and away from his ledgers by Michael O'Hagan, could begin to hope that Oliphant's communication, relating his success, was accurate.

The red-coated Lobsters made up the majority of the first boat and a long glass established there was a marine officer sat in the stern. Casting his telescope over the others, he saw many glum faces, few of them clad in the kind of clothing worn by Jack tars. Indeed, the variety of garments spoke of civilians and not well-heeled ones at that, a fact underlined as they came alongside.

The marines came aboard first, the officer the last to board. Before him Pearce was gifted with a supercilious look under a perfectly white wig, revealed when the hat was lifted both to him and the quarterdeck. In his other hand the marine carried a silver-topped crop with which he struck his lower leg. Pearce thought both the expression and the act lacking in respect.

'Lieutenant of Marines, George Moberly,' was imparted with a languid drawl, 'at your service, sir.'

The formula was rigid and had to be adhered to: he had to introduce himself and issue the required words. 'Mr Moberly, I bid you welcome aboard HMS *Hazard* and look forward to our future relationship.'

'Kind, sir, most kind.'

'I trust you have been given charge of the others in the boats?'

'I have, sir, fetched from the very Tower of London. A rum lot, if I may say so.'

'How many sailors?'

'Not one. They are quota men, sir, to be made into sailors.'

'All of them?' Pearce demanded, failing to keep the jolt out of his voice.

'Yes, sir. Can I suggest we get them aboard and listed on to the ship's muster? I would also suggest it would be an idea that they be fed. They have had nothing so far this day.'

There was no choice but to agree, even if it was done with a sinking heart. Already in his mind, he was composing yet another dose of written misery, to send to Portsmouth, only to then decide to wait until he had once more bearded Peter Parker's opposite number here at the Nore.

CHAPTER SEVENTEEN

It had taken an age to get to see Admiral Buckner a second time and Pearce's mood, unhappy to start with, was positively foul when the two came face to face. This time the admiral was sitting down and had declined to see him alone. He had with him and introduced his flag lieutenant, the message being clear; if he was to be insulted again, there would be someone to witness it for some future sanction.

Unknown to Buckner, that suited John Pearce: he required that what he was about to say could not be denied by a claim of failed memory. Not that he was content to rely on a fresh-faced young fellow who owed his place to his superior. He had in his hand a letter, listing the skills in which he was short, none of which were likely to exist in the men he had just entered into *Hazard*'s muster book.

There would be abilities there yet to be found, but a quota man, supposedly a volunteer, was more often one chosen by his hometown or district from those who posed a burden on the public purse. The act making it compulsory had been enacted to fulfil a requirement promulgated by the government as a way to man an expanding fleet, endemically short-handed. To the municipalities it provided a way to get rid of the inhabitants of the workhouse, men who had fallen into debt and, too often, they would ship out the denizens of the local gaol.

Had the obvious drawbacks of that, which had occurred to him, registered with those who had applied the policy, or was it just another case of Admiralty malice? If the latter, such an action would not serve. It was all very well to forcibly fill a number of vacancies aboard a man-o'-war with such people, but they should not have been sent aboard a ship in which all the necessary specialised duties were uncovered. Without those men, how was he to train the newly recruited in what was a complex artefact?

'Here in writing, sir, is a list of where I am deficient.'

Buckner harrumphed in a melodramatic fashion. 'Every ship in the navy is short, Pearce, and, thanks to the lack of diligence of the towns and shire magistrates in putting the required numbers of their people forward, we will want for a remedy. Best get out to sea and solve the lack of experience in your crew by working them. That is the common way, as I can attest from my own past experience.'

Pearce was treated to a list of the ships in which Buckner had sailed, either short-handed or with an inexperienced crew, which he found impossible to interrupt. All he could think of, for this particular flag officer, was the lack of sea time and battle experience he had acquired, a subject much alluded to by Admiral Parker. Buckner, Pearce was told, owed his present posting to his connections, not his abilities.

'And surely,' Buckner concluded, 'they can get you to a place where you can press what you need from incoming merchantmen?'

That was the last thing John Pearce wanted to do: he'd been a victim of the practice himself at sea as well as on land.

'I suggest that will not do. I have only three men on board who can hand, reef and steer and none of them are topmen, so who is to supervise the setting and working of the sails? Your past experience has no bearing, for my situation is singular.'

That brought Buckner forward, hands flat on his deck and eyes flashing. 'You, sir, are singular, most obviously in your utter lack of respect for a superior officer.'

'I show respect where it is due, sir.' As Buckner swelled up, he threw the letter on the table to cut off his response. 'A copy of this has gone to the First Lord of the Treasury, another the Lord Commissioners of the Navy and a third to the Secretary to the Admiralty.'

Bucker shrugged in feigned indifference. 'That is no concern of mine.'

'It will be if anything happens to HMS *Hazard*, and I say that knowing the possibility to be a high one. With such a useless crew she will either become prize to the enemy, or perhaps founder for want of proper seamen to handle her. There will, sir, be an enquiry. I intend not only to survive but to attend it, also to put forward, as proof of professional negligence, the contents of what I have just delivered, dated this very day.'

'I would order you to weigh immediately if it was within my right to do so.'

'I thank providence it is not. I bid you good day, Admiral Buckner, with the fond wish that you reflect on the fate of Admiral Byng. You are, I suspect, a mere go-between in this, which has the stink of political game-playing all over it. Those who initiated these acts are concealed now, and I suspect will stay that way, should any censure be threatened. It is usually the case, then, that a sacrificial lamb is required to quiet public anger.'

'I am secure in my judgement, Lieutenant, and in my friends.'

'A breed that tend to disappear when trouble in brewing,' was imparted by Pearce over his shoulder. 'As you may find to your cost.'

Which did not apply to Michael, Charlie and Rufus. They were waiting for him on the quayside as was the jolly boat. But also, standing by a two-person coach, was Oliphant. Stance and distance made it plain he had no intention of communicating with the Pelicans.

'You took your time,' came out as a bark from Pearce, still seething from seeing Buckner.

'Damn you, Pearce, I have near grovelled to get you what you need.'

'What *we* need, I would remind you.'

'Well, right of this moment, I need your friends to load a casket into your boat.'

'It does not occur to you to ask them?'

'Best it comes from you. It's the funds we requested as necessary for the mission, a goodly sum in gold and of a weight.'

'Did you sign for it?'

'I did.'

'Then Dundas cannot accuse me of misappropriation this time. It will fall to your account if money is not employed as he would wish. And I can tell you from my own experience, he's damned vague about what that is.'

'Right now, I need to get it to the ship and it's too heavy for me to carry on my own.'

'I wonder which one of my friends will be willing to assist you. I cannot see them inclined to do you any favours.'

'Order them.'

'No. I will merely ask.'

In the end, Michael did what was required and with ease; it was not seen as heavy by the Irishman, who bore the small locked casket on one shoulder as if it were canvas. There was silence in the boat as they rowed out to the sloop, Pearce in a brown study and the others, as usual with Oliphant present, were non-communicative. The former was thinking of how to make the mission work, for there could be no refusal to proceed and that depended on getting his tyro crew to a certain level of ability.

If he had looked each man in the eye as they were mustered, asking them as he listed their names what was their civilian occupation and making notes, it had not generated much in the way of hope. He would need to study what he had written with more care, to see if he could glean any clues to what talents they might possess.

On departing to see Buckner he had instructed Moberly to get the men to the various locations where they would live and sleep and to see them properly clad. The haughty marine had looked as if he was about to decline what was a rather menial duty; the glare he got from John Pearce killed that notion. The purser would have been active in his absence, for each man 'volunteering' had been in receipt of a five-pound bounty.

They were required to pay for their hammocks, bedding and suitable seagoing clothing and, no doubt, he would be loading them with as much tobacco as he could shift, which had Pearce wonder how much of that bounty they would have left when Porlock had finished hustling them.

He should have read to them the Articles of War immediately, but he saw the need to visit Buckner as taking priority, while occupying his mind was the depth of what they would have to be taught and the list was endless. This took him back to his own first weeks aboard HMS *Brilliant* and the man doing the teaching.

In his case it had been the bosun, Robert Sykes, a fellow to recall fondly for his care and patience. Memory of him and his actions provided a blueprint by which he would teach his crew their duties. It would be difficult, but it had to be done. He had already reasoned going any distance outside the Thames Estuary was out of the question; the North Sea was too unpredictable. But the calm waters of the river would be a good place to initiate the men into the very basics of their roles.

Back aboard, he wrote to Emily and composed yet another report to Admiral Parker, trying to sound a more positive note as he listed to him the same deficiencies as he'd given Buckner. He would get HMS *Hazard* to sea and in good shape if it was the last thing he would do. That written, he was then left to wonder how long that would take, which rendered Oliphant's words, once they were alone in his cabin, extremely unwelcome.

'Matters in the Pyrenees are deteriorating. Godoy cannot be relied upon to maintain the alliance with Spain and Dundas insists we shift. He wants us off the Catalan coast, not sitting at the Nore.'

'It's not possible.'

'Why ever not, did I not get you a crew?'

The response, heard all over the ship, settled in every mind – bar the grinning Pelicans – that the man under whom they were going to have to serve was a hard-hearted bastard with a foul temper. There were souls, drummed into their present situation, who had already determined to desert at the first opportunity. The yelling imprecations and references to their lack of anything approaching the ability to sail and fight a ship of war did nothing to dent that aim.

Others, given the tales by which they had been rendered fearful, could imagine nothing but being had up at a grating and flogged to a pulp. There was a third type, the sea lawyer and natural troublemaker. By the time they'd been shown how to sling their hammocks and occupy them without being tipped to the deck, everyone knew who the prime candidate was for that role, he being determined they should.

Harry Teach had very near to an old pirate's identity and it fazed him not that his namesake had ended up with his head on a stake in the Virginia colony. Teach was loud in his low opinion of this noisy tartar of a captain. A finger was poked at the new slops adorning his barrel chest, a firm assertion following.

'He'll soon learn his manners when he comes across Harry Teach, mark my word on it.'

He being a squat fellow, with the manners and build of a bully, no one dared to contradict this.

* * *

In the cabin, Pearce realised he was abusing the wrong person. 'What do I gain by blaming you?'

'A release of exasperation, no more,' Oliphant replied, seemingly unaffected. 'But I would ask, for I do have an interest, how you intend to proceed?'

'First I must address the crew and read to them the Articles of War.'

A raised eyebrow demonstrated that this required explanation, so Pearce provided it in some detail. Said articles covered the behaviour of everyone in the service. How they were to behave in both fighting and ship handling, the punishments for various offences, in a list as long as a man's arm. It was also stated who had the right to administer the penalties and at what level.

'So you can't string someone up from the yardarm?' was the ironic response, accompanied by a yawn. 'What a disappointment, I was so looking forward to being witness.'

'Not legally. But as I hinted before, at sea, there are captains who will interpret their powers very widely. Take keelhauling . . .'

'I'd prefer not to, I will gift that to you.'

'It can be as a good as a death sentence. A body scraped along a ship's bottom comes back aboard with the kind of lacerations . . .'

'Please,' Oliphant protested, holding up a hand, 'no more detail. How about flogging?'

'I'm not in favour and, even if I was, I am confined to two dozen lashes by the articles, unless given permission by a higher authority, though that is rarely withheld. But again, far out at sea, who does a fellow complain to if that is exceeded?'

'So it is as I thought. Barbarous.'

'On land as much as at sea, Oliphant. Chastisement by flogging is common to both military and civil society, something my father railed against all his life. And a day in the stocks can be even worse than a lashing.'

'True. I have never been fond of the practice.'

'Would that be because you might be a victim?'

'I decline to be drawn,' was the composed reply.

'Enough, I have much work to do sorting out the watches, which will be guesswork to begin with. It will also require much adjustment over time to get the balance right. I suggest you find yourself a berth aft on the orlop deck, where the standing officers reside.'

'I had hoped for a cabin?'

'Perhaps, when the junior officers are aboard, you can shift to the wardroom, but such is in their gift, not mine.'

A knock at the door produced one of the new boy servants, to tell him that a boat was about to come alongside with what appeared to be a quartet of young gentlemen aboard. This reminded Oliphant he had the list of names, that being passed over with a comment on their antecedents.

'Would I be allowed to say, have a care of these fellows. They will write to their parents who are, to a man and a mother, beholden to Dundas for their placement. Anything detrimental imparted to them will go straight to the devious sod.'

'How little you know of midshipmen, Oliphant, if they are indeed such creatures. They only write home when a superior is standing over them with birch cane in hand.' He looked at the names, then added, 'But I take your point. Now, it's fitting that I'm by the gangway to welcome them.'

Out on deck a few souls were wandering about, as if lost, which Pearce suspected they must feel, everything being strange and, as yet, no sense of discipline or order in place. If, having been in the same situation himself, he had some sympathy, he dared not let it show. Happy or confused, dragooned or volunteers, these fellows were in the King's service for the duration of the present conflict. The only place they could go until the peace came, barring desertion, was another warship.

Perhaps in time they could be allowed ashore, but that would depend on how they behaved and the degree of trust. He would need to get to know them, not just as a crew, but as individuals too. Likewise, they had to have as much faith in him. They needed to meld into a group, who could work together until they acted as one at all times. There was no other way to sail a ship and fight it. The prospect, given where he was now, was daunting.

He made the gangway as the boat bringing his mids hooked on, their designation called out to him, responded to by an order to come aboard. He watched with a degree of quiet amusement as they made their individual efforts to climb the man ropes and battens. There was no cruelty in this and nor did he offer advice; if the common seamen had a great deal to learn, these young gentlemen had so very much more, if they were to progress to officer rank.

If he failed to recruit a schoolmaster, it would be him, with the help of the master, doing much of the teaching. The basics were mathematics and manners, but then came navigation, the use of a sextant, the ability to set a course by starlight, what was the proper sail plan to get the best out of the ship on any given wind.

In time, they would absorb the collective wisdom of centuries of sailors, information passed down generation to generation, regarding a reading of the weather, both as it existed and what it was about to become. The run of the sea and the depth of the swell, added to the formation of the clouds, would become a map to them, as it was to their forbears.

They must go aloft and be as nimble as the best topmen, able to reef or let fall the heavy canvas as required, in fair or foul weather, while keeping a precarious footing. The likes of the Pelicans would teach some of what everyone needed to know: how to maintain and repair the complex mass of rigging, the application of the correct knots, to be able to carry out rope work as the most adept splicer of hemp. To have a knowledge of the blocks and tackles on both the standing rigging and any temporary rig.

Likewise the hands, which brought Pearce back to his lack of numbers. Some would be allotted to the gunner and carpenter as mates, to specialise in those activities, which did not exclude general competence. Those seconded to work with the bosun would learn from Crocker all the skills needed to undertake the tasks he would oversee, from care of canvas to the proper storage of stores.

Likewise, the master required a coterie of master's mates to assist him in his duties and they would have to show some ability at maths. Application could bring advancement and that had to be stressed; every junior aide to a warrant or seaman of standing rank could one day hold a similar office on another vessel.

In addition, they must be ready to fight. The best of the midshipmen would command a section of cannon, which meant knowing as much about the guns as the men working them. They had to earn their respect, so that when the time came to board an enemy deck, their section would zealously follow them. And swordplay, plus the proper loading and discharge of pistols? Instruction in that could fall to Pearce alone.

With the hands, it would be musket, pike, tomahawk and cutlass. They must learn to employ them as well as to follow commands, in a situation where confusion was more likely than clarity. Good boat work was essential too, for often the task would be the cutting out of an enemy vessel. Added to that, they must learn to kill if required and to grant clemency when that would serve better.

All that ran through their captain's mind as the newly arrived young gentlemen struggled to make the deck, eventually succeeding, to stand nervously uncertain. As their brand-new sea chests were being hauled aboard, to be taken care of by Charlie and Rufus, he invited them to his cabin, where they lined up, in their new and pristine short blue jackets and naval hats.

'Gentlemen, your names, your ages, please, and from where you hail?'

A tall and skinny youngster, with very fair hair and bright blue eyes, named himself first. He was called Maclehose, aged fourteen and hailed from Perth. If he stumbled slightly, that did not detract from the fact of his primacy in speaking, so Pearce marked him as perhaps one to lead the others.

Next came an eleven-year-old called Livingston, from Bathgate, who was in terror, looking to be on the edge of tears when he named his hometown. It was to be hoped Mrs Low, the gunner's wife, with whom he would certainly berth for a year or two, was more compassionate than she appeared.

Mr Campbell, from Argyll, was between them in age, well into puberty, judging by the eruption of red spots on his face. He looked to have something of a pot belly on him, added to a chubby face, which would not last; home comforts did not exist on a ship of war and neither did idleness.

Last came a twelve-year-old youngster from the borderlands, Tennant, a son of the Jedburgh kirk and with a minister father. His voice in reporting was broken, and also low-pitched with nerves, so Pearce could barely hear him.

He had to address them like a surrogate father-cum-tyrannical tutor, with instructions regarding their forthcoming duties and the manner in which they should behave. In doing so he felt like a total fraud. What did he know about midshipmen fresh to the service? The one he knew best from his own past was a poltroon called Toby Burns and he was no example, being a coward and a perjurer.

Others with whom he'd sailed, like Richard Farmiloe, now a lieutenant, had served sea time before he ever met them and was thus experienced. There had been mids on every vessel in which he'd sailed and at every shore function he'd attended. At one end they were intelligent, brave and active, sometimes a danger to themselves as well as the enemy.

Others were dull to the point of stupidity and he had come across sloths who'd been in the same berth for time measured in decades. They were so useless they'd remain there so they would be fed, something not vouchsafed ashore. Which of the two kinds would these lads turn out to be? He was now responsible and the knowledge did not bring much cheer.

'Tonight you will berth in the gunroom with a Mrs Low. She and her husband will see your hammocks rigged and show you how to get in and out of the article without disgrace. It may be you will shift in the coming days, but that will depend on how you take to your new home.'

As he surveyed them, only Maclehose would hold his gaze.

'I have been in your place and know how it can be for good or ill.'

Words meant to reassure, Pearce was aware of his stretching of the truth. He had held the position of midshipman, but in circumstances far removed from the norm. Still, he wished them to behave in a way he knew to be uncommon in most ships.

'I will tolerate no bullying and, if I hear that the contents of anyone's sea chest have been taken without permission, I will have the perpetrator kiss the gunner's daughter and with ferocious application. I doubt I need to spell out to you what the expression means.'

A pause, then a call to Michael O'Hagan to take them below and return with his two companions.

He knew he had to be honest about how difficult it was going to be with this trio of friends. Buckner might send him what he'd asked for, but it was necessary to act on the basis he would not.

'Michael, you will have to take on the duty of master-at-arms. Not how it should be, according to statute, but there's no choice. At least I know, when it comes to keeping order, I can rely on you to impose it without oppression.'

The Irishman nodded as Charlie chipped in, ever ready with a quip. 'There goes the easy life, Michael. No great cabin servant and as much quality grub as you can swallow now. Happen it will slim you down.'

That got Charlie a jaundiced look as Michael spoke to Pearce, his own tone sarcastic. 'Would it be possible, John-boy, that I can try a little oppression, to see how it feels?'

That was ignored. 'Charlie, you and Rufus will have to act as

235

watch captains for now. I need you to find out who is willing and who is slack. I want regular reports on the men you will command, with recommendations as to what useful skills they have and what they might best acquire. I know you didn't sign up for this and I have to offer you the chance to decline. That said, I can carry no passengers, so if you do refuse, I will ask you to vacate the ship.'

'What, John,' Rufus exclaimed, for once to the fore, 'and leave you to try and manage on your own? Might as well save time and send the barky to the bottom right off.'

Agreement followed from the others and Pearce reacted well to that. 'Rufus, it gives me no pleasure to say you're probably right. Now can you assemble all hands, so I can read them in?'

On a well-manned ship that would have happened in half a minute. Here it took an age of cajoling and in some cases shoving to get them all up from below and facing the quarterdeck. They were not silent until Michael shouted that they should be so, in a voice stentorian enough to command attention. Pearce was stood, marines lined up to his rear with bayonets fitted, on the poop: a figure in a blue coat, a total stranger, who had their lives in his hands.

'By the power vested in me by the Lord Commissioners of the Admiralty, I, Lieutenant John Pearce, do take command of HMS *Hazard* and all who sail in her . . .'

As he read out the terms of his appointment, he was looking out at a sea of faces, every eye on him, the ship's boys at the front and his Pelicans, warrants and standing officers, who had heard all this many times before, at the rear. For most, there was palpable concern at this strange new world. An air of false indifference came from one or two.

The Articles of War came next, thirty-six specific regulations and laws with their concomitant penalties; failure of duty, disobedience of orders, drunkenness, espionage, desertion, not pursuing or cowardice in the face of the enemy, false muster and the wasting of stores.

'Article Twenty-Seven. For murder, as on land, death.' That was followed by a long pause and hard look and he saw men swallow hard at the thought. 'The unnatural and detestable sin of sodomy, with man or beast, will be punished by death following a court martial.'

Another fraudulent glare. 'Robbery; punished with death or otherwise, upon the consideration of a court martial.'

On he droned until he had reached the last, by which time many looking at him were clearly fearful. 'You are entered and landsmen at present. But in time that will alter and quickly, for those who put their mind to improvement and learning. You will try things new to you and fail to carry them out correctly to begin with. This I know, for I have been in your place. Some of you, the youngest and most nimble, will find terror in climbing the shrouds and moving out on to the yards. But that will ease with practice. This too I know from experience.'

Pearce talked for another twenty minutes, advising this bunch of novices on watches and how they operated, on how they would be fed as each week progressed, for it was unvarying except in exceptional circumstances. They were told of the allowance of small beer and their daily right to a tot of grog, plus dozens of other factors that would govern their new life, until his voice was hoarse.

'Tonight you may sleep, for the anchor watch will be covered by the men I trust. Tomorrow you begin life as a sailor in the King's Navy. Embrace it and you will come to love it. Fight it and it will consume you.'

Another long look, followed by an order, which underlined he still had no lieutenants. 'Master-at-arms, you may dismiss the men.'

CHAPTER EIGHTEEN

Hodgson walked up the wide stone pavement of Harley Street, Beleau's drawings under his arm, noting it had that luxury which cut off horse traffic from those walking. Such a thing did not exist in most of the streets he traversed, which meant a fellow had to be both watchful and nimble, lest some overexcited coach or cart driver, impatient to progress, paid no attention to the presence of human feet.

In his hand he had Emily Barclay's letter, which gave him the number to look for. That too was so very recent, the numbering instead of naming of dwellings, the latter of which, in any case, was truly haphazard in the rookeries, alleys and narrow backstreets that abounded around the City and Westminster.

Much thought had gone into what might come from this

meeting, prior to setting out as well as on the way, yet it had not formed into anything definite now he was close. The brass, highly polished bell pull had the weight of the newly installed, while the ringing was audible through the substantial front door. It was opened by a fellow in livery, who enquired sonorously of his business and, given he was expected, stood aside and begged him enter when that was stated. His hat and out coat were taken, before he was shown into a well-appointed room on the ground floor.

'Mrs Barclay will be with you presently, sir.'

Surely she had been waiting for him, the time having been arranged and he punctual. He decided, as he gazed out of the window at the world passing by, it was a gambit, to imply he was the supplicant and she the benefactor, which he suspected might be the very opposite of the case. When she did arrive, it was with a footman in tow.

'Mr Hodgson,' came with a nod, but no smile.

His greeting in response was delivered with a cool appreciation that he was in the presence of a very beautiful woman. Added to which, she appeared to have poise; there was nothing nervous or timid about the way she was examining him. Had he been able to see inside her head he would have changed that opinion. Emily Barclay was as tense as a freshly wound clock.

'You came by hack?' was no more than common politesse.

'On foot, as is my habit. Very little can be observed from within a coach.'

'You see a need to observe?'

'Mrs Barclay, it is the kernel of my trade.'

She seemed to take a moment to reflect on that. 'Can I offer you anything in the way of refreshment?'

When he declined, she dismissed the footman, offered him to sit and did so herself, to elegantly perch on a chaise. What followed was a brief period of silence, maybe twenty seconds, which seemed longer. It was one Hodgson was determined not to break. Finally, it was done for him.

'You must wonder why I asked you to call upon me.'

'Not really. I suspect you wish to discuss Cornelius Gherson.'

You had to be a keen observer to see how she stiffened, it was so marginal; a slight retraction of the jaw and shoulders seeming to rise a fraction. This indicated to Hodgson she had not expected him to know of the connection between them.

'I assume Sir Jerrold told you of my interest in the case.'

'No, Mrs Barclay, I deduced that myself.'

Finally, her gaze dropped away to the side, as she seemed to be seeking to absorb this. Hodgson was wondering, as had Sir Jerrold Crossley, if there could be some kind of romantic attachment between her and Gherson, only for the thought to be dismissed. Quite apart from what he knew, which was partial and incomplete, he could not see a woman of the composure she possessed having anything to do with such a creature.

'I was told you were very good at your profession.' When he looked quizzical, she added. 'Sir Jerrold told me so.'

'And is it that which has caused you to invite me to call upon you?'

'In part. He also told me you were the one who bespoke a private cell for the person just mentioned.'

'Would I be right in assuming that was your intention too?'

The look in response was one that indicated she had no desire to answer. 'When first I met him, he implied there was a lady willing to do likewise.'

'Mr Hodgson, can I enquire if you were asking on your own behalf?'

That was a hard question to deal with. To deny the query on the grounds of confidentiality would be an admission it was true. Yet to say he was Gherson's benefactor did not sit well with his pride, so he applied the well-known ploy of answering a question with a question.

'I'm curious, Mrs Barclay, as to why you would think that to be the case.' For the first time Emily smiled and Hodgson knew he had failed to spot a snare. 'What did Sir Jerrold say?'

'That agents for the powerful were not uncommon. He imparted it in such a fashion as to more or less name you as such.'

'More or less?'

'The provision of such accommodation is costly, is it not? Would it offend you if I say your manner and profession are unlikely to mark you out as one who could run to such a bill?'

'Even with a soft heart?' was delivered with the slightest of smiles, no more than a twitch of the thief-taker's lips.

Her smile was more engaging; what he implied was being taken as intended, a jest. 'Perhaps it would be best if I explained to you my motives for seeking to aid Gherson.'

'I would be glad to hear it.'

'Would there be a quid pro quo?'

'My Latin is not good.' For which he meant – and was sure she would get his meaning – expect silence until I decide it is wise to be open.

As she began to speak it soon became apparent there was no intention to allow for assumptions. Hodgson was taken back to the way she had first come across Gherson, as one of her husband's crew, the odd manner in which he had been pressed, moving on swiftly to describe their challenging relationship. Even circumspect, he could discern the deep dislike bordering on hatred his presence had generated.

It came as no surprise when she spoke of her late husband in a detached tone, one lacking in any hint of deep grief. Had she not run away from him? Not that she wandered into anything in the personal line; it was more to do with his taking on Gherson as his clerk and the duties that fell to him.

All the time she was talking, one fact she had imparted troubled Hodgson's already uneasy mind. 'Mrs Barclay, if I may, I would like you to go back to where you began. That is how Gherson came to be aboard your husband's ship.'

'An absurdity, really.'

Hodgson listened intently, though there was no change in his demeanour that she would see. London Bridge, a push claimed, not a fall. The pure luck of landing in the torrents, which roared through the bridge arches on a receding tide, hard by a passing naval cutter, which by pure luck contained a fellow both quick and strong enough to haul him out. Told in the manner of a tale often repeated, it still had the power to amuse her. That was until Hodgson thought it might be a wry reaction to a strong belief. It would have been better for all if that quick and strong hand had been absent.

'He was inclined to deny he was thrown over the parapet, but no one aboard *Brilliant* could accept he sought to do away with himself. He was too obviously a coward.'

'An accident, perhaps.'

Unknown to her, the question was only posed to seek denial, which was swift in coming, for Gherson had never claimed it to be so. Hodgson gently probed a few of the salient points and, as he absorbed those particulars, the facts which had troubled him at Lady Barrington's bagnio seemed to gel, which prompted the next question.

'If I may, Mrs Barclay, I wonder at your reasons for seeking to oblige him in the provision of a private cell, since I sense no great affection.'

The green eyes that fixed him were steady, and the look in them was designed to challenge Hodgson, who had the uncomfortable feeling he had landed precisely where she wanted him to be.

'Perhaps, Mr Hodgson, you should ask the person on whose behalf you are acting?' It was politic not to respond. 'Let me tell you of the relationship between my late husband and his clerk.'

Another lengthy explanation followed, to be given the same level of attention as before, until she came to the nub; the fact that Gherson was engaged in cheating Ralph Barclay.

'But he was not doing so in isolation. He sent me a note from Newgate to say he had information that would nail the other guilty party. I visited him, he provided me with a clue as to the direction of enquiry and that I acted upon. The manner of response hinted at accuracy, thus I felt it would be to my benefit to accede to his demands.'

'Even to the point of his being innocent of the crime?'

'I sense you do not know him very well, Mr Hodgson. I do, but I also have people who know him even better, men who sailed with him and have seen how he acted when the ship was engaged against the enemy: a fellow who sought to hide somewhere safe and gibbered like a madman. If there is a man more cowardly, they have yet to meet him.'

'That does not answer my question.'

'Is he innocent? I don't know. Perhaps you could be engaged to find out.'

'You're offering to employ me?'

'If you are free to act for me, yes.'

She knew about Druce, which was obvious. When thought on, Hodgson realised the connection was not difficult to make. Either in his note, or in speaking to her, Gherson had used the name. If it was easy to come to that as a conclusion, it was less easy to work out how to act upon it.

'Would you permit that is a request which requires a degree of reflection?'

For the first time the smile was genuine. It was as if she could read, not only his thoughts, but his dilemma. 'Would you believe me when I say the lack of an outright refusal is something I take as encouraging? But I would remind you that time is a problem. The Court of King's Bench sits in less than two weeks.'

'There is a backlog of cases; Gherson will not be in the first batch. A day or two, no more.'

'Are you sure I can offer you nothing to eat or drink, Mr Hodgson? Or perhaps order you a cab to take you back to your lodging?'

'Forty-eight hours, Mrs Barclay.'

She took well the fact that he had yet to make up his mind, standing and indicating the door, before holding out a hand. 'Till then.'

* * *

245

'Captain's barge approaching, John-boy,' Michael O'Hagan hissed. 'And the man in command, a captain, is in the thwarts.'

Both the bosun and Pearce were on deck, properly dressed, by the time the approaching coxswain yelled '*Bedford*'. They were soon joined by Moberly and his marines, who dressed into a straight line, ready to present arms. Their officer had his sword ready.

'Michael, get those men idling below. And tell Charlie and Rufus to ensure the men they're instructing keep to their task. I want no gazing or gawping.'

The 'Aye aye, your honour,' was as it should be: crisp and loud.

The well-handled barge swung in a wide and even arc, to hook on right under the gangway, the officer already on his feet and moving through his oarsmen to clamber aboard. The man ropes were grasped and the fellow made his way up the battens with practised ease, to step on to the deck and raise his hat, this as the marine footwear hit the deck and their muskets were raised before each face. Moberly saluting with his sword.

'Captain Sir Thomas Byard, at your service, sir.' This was delivered with a definite middle-of-the-country accent. Pearce in his travels had something of an ear for placement and he had this officer hailing from Staffordshire. 'I assume I'm talking to Lieutenant John Pearce?'

The look was direct, the smile seemingly genuine, on a fellow Pearce put at about fifty years of age and several inches smaller than himself. His face was thin, the skin sallow, which belied his hearty greeting.

'Master and Commander of HMS *Hazard*, sir.'

'Then I have come to the right place.'

Byard said this, with a slight jerk of the head, to indicate if he was going to talk more it should be in private. Pearce was quick to invite him to his cabin and, watched by all on deck, despite the strictures regarding gawping, they made their way aft.

'Damn me,' came the remark on entry, to an officer bent over in an exaggerated fashion, the deck beams far from touching his head. 'I'd forgot how small the cabin on a sloop is.'

'No patch on a seventy-four for comfort, sir. Please, if I can offer you a seat.'

'Obliged.' Byard sat, after removing his scraper and gazed about him at what was a sparsely furnished space. The eyes were brown and seemed large, under a pair of very noticeable bags. 'I see you're not properly settled.'

Pearce was by the wine cooler. 'I've had no time to furnish the cabin properly.'

That got a rather braying laugh and a nod to the cooler. 'Seen to the essentials, though.'

'Some wine, sir?'

'Not blackstrap I hope?'

'No, sir. I made sure of a visit to the Chatham vintner.' Pearce extracted and held up a bottle of Burgundy. 'A stint in Paris made me particular in the article.'

'Paris, eh?'

'Before the outbreak,' was imparted, as he removed the cork.

That got a look at the bottle, which was accompanied by a twinkle in the captain's eye. 'Now it strikes me that a bottle, instead of being sealed with wax, is one with those new-fangled corks. Might have come over the Channel after we went to war, what?'

Pearce poured the red wine into a pair of crystal goblets, thinking this visitor must know corks had been increasingly used in the last decade. It was therefore an attempt at humour.

'I did not enquire.'

'Very wise,' Byard said as he took the goblet. The nose went into it first, to get an appreciative sniff, before he took a sip to pronounce it very acceptable 'You will be wondering at my calling upon you, without I put in a request.'

Pearce had been wondering that since he was told of the approach, but it was impolite to say so. 'Can I say you're very welcome, sir. You are the first of my fellow commanders to call upon me, which makes your presence very special.'

'Then let me wish you good health.' That was accepted, with Pearce thinking, before he spoke again, not many of Byard's peers would share the sentiment. 'I had a letter from Sir Peter Parker.'

'Really!' was all that could be got out in response.

'Him and I go back a long way, Mr Pearce. Got my step from him during the American nonsense. Any road, he tells me you're having some difficulties. Didn't get much detail, but knowing I was due to be in to revictual, he dropped me a line and asked me to find out.'

Pearce was now behind his desk, wondering where this was leading. 'Did he tell you anything else, sir?'

That got him a hard look. ''Bout you. No need, Pearce. You're quite well known in the service.'

'Do I sense disapproval?'

'Got your elevation from His Majesty, did you not? Personal, too.'

'I was lucky in that regard, yes.'

'Same fellow who knighted me.' Out came that braying laugh again. 'So we can't reckon him mad, can we? All I did was take

248

personal charge of the tiller on the royal barge at the fleet review. Old George likes the common touch and he saw that in me, didn't smoke I was damned terrified one of my mids would balls it up and tip us all into the briny.'

'More wine, sir?'

'Don't mind if I do.' Byard leant forward to have his goblet refilled. 'So, are you going to tell me what your troubles are?'

'You're sure you want to know?'

'Damn me, Pearce, I wouldn't have crossed half the Nore if I didn't.'

Byard required a couple more refills as Pearce listed his difficulties, nodding all the while to show he understood.

'In short, sir, I have no more than half a dozen people to teach some sixty quota men their duties and, as of this moment, I am in ignorance of any skills they may have.'

'Best assume none. No town is going to ship you its artisans. Felons and beggars are more likely.'

'I asked Admiral Buckner to make good my needs, but he refused.' There was a temptation to mention Dundas, but it was soon put away. It would probably do more harm than good and, anyway, it would only beg the question as to why he was involved. 'For reasons unknown to me, he declines to oblige.'

Byard was quick to respond and not in a pleasant tone. 'Don't do to treat me as a fool, Pearce.'

'If I have done so, Sir Thomas, it is inadvertent.'

'Forget Buckner. Sir Peter asked if I could help and I am minded to oblige him. *Bedford* is not that well found in that in which you are deficient – I am short over thirty on my muster, but my crew is fully worked up. So, what do you say to me sending over my better midshipmen, as well as my yeoman and master's mates, to teach your lubbers a trick or two?'

To reckon Pearce surprised bordered on understatement. Yet he felt he had to warn Byard there might be consequences, like official disapproval from Buckner.

'I don't sail under his flag, Mr Pearce, but that of Admiral Duncan, who will expect me back on station off the Texel once I am fully victualled. I daresay no harm will come from a delay of a day or two, perhaps even a week and, as for censure, do I not have the ear of Farmer George?'

The braying laugh was really loud now and went on for some time, evidence that the wine consumed had affected Byard's behaviour.

'Then sir, I can only offer you my deep gratitude, while I wonder what I can do to repay such kindness.'

'If Peter Parker rates you, Pearce, that is good enough for me. I will have my people boat over in the morning and we will see what needs to be done. Now, do you have another bottle of this fine Burgundy?'

'I do, sir. It's in the cooler.'

'No damn good in there. Fetch the bugger out.'

If Byard staggered on his route to the gangway, Pearce, following, was in a not much better state. There was no way the man could leave the ship in the manner in which he had arrived, so he had the Pelicans lash one of his new captain's chairs to a whip from the yard, this with a cat's cradle of rope work around the legs, to see the captain of HMS *Bedford* raised in the air then dropped over the side and into his barge.

Not a single man on an oar looked away from their duty, which led Pearce to suspect his visitor was no stranger to the bottle, while his barge crew were not unfamiliar with this condition. Byard began to sing as the oars were dipped, and the words that floated back to the sloop made sure everyone knew the song was filthy.

CHAPTER NINETEEN

Byard was as good as his word. By midmorning the deck of HMS *Hazard* was alive with activity and it was not confined to the ship. His barge crew had come over as well and were in the water, mixing in with the quota men and midshipmen in matching numbers, teaching them how to row and steer the various ship's boats, which looked simple but was a skill not easily acquired.

Timing on the sticks was the key, the rise and fall of the oars as they dipped and left the water, the combined pull, which meant moving men until the force of their muscular ability was balanced. For the mids, steering required a light touch, not excessive turns on the rudder, plus the ability to call for a raise on either side, depending on the direction chosen. If the command was to stop, it required the oars to effect that.

HMS *Bedford*'s yeoman of the sheets was aloft with the men who had shown no fear of the climb, instructing them on moving out onto the yards and the portioning required to let loose the sails. The canvas was left alone; this was a mock drill to get them used to the foot ropes and body positions. Below, Rufus Dommet was working others up and down the ratlines, only as far as the mainmast cap, they being permitted to use the lubber's hole to get a feel for the height, without the fear of a fall.

It soon became clear that some souls were not cut out for duty as topmen, so they were taken below by Mr Crocker to be instructed in the use of the capstan for the shifting of the stores, water and meat in the barrel, which did not require all hands. Michael O'Hagan was in company with Mr Low, teaching a group how to run out a cannon, which came down to a common heave.

Likewise, Moberly was working his marines in the same skill and they showed commendable speed, clearly having done it before. There were times when Lobsters worked the guns and at others acted as sharpshooters or took the lead in boarding. In both cases the more complex act of loading would have to wait, and it would be a long time before powder would be expended on firing.

As the day went on, the senior mid from *Bedford*, in company with Moberly, took *Hazard*'s new quartet to give them lessons in fencing and Pearce joined in when it came to cutlass, axe and pike work for the common hands. Up till then he had been pacing the deck to both encourage and observe, making a mental note where he saw enthusiasm, added to another where he observed slacking.

This happened with a party laying out sails for drying, which was being supervised by Mr Williams, the master, he having no real duties unless they were at sea. In addition, he was lecturing to a confused group about the differing weights of canvas and under what circumstances they were employed. It was the one hanging back and seeking to hide behind another that Pearce approached.

'Your name, fellow.'

'Teach,' came out like a spit.

Pearce ignored the lack of respect, both in the reply and the defiant look that accompanied it and, having eased him away from the others, enquired of the first name.

'Well, Harry Teach, let me tell you there is more satisfaction to be had in a task well executed than work avoided. The latter cannot be disguised, as you will now know, for I have seen you seek to avoid effort.'

'I have rights.'

Charlie was by his ear in a flash. 'You has duties, matey, an' one of them is to show respect to the captain. You may choose "sir", or "aye aye", but you will use one or t'other.'

'Your fellow hands have rights, Teach, and one is that all pull their weight in equal measure. For it to be otherwise is to endanger the ship.' Pearce smiled to take the sting out of his next words. 'It would displease me to have to notice you again, even more if I was forced to act upon it.'

The glare aimed at the back of John Pearce, as he walked away, lasted only for half a second, before Charlie pulled him round by the arm. 'Hark to it, Teach, for if he is not one for the cat, he might make an exception for you.'

The fierce response took Charlie off guard, as Teach pushed his face close and snarled at him. 'Get your hands off me, you sod, or you'll feel my fist.'

Recovery was quick, for Charlie Taverner was far from content to be on the back foot. 'Happen you'll make that error, but it'll be once and no more. A week on bread and water, with the rats eating your toes, will *teach* you manners.'

In his perambulations, in which he sought to stay out of instruction, Pearce was very much aware of the depth of ignorance with which he was faced, worse than he had imagined. Compared to his other commands, or indeed any other vessel in which he'd sailed, this lot looked more set to embarrass him than excite the admiration afforded a crack vessel. And that took no account of what it would be like in a fight.

Considering that and conjuring up a worrying scenario, he reckoned if he spotted trouble, an armed enemy, his only option would be to run, while the thought of a real blow, with a crew so inexperienced, gave him serious worry. As usual, such gloomy peregrinations were assuaged by activity, which is why he took pleasure in the mock fighting taking place on the foredeck, not that it was always pretend.

'Bugger near took my arm off.'

This was claimed by one of the participants, who vigorously rubbed the offended body part before he sat down to his dinner at an overcrowded mess table. Other tables were occupied by the Bedfords, being fed at the expense of the ship, which had raised a complaint from Porlock regarding how it was to be justified in his accounts.

'Reckon his temper got the better of him,' was the opinion of another, a fellow called Simon, for John Pearce had laid about him with gusto, with a short stave standing in for a cutlass. 'He has an evil eye that one.'

'Well, he got my eye,' declared Harry Teach, 'and he knows my name.'

'I'm damned glad he don't know mine,' came from a Tom.

'Which tells me you're afraid of the bastard.'

'As any one of sense would be.'

'I got both sense and gonads, an' soon enough our high-and-mighty captain will know of both.'

The eyes of those opposite Teach were raised, but not to alert him. Already they were reckoning him heading for trouble and deserving of what it brought him. It was the silent approach of Michael O'Hagan that had attracted their attention, as well as their curiosity. Had he heard what Teach had said?

There was no way of telling. Michael merely stopped at the end of the table and enquired after the quality of the grub, to receive general agreement it was good and filling, this delivered with heads bowed over their mess dishes. Anyone looking at his broad smiling face might have noticed his gaze falling on Teach, which would have told them he had marked the man. But he said nothing and moved on.

'Big bastard, that one,' said Simon.

'Big enough to come down hard,' growled Teach.

Above and behind them, John Pearce was also eating his dinner, which Michael had knocked up before going on his rounds. Instead of the Irishman serving him – he had looked after his friend for a long time – the dishes came to him by the hands of a couple of youngsters, which allowed him to enquire more closely into their past, in truth that of their fathers.

If they were a mite cack-handed, they made up for it in their willingness to do right, so he was content. Alerted to an officer asking permission to come aboard, he had to leave his cheese and port to go and see who it was and why. It turned out to be a lieutenant who named himself as Isaac Hallowell in a distinctly American twang.

'Permission to come aboard, sir.' That granted and all the formalities observed, Pearce was in for another surprise. 'I have been despatched to you from Portsmouth, sir.'

'Not surely from Admiral Parker?'

'The very same, but I cannot comprehend how you could have guessed.'

'Second sight, Mr Hallowell. Please, I am just finishing my dinner and it would please me if you would join me in some cheese and a glass of port.'

'Obliged.'

Once he was seated Pearce could ask him his purpose, which turned out to be nothing more than the provision of a junior officer Parker saw fit, and with the competence, to be premier of an unrated ship like *Hazard*.

'I was third on *Barfleur*, sir, presently at Spithead, but Sir Peter has ever been kind to the family. He knows my uncle very well.'

'I know the name. Your uncle would have been at Toulon, yes?'

'And Bastia and Calvi. He presently has *Lowestoffe* and is serving with Sir John Jervis.'

A sip of port was enough to hide from Hallowell that the name Jervis was not one to cheer John Pearce. It was he who'd sent him home from the Mediterranean, in circumstances that screamed good riddance.

'He has written to the Admiralty to recommend that I be appointed to your ship, but of course that is as much in your gift as theirs.'

'Mr Hallowell, considering I don't have any lieutenants at all, you are very welcome.' Noting the querying look, Pearce felt constrained to tell Hallowell why. 'Which may colour your desire to serve under me.'

'I would like to show you that I have the ability to perform the task.'

'I assume the boat you came in has your sea chest?' A nod. 'Then I will see it shifted to the wardroom where you will find Mr Williams, the master. Might I suggest that you change into working clothing tomorrow, for there is much to do?'

The decision to have both Hallowell and Oliphant to supper was necessary as a way to introduce them, as well as to see if they could exist in harmony. Unlike his behaviour with the Pelicans, Oliphant was charm itself and it was noticeable he had the ability to ask penetrating questions without causing offence.

This established that the young fellow had no knowledge of the area to which they were headed and certainly no knowledge of the Catalonian or Spanish languages, which laid to rest one worry. To the suggestion that Oliphant move to the wardroom, he was welcoming.

'You carried that off well,' Pearce said, as he and Oliphant took a stroll on the deck before turning in.

'Did you not pick up on the probing?'

'I know you enquired quite a lot of him.'

'Well a certain amount is obvious. He's a Loyalist Tory, of course, from a quite prominent family, who were forced to flee to Canada when the Americans rose in revolt.'

'That is a subject I shall stay away from. Like my father, I was in support of their grievances.'

'Which marks you out to me as a dupe once more, if you believe all that nonsense about representation. Greed was the true trigger.'

'I wonder,' was the mordant reply, 'if you and I will ever plumb the depths of our differences.'

'It surprises me you have any desire to do so. Now, it strikes me that my presence aboard, with all that is going on, is superfluous.'

Pearce had to fight the temptation to issue a sharp dig, to tell Oliphant he was likely to be in the way, but he held it in check.

'So I propose to reside ashore until matters are resolved. I hope that fits with your opinion?'

'Saints alive, Oliphant,' was exclaimed with gusto, 'we can agree on some things after all.'

It was a rather pinched companion who said. 'I'll bespeak a boat at first light.'

Feeling reasonably pleased with the day, Pearce went to bed in a good frame of mind. The next day saw Oliphant gone and the Bedfords back aboard, working hard. It had to be admitted, also, some of the quota men were showing promise; not all, but in numbers that boded well. Everyone would not reach the same level of ability, regardless of how long they were in the service. But a ship of war could accommodate that, having, as it did, so many tasks to be undertaken.

The late afternoon brought for him another problem in the shape of Lieutenant Peat, the elderly officer who'd written to him days before from Chatham. It transpired he had also petitioned the Admiralty, the latter responding favourably to his request for a place aboard the sloop, subject to approval by the captain.

He was, in every respect, somewhat worse than his written

description. Peat was a bit deaf, which had Pearce wonder if it was something to do with the amount of hair in his ears, a bushy grey cluster, which was replicated above his eyes. There was a sort of belligerent look to his normal countenance, as if he was in permanent preparation for an argument.

In better circumstances he might have sent him packing, but right now any officer, given the duties to be carried out, was better than none. There was also the thought that if he was refused, then the sods in London would send him someone worse. Yet there were other complications: while Peat had to accept that John Pearce was his superior by dint of his position, if not the date of his commission, the same did not apply to Isaac Hallowell.

'I cannot see that the young man deserves to be premier, when my time served is so much greater.'

'You will allow the choice is mine, Mr Peat.'

'I grant you that, but I quote custom and practice. It is in the tradition of the service to respect seniority by date of commission.'

'I have not formally given the position to Mr Hallowell,' Pearce replied, fearing he might have done just that when he mentioned possession of the wardroom. 'So I will take your point under consideration and make my mind up when I see how you both perform.'

The grunt that got showed the depth of the reluctance that went with acceptance. Peat's jaw was set firm in his rather grey face, which was set off by pepper-and-salt hair and watery blue eyes. Pearce felt the need to justify his actions.

'I have looked at your service record from that letter you sent me, Mr Peat. This tells me you have not been at sea, indeed not in employment, for a very long time.'

'A lack of interest, sir, no more. I have no one to plead on my behalf.'

'A point I noted. But I must tell you that Mr Hallowell has been in employment, as well as at sea, continuously from entering as a captain's servant.'

'Which I assume was a favour for his uncle.'

'So you know of Captain Hallowell?'

'Enough to be sure he has the interest to further the career of his relatives.'

Pearce was wondering if he should tell Peat of the way Hallowell had come to *Hazard*. Sir Peter Parker would never send to him an incompetent officer, quite the reverse. He must rate Hallowell highly. Parker fully understood the behaviour of the Admiralty and was quite prepared to apply his seniority to thwart them. Yet that would only evoke in the older man a further claim that Hallowell had the powerful support Peat lacked.

'Well, let it rest for now, given I am due another pair of junior officers and I will need to assess them too. There is any amount of work to be done before we can think of weighing and that will only qualify as a trip round the bay. Now I suggest you settle in, make the acquaintance of Isaac Hallowell, Mr Williams the master and the marine lieutenant. There is a great deal of work to be done with a crew completely lacking in skill. Which we will begin to remedy in the morning.'

'Inexperienced, you say?'

When it was explained to him just how lacking they were as tars, and Pearce agreed the need to be firm, Peat looked as if he had been ordered to quell a mutiny.

* * *

The real problem with the older man surfaced very quickly. He appeared appropriately dressed for toil, in an old uniform coat, so faded from its original blue it would have passed for a French Navy struck by poverty. It was his attitude to discipline that quickly manifested itself, for he carried in his hand a length of knotted rope, to use as a starter, and he was free with its use.

At first, Pearce, busy with Mr Williams and his charts, studying the local waters, had no knowledge of what was happening on deck. It later transpired that Isaac Hallowell felt himself unable to intervene. It was Michael O'Hagan who suggested to his captain that he should come on deck and his expression meant it brooked no delay.

Pearce was just in time to see Peat not only haranguing the fellow known as Teach, but he had been belabouring him with said starter. He was quickly informed that the old sod had threatened some of the Bedfords with like punishment, though he had not actually struck any of them a blow.

The difference in their attitude was obvious, to a man who had observed them over two days. Gone was the cheery enthusiasm, the joshing as they cajoled the men they were instructing to greater efforts: now they were sullen. Pearce was in time to see the starter raised above Peat's hat, but a call to stop it being used failed due to Peat's lack of good hearing. He also saw that the victim, who had been recoiling in order to mitigate the effect, was bunching himself up to retaliate.

The yell to belay, intended for both, did not halt that which was already in progress. Teach, and the Gods had to be thanked for this, did not punch Peat, which might have seen him hang. He merely put both hands on the old lieutenant's chest and pushed him backwards. That he was about to follow that up with said blow became clear as all saw the fists were bunched.

'Mr Peat, come away from there at once,' had to be stated loud enough to register, bringing the head round to aim a vacant stare at his commanding officer.

Charlie Taverner was no fighter, but he had enough strength to restrain Teach, who had taken a small step forward, and shout in his ear what he risked, this while Pearce was striding down the deck towards Peat, his face like thunder.

'What, sir, is that in your hand?'

'The swine laid hands upon me, Mr Pearce, did you observe it?'

Pearce grabbed the starter, which was swinging loose and threw it over the side.

'I will not have such a thing on my deck.'

Everyone had ceased to work and were now standing transfixed, this as an angry Pearce towered over Peat. But there was a dilemma: he wanted to reprimand Peat but to do so in full view of everyone was unwise. In order to do what he must, he first had to control his temper and his voice.

He fought to sound calm as he said, 'Mr Hallowell, you have the deck. Mr Peat, please join me in my cabin.'

'What about this good-for-nothing?' Peat demanded. 'He struck me, you must have seen it.'

'Master-at-arms. Take this man below.'

Peat spat at Teach, now being held by Charlie and one of the Bedfords, 'I'll see you at the grating.'

'An' I'll see you in hell,' Teach yelled back.

'Mr Peat, my cabin, now.'

They made their way along a crowded and silent deck and,

just as they disappeared, Pearce heard Hallowell ordering everyone back to work. Inside, Mr Williams was waiting for Pearce to return; one glance at the pair and the joint looks of fury had him roll up his charts and depart.

Pearce assumed his seat and looked at the old lieutenant, his face leaving his captain in no doubt of his anger. That was being returned in equal measure.

CHAPTER TWENTY

Once the door to the cabin was closed, Peat let fly. 'I do not take kindly to being humiliated, sir.'

'And, Mr Peat, I do not like to see members of my crew being abused.'

'I am perfectly within my rights to correct slacking and the fellow was daydreaming.'

'Correct idleness, by all means, but you looked set to draw blood. I do not approve of the use of a starter, and I tell you I will not stand for it from now on.'

Peat adopted a sly look. 'How is a person to know that when there are no standing orders to show him what is the correct way?'

Pearce was slightly checked by that; it was his job, outside the Articles of War, to lay down for all to see, or at least have read to them, the way he wanted things done outside those regulations, specific to the running of the sloop, and he had not yet got around to it.

'As to blood, it was I who was close to being drawn, sir. That ne'er do well was all set to fetch me a clout. I saw the way his fists were bunched. I suggest it is near worthy of a rope from the yards.'

Pearce was aghast, not only at the suggestion but the look of excitement such a prospect generated on what was usually a closed-up and crabby face. 'You would have Admiral Buckner convene a court martial for such a trivial event?'

'Trivial, Mr Pearce?' Peat demanded. 'It is no such thing. It goes to the very heart of the proper application of discipline.'

'Might I remind you the man in question is a quota man and thus new to the navy?'

'All the more reason to set an example of him. The men must respect me and I will say I cannot see that being boosted by what amounted to a public dressing-down.'

'I did no such thing. I made a point of asking you to leave the deck.'

'You grabbed my instrument of authority and chucked it in the Thames!'

'The instrument of your authority is the coat you wear and the rank you hold.'

Peat reacted like a spoilt child, his fists bunched and shaking before him. His face, too, was contorted. 'He deserves to be punished! I demand the punishment fit the crime.'

Pearce responded in an icy tone. 'I think you'll find that is a decision for me. I suggest you go about your duties and, if you find you cannot do that, repair to the wardroom and stay there.'

Peat opened his mouth to complain. Pearce cut him off with no grace whatsoever. 'That, Mr Peat, is an order, which you disobey at your peril.'

Once Peat had stomped out, the bulkhead door being slammed for good measure, Pearce considered the problem. Teach required to be punished, but what would fit the offence? Laying hands on an officer was serious and, had a blow been struck, it would have had to go to Buckner, where a sentence of death was not beyond the bounds of possibility.

He had to clear from his mind any dislike he had of the man himself, one who'd shown a degree of defiance when addressed. The normal punishments in his armoury – stopping grog, bread and water sustenance or even stapling to the deck – would not do. A boy was called to carry a message.

'Please ask Mr Hallowell to spare me a moment.'

When the American entered it was not so Pearce could seek his opinion; to do so would undermine him. He merely asked him what the reaction had been when he and Mr Peat had left the deck. The answer was a general buzz of chatter and some excitement in the new men, they falling silent if he came too close.

'The Bedfords?'

'Shrugs, sir. In my opinion, they reckon our fellows do not yet know their duty.'

Having thanked him, he asked for Michael O'Hagan. Pearce knew he had to do something and the Irishman felt the same. Pearce had made sure they could not be overheard, so the conversation could be as informal as possible.

'I can see no way out of a flogging, John-boy.'

The look Pearce gave his friend required no words; he was not keen on flogging, having been lashed to a grating himself, albeit his punishment had proved light. He recalled discussing the matter with Nelson, a man also disinclined to resort to the cat. The words he had used were clear in his memory.

'It makes a good man bad and a bad man worse.'

However, even Nelson had acknowledged that, at times, a captain was left with no choice. The men who served in King George's Navy were no saints, and some were incorrigible sinners, with drink at the root of many an offence. The grating was sometimes the only answer.

'If the quota men get an inkling you're soft,' Michael continued, 'we could have no end of trouble.'

'Which would make your life difficult.'

'Holy Mary, mine don't matter, but they's got to know there are things that cannot be borne. Strikes me, Mr Peat will settle for nothing less than two dozen.'

'He would ideally like a hanging.'

'Christ in heaven,' was the response, which came with the sign of the cross, 'for a push?'

'How would you say the rowing is progressing?'

'I'd say it's a bit rough, but they won't drown.'

'Tell Mr Maclehose to be ready to take the barge over to HMS *Bedford*.'

O'Hagan laughed. 'He's Jock the Sock now.'

That gave Pearce something to smile about. 'That was quick.'

'Bedfords started it and our lads lapped it up.'

That was a good thing. If the crew could laugh together, then perhaps they could work likewise. Pearce fretted until he was told his barge was ready, then donned his scraper and boat cloak. The waters weren't choppy this far upriver, but with an inexperienced set of oars it could be damp. To the suggestion he use some of the Bedfords, he declined; time the men he led saw him in close proximity.

Jock the Sock was nervous, but he made a great effort to keep that hidden. Pearce wondered if he knew his new soubriquet and what he would make of it. There was a temptation to tell him that such appellations were usually made affectionately, in fact a sign of popularity not denigration.

It was soon evident, once he'd lowered himself into the boat, that the men crewing the barge were edgy too, which made him wonder if they saw this as a test. It was frustrating: he couldn't say anything to ease their worry. How different this ship was from those he'd served in before, some of which had been more like family, with everyone knowing their place and duty so that the running was relaxed. *Hazard* might be like that one day, but it seemed a distant future.

'Mr Maclehose, haul away.'

The response was crisp, the order to the crew likewise, but the effect was far from perfect. There was no rhythm, so Pearce decided it should be provided, this done by slapping the gunwale and it had an effect as the progress of the boat markedly smoothed.

'You know what your duty requires, Mr Maclehose.'

'Aye aye, sir.'

The shout of *Hazard*, which followed, was pitched at the required level to alert a quarterdeck which would have seen them coming anyway. Unfortunately, the approach to the lowered gangway, which ran from sea level to the entry port, was less so.

Thanks to poor steering, the boat hit the lower platform with a degree of force, unbalancing the already standing captain. This had the young midshipman look at Pearce with alarm.

'Room for improvement, Mr Maclehose,' was his parting shot, as he leapt on to the platform.

'Sir.'

It was, as was common, whistles and stamping marines as he was welcomed aboard by *Bedford*'s premier, to be led to the great and spacious cabin occupied by Byard, the first thing to be apparent the decanter sitting beside two goblets.

'A surprise visit, Mr Pearce.'

'Returning the compliment, sir.'

The decanter was immediately in his hand. 'Which I must do also.'

Pearce sighed as he anticipated a rough tongue and a thick head come morning.

The sloping gangway was welcome when he left. The idea of batten and man ropes did not appeal to a fellow who'd had too much of Byard's claret. He left with two pieces of unwelcome news. HMS *Bedford* was going to weigh to join Admiral Duncan in three days' time and Byard would need his men back the day before to prepare the ship for sea. Just as depressing was Byard's opinion on the problem of Teach.

'You either flog the sod, which you can control, or hand him over to Buckner for what I would reckon to be a sentence much more severe. Navy takes a dim view on assaults of officers and, from what you say of this Peat fellow, he would claim more than just a shove. And I would say, soonest done is best.'

* * *

The calling of all hands the next morning was to witness the punishment. It had to be carried out before the Bedfords came aboard and, having witnessed the act of flogging before, Pearce was aware of another thing he lacked. There was no drummer boy to rap out the call to the deck. Mr Crocker, lacking the usual bosun's mates, had been obliged, overnight, to prepare the cat-o'-nine-tails himself and it would be he who administered the penalty, which had led to a very elliptical conversation.

Every flogging qualified for its own instrument and there was a way for a crew to affect the degree of pain. Tarred and rough rope, riddled with knots, would rip the skin in a trice; soft hemp with a knot or two would hurt like the devil but bring forth no blood. Then there was the level of force used in laying on. With a man he considered friendly, Pearce could have been open. But he and Crocker were not that, indeed his feeling the man was a misery had only grown in the last few days.

So to get the message across, that he wished for as little gore as possible, risked Pearce wandering into territory it was not his right to occupy. If there was doubt as to severity, it would be the collective view of the crew, passed to those working the rope, which would affect matters. In the end he had to leave it be and let Crocker, who clearly found the duty demeaning, to decide.

Teach, who'd spent the night in the cable tier, came blinking into the sunlight of a beautiful morning, one in which Pearce would have welcomed goose-grey clouds. The grating was set at an angle against the poop and, as was standard, Moberly and his marines were in place with their muskets to ensure no one could act up.

Once everyone had shuffled into place Pearce, given the lack of a divisional officer – that too would come in time – read out the crime and the sentence, which would be the two dozen lashes he was permitted as a maximum. At that point Peat stepped forward and asked permission to speak. Much as he would love to have denied the man, it was not possible.

'Mr Pearce, I ask that the sentence be increased. The offence was egregious in the extreme. Too light a punishment will not drive home how heinous it is to lay hands upon a King's officer.'

'I cannot do that, as you well know, Mr Peat.'

The exchanged look implied that he was hiding behind the Articles of War, not enforcing them. A captain could dish out a lot more. A glance from Peat towards Hallowell showed his fellow lieutenant he had no intention of supporting him, not even to the point of catching his eye. The glare switched back to Pearce and the tone of his complaint was persistent.

'You could apply to the C-in-C for the right to apply a greater number.'

The look was challenging: both men knew how often a captain exceeded the limit. Many handed out as much as they chose, then asked retrospectively for permission from a senior officer. It was never denied and, as long as the correct formalities were observed, there was no point, and truly no easy mechanism, by which a common seaman could complain.

Pearce wanted the sod to shut up. First, he was not enjoying this, which Peat seemed so minded to do. Added to that, the discussion was unseemly in front of the whole crew who, if they were supposed to be eyes front and silent, were not: he was sure he could hear murmurs, probably of complaint, and it was moot as to whom they were aimed at.

'Seize up the prisoner, but remove his shirt before you do so.'

That had Peat scowl, not that it was easy to discern the difference between that and his normal expression. But Teach had just bought his slops from Porlock and it would be a double cruelty that he should have to pay to replace a ripped garment.

That duty fell to Charlie and Rufus Dommet, with the former whispering in the Teach ear, as he lifted his shirt over his head, that he had told him so. Teach did not protest as he was dragged towards the grating, but he did manage to look up at Pearce in a way, a hard and uncompromising stare, which implied this was not the end of the matter.

Hands tied, the next command was to call forward the bosun to 'Carry out the sentence'.

Crocker was in his shirtsleeves, the arms of which were rolled up to reveal a set of strong muscles. By the look on his face, pure determination, he seemed set to lay on hard. Pearce had the sudden and disturbing thought that Teach was going to pay with his skin for what the bosun found had become an ill-starred posting. As the cat swung in Crocker's hand, his captain could see the colour of the rope and its outline. It was black with tar and every strand of the nine tails was heavily knotted.

Moberly was looking straight ahead, Hallowell at the bright blue sky. Peat was staring keenly at what was about to occur. John Pearce, who would have dearly liked to have copied Hallowell, was obliged to keep his eyes fixed on the object of the gathering.

The first strike had Teach arch his body and it left a deep red weal across his pale white skin. Crocker had done this before and he knew how to land the next blow right on top of the previous mark. The thwack as skin met rope made more than Teach tense his body. Everyone watching was putting himself in the man's place.

Crocker had his rhythm and he broke the skin on his sixth blow, in a set of marks no more than a couple of inches wide. Pearce knew this was going to be gory: that the canvas on which Teach stood, to protect the deck from dripping blood, was going to be necessary.

A scream rent the air on the seventh strike and each subsequent blow raised the level of agony. By the time Crocker got to the first dozen, that strip of Teach's back was truly lacerated; soon it would be bone they were looking at, not skin. Peat was leaning forward, his lips wetted by his tongue, his eyes bright with concentration and pleasure.

'Enough! Mr Crocker lay up the cat. The man has suffered enough.'

The bosun, his chest heaving, looked disappointed, but that was nothing to the fury which suffused the face of Peat. Nor was he silent, indeed he shouted in a high passion.

'Sir, I protest.'

'Noted, Mr Peat, but the Lord Commissioners did not see fit to give you command of the ship. That they gave to me.' Orders were directed at Charlie and Rufus. 'Cut the man down and take him to the cockpit. Mr Maclehose, please boat over to HMS *Bedford* and request from Captain Byard that we borrow his surgeon. Master-at-arms, dismiss the men. Mr Hallowell you have duties to perform, please go about them, and you, Mr Peat, I will see you in my cabin. Mr Moberly, please join us.'

When the man looked set to protest, Pearce shouted to cut him off. 'At once!'

It was a defiant, elderly lieutenant who entered the cabin, to be faced with a look of stone from his captain. When he made to sit down, he was abruptly told to remain standing.

'Mr Peat, I find that you do not suit this vessel or myself as a reliable inferior. I therefore request that you forthwith pack your sea chest and make arrangements to depart the ship. I will write to the Admiralty with a report on what I consider your unfitness for the responsibilities of your rank.'

'Damn you!'

'Have a care, or you and your dunnage will be trying to get ashore without a boat. There is a man below with a torn back and it's entirely due to your love of a thrashing.'

Pearce knew Crocker was as much at fault, but was not going to say so.

'I will report this to Admiral Buckner.'

'Do so. I care not one jot for what he thinks and you may pass that on to him as well. I now ask what it is you are waiting for. Get out.'

Peat tried to retain his dignity, but the import of what was happening made that hard. He had been beached for so long it had come close to breaking his spirit, this Pearce knew from his pleading in the initial letter. And now he was going to be without employment once more. He could blame that on as many malign influences as he wished, but surely he must know the chance of a place was unlikely to come up again. By the time he made the cabin door his shoulders were slumped.

'And Mr Peat, you best bespeak a wherry. I cannot spare men to row you ashore.' When the door closed behind him he turned to Moberly. 'I think you too can go about your duties. We cannot hang about at anchor for ever. We must weigh and see how we fare.'

For a man who always looked as if little could dent his self-regard or confidence, the thought changed the marine officer's expression markedly.

CHAPTER TWENTY-ONE

John Pearce was determined to see how HMS *Hazard* would fare with the assistance of the Bedfords before they departed to join the North Sea Fleet. Byard, who must have read his mind, sent over a couple of his lieutenants to beef up the aid, while the recipient blessed the luck that gave him a gentle breeze, one sufficient to provide steerage way, without being strong enough to present difficulties.

The mood in the ship was not good and he could feel it, while being painfully aware he had none of the conduits by which a captain could gauge the feelings of the crew. His Pelicans were too obviously close to him and the quota men clammed up when they were in earshot, likewise Hallowell and Moberly, though that was more common, officers rarely seen as being companionable.

Rapport with others was yet to be formed, so he was left guessing. Even Mr Low, the gunner, with whom he felt a certain community of spirit, was unwilling to enter into any conversation that related to such a matter. The best he could do, as much a hope as anything else, was put it down to a general anxiety.

The two Bedford lieutenants went where he directed them, as did the midshipmen who'd been a previous presence, which was to shadow their equals where possible. Young Livingston he kept by his side to act as a messenger. Maclehose he reckoned could manage to look like he had authority. Those manning the sheets, whom he would supervise, required little instruction other than when to pull, release and tie off ropes.

Campbell he put on the capstan: the exercise would do him good and he would be required to shout instead of whisper. Tennant, in the company of a Bedford lieutenant, was given the bitts, to oversee the laying out of the anchor cables as they were hauled in, the stern being the first so *Hazard* would be at single anchor. The next task would be to sail over that and pluck it from the seabed. Catting and fishing the fore anchor was a job requiring skill. Hallowell would be there to oversee a duty that could well fall to him anyway.

Every ship in the anchorage would be watching, with Pearce far from sure if it would go smoothly. But that had to be risked. There was no way to teach certain actions by dumbshow; only the actual handling of the various items would demonstrate the moves required and he was painfully aware that this day would be the last he could expect help. He hoped to be able to repeat it several times.

The paying out of the bow cable went smoothly enough, the

stern cable being brought in at the same rate, to sustain tension. Once that was on board they could proceed to weigh. Pearce was on hand to see the nippers tying on the lines by which it would be hauled in a criss-cross manner between the bitts. The layers had to heave the thick cable, which was weighty, slimy and wet. He returned to the deck to give the orders that would let fall some canvas, the yards being swung enough to catch the wind.

He felt it necessary to use the speaking trumpet to address those of his own men manning the yards; the quartet of *Bedford* topmen knew what they were about. He told them this was an exercise and he had no great ambition that it should be seamless so no risks were to be taken. His last admonishment was that they ensure they kept their footing.

'Know that as a member of the crew you are valued. Nothing would depress me more than that one of you should perish by falling to the deck.'

The orders were simultaneous; the topmast sheets were let fall and, as soon as they billowed, the men on the sheets hauled hard to swing the yards. Below, at the first sign of slack on the anchor cable the order was given to stamp and go, the men on the capstan bars leaning at an acute angle and pushing like the devil to get it moving.

A clean pluck was a combination of wind power and muscle, a bit of decent way on the ship as it sailed over the taut cable being the best method to detach it cleanly from the muddy seabed. If Pearce could barely hear the yells from below, he could certainly hear the cacophony of shouting from aloft, as the *Bedford* topmen cajoled their *Hazard* trainees in the things in which they had been instructing them. At his rear was Michael O'Hagan, acting as quartermaster and gently adjusting the wheel. Mr Williams was beside him to ensure the course he had laid down – a simple one – was adhered to.

A quick look around with a glass showed every other deck with an audience. Some of them even had men manning their tops, no doubt in the hope of being witness to a disaster. They were not to be wholly disappointed, given the manoeuvre was far from smooth. But weigh they did, albeit with the anchor trailing off the bow as the hauling in failed to match the movement. Finally, the anchor was fished and catted: Hallowell saw to that.

The blue light, shooting up from the deck of HMS *Bedford*, brought forth smiles from more than John Pearce. Even if it lost much of its purpose in daylight, Byard was signalling to the whole fleet at anchor his delight that *Hazard* was under way and moving out, at near to high tide, onto the broad reach of the Thames.

It was with caution that Pearce called for the main course, which had the fellow, acting as captain of the main, yelling like a banshee as he cajoled those under his care to loosen the ties and let out a couple of reefs. The heavy canvas did not drop evenly, in fact the lee side was down before the windward even moved, which occasioned much cheering – it was truly jeering – which came floating distantly from other ships.

For all the gremlins, Pearce felt alive; he might barely have steerage way, but it was enough to provide a degree of exhilaration. Looking about him he could see, if not smiles, that exchange of glances between men, one that denotes the feeling they had done well. In short, the mood of the ship had changed.

The more difficult task was to follow; anchoring was a much more complex operation than weighing. Yet he now saw his quota men, for all their errors, going about their duties with enthusiasm. That cheering-cum-jeering, designed to mock them and so diminish their morale, seemed to have achieved the opposite, making the crew more determined.

Even if it was a dog's dinner the anchor had been dropped and it held. The taking in of sail had been a farce, but the whole had been, if not a complete success, enough to prove that with time he would have under him a mostly competent crew, a feeling driven home as they repeated the whole manoeuvre three times.

Once anchored for the last time, with everyone else in the Nore either bored or sated with their derision, he could stand the men down, instructing the purser to issue an extra tot of grog, Bedfords included. In his cabin he poured copious amounts of wine to his guest lieutenants as well as Hallowell, Mr Williams and Moberly, the latter's men having done sterling service on the capstan.

Privately, for all his joy, he reckoned going to sea – which he must do after not much more training – was going to be interesting, to say the least. In his mind he began to compose the speech he would have to make, this in between toasts to *Hazard*, *Bedford*, Captain Byard, the King's Navy, not forgetting to damn the enemy, quite specifically the Dutch.

Having seen his visitors and their hands over the side, he went below to the orlop to visit Teach, who had been accommodated in what would have been part of the sawbones's quarters had the ship possessed one. He had a strong desire that any resentments – and the man was entitled to have them in his view – should not fester. Teach lay face down, his back shining with the ointments put there by *Bedford*'s surgeon, who, before departing, had left instructions to apply it regularly.

'I have come to see how you fare, Teach.'

'As if you care.' It was a snarl.

'I cared enough to save you from worse.'

'What can be worse than to be treated like a rabid dog?'

Pearce took off his hat and sat at the bottom of the cot, which allowed him to see into the man's eyes, deciding to be honest.

'Mr Peat was all for you swinging, but I prevented it.' Seeing Teach preparing to be scathing, he spoke, to ensure there was no further offence that would oblige him to react. 'I ask for no gratitude for doing what I saw as my duty. But I have to say to you, if you persist in the attitude you have shown so far, you will leave me little option but to repeat what has happened to you.'

'Do your worst.'

'A ship of war is not a republic. Someone has to lead and others have to follow and we have been allotted our roles. You are inclined to challenge authority, which will not serve.'

If only you knew, Teach, he reflected silently, *how little pleasure I take in being such a hypocrite* and he knew he was about to indulge in a bit more. He had been nothing but bellicose since the day he'd been pressed.

'It is my view that those most likely to rail against discipline often make natural leaders. When you come back to health, apply yourself to your duty and I will mark it. If the needs of the ship warrant it, you will be rewarded.'

The sound wasn't words, just an audible scoff.

'I have on my desk the reports from various sources regarding how certain men behaved today. Some of them will soon find themselves in a position of authority over their shipmates, so I do not lie.' If Teach had fallen silent, there was no change in his expression; he still looked livid. 'I have done what is my duty in coming to see you and I've spoken my piece. I can do no more.'

Pearce stood and replaced his hat. 'What happens next falls to you.'

Back in his cabin he did indeed have a list of those seen to have performed adequately; well was barely an option, given the depth of nautical ignorance. They would require careful and continuous monitoring, but that was true of any ship. On a plain sheet of paper he played with their names and the position they might fill, with the knowledge that all would have multiple tasks.

The best topman or mate to a warrant would, at times, have to double as a gun captain, even a quarter gunner. He would have to sit and discuss with his standing officers whom they wanted to assist them, with the knowledge of the differing jobs that fell to men on a normal day, and how that altered dramatically when battle was imminent.

Lastly, he wrote once more to Emily to tell her of his progress, aware that he was painting a picture of the day which was a great deal rosier than the reality. He could only wonder if she would be pleased. A repeat letter went off to the Sick and Hurt Board which, having visited Teach, had become to him a matter of urgency. With an inexperienced crew, accidents would be endemic, while treatment for those who could be saved was essential.

That acknowledged, he knew he would lose some hands to falls and other accidents. Every King's ship suffered losses, more from the commonality of sailing a complex vessel than ever expired from enemy action. They had shown some collective solidarity today and he set himself to thinking how that could be supported.

The best way would be to put some prize money in their poke, which was very easy to think of and damned hard to achieve. The thought of facing an armed enemy this early was not to be contemplated. Would it happen when they were properly worked up, and what would be the outcome? There was no way of telling how a crew would act in battle until it was joined.

He had to put into action the next part of their training, which was to call 'All hands', and see how they performed in getting to their stations in darkness.

'*Bedford* weighing, sir.'

'I thank you, Mr Hallowell. Have the crew man the yards. We must give them a proper send-off.'

The seventy-four, third rate, lit by a newly risen sun, showed how it should be done. Byard had a well-worked-up crew and it was demonstrated in the smooth transfer from being static to being under topsails to get moving, then courses on the fore and main by the time she came abreast of *Hazard*. The yards were passably manned, the topmen in place but too many of the rest only sparsely on the ratlines.

That said, it was a gesture and it seemed to be much appreciated. Pearce called for three cheers and it was delivered with enthusiasm as he lifted his hat to Byard, the older man returning the compliment. As the stern began to fade from view, it was time to call the men back to normal duty, to swab and flog dry the decks and to eat their breakfast.

That completed, it would be time to see if they could weigh, sail Mr Williams's course once more, and re-anchor on their own. Everyone was in for another very trying day.

* * *

Walter Hodgson, having taken the precaution of billing the company for his expenses, was waiting to be admitted to the presence of Edward Druce, to whom the amount had been passed for approval, and if his mind ranged over all sorts of possibilities, the thief-taker was calm. He had been faced with many difficult situations in his life. Employers refusing to pay, acquittals where he was sure of guilt were just the surface. There was the threat of violence too; villains did not always want to come quietly.

He had learnt long ago that overthinking what might come his way was of no use. He carried out the given task; how it would all play out was probably preordained. The bell rang eventually to have him ushered in, to face an eager expression from Druce, who seemed to be anticipating good news. The problem for Hodgson was complex; he was unsure what that would entail.

'I took the liberty of ordering coffee, Mr Hodgson. I hope that meets with your approval.'

'Most kind, Mr Druce.'

'Do sit down by the side table and pour for yourself.' There was a lull while this was carried out, but there was no missing the tension in the room. Druce controlled his palpable impatience until Hodgson sipped the steaming brew, before speaking again. 'You have, I hope, something of importance to report?'

Hodgson put down his cup and reached into his folder, producing the twin images as described by Daisy Bolton, these passed over. 'I would ask, sir, if you know either of these two fellows?'

Druce's lips were puckered as he accepted the drawings – either he was surprised or curious, probably both. Laid side by side, he studied them for a while, before slowly shaking his head.

'Am I to deduce they are significant?'

'They might be. Best I tell you how I came to have them drawn up.'

Hodgson took Druce through his meeting with Daisy Bolton, her bagnio and how it operated, sensing a degree of impatience. Being no stranger to erotic entertainment, this was superfluous information to his employer. The thief-taker then moved onto the circumstances of the murder and what Daisy had discovered, finally coming to the departure of the two fellows so drawn, very shortly after the arguing pair left the main salon. To that was added their prior glum behaviour.

'You being an intelligent man, Mr Druce, might wonder at what they were about, two sailor types in a place in which they seemed to find little joy, which is not the way of your common tar. Not much drinking and no interest in the girls.'

'Sailor types, you say?'

'Aye, and Gherson claims he was felled by a marlin spike.'

Unable to comprehend the significance, it proved necessary to remind Druce that Gherson was a one-time pressed seaman and that a marlin spike was as good as a billy club any day.

'He was out cold when Mrs Bolton found him, that is, once she recovered from her shock. I hardly need to tell you a man found in a state of unconsciousness, with a lump on his head, which might have come from said spike, would struggle to carry out that of which he is accused.'

The face, as Hodgson spoke, had gone from relaxed interest to clamping teeth and pursing lips, until Druce said in a voice suddenly hoarse. 'Are you implying that Gherson is indeed innocent?'

'Only that the possibility exists.'

He thought to mention the lack of a knife – after all Catherine Carruthers had been badly mutilated – but decided there were too many possibilities for its absence at the scene of a crime, which had been trampled over by what amounted to a throng.

A slightly strangled note emerged when Druce asked, 'Do you not need to enquire further and find out?'

'I can ask for more, but I am not the law of the land and no one is obliged to answer my questions.'

Druce looked down at the twin images again, going back mentally to the previous attempt to get rid of Gherson and the reasons why. For a man of Denby Carruthers' age to marry a very pretty but naïve woman, thirty years his junior, challenged wisdom and had occasioned much ribald comment amongst his business associates. Druce had shared their reservations, though he never allowed them to be even hinted at in Denby's presence.

He had come across Gherson when visiting Denby and Catherine, though he barely registered, being a fitful presence: an obsequious young man of blonde good looks, employed as a live-in clerk by a man of wide commercial interests. What his confrères had joked about had come to pass; clever and supremely successful as Denby was, he had been cuckolded and humiliated.

It was Gherson, re-emerging as Barclay's clerk, who had given Druce a filleted version of what happened on London Bridge, not having any notion of Druce's relationship to Carruthers, which established to Druce that his brother-in-law had deceived him regarding his intention then. Looking at these two faces, not in truth reassuring, had he deceived him again now? For when he had asked for Gherson's whereabouts it was to again talk of a beating.

He was acknowledging the chance of something he had thought on, but suppressed as too dreadful to contemplate. Had Denby arranged the murder of his wife, in such a manner that Gherson would get the blame? And if that was accepted, what was he to do about it?

'We are in deep waters here, Mr Hodgson,' was produced as a holding remark.

'Indeed, sir.' Hodgson was doing the same, leaving Druce time to think.

Ever since that first request that Gherson should get a beating, Edward Druce had been drawn into a web out of which he could not break, one which had been the subject of sleepless nights. Denby Carruthers too often treated him with insulting and constant condescension, made worse by the way his own wife favoured her brother over him.

She could not see the bully, always prattling on about his kindness, which was a way of reminding her husband how much he owed to the man who had financed him, had made it possible for them to live in more than just comfort. Taking on board what was being implied, Druce could see the solution to several problems at one go, for Gherson, whom he had hitherto for the sake of the agency protected, had become as much of a bane as Denby Carruthers.

'I do not see how any organ of the law could become involved,' was issued as a statement, when in truth it was an enquiry.

Hodgson confirmed that to be true. Justice in King George's realm was a chancy business, one in which he had prospered, there being few officially tasked with the apprehension of those charged. It fell to those in search of bounty and the task was delivery, not enquiry. A felon was issued with a warrant for his arrest and, once that was achieved, it fell to the courts to do the rest, the rest being very little.

'However,' Druce added, with the air of the concerned citizen, 'we would be remiss if we did not continue to seek the facts of the matter, do you not think?'

'So you wish me to continue?'

'What would that entail, Mr Hodgson?'

'We have those faces and they belong to flesh and blood. Happen printed and distributed, we could find these coves and demand to be told of their actions on the night.'

'Would they admit to any?'

'Their faces out and questions raised would get them before the magistrate at Bow Street.'

Druce made a steeple of his hands, the fingertips touching his chin, the brow furrowed. 'One has to examine the consequences, for such a questioning would be unlikely to remain discreet.'

'I would do my best to keep it so.'

'With all of London agog at the slightest detail? I find myself concerned at setting hares running, which may produce nothing, and in that please do not think I cast aspersions on your abilities.'

'Kind of you to say so, Mr Druce.'

'My family, my brother-in-law, has suffered mightily from the manner and loss of his dear wife. It would grieve me to distress him any more and making a printed tract of these fellows, as you suggest, would open the whole matter up to excessive and nasty speculation, of which he has had enough already.'

The steeple was pressed harder into the chin. 'Carry on as you are doing, Mr Hodgson, for I can say without doubt, your efforts to date' – the drawings were held up to be looked at by Druce again – 'they have been exemplary. Your bill I will sign now so you can have it settled. In fact, I will add a decent and well-deserved bonus.'

Which Druce did and it was handed over for him to be told, 'I must advise you there is a limit to what I can do.'

'You can keep an eye on Cornelius Gherson for me, a primary concern, which I dare not engage in myself. And who knows what you may turn up regarding the crime?'

'Would you have me tell him there might be a doubt?'

The eyebrows went up with the hands. 'And raise the poor fellow's hopes? I think that could be construed as cruelty. If and when his innocence can be established, that will be the time to advise him of the good news, do you not think?'

There was no choice but to nod and agree.

'Then, Mr Hodgson, that concludes our business for today, does it not? I do desire you to keep me informed, and me alone, of any developments as and when they occur.'

'The drawings?'

'Best left here. It would not serve that even by accident they should excite comment. They are, I'm sure, fixed in your memory and you are known for your diligence.'

When Hodgson departed Edward Druce went back to studying the two faces. The matter of Denby's involvement, indeed of his guilt, was not fixed, but then it did not have to be for suspicion would be enough. Complicit or not, a mere showing of these would silence him, for he would be as quick as Druce to see the possible ramifications of their public exposure.

Edward Druce was not a man much given to laughter but he

could not avoid it now, and it was no mere chuckle, indeed it was so full-throated he had difficulty in saying out loud what had set him off.

'Your days of treating me a dung on your shoe are over Denby, and for good.'

The thought of Gherson did surface next, but he reckoned mere inactivity would take care of that problem.

CHAPTER TWENTY-TWO

Pearce got his surgeon, a Mr Cullen, plus two assistants. This time, coming as they did from the Sick and Hurt Board, there was no seeking to land him with the dregs. Cullen seemed sober and competent, while he had an immediate patient in Teach who, still in pain, would surely be grateful for their ministrations. He was still short two lieutenants but was determined, if anything supplied was to be like the now-departed Peat, he would willingly do without.

At least, thanks to Admiral Parker, Hallowell had been confirmed and that influence was applied, once more, to gain for him a just-passed midshipman called Worricker, who arrived only hours after the surgeon. He hailed from Hastings, the scion of a family of fisher folk of the better sort, those who owned several boats and employed people to sail them.

A seaman to his fingertips, at sea since he was breeched, Worricker was, like Hallowell, a real asset, which led his captain to think the Admiralty had made a mistake. The two hit it off immediately, which boded well for the future, as did a wardroom nearly complete in its complement.

Not that all was entirely rosy for, without the Bedfords, the pace of learning slowed markedly and on one or two occasions – it was not entirely unexpected – the manoeuvres of weighing, sail work and anchoring had been very close to embarrassing.

The decision to depart to Nore was taken for two reasons: wind favoured the move while, at another anchorage, continued exercises could be undertaken without the constant oversight of their naval peers, with Pearce sure it was affecting his men. Not that he intended to go far. He would give the north shore of Sheppey a wide berth on a course plotted by himself and a worried Williams.

A letter was sent ashore to Oliphant, advising him to move to Faversham immediately, as Pearce intended to anchor just off the creek of that name. It lay at the point where the Swale rejoined the Thames, on the east side of Sheppey. But he kept to himself another aim, knowing Faversham was home to the government powder factories. He was keen to see how his crew handled the cannon when they could at least feel the blast and smell the burnt remains of a discharge. He would allow balls only if a certain proficiency was established.

He was fully supplied with powder and shot and could justify a certain amount for the purposes of training. But what he had in mind went beyond that. Finding a way to provide was not something he wished to have recorded in the ship's ledgers, either his own or that of Mr Low, the gunner. Obscuring overuse was near impossible when, at some time in the future, said logs would be compared and he as captain could be billed for what was seen as excessive expenditure.

To creep away in darkness was a risk, but the tide was right, falling from its peak on a night with a near-full moon, added to a medium strength south-westerly. The reflected glow of said moon on the river, coming from the east, almost gave him a bearing to follow. In addition, the shores of both Kent and Essex were inhabited along its length, so there were pinpricks of light to act as landmarks.

The crew off duty had been roused out twice before at night, but had only moved to their allotted positions, not acted upon them. When they were given the same orders as had been issued in daylight, there was a ripple of apprehension. Hallowell and Worricker began yelling the requisite commands which, when executed, were carried out with an annoying amount of noise and confusion.

'So much for departing in secret, Michael.'

O'Hagan was standing by his side, as was the youngster Livingston, who was, during the day, being educated in mastering the signal flags. Mr Williams had insisted, on this occasion, he would take the wheel, with a man to help him.

'Sure,' Michael hooted, 'they'll reckon the Dutch are in the offing. There's enough row to have the fleet beating to quarters.'

Sure enough there was lantern movement on various quarterdecks, but that had to be ignored as, more slowly than he would have hoped, *Hazard* got under way. The familiar creaking of timbers, the stretching and hiss of the wind through the rigging, was somehow reassuring. To begin with the yards had to be braced right round, to get them clear of Garrison Point, the flaring torchlights of the fortress on the peninsula giving a clear indication of distance.

Once out in the broader Thames, Pearce, or more importantly the master, felt secure in putting down his helm, bringing the yards round to take more wind. Williams had put a man in the bows to look out for other vessels, which amused his captain. No sensible merchantman, Pearce thought, would make their way beyond the mouth of the estuary after nightfall.

It was the hunting ground of press gangs from individual vessels. To do so risked having half the crew forcibly removed, but Williams worried the sloop might run afoul of someone anchored on a deliberately darkened ship in order to avoid such a fate, and insisted on taking all precautions.

There is something ghostly about sailing at night, better in moonlight than under cloud cover, which had Pearce wonder if any of these men new to the sea were prey to superstitions. If they suffered such an affliction, they'd find happy company in the navy. He had never met such a bunch of old women, who had a curse ready to fit every ordinary act. That said, it was a brave man who scoffed, not for fear of the supernatural but as a precaution against the Jeremiahs, men who'd put the whole ship on edge with their fancies.

There was another fellow in the chains to cast the log, a runner of a ship's boy sent back to tell Mr Williams how many knots they were making, rarely more than two. At each message, once the slate was marked, the master would retire to his cabin, employing his dividers to check their position. Amidships, Charlie Taverner was casting for depth of water, for in the Thames lay a mass of ever-shifting sandbanks. In this Pearce was as concerned as Williams; to run aground would be humiliating.

'Time to put up our helm, Captain. Happen you'd care to check.'

Which Pearce did; it was expected and, in truth, he was keen to show his ability at navigation, even if he lacked the depth of knowledge that would have come from a more normal induction into command.

'I rate your calculations spot on, Mr Williams.'

He left behind a man swelling with pride, which he held to be a touch excessive.

Back on the quarterdeck Pearce gave an order to Livingston. 'Please go to Misters Hallowell and Worricker and advise them we are about to alter course to the south.'

'Aye aye, sir,' he squeaked, before dashing off.

'That one's even younger than his years,' Michael said.

'I'm sure he'll grow to be what the service requires,' was the only thing Pearce could say in reply.

The hands, who'd been below, were brought up to man the falls, to swing the yards once more, while Williams spun the wheel as he gave instructions to the topmen to clew up the topsails a reef, careful to tell Pearce why he had acted so.

'We're heading for shore, sir. Wouldn't do to be beached.'

'My sentiments exactly, Mr Williams.'

Dawn found HMS *Hazard* off the mouth of Faversham Creek, safely at anchor, in deep water, with the hands going about their normal duties. A pair of East Indiamen, down from London on their way to the Orient, lay close by. They were there, no doubt like him, to take on powder, in a place where the press of all kinds were forbidden to operate. Shot would have been loaded upriver, coming as it did from any number of foundries around the country.

Once the men had breakfasted, Pearce called for his barge to take him ashore, his intention to visit the official who oversaw the working of the powder factories. He took with him a marine corporal and two of his men. Once they made the quay and he had disembarked, Maclehose was instructed to return to the ship, to avoid the chance of anyone deserting.

There were several powder factories around the Faversham area, but the management office lay between the quayside and the town centre, though he had been obliged to enquire as to its location. His aim was to find what he wanted to purchase and how much it would cost. Another enquiry was needed: the location at which the coaches passing through the town en route to Canterbury tended to stop.

Pearce was no stranger to the price of the product he was seeking; it was listed as a per-barrel item in his ledgers. That was as a government product, from a government factory for the military arm of same. He feared, and was proved correct, that the price was higher for private buyers. Not that he had any intention of dipping into his own funds.

He waited for Oliphant at the Bear Inn who, when he arrived, declined the notion of going aboard and so took a room. They had enjoyed some food, as well as ale from the local brewery before Pearce made his opening gambit. It did not go down well, in fact he ran into a wall of opposition.

'Might I remind you, though I cannot see why I have to, that I signed for that cask of coin from Dundas?'

'Three hundred in specie you tell me, Oliphant, with no idea how it is to be disbursed. Is it to be used to bribe, to buy support or just to expend on necessary expense? It matters not. As I found in the Vendée, there is no way to properly account for how it is employed. I also say that what I propose is a worthwhile purpose.'

'It was not meant for the buying of powder.'

'Let me take the responsibility. I will include the bill in any returns we are required to make and accept responsibility.'

'He could demand you pay it back.'

'Dundas can demand away. I have sidestepped that threat before and I'm sure I can do so again.'

'And if he cannot get satisfaction from you, what then?' A finger was pushed into the Oliphant chest. 'He will come after me.'

'I am in command of a ship which, as of this moment, is only just getting to the point of being able to sail.'

'And you want me to come aboard,' was the arch response. 'No doubt you'd have me haul on a rope.'

'When we set off you might have to.' Said to shock Oliphant, he soon realised it was a joke but what came next was deadly serious. 'Sailing will improve, of that I'm certain. I can already see signs of a group beginning to work together. What I worry about more is our ability to fight.'

'Then work out a strategy to avoid the need.'

'You talk as if that is in my hands, but it might not be. I cannot command the wind. And nor can I guarantee to you we will not come across an armed enemy vessel, one that has the weather gage on *Hazard*.'

'You are a master of nautical verbiage, Pearce.'

'While you are an incorrigible lubber, my friend.'

The tankards were employed by Pearce to explain what he meant. It had always amazed him that landsmen were so ignorant, as he had at one time been himself, that the wind dictated everything at sea. That applied to nothing as much as fighting. It was the primary task, be it a fleet or a single ship action, to get to windward of your enemy, because that allowed you to control what came next.

Oliphant made a good fist of looking bored by the explanation, but Pearce reckoned he could not help but be interested, especially when the man explaining matters to him went on to relate the possibility of him suffering from the outcome. A loss in battle might not see him wounded or killed, but it would most certainly see him taken prisoner.

'The King's Navy relies on firepower in battle. It is the French habit to stand off from close engagement and to seek to disable their opponent by shredding the rigging. We seek to close and batter them into submission by the sheer rate of fire. We run in our guns and reload, ready to fire, on the basis of two-to-one advantage. Sometimes, on a truly crack frigate, even more.'

The tankards, representing ships at sea, were near to touching now. 'Such a rate often upends the cannon, and it drives the enemy gunners away from their weapons. Those firing on the upper deck, in the case of *Hazard* it would be the swivels, will try to decimate the enemy command by fusillades aimed at the quarterdeck. Then, if they don't strike, we board.'

'You make it sound as if we never lose, which I know from the journals is far from the case.'

Pearce slapped the table. 'We lose when the conditions are against us, when we are outnumbered, and when the gun crew training is neglected, which takes no account of poor captaincy.'

'I am still disinclined to oblige you.'

Pearce was encouraged by that; the flat refusal had been moderated. 'Even with an inexperienced crew, I back myself to get close to anyone we have to fight.'

'You do not mention flight, just fight.'

'I will and have sought to avoid battle where the odds did not favour me. But I can tell you of one occasion, in the Mediterranean, in which every attempt to avoid engagement was thwarted. Had I not been lucky, I might have ended up as a galley slave.'

'Tell me of it.'

Oliphant was prevaricating and Pearce was having none of it. 'I would suggest if we faced the same conditions against a Frenchman, you would take capture by Barbary. What would the people who know of you in Paris, the ones who would address you as Bertrand, mete out? Perhaps, given you are so keen on tales, you would like to tell me what is the provenance of that name?'

'While I would say that is none of your affair.'

'Is it not? I went to Paris in your company, thinking I was in the company of a man called Oliphant, as I am now. And yet I'm uncertain if that or Bertrand is your true name. What we were engaged in was dangerous enough, without additional and concealed concerns.'

The response was pugnacious. 'You are a sailor, Pearce; I am what I am. Oliphant will serve.'

'Which comes close to an admission that's not your true name either. In truth, while it worried me once, I have ceased to fret on it. I realise you have abilities I do not possess. Would you grant the same in reverse to me?'

If he was reluctant to do so, he stayed silent, for conversation continued in the present vein was not only uncomfortable, it was in danger of becoming too revealing.

'I have no more mind to perish in battle or be taken prisoner than you. What I am asking for is that which will lessen the chance of it happening.'

'How much do you require?'

'Fifty pounds would serve.'

'And you're sure it is necessary?'

'Wise. Only time will tell if it's necessary.'

'Would you be willing to put the request for the funds you require in writing, and with the reasons?'

Pearce was reluctant to do so, for obvious reasons. It made no odds if it was the Admiralty or Dundas seeking recompense, he would be on the hook for the money. What decided him to agree was one possibility. The need might not arise with Dundas, whereas it was a certainty with the naval administration. And then there was the old adage, there's many a slip betwixt cup and lip. He had no idea what the immediate future might bring and neither did his companion.

'I will ask the innkeeper for quill and paper,' Oliphant insisted, when Pearce nodded.

The requirements were met and the details agreed, before being listed. 'I offer you a chance to reconsider.'

'No. But do not extract the cost of your staying here, as well as the services it provides, from the same source.'

That got a sharp rejoinder as the paper was signed. 'The navy feeds you, Pearce, who is to feed me if not Dundas?'

'I require the key, unless you are intending to accompany me?'

'Be assured,' he said, fetching the key from a waistcoat pocket. 'I trust you not to cheat.'

It would not help, Pearce thought, to deny him the same.

Faversham was well equipped with hoys, supplying as it did an endless number of vessels calling to take on powder. He insisted on inspecting his purchase, payment on delivery, for quality, despite the assurance that, in providing for the armed forces, it was guaranteed as the best grade available. He not only ground the product between his fingers, blacking them with the charcoal, he sniffed for the level of sulphur and saltpetre.

That afternoon, when the ship's company had dined, the shore around Faversham Creek resounded mightily to the firing of cannon, in which the new men took great pleasure. For every discharge, the weapons were pulled in a dozen times, the act required to load, run out and fire them rehearsed. The actual addition of a powder charge was being used as a reward for a shortening in timing, this overseen by Hallowell and Worricker and reported to their captain.

'The aim, gentlemen, is for two minutes. We are very far from that.'

Finally he had balls fetched up and chipped where required, and an empty powder barrel floated off to act as a target. Not one hit it, but several landed close, sending up great plumes of water, bringing forth hurrahs from the aiming gun crew.

The firing lasted until he was informed, by a powder monkey, that Mr Low had run through his purchase and, if he wanted to continue, it would be from the ship's own store. So the cannon were wormed and washed down, some of them requiring blacking.

Once housed for the night, the information was passed on that tomorrow would be a return to sailing and anchoring drill.

Pearce knew he was running out of time. Soon he would have to get out to sea, even if he was unsure the crew were fully ready.

CHAPTER TWENTY-THREE

Walter Hodgson was sat in another office waiting to be seen, this time that of a lawyer called Thomas Southouse, a man with whom he had had many dealings before and one with whom it was wise to make an appointment. He was not the only one waiting: Southouse had a busy attorney practice, with several apprentices under his wing. These youngsters bustled in and out of various rooms, all carrying briefs and all in a hurry.

Part of the thief-taker's trade was patience, so there was no annoyance in being kept waiting. Besides, he had much to think about, not least his interview with Edward Druce. There were things he was not being told, but then he didn't need to be. He had to reckon that as far as Druce was concerned, the name of Denby Carruthers was only known as his being the husband of the victim.

Head on chest he failed to notice that Southouse had come out to fetch him.

'You slumbering, Mr Hodgson?'

The head came up slowly and with it a smile. 'Never sleep, Mr Southouse. If I did I never collar any of the rogues I'm sent to find.'

He had a habit of cocking his head to one side and Southouse did that now. 'You obviously wish to see me?'

'If you have time.'

'I rate it interesting, if you've come without prior notice.'

'And I think it'd be right to do so, for the subject merits it. But I must warn you it might take time.'

The lawyer looked around the crowded waiting room, at a series of expectant faces holding bundles of papers, which fell somewhat as he said, 'There's nowt here that cannot be dealt with by my assistants. Best come in.'

Southouse had taken his seat before Hodgson, having picked up his folder, got through the door, which had the thief-taker wonder how he had managed to weave his way through the masses of files, both those piled up and the rest, which littered the floor. It was not necessary to allude to his being busy; he had been that since Hodgson first met him.

'Where have you been these last two years?'

'Here and there.'

The lips twitched for the coming pun. 'From what I hear, it's damn near everywhere.'

'Surprised you noticed.'

The hair had thinned since the last time they had met, and the ends of what remained, which hung long on either side of his head, were grey at the tips. A finger was used to push a thin pair of spectacles up his sharp bone of a nose, not that they would stay there. If Hodgson was to remark on his pallor, he would also have to acknowledge how rarely the Southouse visage was exposed to sunlight. He was either in this dingy office, the back of a hack, or shut up in the law courts.

'Can't but take an interest when someone of your stamp disappears off the map. Not disappears, but set on a strange chase, I was told, which seems to never end and one no one could work out the purpose of. That's not your style – quick to nab is more your way.'

'Employed by one client, Mr Southouse, all that time.'

'Must have deep pockets.'

'Bottomless, more like.'

That pricked his interest; Southouse always claimed money meant nothing to him compared to justice, which would have held true if you made exception of the level of his fees. If there was a more expensive set of chambers in London, Hodgson didn't know of it. Against that, few could come close for successful results.

'Are you here on his behalf?'

'Not exactly.' The expression in response to that was silent curiosity. 'Truth is, I am not certain of how to proceed on a certain matter.'

'And you want my advice.' Hodgson nodded, which got and avaricious grin. 'Just sat there you have expended near half a guinea.'

When Hodgson replied, he had to hope he was right. 'I doubt fees will be a problem. You will know of the Catherine Carruthers murder?'

'I'd have to be deaf, dumb and blind not to. But that is a done and dusted case, perpetrator at the scene. The name of the butcher escapes me.'

'Gherson. There are grounds to think he might have been as much a victim as the poor woman.'

A hand was clutched over a fist as Southouse sat back, the expression one of bland enquiry. 'You intrigue me. I'm listening.'

'It is one of those affairs where I seem to be sitting in the middle of a web . . .'

Southouse was quick to deduction; it was what made him so successful 'Which I take to mean you know things, or reckon you do, that others don't.'

'Nail on the head, as ever.'

'Do I sense uncertainty?'

'Always best to be that, I have found. Times I've gone wrong, thinking I know matter top to tail.'

Southouse pulled out a hunter from his waistcoat pocket and flicked it open. 'I have missed my dinner, Walter. What say we repair to the Ye Old Watling and avail ourselves of a couple of their pies?'

'It'll be a damned expensive fillin', if I'm half a guinea down already, as I must be.'

'Then let us make it a social visit, two old friends enjoying a feed and some porter.'

'Can't fault that.'

'I'll take the bare bones on the way.'

Hodgson wondered, by the time they got to Ye Old Watling and secured a seat, if he had managed to tell his tale properly. Weaving through the crowded streets had seen them parted by other people more than once and Southouse, for all his slight and bony frame, moved at a pace, which left the more bulky Hodgson breathing quite hard by the time they got to a seat. There was a pause while said pies and ale were ordered, and it required a deep gulp of ale before the lawyer returned to the subject.

'So you sense two attempts at the same cove's life, if what this lady you mention says is true?'

Hodgson had been careful with names. None of those in his web had been identified, they had all been a certain party or a lady I know. The only person named was Daisy Bolton: no sense in concealing that, if the murder was carried out on her premises. There was a point where other names would surface, but it was not to be yet. It was just as telling, when Southouse enquired, what he did not bother to ask – like how come a lady knew so much of someone pressed into the navy.

'It would seem real enough.'

'Gherson could tell you, if you asked him. I take it you are in a position to do so?'

'I am, but I need to know which way I'm going to proceed afore I do that.'

'So what's in the folder you're carrying? Must be germane, or you could have left it in my office.' As Hodgson made to reply, Southouse held up a hand to stop him, a look of sly humour on his face. 'I would guess, by its size and shape, it is likenesses of those two fellows reported to you by the Bolton woman. Do tell me I'm right.'

'Copies I had made, yes.'

Their mutton pies arrived as the folder was handed over, which Southouse laid on a vacant chair, unopened. Two more pots of porter were ordered and the crust of both pies speared before he spoke again, this time through rising and meaty steam.

'Why would the man who employs you not wish for them to be publicly flushed out?' He was quick to answer his own question, given time, because Hodgson was dealing with a mouthful of his own piping-hot mutton. 'Who is he protecting and why? These are questions you've asked yourself and I reckon you know the answer.'

Hodgson shrugged and mouthed another forkful. He knew Southouse of old as a man who liked to follow his own line of reasoning, liked to deduce from fragments some kind of whole, and if he was brilliant at it, the same could sometimes blind him to what was really the case.

'You said fees would be unlikely to present a problem. Would they run to the services of both myself and Garrow?'

'Possibly, if Gherson is to have a chance of being freed.'

'Is that what you wish? Or should I say, is that what one of these two interested parties wish? My guess? For one of them the answer is yes, for the other it is no.'

'The drawings, Mr Southouse.'

'They are superfluous unless identified, and that has not yet happened or you would have said so. The question, to my way of thinking, is this. How did Catherine Carruthers come to be at the bagnio in Long Acre? What would a fellow do when he was far gone in drink and being tongue-lashed by a woman he'd had a carnal liaison with at some time in the past? She was still warm for him, by your account, was he still warm for her?'

More pie followed and Southouse looked to be chewing on that as well as the possibilities simultaneously, with Hodgson wondering how he could have absorbed so much of the conversation on the way, given how fractured it had seemed to him.

'She was a married woman and admitted as much, with a complete want of discretion. That is if the Bolton woman's testimony is to be believed. Does she have a reason for invention? I think not.'

More pie was consumed and chewed. 'Could the Gherson you describe have resorted to foul murder and mutilation of a one-time lover, a refined woman by all accounts, and why? It is possible, I grant, but you say he is of a weak disposition. Which begs the even bigger question of how it could be done, if he was found unconscious? You say there was a club in the room?'

'There was and it's been taken by Bow Street for the trial. I could ask to see it but to what purpose? A knife was employed, obviously, but no sign of it emerged. There was a mob in that room afore Gherson was carted off.'

'So you discount it, given it could have been taken by anyone?'

'I do. Could Garrow get him acquitted?'

'On the Bolton testimony, I would hazard a yes, though you know as well as I do nothing is certain in a court of law.' He tapped the folder on the chair. 'But as for the real culprits, if indeed it is they who are drawn here, that would be impossible to prove. You say they left the salon and no one saw them subsequently?'

'Except the fellow on the door, who could have seen them depart?'

'To be considered, Walter. But you have observed many a trial and any number of juries. How often is the claim made for some strange and mysterious third party as the villain in a crime? How often is it given credence by our forty-shilling freeholders? It would serve as no more than a last throw, and a poor one at that.'

If Hodgson's instincts were to save Gherson, given he was

inclined to his innocence, he had other things to consider, not the least his own prospects. No honest soul liked to see a man or woman hang for that in which guilt was in doubt, but it happened, if infrequently. The law was a blunt instrument at best; he knew it and so did Southouse.

His meeting with Druce had left him with two ways he could act and he had to work out which was best, his own well-being high on the list. Southouse was watching him as he ruminated on this, slowly wiping his mouth and chin with a napkin, and he nailed what he suspected lay at the heart of the dilemma.

'So, Walter, for whom are you going to act? This mysterious lady or the fellow hiding the real promoter of the crime?'

This time, in the smile, the lips were so compressed they disappeared.

'Imagine a verdict of not guilty, which puts another as the miscreant? What if you were to expose him? I assume a he, of course, not a woman. All those lurid penny pamphlets wrong by a mile. This will be a case to remember for years to come and it could make you, the one who solved it, famous.'

'Let me settle for the pies and ale.'

That got an effusive protest, hands criss-crossing before his face.

'Never in life. The tariff falls to me. I am about to wager which way you will play the game, and I have come down on the side of substantial fees for my practice. Call it an investment.'

'One more call to make and I will advise how it goes.'

This time he did take a hack to Harley Street. Druce had paid him well and, besides, it was dark. He was taking a chance that Emily Barclay would be there, given he was within the time stated to

311

respond. The fellow who answered the door informed him Mrs Barclay was occupied. Before he could say at what, if he even intended to, and that was far from certain, the cries of a baby came floating down to the hallway.

The look on the servant's face, of something revealed that should not have been, told a man like Hodgson much, and he could add to that what he knew. An estranged husband and runaway wife, the rumour of it being in the company of a lover.

Druce sending him to Frome to look for denigrating information. The presence of a child not having been mentioned on his previous visit. Surely if it was Captain Barclay's, it would have been in order to name it to evoke sympathy.

'Can I ask you to wait, sir?'

'Outside?' Hodgson enquired.

The fellow was embarrassed. 'If you please.'

He stood under the gaslight that fully illuminated the wide top step, thinking how novel such a device was, common in playhouses now, but still rare in dwellings. A hand was slid over the varnished oak of the door, the complex design of the heavy knocker fingered, both signs of the wealth to which he, like any other soul, aspired. Was Southouse right and with his imagined fame would there come prosperity? His hand was still on the brass when the door opened and he was silently invited to enter. She was at the bottom of the stairs, the infant in her arms.

'Mrs Barclay.'

'Do I judge by your early return, you have good news for me?'

'I may.'

'Please take Mr Hodgson's hat and coat, Cotton, and show him into the drawing room.' Turning back to him she added,

'I will be back soon, once I have laid my son down.'

Then it was Cotton again. 'And I'm sure we can give the gentlemen anything he desires as refreshment.'

She went up the stairs and he went to where he was directed, happy to take a decanter of wine and a tray of biscuits while he waited. She had put on a touch of rouge before returning, unnecessary to his way of thinking, but he reckoned it was there to hide any sign of a blush.

'Please say if you want more wine.'

'This will serve, Mrs Barclay.' It was slightly unkind to then remain silent, to play upon her anticipation. 'I wish to lay out a case to you, so you can decide how you wish to proceed.'

She sat down, as she had before, on the chaise, hands clasped in her lap, a sign to proceed. 'There is a chance that Gherson could be found not guilty. The question is, do you wish that to be the case?'

The response reminded him she was clever. 'You pose a possibility, not a certainty?'

'Certainty is not attainable in any legal proceedings, as any lawyer will attest. I would guess you have little experience of the law, Mrs Barclay, and none whatever of the King's Bench.'

'In that you would be correct. But surely guilt and innocence are polar opposites? The accused must be one or the other.'

'There are many factors in the drawing of a verdict.'

Emily listened as he outlined the several influences that affected a trial, first the opinion of the judge, most notoriously the Lord Chief Justice, Kenyon. With him politics would intrude if it was that kind of case; he would free his friends and direct the jury to condemn his enemies and it was a bold foreman who would defy him or any of his fellow judges. Others were dyspeptic and irascible, so opinion of counsel played a part.

A good lunch could more explain the way the jury was directed to acquit, a bad cold or a rumbling gut send the accused down to transportation or the gallows. Then there was the jury itself, what were their opinions and prejudices? That could not be foreseen for there was little control by counsel over choice.

'But all that notwithstanding, a case can be made?'

His folder was opened and laid before her. 'It can, but certainly only lies in the fact that, if Gherson was not the perpetrator, someone else must be. I ask you to look at these drawings and tell me if they trigger any memory.'

'You think them involved?'

'I think it possible.'

She took her time, as befitted the seriousness of the situation, but finally shook her head. 'I am curious as to how you came to suspect them?'

'A certain pattern of behaviour on the night Mrs Carruthers was murdered, which makes it conceivable they are the true offenders. But if you can't name them, then Gherson is left with what I have at present.' The pause was deliberate, the look that went with it equally so. 'But have you considered what will happen if he is acquitted?'

'I suspect that's not a question you have put to Mr Druce. If you had, you would not be here.'

He had to smile; she was so quick to see what lay behind his being here and he responded with a shake of the head. It was time to be open. 'I have a suspicion that it is not an outcome Mr Druce is much concerned to bring about.'

'Because a dead Gherson cannot attest to his peculations?'

'There may be other reasons.'

The slight forward jerk indicated she was about to ask for details, but she checked herself, realising the way Hodgson had said that meant he had no intention of enlightening her. He went on to tell of his meeting with Southouse, though he filleted their conversation, keeping to what mattered, mentioning Garrow and how he could plead an erroneous charge. It was a name which registered.

'Let us assume a positive outcome and you are the person to engineer it,' he said.

'Pay for it would be more precise. I cannot believe William Garrow comes cheap.'

There was no need to confirm that. 'You would then anticipate Gherson becoming a source of information to you.'

'Naturally.'

'Then if you will forgive, Mrs Barclay, you are being naïve. If I suggested to you that Gherson knows very well who arranged for the murder, would that surprise you?'

'It would surprise me he has not pointed the finger of accusation.'

'Then I would posit you have not appreciated how devious he can be.' The scowl took issue, but again she did the right thing, which was hold her tongue. 'A name could well surface at the point where he is about to be found guilty and, with it, some evidence of another's guilt.'

'Which would be?'

'Only Gherson knows that for certain. But when you related to me the tale of his impressment, I admit to being taken aback. It told me many of the assumptions I had made were wrong.'

315

Hodgson trusted her to get the drift, without it being explained. The same person who sought to dispose of him on that occasion had to be the person who conspired to have him hang for the murder of Catherine Carruthers. She might even produce a name, but she would not hear it from him.

'He has no employment and no prospect of any, so a freed Gherson will sell his soul to the highest bidder.'

'That would be in his nature.'

'Then we must ensure that no bidding can take place. If I am to act for you, I see it as my primary task to extract from him everything he knows, before he's made aware of Garrow and the defence.'

'And how, Mr Hodgson, will you do that?'

'Two people can play a double game, Mrs Barclay, but I admit, with a fellow like Gherson, it is going to be challenging to match him.'

CHAPTER TWENTY-FOUR

The crew of HMS *Hazard* had so far spent time in waters that were tidal but calm. Even in a bit of a blow the wind never did much to disturb the surface of the Nore and Faversham had been likewise. Moving out towards Margate, under topsails, took the ship into a running sea, albeit one not very lively. Pearce held a straight course, the run of the waves striking just off the larboard bow, with a very good idea of what was about to happen. As soon as the ship began to pitch and roll, seasickness struck. Others, yet to succumb, found they could not keep their feet on the ever-moving deck.

He intended the cruise to be a gentle affair, so that a change to sail down past Ramsgate involved no more than hauling on the yards. Yet he knew difficulties would arise when he was required to come about, given there was not much sea room between the

317

North Foreland and the Goodwin Sands. When the time came, the crew would have to be driven to their tasks, regardless of how they felt.

Too many people saw seasickness as a weakness, but Pearce had suffered it himself in the Mediterranean, if only briefly. Even the most experienced sailors could become afflicted, usually on leaving harbour after time spent ashore. Likewise, it was strange to be back on terra firma, when you'd been at sea for weeks on a lifting and falling, as well as a seriously tilting deck.

Right now, he was absorbing the movement with his knees and that would come to others as they became accustomed. He had noted that Hallowell was a bit green, though hiding it, Worricker seemed to be revelling in the motion, while all four midshipmen were stricken. Rufus Dommet would be laid low as he ever was, while Charlie would be mocking the afflicted, which included his fellow Pelican. Oliphant, now aboard, had not appeared, which had Pearce wonder at his condition.

'It wouldn't be so bad if the sods could hit the buckets.'

O'Hagan posited this, in response to a sympathetic aside from his captain, a statement he'd made so often in their time together it was reckoned a mantra. But he had the right of it: nothing was worse for an already troubled gut than the sight and smell of vomit.

Off their starboard bow lay true white cliffs, so much purer in colour than those around Dover, as well as the entrance to the River Stour bracketed by a marsh floodplain. He would have to make his turn before he came abreast of the Sandwich Flats. Anticipating it to be a slow process, he called everyone up from below with ample time to spare. He watched to see how many of his topmen looked nimble and for others who clambered up the shrouds like a crab. There were too many of the latter.

If *Hazard* groaned as she wore round, so did her captain, as well as anyone used to the sea. It was so slow in execution, she nearly failed the full turn, a lucky and slightly stronger gust of wind bringing her head round in time to avoid missing stays. On her new course, the waves slapping into and lifting the stern changed the nature of the pitch and roll, to no doubt claim new victims.

The cruise, if it could justify that description, took nearly the whole of the day and, once more at anchor off Faversham Creek, the job of cleaning the ship became a priority. The smell of vinegar soon overpowered that of sick, but it was a weary crew who took to their hammocks, Pearce having decided that for this night, an anchor watch would serve, so as many as possible could rest.

'How do you fare, Mr Livingston?'

They were sharing a watch, not that Pearce was required to, but such times, when the ship was quiet and there were few people about, provided a chance to get to know a person like the midshipman.

The 'I fare well, sir' was a fib.

'You will overcome it, be assured. Seasickness passes.'

'Aye, aye, sir.' This sounded unconvincing.

There was a temptation to enquire into how he was faring with his fellow mids, but that had to be suppressed. The three older lads had moved to the orlop, but being so tender in years, Livingston had stayed with Mrs Low. While that would save him from off-duty bullying, it did not bar it during working hours. As a source of endemic harassment, few places could compare with a midshipman's berth, which had Pearce bless his good fortune in having a quartet of real youngsters.

There were fellows in their thirties who still clung to the position, sitting and regularly failing to pass for lieutenant, kept in place only though their connections. Taken aboard by a captain, it would usually be a favour to a relative, a close friend, or the man's own patron, a senior officer or some titled peer.

Would he have passed if he'd had to sit the exam? There was no way of telling, yet had it been at the time he was promoted, it would have been highly doubtful given his lack of time at sea. Odd, that then all he could think about was getting out of the navy, which foundered on several things, the key one being the need to aid his Pelicans not cheered at the prospect of life ashore.

Nothing had prepared the young John Pearce for anything other than as a radical opponent of monarchical government. Even that had fallen somewhat after what he saw as the debacle of the French Revolution. How high had been the aspirations when the Bastille fell, how low it had sunk in the bloodbath of the Terror, which had dispirited and consumed his own father.

It was gloomy introspection again, so he was glad when the bell rang to bring Mr Hallowell on deck to take over, along with Campbell. Entering his cabin he found Oliphant, who should have at this time been asleep, waiting for him, drinking his wine and eager to tell him it was time they got on with their mission. He even referred to the overused cliché of time and tide waiting for no man.

'Did you witness our efforts today?'

'I stayed out of the way, kept to my cot, but by the mood in the wardroom, I can guess it was not, what should it be called . . . ?' He paused, his eyes lighting up, 'Plain sailing?'

'Not funny and neither was the experience.'

'We can't delay for ever, Pearce. Dundas must think we're on our way already.'

'He can think all he likes, he is not on board.'

'What if matters are resolved before we weigh?' The look Pearce was getting had no humour in it now, more proper concern. 'What need then of us and this ship? He made it plain to me, matters were close to becoming critical.'

'I see no advantage in us foundering for want of skill.'

'Can I ask if you are exaggerating that possibility?'

Pearce had to admit it was possible he was being overcautious. Plenty men-o'-war put to sea with crews at less than full competence and managed to get to their destination. Quite a few even went into battle in such a condition. There were any number of things that could cause a vessel to founder but, outside an unexpected hurricane, poor handling was rarely the cause.

That did not take into account being driven onto a lee shore, running aground where the hull could be damaged, fire, which was much feared for the speed at which a vessel could become very like a torch, or losing masts in a gale. All were everyday risks, but in normal sailing things could go less than perfectly, damage could be sustained, but ships were built to stay afloat so any situation usually left time for retrieval.

'I will discuss the weather with Mr Williams and gauge his opinion.'

'Which sounds like an excuse to do nothing.'

Another cliché came to mind about being caught between two stools. Oliphant was right, they could not delay indefinitely and never mind Dundas. His conversation with Sir David Rose at Gibraltar had more than hinted what Britannia feared could quickly come to pass.

'I will try to get away in the next few days.'

'The next two days would be more comforting.'

'Speaking of comfort, how is the wardroom?'

'Your surgeon seems a decent cove, Williams is an old woman, Hallowell and Worricker are too young to be interesting and Moberly is a bore. Did you know he played the flute?'

'I could hardly fail to hear it.'

'What you will not hear is anything approaching a tune.'

'Well, you will oblige me by returning there. I have letters to write. Another thing, send ashore tomorrow for some personal stores of your own, not least some wine.'

The letters included a repeat communication to the Admiralty, the fourth on the subject, for another lieutenant and a master-at-arms. The latter, should there be a choice, someone recommended for the position by a respected officer under whom he had served.

The quill paused as he thought of Michael, presently doing the job, and the description in the regulations, which said any person, so put forward, should be sober, orderly, respectful and obedient. O'Hagan qualified for orderly, but nothing more. It brought forth a soft chuckle. Next, he penned another letter to Emily, which Oliphant could take ashore in the morning. She would be getting his; he was not getting replies, if indeed there were any.

Sat in a nightgown, she was writing at the same time as he, replying to his last letter sent from Chatham, with gossip regarding Adam and his almost magical progress, which amounted to increased smiling and his disinclination to sleep through the night. He was the reason she was awake. She told him briefly of what had happened regarding Gherson, though she was circumspect about Hodgson and what he intended. This he had vouchsafed to her before he departed.

John would not approve of her getting involved with Gherson. He would certainly disapprove of what Hodgson had got her to pen before he left. Sanded and sealed with wax, and with Adam now asleep, she went back to bed.

Walter Hodgson set off for Newgate early, knowing he was in for a testing meeting. He had decided, on first acquaintance, he disliked Gherson intensely, and all that had occurred since did nothing to change that opinion. As for him hanging, his view was that if he was not to swing for Catherine Carruthers, there was probably, in his past, enough villainy to justify a rope; he was the type for crime.

Druce was protecting his brother-in-law, that was obvious, and he knew what it meant for him. He would soft-soap him now, hint at more paid employment, but once Gherson was disposed of, he would want any connection severed. That was still in his mind when he entered Gherson's cell to find him being shaved. He nodded and sat on the cot to wait.

'Do you have a spare coin for the barber, Mr Hodgson?'

This came with a knowing look, yet there was no surprise for the thief-taker that his name was out. He had dealt with Crossley and that could not be done without it being noticed. Warder gossip would take care of the rest. Likewise, the request for money was done to assert Gherson's dominance but it was not worth the concern to refuse. Very shortly he would knock him off his perch.

'Had you told me you were calling, I would have delayed my breakfast.'

The coin was passed to the barber and he departed, shutting a door it was unnecessary to lock; no one sought to escape from the State House.

'And you are obliged to sit on the bed. I really must demand another chair.'

'Perhaps for Denby Carruthers.'

Gherson tried to hide the jolt the name engendered. He failed, though it had to be said, only for a moment. That irritating smirk was soon back. Dislike him he might, but Hodgson still had to acknowledge his cunning.

'Who is he?'

'Please, Gherson, do not insult me.'

Such was his arrogance, he couldn't resist the sneering rejoinder, and for Hodgson it showed his Achilles heel.

'Why ever not? Is that not what you're here for, to take insults for another?'

'You'd be a fool to think so and I don't rate you that. But I do wonder, if you were acquitted of murdering his wife, what do you think Carruthers would do?' There was no response. 'Or is it you think you and he might be exchanging places?'

The smirk was gone now and a long silence ensued, coupled with an unblinking stare. There were things that did not have to be said to Gherson for he knew them already. Carruthers, rich, betrayed and furious, had sent his wife to find him. He had also sent the pair of brutes to see her atone for her sin.

'If you now know my name, you will also be aware of how I make my way in the world. But you will be in ignorance of one fact. I was engaged to search for you and the fees for my work came from Denby Carruthers. Would you care to tell me why that would be?'

'I would not.'

'Which makes even stranger my actual instructions were to fail to do so. My hunt was a pretence.'

'Instructions from whom?'

'I doubt you require me to tell you.'

Gherson had made a great effort to remove any clues to his thoughts from his expression; nothing was to be given away by reaction.

'Let us go back to Carruthers, the man whose wife you rogered. How upset was he? Angry and humiliated enough to go to extremes, indeed to seek to dispose of you off London Bridge. Why not a second time when that failed?'

That furrowed Gherson's brow; he was well aware of what was being referred to, he just didn't know how Hodgson had acquired the information. Only those on HMS *Brilliant* possessed any knowledge and that was partial – what he chose to tell them, which was not the whole truth.

'The question surely occurs to you?'

'It may.'

'It must. You were carousing in Covent Garden when Catherine Carruthers found you. It's doubtful she would have friends or spies in such a location, so who told her where to look? Her husband, perhaps, but who told him?'

Silence and a pinched look. He had left Druce's office,

325

telling the prize agent where he could be found. He had no idea Hodgson was guessing and his observation was something of a shot in the dark.

'Yet you seem to be relying on that source to get you freed.'

There being no point in more obfuscation, Gherson spoke plain and, in doing so, vindicated Hodgson's guesswork. 'It would be in his interest to do so.'

'Which could only be true if you had evidence of Carruthers' involvement and I doubt that to be the case. The question is, if you seek to bluff Druce, will he fall for it? You see yourself as clever and I admit you have certain abilities in that area. But happen you might be too clever by half.'

'You flatter yourself to think so.'

'Do I? You sent a note to Mrs Barclay . . .'

'How do you know about that?' he barked, composure gone.

'If you are free to do so – not in prison, say – it is possible to find things out.'

'So it was she who told you about London Bridge.'

'Just as you told her about certain doubtful trades being carried out with the Barclay funds, something that imparted directly and before the crime could have had little effect, given you would be incriminating yourself.'

Hodgson had to leave him room to react, but he was not surprised by his silence.

'You did so, knowing full well she would challenge Druce. He would smoke her suspicions and the source. From there it was a short step to him giving you what you asked for through my agency. That you did not anticipate, you expected him to come and see you himself. I'm sure you would have promised him your silence, knowing he would not believe you. When were you going to threaten him with the rest?'

'You assume a great deal.'

'Because I know a great deal. You think Druce will sacrifice his brother-in-law to save you.'

'To save himself. I have the means to ruin both him and Ommaney and I will have my chance to do so in court. That pamphlet you threw at me tells me my words would be widely disseminated.'

'Ah, the right of the accused to speak. And Mrs Barclay?'

'I owe her nothing, less than nothing. Wrong, I owe her my contempt.'

'Handy, when you reckon to have the means to blackmail her.' When he didn't respond, Hodgson merely said. 'The child.'

'The bastard child.'

'What if it is she who could save you?'

'I cannot see how.'

'I can tell you now, Druce will not lift a finger and he has done nothing that might prove help to your innocence, even given the chance to do so. I showed him the drawings I brought to you, two of which are true likenesses of a pair, sailors by their garb, who left the Barrington salon minutes after you and Mrs Carruthers. They could be the men who laid you out and ravaged the poor woman, no doubt on instruction but for foul satisfaction as well. I put forward the notion they be printed and disseminated. He declined that suggestion.'

'Where are those drawings now?'

Hodgson responded with a humourless smile; Gherson was getting to where he needed him to be, any sense of his being in control evaporating.

'In his possession, where I suspect they will stay. That is unless he destroys them or allows Carruthers to do so.'

His scheming was falling apart but he was reluctant to admit it and his response was petulant. 'I shall have my say.'

'Last words, which might raise questions about Ommaney and Druce, but they will be laid at the door of an aggrieved associate who may be a swindler. Accusations against Denby Carruthers will prove nothing and be a nine-day wonder.'

'I pray it to be more than that.'

'Even if he is brought to justice, what good will that do you in your pauper's grave? And that you will be lucky to get if you are freed. A man who has tried to kill you twice will not be afraid of a third attempt. And, now you are famous, your likeness in all those pamphlets, it will be impossible to hide.'

A full minute of reflection followed, Gherson gnawing on his prospects, the thief-taker wearing the wry smile of certainty.

'What are you proposing?' he whispered eventually, like a broken spirit.

'I have consulted a lawyer and he is of the opinion that the right person pleading can get you acquitted.'

'Who?'

'They will be named once you have listed for me all the dubious transactions you entered into with Ommaney and Druce on the Barclay account, a document I will have attested by a notary public.'

'To do so would be to surrender my leverage.'

'You don't have any leverage, Gherson. But Mrs Barclay, with that information, has a great deal and it will be used to benefit you. That will include your well-being when you are released, for she will not chase for a public shaming, only reimbursement. In short, the reputation of Ommaney and Druce will remain unsullied.'

'Why?'

'I do believe you pleaded Christian charity when you met her. If there is doubt about your guilt, she cannot countenance an innocent man going to the gallows, even one she dislikes with all her heart.'

'She hates me.'

'That is not a sentiment she allows herself, for it is a sin.'

'I will still be at risk.'

'True, but ask yourself what Druce both wants and needs. Then ask who has the means to stay Carruthers' hand?'

'How will I know he has succeeded?'

'You won't.' Hodgson reached into his pocket and produced a folded letter, which he opened and began to read. 'There's much here about Captain Barclay and what a fine and upstanding officer he was . . .'

'Forgive me if I jeer. The man was a fool and such a person and their money are soon parted. In the case of that dupe, it was he and his wife who were even sooner parted.'

'Enjoy your joke, but listen: "I feel it my duty to recommend to whosoever reads this reference that the good character and abilities of Cornelius Gherson cannot be overpraised. He served my late husband diligently and well, bringing to him not only his skill with accounts and ledgers but, having served before the mast, an acute knowledge of how to work and sail a ship of war."

'There's more, but you have no need to hear it. Such a saint will seek to ensure you are not the victim of a murder.' The letter was folded and returned to the pocket. 'That will be signed as soon as you provide what Mrs Barclay requires. All efforts will be made to get you free and at the expense of Edward Druce. Once that is secured, such a recommendation should get you a place with another ship's captain.'

Gherson was staring straight ahead, thinking hard.

'You hid from me at sea, so I would never have found you even if I had desired to do so. I would say that could be the only place you might be safe.'

CHAPTER TWENTY-FIVE

The two days were up and with Oliphant badgering him, Pearce decided he would have to get away. The day before, for the first time, he had managed two consecutive sailing and anchoring drills, which had gone reasonably smoothly. The most notable thing was the lower level of shouting; the men were beginning to function as a collective instead of individuals, and when asked over dinner in the great cabin, Hallowell and Worricker pronounced themselves pleased. On the excuse of a conference to examine the same subject he called Michael, Charlie and Rufus to join him over toasted cheese for an opinion.

'I spoke to Mr Williams and asked what weather we might expect in the coming days.'

'Sure, we've had it forgiving, John-boy.'

Charlie countered O'Hagan. 'For my money, Michael, that begs a wager: the elements will turn.'

'What did Crock of Shit say?' Rufus asked.

'Has everybody been given a new name?' Pearce chuckled, though; the bosun deserved his moniker for his general misery. 'He declined to be drawn.'

'Hanged, drawn and quartered would suit.'

'Let's agree no certainty is possible,' Pearce insisted. 'But it can only be guessed at. Mr Williams is of the opinion the recent weather should continue and I don't feel qualified to argue with him. More important is your opinions on how the crew are shaping?'

The question was aimed squarely at his temporary watch captains, not O'Hagan. They were closest to the men, working with and supervising the duties they undertook.

'Some are shaping up a bit,' was the opinion of Rufus. 'I would recommend Foster to be yeoman of the tops, he being a real worker and keen. There's good among the dross. Others, well they'll never make a sailor as long as their arse is pointing south.'

'Usual mix, John, good to useless.'

'Charlie, I'm asking if I can take us out to sea.'

'Only doing it will tell. Reckon Bastard Barclay thought the same when *Brilliant* weighed with us aboard.'

'Jesus,' Michael cried, 'do you recall it!'

'It was learn quick, all right,' Rufus said. 'Had my back struck a dozen times with a rattan those first days.'

'Got off light, then,' Charlie joked, only it was not really funny.

Recalling his own imposed service, Pearce realised in recollection just how much he had absorbed in their first few days at sea. A man-o'-war in service had a rhythm to the day and it imposed itself on all aboard, top to bottom, from the men being roused out of their hammocks to the master-at-arms dousing what lights were not required at day's end.

Barclay had crept down the channel, with older hands willing to talk to the newcomers, pointing out there was always a harbour or an anchorage in the offing for which to run, all the way down to Falmouth. It was then helm down for Ushant and by the time they had weathered that Breton Island, some of what was being drummed into, and occasionally beaten into them, had been absorbed. Would his crew be likewise?

The tempo of shipboard existence imposed itself. A bell, which tolled throughout the day and night, each clang pointing to some duty or other – high wind, foul weather or an enemy in the offing – being the only thing to break the pattern. Rise and shine, swab and flog were daily; other duties were worked out over the days, sometimes in weeks and months, but would it be the best way to instil experience into the crew of *Hazard*?

'We have to weigh and get to sea, which we will do in the morning just after the tide peaks. So anyone who has letters to send, best get them penned and ready to go ashore.'

'I don't think he's talking to us, lads,' said Charlie.

The news they were leaving could not be kept from the crew – few things could – and it was telling that, while some were excited, as many were worried to varying degrees. Pearce took to the poop after the deck was swabbed, to talk to the crew before they went to breakfast – not the best time, given rumbling bellies. He had them gather aft as they did on a Sunday, a sea of expectant faces, who reckoned they knew what was coming: a rousing speech 'to raise their spirits'.

'A tot of grog would do that.'

It was Teach who voiced the complaint. Back on light duties, he had not lost his ability to make everything sound like an imposition. But that same flogging had blown away some of his bluster, while those he messed with were less unhappy with their lot and, it had to be said, less inclined to defer to him.

'Belay that blathering,' called Michael softly, well aware of who to target. Teach's head shrunk into his shoulders.

This time there were no marines at Pearce's back. They, with Moberly, had been lined up at the rear, out of the line of sight, that being a less threatening location. His lieutenants and mids he had lined up at the front, backs to the hands. Pearce wanted no sense of intimidation to blunt his message. Once on the poop, looking into that sea of faces, he was assailed with the notion, a recurring one in his life, that what he was doing was fraudulent.

'A good morning to you,' he began, taking off his hat to underline this was to be informal. 'As yet I do not know all of you, but you know me, or at least what I look like. How many of you take pleasure in what you see, I will leave unspoken.'

Some chortled, most did not; it was not, in truth, a very good quip. 'We are about to pluck our anchor, as we have done many times days past, but with a difference. We will not be coming back to Faversham Creek.'

Some looked surprised, which Pearce took to be play-acting. The ship had been abuzz since dawn. 'I will not tell you our destination, but it is a long way off and, by the time we get there, I expect you to be as capable a crew as any in the service.'

Dropping eyes gave a lie in many minds to that possibility. 'I sense many of you doubt it, but I speak from having been where you are now.'

How many knew his story? He suspected most, if not all, for it was no kept secret and some would have plucked up the courage to quiz the Pelicans about him. It was a case then of tell one, tell all.

'Being at sea, where this ship belongs, will bring on your skills at a speed you would barely credit, again something I know from having been through it. The plain fact is I will depend on you and you will depend on me. That is how a ship works and there is no other method that will keep us safe and certainly none that will make us effective in battle, which I am determined we should be. I wish you good luck. Mr Hallowell.'

'Mr Crocker,' Hallowell called, 'pipe the hands to breakfast.'

'I am so tempted to applaud, Pearce,' Oliphant said, coming from where he had been resting, with his back to the taffrail. 'Not a fighting speech but . . .'

'We weigh in two hours. I suggest you put in your gut what will shortly be spewing out again.'

He looked about to deny he had, like many of the crew, suffered that day when they had sailed past Margate, but then thought better of it.

The wind was in the prevailing direction, still in the south-west and stiff enough to promise a swift exit to the Channel, their route out of home waters. From there it would be necessary to tack and wear but that would suit Pearce. It meant constant work on the yards and should mean some adjustment to the sails, the very thing he wanted. There was no coastal creeping this time; he wanted to be far out in deep water, which would take him closer to Flushing than the Kent coast.

He could then head down the Channel towards the Lizard, knowing – the narrows apart – he would not be short of sea room. Men were sick and they hit a running sea, but fewer than on the previous occasion, another cause for optimism. This was easy to maintain under a sky of slow-moving clouds, interspersed with patches of blue sky, the sea switching from green to blue as it reflected what lay overhead. Everything was going to be fine.

'All hands to come about.'

Mr Williams was by the binnacle, Michael was on the wheel. The men let fly the sheets and hauled round the yards, to reset them near fore and aft. A couple of reefs were taken out of the courses to gain more way, needed given the wind, which had been off their stern and was now on the beam. Once round, the deck canted over some ten degrees, which caused much staggering gait, this as the prow rose and fell in harmony with the run of the sea as they made for the South Foreland.

The day wore on and slowly but steadily they progressed into the narrows, both shores now fully visible from the tops, and it was up there Pearce chose to take himself, clambering up the weather shrouds. All of his midshipmen were at his back, young Livingston climbing for the first time, it being a good idea to let the men see that those who exercised authority, which was total in his case, nervously applied by the youngsters, were as capable and as fearless as any man aboard.

'Mr Livingston, you must keep up,' came the call from the mainmast cap.

'Aye aye, sir.'

The Mite, as Pearce saw him, would have struggled to do so regardless, with his lack of height and reach, but there was reluctance as well.

'The wind is on your back. As long as you are clapped on with one hand, nothing bad can befall you.'

Was it the word 'befall' that took his feet away? Pearce had no idea, only that Livingston, halfway up from the bulwarks, was reliant on that one hand while his shoes were waving in thin air. He was heading down in a flash, glad to see that Worricker, who had the deck, was racing to get to him from below and he got there first, to take the boy's weight and get him safely fixed hands and feet.

By that time his captain was right above him, looking down at a face full of terror, telling him not to look down but up and proffering a hand. That was taken to be firmly gripped, the pull bringing him closer and, the shrouds still being wide enough, alongside. From there it was ratline by ratline until Livingston could be pushed through the lubber's hole, his captain joining him to find the boy trembling.

'I beg forgiveness, sir.'

'For what, a slip of a shoe?'

'Which did not happen to the others.'

'Stand up and look,' was obeyed, Pearce pointing out the coast of England and France. 'There. How many people in Bathgate can say they have seen such a sight?'

'None, sir,' was the tremulous response.

'It is your first. Would you believe me when I say that in a few weeks' time you will have me yelling at you and promising a feel of the birch for skylarking in the rigging?'

The direct look, in a pair of blue eyes full of purity, as he gazed up at a smiling Pearce, denied such a thing was possible.

'Do you feel able to make the crosstrees with me at your back?'

This was a test and, if he failed it, John Pearce would have a problem. The Mite had to be given time to grow and find his way, but he could not keep a midshipman that failed to match his topmen. An aspiring officer had to be able to do everything on a ship in the same way and to a matching standard as the crew. It was his job to make that happen and he had an idea that might help.

The boy was on his own too much and, if the gunner's wife was not his mother – he hoped for a kinder and more comely soul in Bathgate – she was too close to the reality for him to know he was in the navy. Separating him kept him away from bonding with those with whom he would serve.

'It occurs, Mr Livingston, that you should shift from under the care of Mrs Low and join your fellows on the orlop.'

It was not taken with glee, more confusion, so there was no telling if he was sad or glad. All Pearce could do was take him to the next set of shrouds, give him an encouraging look and oblige him to climb, thinking one day he might have this happen with Adam, who could be just as fearful. It was not a thought to cherish.

As they climbed, he called to the other three to shift out onto a yard and vacate the crosstrees so the Mite could occupy the space. They sat, looking down at a prow dipping into the sea, throwing up white water, some of which wetted the foredeck. Men, looking like ants, were working, for there was rarely a moment of inactivity at sea. On deck the master was looking up, which was in itself a message.

'We must go down soon, as we'll be coming round onto another tack. I will not permit you a backstay, Mr Livingston, you must go the way you came. And since I am an old crock, I reckon to do likewise. Probably best I go first, for if I tumble onto you, I cannot expect you to catch me.' The chuckle was manufactured. 'I'll take you all the way to the deck, for sure.'

'Sir.'

A call to the others saw Jock the Sock and Campbell use a backstay, to speedily make the deck, while Tennant used the lee shrouds, not good practice, but which would pass without comment. There was no shame in that yet, but the time would come. He went down slowly, repeating the mantra of one hand clapped on, his own free hand hovering below the Mite's feet.

'Any sign of Mr Oliphant, Michael?'

'None, the Holy Trinity be thanked.'

He was in his cabin, encased in the endless paperwork, when the marine sentry knocked, opened the door, then called to announce the master.

'Mr Williams?'

'Bit of a drop in the glass, Mr Pearce, if you'd care to look. We might be in for a blow.'

So much for no change in the weather. Pearce stood to look and tap his own barometer which, by the level of the mercury, confirmed what Williams was saying. 'It's not precipitous, but we'll keep an eye on it.'

'English Channel,' was intoned as Pearce went back to his desk to sit down.

These were words that had him look up, obviously in deep

thought, and there was no need to add more. For sudden storms, there were few places more disposed than the sea between Normandy and England. There was an option to run for a safe harbour if danger threatened, not that he was so inclined. His crew would have to face bad weather sometime and, if soonest was not ideal, it might just serve to blood them early.

Dover, the closest, was tricky to enter and he worried about how his men would fare at what would be a complex manoeuvre. He could make for Deal Roads and the protection of the Goodwins. Yet approaching those sandbars, if the sea cut up rough, was fraught with peril, even if the tide was likely to be low and much would be visible. As a graveyard for ships, it was without parallel on the coast of Britannia. Dover was the lesser of twin evils, but that would mean coming right up into the wind, which would make progress near to impossible.

'As I said, we will keep an eye on it.'

Which he was later to acknowledge was one of the worst judgements he had ever made as a commanding officer. Busy with ledgers he failed to keep an occasional eye on his own barometer. When he finally got round to looking, the mercury had dropped at an alarming rate. In consultation with Williams they agreed seeking harbour was getting less possible by the bell and they were running out of daylight, which made Dover too risky and Deal positively deadly.

Hallowell and Worricker were called in to give a view and it was agreed to come about while it was still a relatively straightforward exercise, not that it was as simple as it had been only a few hours earlier. They could use the huge amount of sea room that afforded and, if required, they could run for the expanse of the North Sea.

It was a blessing, and the only one, that as the weather deteriorated they had time to make things secure. This put pressure on those who could do what was required without instruction. Even getting the chicken coop below turned into a major crisis when the birds got loose. Down below extra straw was being laid in the manger to protect the pigs and the goat.

Foster, newly appointed as yeoman, along with the bosun and the master, had storm canvas hauled out for the topsails and foresails, the normal suits brought down and stored; everything else would be clewed up. Getting that aloft and bent on in the increasing pitch and roll, plus a strengthening wind, taxed what little ability existed.

Pearce had no choice but to leave them to it. The swivels had to be struck below, as well as any round shot from the deck rings, the cannon trunnions secured with double lashings tight against the gunport cover. In addition, Hallowell and Worricker were rigging extra stays on the masts, while down below everything moveable was either being tied down or struck into the hold, where it should be jammed to keep it secure, this accomplished with anything which would serve.

Luckily the boats were inboard, so extra lines were all they needed. Oliphant was roused out of his cot when the panels arrived to cover the casements, so if the glass was stove in no water would penetrate. Relieving tackles had to be rigged on the rudder, to help those on the wheel, which would become a burden to spin. But what slowed matters was the utter lack of basic seamanship.

The crew were willing, many more than that, but everything requiring to be done had to be preceded by a shouted instruction and it was inevitable confusion gained the upper hand. Some canvas meant to cover one of the hatchways went over the side due to poor handling. Barrels that should have been secured got loose and, being full, were a cause of injuries as men tried to stop them without using a pair of oars or some kind of a lever.

By the time darkness came and the wind in the rigging had turned to a scream, they were running north-east ahead of a sea that only these waters could produce. The waves were not as high as ocean waters, it was the lack of room between the caps that made it dangerous. And then the rain came, blown near to horizontal, to run in rivulets off the men in oilskins, hanging on to the huge steering wheel to keep their feet as much as seeking to control the ship.

CHAPTER TWENTY-SIX

In full darkness, for those on the quarterdeck, the world shrank to what could be seen by the light of the binnacle and that was barely enough to show another body never mind anything outside its arc. Being clad in oilskins provided some protection but nothing could stop flying spume from finding the gaps in any garment, so everyone had cold water running in, to soak their inner clothing.

John Pearce, the master, Michael O'Hagan and a trio of the strongest men aboard fought to keep the head from falling off, which would expose either beam to the waves, while down below men hauled on ropes, at commands passed down, to work the rudder. Nowhere was dry: *Hazard* was shipping water with every wave as the following sea lifted the stern and drove down the bow. This allowed the sea to ship masses of water over the foredeck, a great deal of that making its way to the lower decks, to swill around before it seeped through to the bilge.

If conditions on deck were harsh, down below was not much better. The clanking of the pumps could not be heard by the wheel, but they were a permanent noise below as teams of tars and marines, overseen by Moberly, took turns at keeping the right equilibrium between what was coming aboard and what was being discharged, with the carpenter continually checking the level in the well. Oliphant, with no duties to perform, stayed in his cot, which being slung from the deck beams remained fairly static as the ship pitched and bucked like an unbroken steed.

If it was a baptism of chaos for the crew, it was worse for the midshipmen, called to various duties with only the vaguest instruction from Hallowell and Worricker as to how to carry them out. They must ensure various artefacts stayed where they had been stowed, gather a party if called upon to take an injured seaman to the cockpit, there being a constant run of accidents from the slight to the broken bone.

At the same time and no doubt in fear of drowning themselves, they had to look unconcerned as they staggered from place to place, always with one hand clapped tight on to a man rope, checking the trunnions and cannon remained secure, ensuring no rigging had frayed or blocks had parted from their tackle.

Another task, accepted in turns, was to take to the quarterdeck the approximate speed the ship was making, accuracy being impossible, to see relieved the man casting the log into the boiling sea, a duty that could only be maintained for a very short time. It was a task for which no one would volunteer, so they found for the first time the misery of dealing with truly sullen resentment.

Cullen and his assistants, under a swinging lantern, stitched, bandaged and splinted as required, with Mr Livingston required to take to the captain a list of those afflicted: if it was someone he had promoted to a position of some responsibility, they had to be replaced and all Pearce had was a memory of the muster from which to choose.

Not all the marines were engaged in physical toil. A double and regularly changing guard had been placed on the spirit room. If quota men lacked time at sea, they would share with every tar the notion that if you were going to drown, it was best to do so blind drunk. When called on deck, as they had to be from time to time, it must have appeared to the crew as though hell had come from the deep to claim their souls.

'We must seek to establish our position, Mr Williams.'

For the first time in an age, John Pearce could communicate in something approaching a normal tone. Outside the master's chart room, into which they had slipped to talk, the screaming of the wind through the rigging meant even a full shout might not be heard. Williams had been recording the supposed speed every time one of the dripping mids reported. He had brought the slate inside and on his desk lay the chart that showed the area he reckoned they had been driven into. Pearce noted they were now past Gravelines, which, on the mainland coast, marked the point where the English Channel gave way to the North Sea.

Pearce could see, without being told, that a slight change of course was required. It could not be certain, the plotting was far from precise, but HMS *Hazard* appeared to be heading too close to a lee shore for comfort, which meant calling all hands on deck to haul on the sheets and bring round several degrees the scrap of storm canvas, which was all that was driving the sloop forward.

The notion of coming about and sailing head-on into the wind was not possible. It might have been on a ship with a fully worked-up and long-at-sea crew. But to get aloft what was needed to retain motion on the vessel was beyond the men he had under his command. Pearce was tempted to ask Williams for an appreciation as to when the wind might moderate but stopped himself. He would be asking a fellow who had predicted benign sailing conditions before they weighed and the older man might take it as a criticism.

It did ease as the hint of a grey dawn hit the eastern sky. Then, with the kind of suddenness with which it had come upon them, it began to blow itself out, leaving behind it very disturbed water and an exhausted crew, from captain to nipper. A day of cold provision had done nothing for the mood, even if few could have kept much down, so it was a blessing to see smoke coming from the chimney as the cook got his coppers firing.

There was no time for rest: HMS *Hazard* was a man-o'-war and, as such, had to be ready to engage an enemy at all times. Their position seemed to put them north of Flushing in latitude, which showed just how far they had been driven. This put the ship off the shores of the so-called Batavian Republic, enemy territory. Even if Admiral Duncan's fleet should be not too far off, guarding the Texel, danger could threaten in a trice.

It was not possible to run out the guns at dawn, the deck was still heaving, but that did not mean avoiding the ship standing to until Pearce was sure he could see a grey goose at a quarter mile, to ensure there was no enemy in sight. Likewise, clearing up both on deck and below had to be undertaken at once, for a vessel all ahoo was in no condition to fight.

His crew grumbled, but John Pearce set a well-practised face against such belly-aching. He had been obliged to impose exacting conditions in previous commands and this would be no exception. So, as the day wore on, with only a minimal break to eat, everything was put back in order. The pumps were kept going until Mr Low was satisfied the well was at the level it should be.

The last task, now that the sea state seemed to be settling, with the wind shifting to an easterly, was to come about under what they had aloft. The storm canvas was exchanged for a lighter weave, once they had got up the topgallants. This required the use of the capstan, combined with complex execution to get them seated and secured. Soon *Hazard* was heading south again under a proper suit of sails.

'Michael, I would ask you to oversee the pantry,' Pearce said. 'I believe I owe my officers and mids a capital dinner. I doubt the skill exists at present to provide it.'

'Sure, I'll grow another pair of hands, John-boy,' was the acerbic response. But he agreed to oversee the preparation of the food, at which he had, in the past year, become very adept.

Before any dinner, and as the sea calmed, he had to hear, in turn, the reports of his inferiors as to how the men had functioned; who had been attentive to any duty required of them and who had proved less than willing. The name of Teach came up from Jock the Sock when it was his turn, Pearce having to cover a sigh: the man was a nuisance.

'I ordered him to take a turn on casting the log, sir, and he refused.'

'Outright?'

'To begin with, then he claimed to not yet be fit for the duty.'

'But he went to it in the end, I hope?'

'He did, when I said I would have no choice but to report his behaviour to you.'

He was impressed with Maclehose. Given his age, it could not have been easy to stand before a grown man and, having given an order, hold his ground in the face of what amounted to rebuff. Pearce wished he could have been a witness to the exchange, to have seen how both parties played out the clash of wills.

'Your recommendation, Mr Maclehose?' There the youth of the lad showed itself; he was unsure how to respond. 'Do you see it as insubordination?'

'I lack the knowledge to answer, sir.'

'It comes down to how you rate his actions in terms of possible punishment?'

'I had not thought on it, sir.'

'I would request you do so now and please feel free to come to your own decision. I will not think the better or worse of you, whatever it is.'

Maclehose blinked. The uncertainty was palpable. 'I believe he was afraid, sir, as were many of the crew throughout the storm. It was mayhem below and even worse on deck and I cannot find it in myself to condemn a man for hesitation.'

'I hope you were afraid yourself.' Several more blinks followed as he sought to take that in. 'I admire bravery but abhor stupidity. Anyone who was not concerned for their life over these last hours, I would place in the latter category. So, Teach?'

'Would it be appropriate to stop his grog?'

348

'I don't think you understand, Mr Maclehose. You are required to recommend an action to me.'

'Then will that suffice, sir?'

'Only if you're content.' Pearce looked him up and down, taking in his working clothes, streaked with dried salt. 'Now I suggest you return to your berth and spruce up. I do not desire to entertain scruffs to dinner.'

With the private storeroom full from Faversham, Michael was able to cook two brace of duck. Pearce had also acquired some Kent cherries, a pricey fruit in London but an abundant and inexpensive crop locally. The host was determined at this, the first occasion he had invited everyone, to be generous with his store of wine.

It was a cramped affair – he had to borrow chairs from all over the ship – but it soon turned convivial. Even Oliphant was in the right frame of mind and over his *mal de mer*, no doubt relived to be able to fill his belly without the prospect of subsequent retching.

'Gentlemen,' Pearce said, when the ducks were no more than stripped bones, 'I wish to congratulate you all on how we managed in the recent blow. I must admit to misgiving that we would come out of it so well.'

He went round the table bestowing gratitude individually: the master; Mr Cullen, who had dealt with fourteen casualties with varying injuries: gashes, fractured ribs, any number of cuts and abrasions and one broken leg. Hallowell, Worricker and Moberly were singled out and then he came to the midshipmen, who had been silent, overawed by the occasion and slow to the bottle, fitting given their age.

'I must praise you, young gentlemen, and I would ask that we, your seniors in age if not wisdom, charge our glasses for a toast to you. You have faced a crisis and come through it with colours flying.'

'Jesus Christ, John-boy,' Michael O'Hagan whispered from the pantry, his words covered by the loud agreement at the table. 'I have employed a trowel in my time, but never with so much shit on it.'

'Sorry, Mr O'Hagan?' asked one of the boys who'd served at table

This got a shake of the head and an admonition to, 'Get those vittels down you, son.'

Given the amount of effort expended, Pearce reckoned it wise to shorten sail overnight. He wanted the crew to rest, so the watches were skeleton – just enough hands to see to what was needed and regularly relieved. But everybody was roused out before dawn and, this time, the guns were run out and ready to take on anything that appeared out of the darkness.

Slowly a set of sails took shape and Pearce ordered the helm put down to close. Full daylight revealed a fully laden merchant vessel lumbering along under the yellow cross on a blue background, the flag of the neutral Kingdom of Sweden. They may be non-belligerent but what were they carrying and who were they supplying?

Pearce kept his telescope to his eye, thinking the sea state did not permit for too close an approach and there was a chance to see how a boat crew would behave in what was a really heavy swell. Having called for the backing of the sails, he gave an order to an expectant premier.

'Mr Hallowell, prepare to cross and check the Swede for destination and cargo.'

The capstan was manned again and in number, for it was no

easy lift to get the cutter off its chocks, swing it over the side and lower it into the water with four of his men in it already. The rest of the rowers, as well as Hallowell and Campbell, joined them and Pearce watched how they performed, for this was boating out in the open sea, which called for precise oar work.

There was a degree of reassurance that all was as it should be; the merchantman was making no attempt to evade inspection and, as Hallowell was brought alongside, the gangway was opened to permit him to board, leaving his boat crew and the midshipmen bobbing in the water. His premier was aboard for some time, more than his captain would have reckoned necessary, but he eventually reappeared and clambered down to be rowed back to *Hazard*.

When he came back aboard Pearce noticed his rather flushed face, so instead of enquiring on deck he called for the premier to join him in his cabin. Hat off, Hallowell made his report; the vessel was indeed a neutral with a mixed cargo, heading for the Thames Estuary and London. The cargo was timber, high-quality pine for panelling and untreated poles of the same wood suitable for upper masts, turpentine, iron ingots from the northern mines and salted cod in the barrel.

'I sense our friend also had aboard a quantity of spirit,' Pearce suggested.

Hallowell went a deeper shade of red. 'He did indeed, sir. A fairly fiery spirit he claims he distils himself.'

'Which he invited you to try?'

'He has a cousin in the American colonies, sir.'

Pearce was about to remind Hallowell they were no longer colonies or possessions of the British crown. This was halted by his

351

feeling the likes of the Hallowell family would scarce accept they were lost for eternity.

'He was keen to know about the nature of life in Pennsylvania, where his cousin resides.'

'And how many glasses of fiery spirit did that take?'

'The captain was a very insistent fellow.'

'Well, I too am an insistent fellow, Mr Hallowell, and it pleases me that my officers should be sober, which I take leave to point out you are plainly not.'

I'm playing the damned hypocrite again, Pearce thought, as he looked at an abashed Hallowell. *What state was I in, when I came back from visiting Byard aboard HMS* Bedford? Truly, command obliged a man to be dishonest.

'I will make no further reference to it now or in the future, Mr Hallowell, but I hope you take note of my displeasure.'

'Sir.'

'Now, I would suggest there are duties requiring your attention.'

In what were busy sea lanes they saw, over the course of the morning, several ships, Pearce choosing to ask their business through a speaking trumpet, for none shied away, a sure sign of their being blameless. He was, like the crew, eating his dinner when another sail was sighted, this one well ahead of a course that would cross their bow. It would require to be checked but his informant implied he would have ample time to finish eating. He was consuming an apple when the knock came.

'Mr Hallowell?' was the enquiry. His interest pricked.

'The ship ahead, sir. It's flying no flag, has raised more sail and altered course to the south.'

'Her previous course was for home?'

'Mr Williams says most certainly yes.'

'If she was crossing our bow, from where was she coming?'

'The master consulted his charts and did a bit of guesswork.'

Pearce was slightly irritated at having what little time he had to himself disturbed, which resulted in him speaking more forcibly than was warranted. 'Are you asking that I do the same?'

Still seeing himself under a cloud, Hallowell flushed, which got him a full and immediate apology. 'So, what did Mr Williams come up with in his conjecturing?'

'He reckoned the port from which the ship could have come was Gravelines.'

The speed with which his captain was out of his chair and heading for the deck surprised the premier and, when he followed, it was to see John Pearce, coat thrown off, with a telescope being jammed into his breeches, on the way to the shrouds. Soon he was climbing at pace, all the way up to the crosstrees, to sling a leg over the yard and, hauling out the glass, to train it forward.

It told him little to nothing at this distance; not even the name could be made out as the stern was covered with canvas, no doubt a sail being dried after the storm and a good place to do it. But the alteration of course and the putting on of extra sail on the upper spars was curious.

CHAPTER TWENTY-SEVEN

Pearce reckoned everyone on deck would be wondering, first what he was about and next what, if anything, was coming. They were not to be disappointed: even if there were good reasons to do little or nothing, he could not pass up an opportunity to behave, as he would and should, had the ship ahead been an enemy merchantman. He called down his orders.

'Mr Williams, I require that we alter course to close with yonder vessel and I suggest we will need aloft all we can bear. Mr Hallowell, once we have the canvas rigged and drawing, I want you to be ready to clear for action.'

It was gratifying to see the deck burst into a mass of shouting and activity: having no idea there was no threat, everyone was acting as if one existed. The orders rang out and the numbers doubled as the watch off duty came tumbling up from below. He knew he must get down quick: once the topmen started about their duties, he would be in the way. The whole ship was then treated to the sight of a ship's commanding officer, sliding hand over hand down a backstay, with all the freedom of a fourteen-year-old skylarking.

Soon he was back in his proper clothing and place, on the quarterdeck and saying as little as possible: he wanted to see how things worked out without too much intervention by him. The Mite, who had come to take station beside him, was ordered to make a note of the time, as well as a rough reminder of the ship and its position for later writing up in the log. What details were needed, or in this case those he wished to be seen, Pearce would add later.

As the necessary duties were carried out, he knew he was the object of much interest. Had they been able to feel his pulse they would have noted his heart was pumping marginally faster than normal due to several factors. The first was the ship under his feet and what she could do, something about to be proved and for the first time. A chase was one of the operations for which the Cormorant class of sloops had been built. She would be fast on a bowline, thanks to a narrow hull, a shallow draught and a lot of top hamper. In the case of HMS *Hazard*, never having been required to serve in warmer climes, could be added relatively clean copper on her bottom.

For John Pearce, the second thing to mildly affect his heart rate was the sense of excitement rippling along the deck as well as aloft once they became enthused. The sky was clear, the swell far from heavy, which on its own had done much to dissipate the misery of the last thirty-six hours. It was only later he realised even that had done something for the collective feeling of the ship. It was as if the crew, new and fearful of what this unfamiliar life held for them, had confronted their personal demons and faced them down enough to modify their attitude.

'I have been told to vacate the wardroom, Pearce, so what are we about this time?'

Oliphant had got on to the quarterdeck without being seen and it was not a place he should be. As a civilian, his only contribution would be the ability to get in the way. About to tell him so, Pearce checked himself, to explain patiently and quietly the situation, thinking he was probably the only other person aboard who could make the same connections, those that had occurred to him when he was aloft.

'A possible smuggler?'

'Possible, yes – far from certain. The course it was on would be appropriate.'

'And if not?'

'Any number of things too numerous to mention, including a perfectly innocent neutral or British merchantman, which has, like us, been blown off course and is seeking to get to where it should have been two days past.'

'You said it flew no pennant.'

'We're much closer to the French shore than our own. The lack of a flag might be a precaution and there's no certainty they have seen ours with the wind as it is.' Oliphant looked aloft then, to see both the ensign and the Admiralty pennant blowing almost straight from stern to bow. 'We will find out when we close.'

John Pearce took pleasure from watching new canvas being bent onto the hitherto unused topgallants as well as the busy application of the topmen as they worked on the yards. The wind, the rising and dipping of the prow, which was evident if not excessive, was having no effect on their activities. It was as if they had ceased to notice such things.

When the ship had settled down, on its course and with nothing left but a sense of anticipation, the lack of activity soon came to bore Oliphant. 'I don't suppose I can hide away in your cabin?'

Pearce had great pleasure in shouting to Hallowell, who went into action immediately. Before answering Oliphant, he took out his fob watch, to open it and verbally mark the minute.

'I think you'll find my cabin will have ceased to exist almost before you get there. We are about to clear for action.'

'Is that not excessive, and I say that as what you term a "lubber"?'

Again Pearce spoke quietly; what he said was for this man's ears only. 'This sort of activity will serve as a drill and one that looks and feels real.' Seeing scepticism, he felt the need to add, 'Besides, I'm not one to take chances. If that is a smuggler, he has cannon and perhaps he will not give himself up lightly.'

Pearce knew he was talking nonsense, Oliphant did not. It was possible several people aboard wondered what he was about in running out his guns, not least Hallowell and Worricker, but also the bosun and the master, for no contraband ship would dream of taking on the navy.

He fully expected to see the Red Duster break out well before they got in range of long cannon shot. If the King's ship came on, and they were running contraband, they would have aboard all the false papers needed to convince the Revenue they were engaged in legitimate business. They would also expect no deep examination to ensue from him, relying on naval vessels having no interest in getting involved.

Their Lordships at the Admiralty were adamant that it was not the job of their ships and their men to act in that capacity. They defended the coast and attacked the enemy wherever they found them at sea. Let the Revenue Service, set up for the interdiction of smuggling and the failure to pay taxes, do its job and the navy would do theirs.

Bringing in a smuggler was in no way comparable to taking any kind of enemy vessel, merchant or warship. They would be accounted as prizes, with value in both what they contained and the hull: cargo, men, cannon and stores. Contraband attracted no such reward. The Revenue would say thank you very much, we will take both ship and cargo, to sell for our own purposes. Any shot expended or canvas damaged in the process, not being seen by the navy as properly employed, could well find the man in command out of pocket.

That they would close was not in doubt; few vessels could outrun a properly handled ship-rigged sloop. But to do so took time and the sense of resolution mixed with anticipation began to drain away from most of the crew, as time seemed to stand still. Pearce would have gone forward with a telescope anyway, but there was no need for the purposeful glare and the determined step with which he progressed, the Mite at his heels. Naturally Hallowell, as premier, took his place.

Stood in the bows, he trained the glass on the deck of the other vessel. The figures around the wheel were tiny dots and there was still no identifying flag, as there should have been by now. Could it be they were French or Dutch, which would change the whole nature of what he was about?

He stood for an age, resting himself against the bowsprit

gammoning to aid his balance, alternately lifting and dropping the telescope and feeling slightly perplexed; nothing anticipated had occurred. He thought about firing off one of the swivels just for the sound as well as the cloud of smoke it would portray. He was slightly annoyed: it seemed as if this merchant sod was mocking him.

Under his feet, Jock the Sock had command of the forward cannon, so he leant over the bulwarks and he called out to him, 'Mr Maclehose. I have a hope your number one 6-pounder is ready to be trained well forrard.'

'Sir?' A head poked out of the gunport, the cannon was still inboard. 'It is, sir.'

'Then, when it is run out, give it maximum elevation and be ready to fire as soon as it bears on the chase. Mr Livingston, back to the quarterdeck and ask Mr Hallowell to let the head fall off a fraction, so I can send our friend yonder a message.'

The Mite scampered off as Pearce raised his glass once more, to look at those figures surrounding the wheel, bigger now but still indistinct, feeling the change in motion and aware of the shifting bowsprit. He could picture Maclehose below – or would it be his designated gun captain? – peering along the cannon and through the gunport for sight of a hull not seen since they had cleared. It would come into view slowly and, had it been him, he would have waited till he could aim amidships.

Jock the Sock let fly a bit early. The ball was visible as it arced through the air to plunge into the blue-green of the sea and send up a great plume of white water. The effect was immediate; the expected Red Duster broke out at the masthead and now Pearce, as *Hazard* came back onto its original course, had to decide how to proceed.

Under normal circumstances he would have got close enough to hail the captain and ask his business, cargo and destination. But he was aware, by his previous actions, he had raised expectations of something unusual, while they had carried out that drill several times this very day. Something different would be more interesting, which precluded sending Hallowell off in a boat again.

Giving the duty to Worricker was similar, though it would be useful to see how he handled the task, so he decided that would have to suffice. Pearce went for a last look at the bugger who had messed him about, thinking it would serve him right if he was forced to heave to and have a naval officer, backed by a party of marines, to deal with.

'Give the sod a fright,' he said to himself.

'Sir?' asked the Mite.

'Nothing, Livingston,' he replied and, to cover a touch of embarrassment, he raised the telescope for a last look only to freeze. Now he could just make out the faces of those around the wheel, Pearce doubted what his eyes were telling him. The telescope stayed fixed as the distance continued to close, until he could be sure that what he had supposed to begin with, and actually dismissed as absurd, was fact.

'Mr Maclehose. Drop your elevation and on the next yaw, put ball as close to the hull of that sod as you can.'

The Mite was sent back with his instructions to the premier for a repeat manoeuvre and Jock the Sock executed his orders to perfection. The ball struck a flat trajectory to bounce forward twice, before sinking into the sea fifty yards off the scantlings, which brought about an immediate backing of its topsails. Pearce headed back to the quarterdeck, calling for the cutter, now being towed off the stern, to be brought forward.

'Someone fetch my sword and pistols. Mr Moberly, I want a party of half a dozen marines.'

'Am I permitted to enquire what you have seen, sir?' asked Hallowell.

He got an answer because the proposed reaction was exceptional. Whether he made sense of it was another matter. 'I have seen the Devil, or to be more precise, Satan and his dark angel.'

'What in the name of creation are you on about, Pearce?' Oliphant demanded.

'Get off the deck,' was the angry response. 'You have no business here.'

'He's right, sir,' Hallowell added in a more emollient tone. 'I'll have someone direct you to the orlop.'

The bustle that followed included Michael O'Hagan who, as he had done so many times in the past, fetched Pearce's weapons. The marines were called from their station manning two of the cannon to hurriedly get into their Lobster uniforms, pick up their muskets and make for the gangway. Pearce was halfway down the man ropes before the cutter was in position to receive him, the Mite at his back.

'What is going on, Mr Hallowell?' Oliphant enquired.

The Yankee drawl was very evident in the mystified reply: the premier had no idea. He did know his duty was to back the sails and let *Hazard* glide to a halt, lest they run down their own men. Mr Campbell appeared to lead Oliphant to what was a place of safety in battle even if they were not in anything of the sort.

The marines manned the boat as soon as the dozen oarsmen were in place and it pushed off, with Pearce in the thwarts, wearing a face like thunder. Visible from the deck, once the cutter cleared the bows, but not from a boat low in the water, was the sudden burst of furious activity on the merchantman. Hallowell had a telescope on the tall and burly figure still at the wheel, and had the impression his telescope was aimed at the cutter.

The first cannon fired before Pearce was a third of the way. It sent up a burst of spray so close some of it fell on the cutter, in fact too close for comfort. Added to that, musket balls began to pepper the sea, luckily no threat, given the range was too great.

An alarmed Pearce realised he had made the same mistake as that buffoon banging on the door in Gravelines. He had allowed his temper to dictate his actions, charging like a bull where subterfuge would have served better and, in doing so, he had brought into real risk of death or injury his oarsmen and marines.

As he called for the cutter to be swung round, he wondered what Hallowell would do. How would he react? At least Moberly's men knew what was required. They began to load their muskets, difficult to carry out sat down and with no room, but a proper response to a threat. Pearce hardly had to call for effort to get back to the ship; the men were hauling like madmen, halfway off their perch on the pull.

Having backed the sails, the run of the sea had swung *Hazard* round several degrees. It mattered not who had the wit to respond, but two of the amidships cannon spoke. The aim was well wide of the target, it being for show and taking care not to endanger him and his men.

'The other ship has reset its sails, sir.'

'Get down, Mr Livingston, at once,' he shouted to the mid, who had stood up in the middle of the boat. The Mite looked at him slightly confused as a hand took away his legs. He tumbled backwards, a scream of pain following, this as a pair of cannonballs hit the water, bracketing the cutter.

Those two main deck cannon spoke again, this time firing high, soon to be followed by the whole of the larboard battery, which left the sloop wreathed in smoke. The balls went over the *Hazard* and into the sea, watched by a captain twisted round to see the fall. It had been designed to be short and would have been, even if the chase had not been opening up the gap.

Hallowell chose to wait until the cutter was hooked on before he gave the order to man the sheets and get the sails drawing again. Pearce came back through the gangway, no pipes this time, to find his subordinate looking at him in a state of total confusion, for this should not be happening.

'Orders to Mr Worricker, Livingston. We are going to close with that bastard and take out his rigging. Chain shot from now on and I want no waste.'

'Sir?' his premier said, obviously in search of an explanation. He was not alone. Williams and Moberly were staring at him for the same reason.

'Pay no heed to that Red Duster, Mr Hallowell, it is false. Besides, the swine has forfeited any protection it might have afforded him. He has fired on a King's officer.'

'But why would he do that, sir?'

Pearce could scarcely tell him it was his presence that had caused the cutter to be fired upon, so he gave the only reply he could. 'He is a smuggler.'

'Are you sure, sir? I know it has been speculated that might be the case, but how can you be certain?'

'Who else would fire their cannon?'

'By custom he has nothing to fear from us, sir, we are not the Revenue.'

He was tempted to tell Hallowell to shut up and mind his own business, the trouble being, it was his business. For all the power a captain had, he had to act in a way that made sense to his inferior officers and that was not happening right now.

Now HMS *Hazard* was under way, the timbers creaking as the sails filled with wind, Pearce was mentally composing what to say in his logs, an explanation of why he had taken to the cutter. He could hardly admit the reason was personal, that the faces he had described as Satan and his Dark Angel belonged to men who had tried to murder him.

Besides that, the names of Jahleel and Franklin Tolland would mean nothing.

CHAPTER TWENTY-EIGHT

If there was doubt about the motivation of John Pearce, there was none about the outcome and the Tolland brothers knew it. They had come round on a south-westerly course, which, given time, would have beached them north of Calais, only that time was not going to be gifted them. Even if his anger had not abated, it had receded enough to allow consideration of what he was about, as well as what would happen once he had the swine under his guns.

'Mr Williams, put me inshore of the chase. I wish to deny them an escape. Mr Hallowell, we will hold our fire until we are close; the orders I will issue personally.'

Pearce was acutely aware he could not talk or explain his actions to his inferiors: the Pelicans required none, for they knew the story only too well. He sent Livingston to request Oliphant to come on deck. When he arrived, the chase was pointed out to him. Given he had been below during the firing of cannon, he was also treated to a brief outline of what had happened and, having given an order to keep him informed, Pearce took him into the now clear area which had been his cabin.

'I need your opinion.'

'How refreshing.'

'This is no time to exercise your wit.'

'I was unaware I was seeking to be humorous.' Seeing Pearce suck in air to let fly at him, Oliphant quickly added, 'Opinion on what?'

Having decided to use him as a sounding board, Pearce was now wondering how much he should say. For instance, what had been curiosity, in closing with a ship behaving oddly, had now become personal. The Tolland brothers had tried to kill him on more than one occasion, suffering under the erroneous belief that he had, sometime past, stolen their ship and cargo. On the last attempt he had outmanoeuvred them, to the point of handing them over to the Impressment Service, only to subsequently discover they had somehow bought their way out, obviously to go back to their old game.

It was a complicated tale and one that did not reflect too well on his judgement. Was the telling of it likely to affect Oliphant's point of view? He was now looking inquisitively and waiting for an answer to his question.

'I told you I had been in Gravelines before. There are men aboard that ship whom I know from that time. They are people who think of me less than fondly.'

Oliphant could not resist it. 'Such folk are, I have found, numbered in legions, so what is so special about the here and now?'

Pearce ignored the barb and answered in a soft tone, 'The vessel they are on.'

'I don't follow.'

Oliphant was treated to a quick explanation of the naval attitude to smuggling and smugglers, before Pearce admitted the reason they had fired on the cutter was the sight of him in the thwarts.

'You?' he replied, clearly astonished. 'But if what you say is true, regardless of the naval attitude to the Revenue, then what they have done is madness.'

'They have good reason to fear I will hang them, for the very simple fact they have tried to kill me twice and would attempt to do so again, if they were afforded the chance. I, in my foolishness, admittedly unintentionally, offered them just that opportunity.'

'They cannot, I assume, get away. We will overhaul them?'

'I would reckon within the next hour.'

'So, will you hang them?' was posed with a concerned frown.

'That is part of my asking you for an opinion, but it is more than what I do with them. It is to do with the ship and its cargo.' Seeing the misgivings still on Oliphant's face, Pearce added with a sardonic smile, 'I won't hang them. I can't.'

'Thank God for that,' came out with palpable relief. 'I doubt I'm alone on this ship in not wishing to be a party to what would surely be murder.'

'Do you really think I would?'

'I recall what you were never tired of telling me about the powers of captains at sea.'

'The ship and its cargo. What I should do is put a crew aboard and take them to a home port, where both can be handed over to the Revenue.'

'The crew aboard now, you don't mention them.'

'They would be pressed into the navy. Smugglers are usually experienced seamen.'

A cough had him turn. There was the Mite to tell him they were between the chase and the shore, as well as closing to within range of chain shot.

'They appear to be chucking stuff overboard, sir. Mr Hallowell says he can't be sure, but it appears the name board that was under canvas has gone from the stern.'

'I will be on deck presently, Mr Livingston.' When the boy had gone, Pearce looked hard at Oliphant. 'While I'm dealing with taking possession, perhaps you can think on the matter. Feel free to help yourself to some wine.'

On deck the tension had not eased, nor, even if it was not voiced, the curiosity. Or was it concern at what they were about to do, for none were sure it was worth the effort? There was wonder when Pearce picked up the speaking trumpet and hailed the other deck, to tell them he was in command of HMS *Hazard* and ordering them to heave to.

Two cannon, probably all they had per side, blasted off simultaneously, badly aimed. His ship suffered no damage, so Pearce, having got *Hazard* round until his cannon would bear, ordered his main deck to reply. The ship recoiled slightly, as the fire rippled down the side, each 6-pounder going off a second after its nearest neighbour.

As the smoke from the broadside cleared away, they could

see the rigging on the merchant vessel was badly shredded, sails ripped, blocks dislodged and ropes cut in two, not least one of the stays securing the foremast. There was no one on the wheel, which had Pearce wonder – in truth he hoped – whether some badly aimed chain shot had cut both the Tollands in half.

'They're abandoning ship, sir,' called Hallowell, his telescope trained on the target.

'Hardly surprising. Mr Livingston, tell Mr Worricker to house his guns. Mr Hallowell, a boat party to take possession, if you please.'

'And the crew, sir?'

'I don't think they can outrun us, do you?'

Hallowell grinned, the first time for a while. 'Prime hands, smugglers, sir, be a good addition to the crew.'

'We shall see.'

As soon as Hallowell and his boat crew had got away, *Hazard* went in pursuit of what was no more than a forlorn hope. By the time they overhauled them, the long beach between Gravelines and Calais was just visible. Moberly had his marines lined up on the bulwarks, muskets aimed and awaiting the order to fire, which John Pearce had made his own.

They had tried hard, those rowing, collapsing over their oars when the sloop closed in, to tower over their boat. John Pearce went to the open gangway, to call down to the only two looking up instead of down. There was Jaleel, ugly, his choleric, pockmarked face as unchanged as his ill temper. And little brother Franklin, of a softer more becoming visage, marred by the deep scar Pearce had inflicted.

'We meet again.'

He had to jump backwards as Jaleel Tolland whipped up a pistol and fired it off, the crack of the passing ball audible, Pearce shouting to the marines to hold their fire, which was obeyed. He was back at the gangway in seconds, favouring them with a wolfish grin.

'It appears you wish me to string you up.' The elder Tolland had a gravel voice, which invited Pearce to do his worst. 'Mr Moberly, please drag these scum aboard and see that the master-at-arms puts them in shackles. Mr Williams, as soon as you can, let us rejoin Mr Hallowell. I am keen to see what we have acquired.'

It soon became obvious what they had been throwing into the sea, as reported by the Mite. While men were set to repair as much of the rigging as possible, Hallowell had searched for paperwork and found none, which indicated that whatever it had contained was information they had no desire should be seen, material to fool any inspection by the Revenue. Ownership documents, forged bills of lading, which would include made-up evidence of what had been purchased, from whom, and for how much. Like the name board, it had all gone to the bottom.

Hallowell had not been idle; he had been in the holds listing the cargo. 'Brandy, wine, tea, bolts of silk and lace. Worth a mint as a prize and none of it ours.'

The last bit was delivered with an odd expression: not glum as it should be, but as though he was wishing it could be otherwise. The list was handed over to Pearce, who gave it a cursory glance, then put it in his pocket.

'Stay in hailing distance and set your course to follow ours.'

That acknowledged, Pearce took a boat back to *Hazard*. Once both vessels were under way, with instructions to sail a circular course, maintaining not much more than steerage way, he sought out Michael O'Hagan. He issued instructions to separate the Tollands from the rest of their crew. Back in his cabin he found Oliphant, feet up in Pearce's own chair, a glass of wine in his hand and, judging by the state of the bottle, far from his first one.

'Have a look at this.'

The list was handed over, while a look was enough to have Oliphant move to another chair, where he sat examining it.

'You will no doubt duplicate my premier, who termed it worth a mint.' That got an emphatic nod. 'So now we come to the question of what we do with it – either send it and the ship to the bottom, or sail for somewhere like Ramsgate to hand it over to the people who have done nothing to deserve it.'

'Seems a shame either way – but no choice, I suppose,' was the sad conclusion, as Oliphant drained his glass.

'What if it was taken as French?'

That had Oliphant sit up. If there were many things about the man Pearce did not like, he could not fault his quick intelligence. It was almost possible to see the brain working.

'Can I tell you, there is many a rumour that, over the years, what I'm going to propose has happened before? Not that any actual evidence exists, it's all apocryphal and hearsay, but strong nevertheless.'

Pearce expected Oliphant to understand the difference between what should happen and what did, a gap that existed in every walk of life. The Articles of War and the regulations sounded as if they left no room for manoeuvre: everyone in the King's Navy knew that to be untrue. Bending the rules was not only endemic: it was essential and no more than in the taking of prizes, which was seen as an ordinary function for an officer wishing to prosper. Many – not all, it had to be admitted – spouted enthusiastically as well as hypocritically about their love of country. For a goodly number, their love of a full purse took precedence.

'As long as you're not going to suggest selling it in Calais.'

That made Pearce grin. 'The notion did occur. That we could beach the ship, at high tide, by arrangement. And I reckoned you might like to revisit the lady you called Marie, not I assume her real name.'

That got Oliphant a cold stare, one to which he declined to respond.

'But making it happen is fraught with risk, you going ashore being the most obvious and difficult to explain. The real worry being it could be construed as treason.'

'So the other possibility is?'

'When we first sighted her, she was under no national ensign. The sods only raised a British flag when we sent a couple of balls in her direction, which is very much something an enemy vessel might do to seek to humbug us. The board with the name of the ship and its home port was covered to begin with, with what I took to be airing canvas. But it was then dumped in the sea, along with every scrap of documentation. So, we have a vessel that was and still is a mystery.'

'And if it's a prize ship?'

'The hull and everything aboard will be sold, to be shared by the ship's company.'

'Which does not include me.'

The response was delivered with deep irony. 'I admire your generosity towards your fellow human beings, it's so like you. But I can rate you as a midshipman so you do share.'

'Even I know they don't get much of that.'

'Since we're not sailing under a flag officer, I will get the admiral's eighth, so I can gift you enough of a reward.'

'That I'd like in writing,' was imparted as only half a jest.

'Oliphant, you're not navy. I think I can get the others to agree with me, but they will know you need to do so as well. If it ever came out that we engaged in subterfuge . . .'

'Don't you mean fraud?'

'I suppose I do. But it's not just the officers who will gain, the crew will as well. Coin on their first outing.'

'Which will see them eating out of your hand.'

'Again, you're ahead of where I thought you would be.'

'And what about the smugglers chained up below?'

'I have a solution for that.'

The conference, in the cabin, saw the same crowd as had sat down to dinner. Now they stood listening to Pearce outlining the same options, *sans* Marie, as he had to Oliphant. He was relying on two factors: their own self-interest, as well as a knowledge of the rumours of deception previously practised. Then there was getting one over on the Revenue. All must agree, without exception, so all could share. They nodded at his point about the vessel having no name and no home port, so it could be from anywhere, which was heartening.

'I will record in the log that she carried no flag and, on boarding, possessed no papers. Given we had no idea of her nationality, and we took her so close to the enemy coast, we are assuming her to be a French merchantman and therefore a prize.'

Moberly posed the same question as Oliphant, to get the same reply, but no actual details as to what Pearce intended. He undertook to reveal that at the appropriate time.

'Ultimately, I have responsibility and I'm damned if I'm going to be dunned for the price of powder and shot for taking a smuggler.'

If there was any wavering that acceptance of accountability snuffed it out.

'Mr Hallowell, it falls to you to take the prize into harbour. I would suggest it would be good that Mr Maclehose accompanies you. I leave you to pick the crew you need.'

'You will not sail with us, sir?'

'Not to start with, but I may catch you even before you drop anchor. If not, it will be a very short time until we're reunited.' He looked pointedly at Oliphant. 'Then I must tell you, we have a task to perform, one of which I cannot as yet give you details. So, we will touch at Ramsgate only for as long as is necessary and no longer. Time and tide, as the Bard said.'

The level of curiosity was at a high pitch; no one had any inkling of what Pearce had in mind. Much time was spent repairing the capture's rigging, but it was done in such a way as to show it had been seriously shredded. Authenticity was all. That done the pair parted company, Pearce waiting till his 'prize' was over the horizon before ordering a course to take *Hazard* north.

If they were mystified before, it was even odder now and enlightenment was not forthcoming, even when they sighted the topsails of the North Sea Fleet. One of the swivels gave the required salute to Admiral Duncan's flag, but it was for HMS *Bedford* that the sloop was headed. Under the control of Mr Williams, John Pearce was with the Tollands, chained up just between the bottom of the hold and above the bilge.

They were three people who, under the light of a lantern, only had in common the expressions on their faces, one of undisguised hatred. Pearce had come to tell this pair how wrong they were about their grievance. One look and he decided not to bother: he knew he would be wasting his breath.

'You got away from the fate I had in store for you once, but not a second time.'

'So no rope?' Franklin enquired, which got him a blast from Jaleel.

'Don't beg. If he wants to stretch our necks, let him do so, and I'll curse him yet as I drop.'

'I would prefer to drop you overboard with a round shot in your breeches. Much as I'd like to, I am barred from doing so.' Then he called out to his Pelicans. 'Unshackle them and get them into a boat with a chain round their feet.'

There were three boats in the water: barge, cutter and jolly boat, with the Tollands' crew split up into groups. As soon as the brothers and Pearce were aboard, they set off for *Bedford*, which had Byard at the gangway well before they hooked on.

'An unlikely call, Mr Pearce.'

'A welcome one, I think you'll find, sir.'

Everyone was left in the boats, as Pearce clambered aboard and went through the rituals, which inevitably led to Byard's cabin and a bottle of wine. Following that was an explanation.

'If you will forgive my lack of a full clarification, I cannot have these twenty men about HMS *Hazard*. In their numbers I would fear mutiny, but on a third rate, with a crew of over five hundred, they can be absorbed.'

'Would they be inclined to mutiny?'

'I will point out to you a pair that would be ringleaders if the occasion arose. I would not see any of them being allowed ashore.'

375

'I trust very few ashore. This is a singular gift, Pearce, especially in these times.'

'You were kind enough to help me in my hour of need. I see it as repaying that. All I ask is that they be exposed to a proper degree of discipline.'

'Which they will be, by damn. Mutiny, indeed.'

'Now sir, as I am on Admiralty orders and have an assignment . . .'

'You wish to be away?'

'I do.'

'Well, you're not going afore we empty this second bottle.'

Pearce stood by the gangway as the Tollands were brought aboard, a smile on his face designed to annoy them, which succeeded, more with Jaleel than Franklin, the former in receipt of his parting shot.

'I will wager you'll be at the grating before the week is out, and I can tell you, Byard is not just a two-dozen man.'

'And you,' Jaleel spat. 'Hell will freeze before you can rest easy.'

The starter hit him hard across the back and a rough voice told him to stow his tongue. This had Jaleel spin round to retaliate. He found himself looking into the face of a bosun's mate, inviting him to try.

EPILOGUE

HMS *Hazard* made Ramsgate in two days, to find Hallowell and Jock the Sock on board the prize and anchored outside. The tide left the inner harbour as mud, with not much deep water for anything of a size in the middle. Besides, they could not let the men off in case they deserted, so had been obliged to stay aboard themselves. Pearce likewise anchored in Joss Bay and went to see them.

'We have not yet properly reported to the Port Admiral, sir, but an officer came out to us and we have declared the prize. We have been promised a crew to take it up to Greenwich, where it can be valued.'

'I am bound to visit him anyway. Do we have a name?'

'Admiral Vereker, sir.'

The admiral was housed in another one of those comfortable buildings overlooking the harbour, which had been built in the time of the early Georges, while the occupant was probably, by his name, a descendant of those who had come over with William of Orange in the last century. Bluff, fat and hearty, he looked Dutch, with his big head and high colour.

Dinner was essential, as was the tale of the taking of the capture, which tested Pearce's powers of invention to make it interesting, and it was held to be a pity the crew of the capture, so close to the Calais beach, had been able to take to boats and get away. Vereker was honest enough to bemoan he was not the responsible flag officer, so would not get his eighth. Pearce was dissembler enough to commiserate with him.

'Lucky to catch me, Pearce, I was up at the Admiralty for the last week.'

'I hope they treated you with respect, sir.'

'Odd thing to say. Mind they can be damned awkward. Nepean seems sound. Never took to Sir Philip Stephens, no salt water in his veins.'

'I wish I had time to go to London, sir, but my duty forbids it.'

'Then you'll miss the sensation of the season. Everyone's talking of it.'

'And what, sir, would that be?'

'That murder case, the one where that woman was ravaged and cut up. In Covent Garden.'

That required a bit of swallowing and he wondered if Emily was somehow involved, not that he could mention it, but he had to say something.

'The culprit was a fellow called Gherson, I recall.'

'Not so. That clever lawyer fellow, Garrow, got him acquitted.'

'Really?' was all Pearce could say. 'How interesting. I wonder: if he didn't do it, who did?'

'Nine-day wonder, Pearce. No one will care in a week.'

After dinner, all arrangements in place and a letter posted to Alexander Davidson to tell him of his good fortune, as well as to ensure all was properly done, Pearce made his way by barge back to HMS *Hazard*. Hallowell had welcomed aboard the crew who would take the vessel upriver and left to rejoin the sloop. Now everyone was aboard and no leaks could occur, he invited his officers to a glass of wine and told them where they were off to.

'We will weigh in the morning, gentlemen. Our destination, I can tell you, is the Mediterranean. And I hope it will be a happy hunting ground.'

Gherson had come out of the Old Bailey, to face a crowd who had fully expected to next see him at his hanging. Fickle as the mob is, they cheered him to the rafters like a hero, if indeed that could be done outdoors. Walter Hodgson had hired a trio of sturdy men to get him to a hack and away, which was not easy when his new supporters wished to hoist and carry him on their shoulders. At Charing Cross he was put on the Portsmouth coach; once there he would be on his own.

'Keep low until you get a place,' Hodgson advised him. 'Don't go gallivanting about and whoring, or they'll fish you out of the harbour.'

'And if I can't get a place?'

'You're a survivor Gherson, so survive.'

* * *

Edward Druce looked at the bill he would be required to meet to satisfy Emily Barclay: a hefty one, which was not just reparation for the questionable trades. Included were the substantial costs of Southouse and Garrow. She had asked the funds to be remitted to her local bankers in Frome within seven days or she would instigate court proceedings in a case, thanks to Gherson, the firm could not win.

Her business was now with Davidson, which had not pleased Francis Ommaney when he was told of the loss of the client. What would he say to this? It was clear Hodgson had played his part and betrayed him. When challenged he had asked Druce to examine his conscience.

'Damn you, Denby,' he cursed out loud. 'You can meet this. And if you decline . . .'

The result of that was left hanging: threatening his brother-in-law, now raging on about Gherson being at liberty, was not to be undertaken lightly. And the real worry was what he would do now.

DAVID DONACHIE was born in Edinburgh in 1944. He has always had an abiding interest in the naval history of the eighteenth and nineteenth centuries as well as the Roman Republic, and under the pen-name Jack Ludlow has published a number of historical adventure novels. David lives in Deal with his partner, the novelist Sarah Grazebrook.

To discover more great books and to
place an order visit our website at
allisonandbusby.com

Don't forget to sign up to our free newsletter at
allisonandbusby.com/newsletter
for latest releases, events and exclusive offers

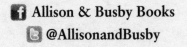 **Allison & Busby Books**
@AllisonandBusby

You can also call us on
020 3950 7834
for orders, queries
and reading recommendations